NIGHT LORE

GENESIS BATISTA

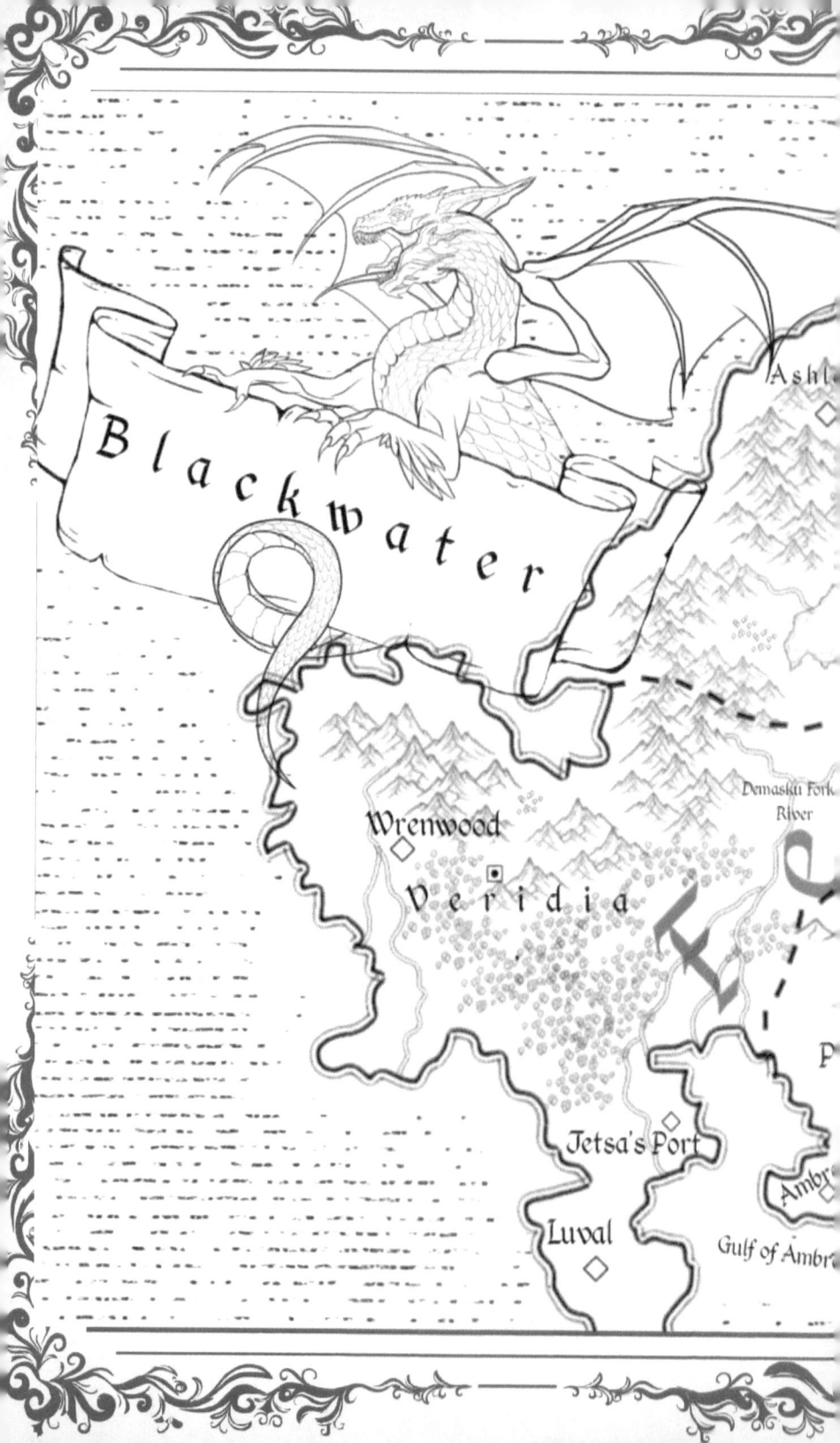

CONTENTS

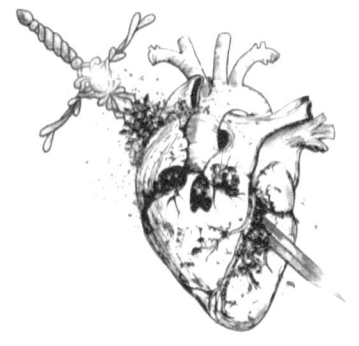

WARNING

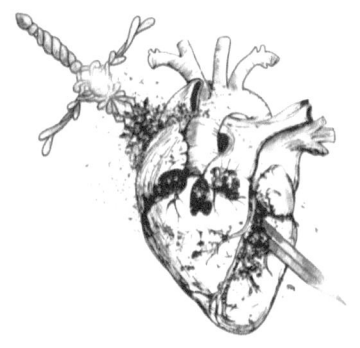

PROLOGUE
THE WAR OF FALLEN SKIES

The war was over.

Ash drifted from the heavens, a soft, silent snow of gray that dressed my warriors in a cloak of sorrow. Their once shining armor, now dulled beneath the remnants of battle, still caught the fractured sunlight that dared to pierce the smoke-choked skies. Around us, the field lay littered with the fallen—their spears jutting out like accusing fingers from the hills of the slain, banners that had once soared with pride now a somber dance upon the gentle breeze. The symphony of the dying, a chorus of ragged breaths and whispered goodbyes, filled the air, underscored by the raw, keening cry of a dragon in its death throes.

My legs, unsteady as a fawn's, betrayed me, sending me sprawling over the twisted form of a wyvern. Not just any wyvern—Zaezar. Her wing, a once-magnificent canvas of strength, lay severed beside me. A gasp tore from my lungs, a silent prayer escaping as I frantically sought out those I called kin within the carnage.

The war had ended.

And we lost.

A glint of silver in the hellscape caught my eye. There, tangled amidst the corpses of a Solaris knight and a fallen Blackwater guard, my world came to a shuddering halt.

Aislinn.

Aislinn—my fierce, indomitable Aislinn—lay before me, her brown eyes void of the fire that had once set the world ablaze. The disruption of her life had been extinguished as quickly as a candle's flame snatched by the cruel fingers of Death.

A scream clawed its way up my throat, a raw, animalistic sound that tore through the silence and declared my anguish to the gods who had forsaken us.

Gaelin came from behind me. "The enemy may yet scour the field, and we are not yet so broken that we should offer them our necks."

I snatched him by his throat, lifting him a few inches off the ground. His eyes widened in shock, disbelief etched across his face as he gasped for air. But my grip only tightened, the fury within me eclipsing all reason. "How can you say that?" I hissed through clenched teeth. "How can you stand there and talk of leaving when she lays here, lifeless?"

Gael clawed at my hands, his legs kicking futilely as he struggled to speak. "El... Eldra," he choked out, the name cutting through my rage. I blinked, the fog of anger slowly dissipating, and I realized what I was doing. With a shudder, I released him, and he collapsed to the ground, coughing and gasping for breath.

I collapsed beside Aislinn, my hands trembling as they hovered above her eternal calm. Hot and unbidden tears blurred the lines of the desolation that cradled us. My fingertips brushed her pallid cheek, the icy touch a lance through my soul. "I'm so sorry, Aislinn," I murmured, a broken whisper in the void.

She was never meant to be among the casualties of war.

She wasn't supposed to be here.

"I told her to stay back," I whispered. "I told her to stay where it was safe."

Gael rose to his feet, his face a mask of pain and exhaustion. "Eldra, we can't stay here. The enemy may return if they find us with the dead..." He trailed off, his face haunted.

"Where is Seraphix?" I asked.

He shook his head. "The Blackwaters chained Aislinn's beast and dragged him to their vessel. He is alive. We need to go, Eldra. Ramses will come back and finish us off. There is still time to escape," he pleaded.

The mention of Seraphix, Aislinn's bonded beast, reignited my urgency. The bond between a rider and their dragon was sacred, unbreakable—and with Aislinn gone, Seraphix would be untethered, a creature of immense power and grief. The thought of him chained and captive, subjected to the whims of the Blackwaters, fueled a new kind of fury in my blood.

"Ameria, Emery, and Madsen are already on the retreat to the safe grounds," Gael stated.

I leaned down, pressing a kiss on Aislinn's forehead—a promise, a vow. "I will return for you," I swore into the stillness. "I will carry you from this place of death, and you will rest among the stars."

The Gods are cruel.

The vow etched itself upon her exposed collar bone—a mark of a Fae bargain struck—a black four-pointed star no larger than a snowflake.

And with that solemn promise, sealed by the ancient magics that bind the Fae to their word, I rushed to find anyone else I could save.

But then, Ramses' mist of death was already creeping back across the land.

"Come on!" I called out to the soldiers, my command cutting through the thickening fog. "We must leave this accursed place!"

The mist, a living entity of malice and sorrow, slithered across the battlefield, swallowing the forms of the fallen as it advanced. I knew the time for escape was upon us, but the bond of my vow to Aislinn rooted me to the spot. I had promised to return for her, to carry her from this place, and the Fae mark upon her collarbone was a testament to that oath.

But as I reached for her, the mist enveloped her body, and in a whisper of darkness, she was gone—stolen from me. A hollow emptiness gaped within me as if the fog had torn away a piece of my soul and her.

"Eldra!" Gael screamed, pulling me back from the brink of despair. "We must go now!"

Aislinn had lain, where now only the mist danced in a cruel mockery of my loss.

I turned and ran, the mist nipping at my heels like a pack of hungry wolves.

One by one, those who could still move began to rise, realizing the impending threat. They were the lucky few, spared by fate or chance, but even they bore the scars of the battle around them. The echo of clashing steel and the roar of beasts had faded, replaced by the ragged breaths of the living as we cut through the remnants of war.

"Around me!" I shouted, a rallying cry. "Protect the retreat!"

The soldiers formed a protective circle, shields interlocked, spears bristling outward like the quills of a great beast. Each warrior stood shoulder to shoulder as they trotted backward to keep up.

With a strength born of desperation, I bent down to lift a young soldier whose leg was broken, slinging his arm over my shoulder. Gael did the same with another, and together, we ushered them toward the safety of the trees—where Emery had put in place a barrier. Gael shouted my name, laced with panic and fear, as the mist swallowed everything in its path. In the distance, the thunderous roar of draconic fury shattered the eerie silence.

Seraphix, Aislinn's bonded dragon, was calling out—a cry of anguish that speared through me. I chanced a glance to the see. The Blackwater vessel loomed large, a hulking shadow against the dimming light, its sails billowing with dark magic. Seraphix's incredible body was chained. There was nothing I could do for him. I only had a small amount of strength left in me.

The forest's edge was in sight now, the trees a dark wall against the encroaching mist. I could hear the rattling breath of the fog behind me and feel its chill seeping into my bones. But I would not falter. I could not. With a final burst of speed, I broke through the tree line, the mist curling back as if repelled by some unseen force. Emery's arms were outstretched in front of her, arms shaking, nose bleeding, as the mist snaked its way along her barrier, trying to find a weak spot.

Warped popping noises filled the air, and I knew without looking that my soldiers were jumping through Hisen's makeshift portal. The portal was a circle of blue light that flashed and sparked with energy. I turned to ensure no one was left behind, scanning the clearing rapidly. That's when I saw a silhouette emerging from the mist, a figure shrouded in the power and malice that could only belong to one man. Ramses.

His presence halted me in my tracks, a cold dread settling in my stomach. He stood there, the mist parting around him like a curtain, unveiling the final act of a tragic play. His gaze found mine, and time seemed to stand still at that moment. "Eldra," he called out, cutting through the silence with the sharpness of a blade. "Do you think you can escape me?" I felt Gael's hand on my shoulder, a silent warning that we needed to move, to disappear through the portal before it was too late.

This was the man that took my Aislinn away from me.

Then, just as I stepped toward the shield—to sacrifice myself for the chance of victory—the unexpected happened. A sudden, powerful gust of wind swept through the clearing, so fierce it uprooted trees and sent debris flying. And I felt myself being lifted, not by my power but by a force beyond my understanding.

The wind enveloped me, and I could hear Gael's muffled and distant shout as the world around me blurred into a vortex of color and sound. The last thing I saw was Ramses' face, a look of surprise etched upon his features before I was swept away into nothingness.

●

My feet sank into warm sand as waves crashed against my skin. Seagulls shrieked overhead, the sun beating relentlessly on me. A hand closed around mine.

Calloused fingers interlaced with my own. A fisherman, his face a map of lines and scars, hauled me to my feet. I stumbled, the world spinning. New Solara. This wasn't where I was supposed to be.

The fisherman's gaze held no surprise. "Welcome back, King Eldra," he rasped, as if my arrival was expected. Not a question, but a statement.

I managed a whispered "thank you." His calm acceptance offered little comfort. The turmoil inside me roared like the sea.

Aislinn. Her name was a scream in my mind. My knees gave out, the sand a poor substitute for the blood-soaked earth I'd left behind. I had to move. Had to escape.

With each step toward New Solara's heart, grief and responsibility threatened to consume me. The city's laughter and clanging pots were a distant hum, a world away. A world where Aislinn still lived.

I found myself in the central square. People milled about, oblivious. Today, I was alone.

The sky turned a sickly shade of green. My heart, a heavy stone, threatened to shatter. A sob tore from my throat, and the skies opened up. Rain, like tears, poured down.

People scurried for cover, but I stood there, letting the rain wash over me. Wash away the facade. Here, I could grieve.

The rain wouldn't bring her back. Wouldn't fill the emptiness to come. It should have been me. I wish it were me.

Years of secrets, of moving my people here, of spinning illusions... and I couldn't save her. The rain drummed against my skin like an accusation.

Citizens watched from doorways, their faces a mix of confusion and concern. Then, a little girl. She approached hesitantly, a bedraggled flower clutched in her small fist. She placed it before me.

The spell was broken. The crowd surged forward, each adding to the girl's offering. A lavender sprig, a red rose, daisies. The flowers were a riot of color against the grey stone.

I stood there, tears mixing with rain. The weight on my chest eased. They understood loss. They'd sacrifice with me, for me.

New Solara wasn't just magic. It was hope, made flesh. A city born of determination, of the will to survive. Ramses would never find it. I knew that.

The rain slowed to a drizzle. I looked at the sea of faces. "Go home," I rasped.

Silent nods. Slowly, they dispersed, leaving me alone with the flowers. Aislinn's favorite had been daisies. A sob clawed its way up my throat. I fell to my knees, surrounded by the tokens of my people's grief.

The stone was cold and wet beneath me. I scooped up a handful of rain-soaked daisies. They smelled of nothing. Not of her. Never again.

I screamed. The sound ripped through the square, echoing off the buildings. I screamed until my voice was gone, until all that was left was the rain, drumming against the stones like a funeral dirge.

The flowers remained. A sea of white and yellow and red. I lay down amidst them, surrounded by tokens of grief, of loss. Of my failure.

The rain finally stopped. I stared at the flowers, my vision blurry. The city was silent. Waiting. For their king to lead again.

I had to get up. Had to keep going. For them. Not for her. Never again for her.

With a roar, I surged to my feet. I walked away from the flowers, from the square. Left Aislinn behind.

I couldn't bring her back. But I could keep her memory alive. I could keep our people safe. I could make sure those left behind avenged those who fell.

The sun broke through the clouds. Not warm, but a cold, hard light. The type of light to see things as they truly were.

The enchantment shrouding New Solara wasn't just a bunch of arcane or mystical gestures; it was the shared determination of a community set on persevering, forging a new existence far from the shadows that had almost devoured us before. It was like our collective wishful thinking had taken physical form, a city pulsing with life, boldly standing its ground amid the ruins that once threatened to obliterate everything.

It's all stitched together by the very essence in my veins.

Ramses would never find this place. I knew that with absolute certainty.

●

The people celebrated. They celebrated having been saved from the destruction of Old Solara in what was once Veridia. Music and singing filled the air as they feasted and danced. I sat in the city square, listened to the music, and watched the people dance. Some held up our banner, others held up the gold helmets of the men who hadn't returned from battle, and others shuttered themselves quietly away in their homes to grieve.

Aislinn had loved to dance.

Her absence was a gaping wound, and the thought of her dancing, her laughter once mingling with the music that now played, brought an ache that no amount of song could soothe.

Hisen, Ameria, Gael, Emery, and Madsen shared the weight of silence with me, their faces a mixture of relief and remorse. Each of us was grappling with our own ghosts, our own catalog of could-have-beens and should-have-dones.

"I thought we would win," I found myself confessing, the words slipping out like traitors from a fortress of denial. "I truly believed we would beat Ramses and force him into submission. But he... he wielded powers beyond our understanding and anything I had ever seen." My eyes settled on the empty spot where she would have sat, between Madsen and Ameria. The space was still between them, and neither was willing to close the gap.

The others nodded, their expressions grim. They, too, had witnessed Ramses's unnatural might unleash upon the battlefield, turning the tide in ways we were ill-prepared to counter.

"It wasn't just you, Eldra," Hisen said, his voice low. "We all believed. Our strategy was sound; our forces were strong. But Ramses..."

Ameria reached out, placing a comforting hand upon mine. "We did what we could," she said gently. "We saved as many as we could. And now we have New Solara, a new beginning. The lives lost are not on your shoulders alone. We all share in this burden." They all had opted to wear funeral shrouds, and still, Ameria was trying to find the brighter side of things.

There was no bright side for me.

Gael added, "Eldra, you led us with honor. You gave us a chance to fight another day. Ramses may have taken much from us, but he has not taken our spirit. Nor has he taken our will to make things right."

The loss of Aislinn meant the end of the Furian line. Without an heir to continue the Furian legacy, Tor's fate was left to Ramses' mercy.

We had tried to gather as many of her people as possible to join us in New Solara, but there were stubborn ones. The Tor saying was that death is not the end.

How fucking ironic.

The Blackwaters, now emboldened by Ramses' dark sorcery and conquest of Ember, would undoubtedly seek to extend their dominion over Tor. The void left by the fall of the Furians was a breach in the defenses of our lands, an opportunity for the Blackwaters to seize control and spread their tyranny.

The land of Ferenz would be lost to him now.

"The Furians have always been the shield of Tor," Hisen said solemnly, his vacant expression reflecting the flames of the celebratory torches. "Without Aislinn, without their line, we must prepare for the struggle ahead."

Ameria said, "The Blackwaters may believe they can claim Tor, but they do not know the will of its people. We will stand with them, fight with them, and ensure that Aislinn's sacrifice was not in vain."

"We do not have the numbers," Madsen scoffed. She ran a hand through her blue hair and scrunched her nose. "We cannot stand against them alone. None of the other great houses could withstand him."

Gael clenched his fist, and I saw a fire kindling within him. "Let Ramses come," he declared. "He will find not a land ripe for the taking but a united front ready to repel him. We are the legacy of the Furians now, and we will hold Tor against all who dare threaten it."

"No," I sighed.

"The Hell do you mean?" Gael asked, his expression incredulous.

"We must seek allies among the Tyrens of the Paladin Plains and the Old Solaris of Veridia," Ameria suggested. "The balance of power has shifted, and we must shift with it. We can forge a new alliance to counter the Blackwaters' advance.. "

"No," I said again, more loudly.

They all turned to me then.

I could feel the weight of their stares, the confusion and disbelief etched on their faces as I negated their calls to action.

"New Solara is safe," I began, "For now, our focus must be here, within these walls, within this sanctuary we have fought so hard to create. The world outside," I paused, my gaze meeting each of theirs, "belongs to Ramses now."

Ameria's brow furrowed. "But we cannot just sit idle while Ramses destroys everything we—"

I raised a hand to halt her words. "I understand the impulse to fight, to take back what has been lost, but we cannot be hasty. Our people here in New Solara need stability and hope. If we rush to confront Ramses without preparation, without certainty, we risk everything. We must be the shield now, not the sword."

Gael's knuckles were white as he gripped the edge of the table. "And what of the lands that Ramses will ravage? The lives he will take? We cannot—"

"We will not abandon them," I interjected, my resolve hardening. "But we must be strategic. We must rebuild our strength, gather intelligence, and strike when the time is right. If we act out of vengeance or pride, we play into Ramses' hands."

Hisen, thoughtful as ever, nodded slowly. "Eldra is right. Our first duty is to protect what we have here. New Solara must become a beacon of resistance, a place where hope can thrive despite the darkness surrounding us."

Madsen let out a frustrated sigh, her gaze lingering on the gold helmets. "And what of Tor? Will we just watch as Ramses' shadow falls over it?"

"No," I replied firmly. "We will not watch. We will work to undermine his rule, support those in Tor who resist, and ensure that Aislinn's legacy endures. Our fight is not over—it has merely changed. We must adapt, and we must be patient. The Furian saying holds true: Death is not the end. And neither is this."

Emery hissed something in Arathi, shaking her head. "That could take years!"

"It could take a hundred years. A thousand years," I said sadly. "However long it takes, it must be done."

●

One year later.

The problem with living in a secluded place was keeping up with the people's needs. We relied heavily on fishing and hunting. Currency was not a coin but trade.

I strode into the verdant embrace of the forest, the morning mist hanging low, obscuring the path. Emery followed closely, her bow at the ready, scanning the underbrush for any sign of game. We moved with the silence of shadows, communicating with hand gestures more than words.

She halted and gestured towards a thicket where a deer grazed.

Emery raised her bow; the arrow nocked and ready as her gaze fixed on the deer. I watched from a few feet away, appreciating the absolute stillness that had settled over her. Calm and dangerous. But before she could release the arrow, a piercing shriek rent the air. Birds erupted from the trees, and the deer, startled into a blind panic, bolted.

Webs shot out from the trees, aimed at our deer. It made a pitiful bleating noise as it tumbled over raised roots and entangled further into the webs.

My hand went to the hilt of my sword, scanning the trees above us for who I knew to be coming.

They emerged quietly down on silken ropes, so slowly.

The Aranha descended with a grace that belied their monstrous size, their eight legs and two arms working down large tree trunks. Emery hissed at them, crouching low. The Aranha surrounded the ensnared deer, their pincers clicking softly as they worked to secure their catch.

Emery, her body taut and ready for any sign of aggression, looked to me to make the first move. Our people, the Fae, were only sometimes seen favorably by the Aranha, mainly since we had settled in land they claimed as their own. Their grey skin, which allowed them to blend into the tree bark, changed to shades of greens and browns to match the forest floor. Their eyes, numerous and sharp along their puffed cheeks, flicked back and forth between Emery and me, assessing whether we were a threat. They were hairless, save for long braids of bright-colored hair—their bodies scaled in some places and brimmed with hard armor of bone. Slings made of animal hides cradled throwing spears and atlatls on their backs.

I could tell they were all males. The males were smaller than the females. I had only ever seen two females in the year we lived on the island, and that was enough for me not to want to go further into their lands. We could keep our outcrop by the sea—Ameria shrieked at spiders smaller than my thumbnail—I could only imagine what she would do if she saw the Aranha.

Aislinn would have loved them. She embraced all creatures, furry or scaled. I blinked—hard—holding back the grief that threatened to swallow me most nights.

One male raised himself on his back four legs, his large thorax vibrating at us. The others circled, clicking and vibrating.

The tension in the air was palpable, as thick as the webs that the Aranha spun. They all stood—straight-legged and thoraxes high. Attacking one of them would do us no good—we were outnumbered, and I did not want to ruin the fragile peace I had found for our people on the island.

Emery stepped back on a twig—the sound might as well have been a lightning strike.

A mistake. We were never to show them we were afraid.

An Aranha male with an opulent blue body reared up on his hind legs, looming more prominent than the others. His upper body swayed like a cobra about to strike, his pinchers opening and closing with a sound like dry wood snapping.

He charged, legs a blue blur as he upturned rocks and logs to get to Emery.

"Don't move, Em," I hissed as she reached for the dagger at her side and widened her stance.

The Aranha male halted his charge mere inches from Emery, his pincers still snapping in the air between them. The sudden stop sent a cloud of debris skyward, leaves, dirt, and twigs disturbed by the force of his movement. He chuffed in her face, small mouth between his pinchers snarling, red orbs flashing. He tilted his head, studying her pale green skin with interest—noticing the differences between her and me. Her fingers twitched at her side, and she bared her pointed teeth.

I had seen enough of the Aranha on my hunts to know they often performed bluff charges. He seemed to rethink his stance, slowly stepping back from us.

But then the Aranha stumbled back. Their multifaceted eyes darted beyond Emery and me, and their bodies tensed. High-pitched cries, unlike any I'd heard from them before, pierced the air as they leaped into the trees with astonishing agility.

Behind us, a low growl resonated, vibrating through my very bones. Emery and I turned in unison. There, emerging from the underbrush, was a creature—a giant cat with batlike ears that swiveled independently, capturing every sound. Its fur seemed to shift in patterns and colors, blending seamlessly with the forest around it, a natural chameleon. Two sets of eyes focused on us, viper-like teeth dripping with the promise of death.

A Whisperfang. It was too late when you realized you were being hunted.

Emery cursed in Arathi. "Move, don't move?"

"Fucking run!" I shouted.

Emery and I bolted through the forest, our feet pounding against the earth as the Whisperfang's growls echoed close behind us. Emery, not one to flee without a fight, began to conjure her magic, her hands weaving through the air in swift, intricate patterns. Spirals of fire burst from her fingertips, hurling toward the Whisperfang.

"You think we haven't tried using magic on one? It doesn't work on a Whisperfang!" I yelled at her while we ran, dodging low-hanging branches and leaping over roots.

She reached for the dagger at her side—a blade that had felled many men before. "What about steel?" she shouted, her arm swinging wide to send the dagger spinning toward the Whisperfang.

The dagger sailed through the fragmented light of the forest and bounced right off the Whisperfang's shoulder.

"To the cliffs!" I called to Emery, remembering the sheer drops not far from where we were.

We veered sharply, the canopy above barely registering as we sprinted for our lives.

"You didn't think to mention this Whisperfang when you cased this place out?" Emery shouted.

"It's only a problem this deep in the forest—not by the shore," I panted.

The cliffs came into view, a sheer drop to the roiling waters below. We skidded to a halt at the precipice, loose stones tumbling over the edge and into the white caps of the waves.

Emery said something in Arathi. "Tou faust!"

My head swiveled to her. "Did you just call me stupid?"

She laughed incredulously. "*That* you understand?"

I peered over the edge, then back to the tree line where the Whisperfang had broken through, now stalking toward us with an open maw.

I turned to Emery, saying, "Fish tonight?"

She groaned.

We jumped.

❋

"That was too close," Emery gasped, spitting out a mouthful of saltwater.

"Too close? That was madness," I replied, kicking my legs to stay afloat. "You should have seen the look on your face."

I shifted in the water, looking for where New Solara began. I spotted a slight indentation to the east, where the rock face appeared less steep. "There. If we can reach that cove, we might climb up."

Emery followed my gaze, squinting against the sun's glare on the water. "You sure that's not just another one of your illusions?"

I shook my head, the water lapping around my ears. "I would know, wouldn't I? *Tou fast.*"

"If you are going to call me stupid in my tongue, at least say it correctly," she snapped, sending a small wave toward me.

We swam towards the cove, aching muscles and the cold bite of the sea slowing us down.

We dragged ourselves onto the stone-strewn sand, our breaths coming in heavy pants. I turned to look back at the forest, half-expecting to see the Whisperfang emerge at the tree line, but there was nothing but the gentle sway of trees in the breeze.

Emery collapsed beside me, her chest heaving. "Never again, Eldra," she said between breaths. "I mean it. Next time you suggest we hunt in the deep forest, remind me to punch you. I don't care if we have to have just fish for the next fifty years."

"Duly noted," I chuckled.

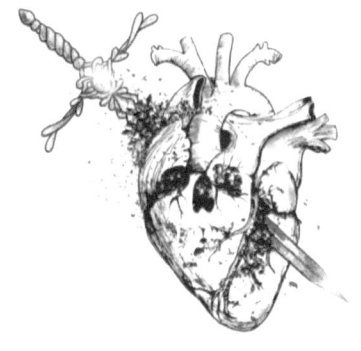

CHAPTER ONE

ATREYA ... 50 YEARS AFTER
THE WAR OF FALLEN SKIES

F loating in the void, my consciousness drifted aimlessly through an expanse of nothingness. There was no up or down, no sense of time or place—just an infinite stretch of darkness that enveloped me. My earliest memory flickered in this boundless void, a lone beacon against the black: a green light, soft and unassuming, pulsing gently like a heartbeat in the darkness. It wasn't attached to anything, just a glow that existed

"In the hush of twilight's room, a curtain of dark hair,
A melody whispered, tender and fair,
A lullaby soft as the evening's cool breath,
A newborn's first cry, piercing the veil of death.

My nursemaid Joslynn's lullaby, drifted over me as I tried to grasp the strands of sleep. I understood her thick accent enough to understand the words she sang, but I never fully understood them. An old song, she would say.

A promise made by a stranger, cloaked in the night,
A vow to protect, to guide towards the light,
With whispered oaths that echo in the stone,
A pact sealed in shadow, a future unknown.

Sometimes, if I closed my eyes hard enough, I could see that green light again. Sometimes that green light shifted and gave way to my dream world. Soft beaches of sand and an ocean that splashed up against rocky cliffs.

"Beneath the castle, where secrets dare to dwell,
Lies a beast in slumber, bound by a spell,
Its wing beats a rhythm, a thunderous drum,
Awaiting the moment its freedom will come."

Other times it sucked me deep into nightmares. Where cold was relentless, and the light of the moon filtered through a small crack.

"Above, the dove dons the raven's dark attire,
Proclaiming peace, yet fanning secret fire,
Its gentle coo, a guise for sly deceit,
Veils the shadowed soul where light and twilight meet."

I told Joslynn about the green light. She said it was just a dream.

"The curtain, the tune, the tears, and the lies,
The beast, the bird, the castle's old ties,
All woven together in life's intricate weave,
A crown, a throne, a Kingdom of thieves."

She told me never to speak of it. That dreams were private, and I would dream less as I got older. I did not tell her about the dream I had of her dying.

"In the chasm's embrace, where no light dares to thread,
A babe from the shadows, its destiny spread,
Born from the dark, where life inverts death,
A whisper of power in each tiny breath.

The darkness of the room ebbed with the cadence of Joslynn's singing, each note a gentle rocking that cradled my thoughts. Even in the dim light, the outlines of the chamber seemed to soften, the edges of reality blurred by the magic of her song.

In olden days, when magic breathed,
And noble hearts were oft deceived,
A tale was spun, so bittersweet,
Of love and loss, of dark deceit.

The green light came less and less as I got older, just as Joslynn said. No more nightmares of cold stone floors or the moonlight. No more beaches or the ocean. No more nightmares of Joslynn lying in the rain.

A crown for the child from the depth of despair,
A throne for the one with night's own stare,
A kingdom awaits for the heir of the night,
To rise from the shadows and claim their right."

I drifted on the edge of sleep until it finally claimed me.

●

"Where are we going?" I asked Joslynn, barely above a whisper. She wove through the corridor, her dark hair bouncing with each step. I hurried to keep up, the gossamer gown she'd forced me into rustling with every move.

"His Majesty has summoned for you; it's best not to keep him waiting," she answered, her accent lilting.

I shivered. "What does His Majesty want with me?"

Joslynn shot me a look. "Does it look like I am full enough to ask?" Her brow was furrowed, her mouth a thin line. "Dat man is all teeth."

"Fool," I corrected, earning a wave of her hand.

I fell silent, knowing better than to press. Joslynn had been with me since I was a babe, her sternness a constant. But beneath that, I knew there was warmth, reserved for few. I was one of them, and her concern wasn't lost on me.

We reached the grand doors of the throne room, the guards nodding to Joslynn. She fussed over me, smoothing my hair, adjusting my gown. "You must look pleasing to 'im." Her hands cupped my breasts, lifting them indecently high. I swatted at her, earning a glare.

The heavy oak doors creaked open, revealing the vast chamber. The air was thick with the scent of oiled wood and incense, the stained-glass windows casting kaleidoscopic patterns on the floor. At the far end, on his elevated throne of Pearl Glass, sat His Majesty.

Joslynn's hand was a steady pressure at my back. I felt my heart thud in my chest.

She bowed low, never rising, and I followed suit, but she stopped me from going to my knees.

His cheekbones were high, his jaw hewn from stone. I drew in a breath, held it.

His smile revealed the glint of fangs, the concealed armaments of a predator. A river of ink coursed up his neck, flowing to his jaw.

I exhaled slowly, twice.

"Atreya," he said.

I dipped my head and curtsied as I'd been taught.

I looked up at him, something I'd been told never to do. His eyebrow twitched, and he smiled, a predator's smile. "You have courage," he remarked, approval in his tone. "It is a trait that will serve you well." He leaned back, tilting his head. Contemplative.

"Or ignorance, your Grace," someone said from the side.

She was my age, maybe, in robes of red and gold, her red hair braided about her head, her face powdered and painted to appear older. Beside her stood a man in black and silver, his white hair pulled back in a bun.

"I did not mean to offend," I stammered.

"Corina, you ignorantly speak out of turn, cousin," His Majesty said, his voice mild. Corina's cheeks flushed deeper red, her braid swaying as she moved to lean into her companion.

His eyes, a striking steel grey, watched the exchange with detachment, as if well-versed in courtly intrigues. His serene expression suggested indifference, but I sensed calculation behind it.

His attention returned to me, the interruption dismissed as if it were no more than a buzzing fly. "Atreya," he continued, his warmth returning. "How have your studies progressed?"

I blinked. Had he summoned us in the middle of the night to ask about my schooling?

Joslynn pinched my ankle, and I jolted, answering, "They are going well."

Corina's companion snorted, and His Majesty turned to him. "Servat. You have something to add to that?"

The man shrugged, looking bored. "Her archery is atrocious."

Corina snickered. Joslynn's fingers tightened on my ankle, a silent plea for restraint. I swallowed the retort that threatened to escape, studying the intricately woven rug instead.

His Majesty's chuckle reverberated through the room, terrifying and captivating. "Atreya, is this true?" he asked, amusement curling his lips.

I glanced up, embarrassed. "I may not have the aim of a seasoned hunter, but I am improving."

"Improvement is all we can ask for," he said, nodding thoughtfully. "And I trust that you will continue to strive for excellence in all your endeavors, not just archery."

I nodded. "Of course, Your Grace."

Another pinch from Joslynn.

"Ouch," I exhaled. She let out a panicked breath.

"Something the matter?" His Majesty asked, resting his chin on his knuckles. I shook my head. "Good. Tell me... have you had any strange occurrences?"

I shook my head again. "No, your Grace."

"Not with your... body?" He pressed.

I blushed deeper red than Corina. I looked down at the carpet, the muted colors a welcome distraction. "I have...bled," I stuttered, the words rushing out.

"You are fifty winters."

Not a question, but I nodded anyway. He clicked his tongue, turning to Corina. "When did you start bleeding, Corina?"

"About the same," she answered briskly. "Earlier, even."

"And this is a...normal occurrence then. For girls your age?"

"Fae females start their blood at different times. Some as young as thirty years. I have seen some as old as one hundred. For humans, it's even faster. Eleven. Some to seventeen," Corina offered.

"Fleeting creatures," His Majesty added, "Insignificant."

I waited.

"And there is nothing else you have noticed?" He asked.

I stopped myself from complaining about my sore breasts, wondering what else he expected.

"No, your Grace."

His Majesty stared at me, unblinking, as if trying to peer into my soul. "Very well," he finally said with a hint of impatience. "The reason I summoned you is more... nuanced than a mere inquiry into your health or skills."

I straightened, trying to appear composed. Joslynn's grip on my ankle had relaxed, but I could still feel the ghost of her warning.

"The blood signifies more than just maturity. It marks the awakening of potential—a potential that I have been waiting for."

He sounded displeased, as if I'd kept him waiting.

Corina and Servat were still now, their earlier amusement replaced by intense focus. It seemed they, too, were unaware of this so-called potential I possessed.

"Your Grace," I started but stopped, feeling Joslynn's grip tightening again. I had to stop myself from yanking her. I bit my lip, waiting.

"It is of no matter now. See yourself in bed. I shall speak to you first thing in the morning and every morning and night after that until I am satisfied." His Majesty strode from the throne room, the door closing behind him with a resounding thud.

●

The walk back to my bedchamber was a silent one. Joslynn was all stiff-backed and formal, wringing her hands in her apron. When we were finally inside, she let out a shuddering breath and turned to me.

"Arrogant and *foo*-lish," she snapped, emphasizing the word I had corrected her on earlier. I turned to stare at her, my mouth agape.

"I thought you were going to tell him da days of your cycle, da way you ramble on! And speakin' outta turn? Have I teach you nothing?"

Her reprimand continued, a torrent of concerns and admonishments, in a language I vaguely understood, and I could only murmur a correction under my breath, "Taught."

Her eyes snapped to mine. "You know what I say," she retorted, frustration fluttering her jaw.

Her outburst caught me off guard, and her usually contained composure crumbled before me. Her face was flushed with anger and concern, and it dawned on me just how much she feared the consequences of my naivety.

"I'm sorry, Joslynn," I stammered. "I was caught unprepared and... and I didn't know what he wanted from me."

Her expression softened slightly, and she let out another weary sigh, her anger dissipating as quickly as it had flared. "Atreya, my dear," returning to her usual sternness but with a hint of affection, "'Tis are dangerous times, and His Majesty is not one to be trifled with. You must be cautious wit' your utterances and actions."

Joslynn moved closer, placing a gentle hand on my shoulder. "You are more than just a ward of the court, more than you even know."

"I-I don't understand," I said.

Her lips pursed, weighing something in her mind. "Men *see* you. D'ey notice you. You are of age. You are beautiful. Arguably da most beautiful of all da girls in da kingdom, and you have bled..." She stopped, shaking her head. "The King is not blind to dis. Aye, he is not blind to you. He has wanted you from da moment your cry came into dis world, and for reasons dat are his own."

My earliest memory was of a wooden rocking horse in a large room. Joslynn coaxed me to sit in the saddle. Whenever I asked about my mother, Joslynn said she did not know her. I had lived under the assumption that I was orphaned, a ward of no consequence who had been granted the king's mercy. Yet Joslynn's claim painted a different picture, one where I was not merely an object of pity but a person of interest to the king—a person of enough importance that my very existence was intertwined with his desires.

I twisted the gossamer in my hands, unable to look at her. "Are you saying... the King desires me now?"

Joslynn's gaze intensified, and she took a moment before responding, choosing her words carefully. "It's not desire as you might tink of it, Atreya. His interest in you goes beyond da superficial," she said, her tone serious. "Your beauty is but a facet of you. It is what you represent, da power dat lies within you, dat he seeks to 'arness."

Harness.

I held back my correction. Confusion etched across my face. "But why? What power could I possibly have that would interest the king so much?"

She opened her mouth to say something, anger flaring, but stopped. Her expression shifted, paling to a ghostly hue, her hand flying to her throat, clawing at it. Horror clenched my gut as I realized she couldn't draw breath.

Joslynn lay crumpled on the floor, her body trembling as she struggled to draw air into her lungs. Her eyes, usually so sharp and full of fire, had rolled back in her head, leaving only the whites showing in a terrifying display.

This wasn't the first time I had witnessed Joslynn's strange affliction, a disorder that came without warning, seizing her breath and consciousness in an iron grip. At times, she would faint, her body going limp as if the strings of her life had been cut, only to awaken moments later, gasping and disoriented.

"Joslynn! Joslynn!" I shouted, covering her hands with my own. She came to a few moments later, unfocused. I knelt beside her, placing a hand on her back, waiting for her to regain her breath.

I remembered the first time it had happened, in the gardens on a day when the sun had been particularly unforgiving.

Joslynn had been instructing me on the proper way to address the courtiers, her tone strict as ever, when suddenly her speech had faltered, her hand flying to her throat. I had watched in horror as she had collapsed, a delicate flower wilting in the heat.

Since then, these episodes had come at odd intervals, sometimes months apart, occasionally mere days. The court physicians were baffled, unable to diagnose the cause, and their treatments did little to prevent it.

She had said that their medicines could not fix what was inside of her. Not even the humans had an answer.

Gradually, the color returned to her cheeks, and her breathing steadied. She coughed a rough sound, music, to my ears because it meant the air was reaching her lungs again. She groaned as she fought her way back to consciousness.

"Joslynn, can you hear me?" I asked as she slowly oriented herself, her gaze fixing on me with recognition.

She nodded weakly with a raspy whisper when she spoke. "I'm here, child. Forgive me."

"There's nothing to forgive," I said, helping her to sit up. "You mustn't apologize for this."

She took several gulps of air. "Oh, child. For all da world you look so young, and I fear da innocents be stripped away from you. I fear da world will tear you down to no-thing, and you will not know yourself."

I shook my head.

The ramblings of an old Fae, her mind must be sick.

"Hold onto that little light in you 'Treya when da world is dark. Hold onto it and let it shine," she whispered.

I hushed her, bringing a blanket from the chaise in the corner and laying it over her.

I watched Joslynn's chest rising and falling with each labored breath, her ramblings lingering in the room's stillness like a silent prayer. Her moments of breathlessness had become more frequent, and my concern for her deepened with each one. She had always been the pillar of strength in my life, unwavering and steadfast, and to see her so vulnerable...

"Joslynn," I said softly, brushing a strand of hair from her forehead, "you must rest. We will speak no more of this tonight."

"Promise me, Atreya," she rasped, "promise me you will remember what I say. The light within you is precious, and it will guide you when shadows fall."

I squeezed her hand, a promise forming in my heart. "I promise, Joslynn. I will hold onto it. I won't let the darkness take me."

Ramblings of an old Fae. There was no darkness in Ember.

●

"Stand before the King," a soldier ordered from my bowed position. It was early morning, and the sun was breaking through the morning mist, casting a golden glow over the throne room. I wore my finest clothes: a pale green gown that clung to my curves and a black ribbon tied around my waist. The bright and colorful beading spiraled around the hemline into bouquets. I left my hair loose, the ebony curls falling past my shoulders, and my eyes were lined in dark kohl.

Joslynn had said to leave my hair out. That it was more sensual that way.

The way the King looked at me now, I knew he appreciated it.

As I stood and approached the throne, I could feel the weight of the King's stare upon me, measuring, calculating.

With each step I took towards His Majesty, my heartbeat quickened, but I focused on maintaining the grace and poise Joslynn had drilled into me since childhood. The gown's fabric whispered against the marble floor, a soft counterpoint to the tension in the air.

I stopped a respectful distance from the King, my head bowed slightly in deference. His Majesty's throne, a towering structure of carved Pearl Glass and gilded embellishments, seemed to loom over the room, catching what little light streamed in through the tall windows. It was a perfect throne, a halo of light surrounding it.

"Your Grace," I began, trying to keep my enunciations clear and steady despite the fluttering in my stomach.

The intensity of his stare made my throat dry. "Atreya," he greeted, "You are a vision this morning."

"Thank you, Your Grace," I replied, a flush warming my cheeks at his compliment. I remembered Joslynn's warning about the King's interest in me, about the potential he saw within. It was a dance of courtly manners, and every word and gesture held meaning.

The King rose from his throne of Pearl Glass, the light reflecting off the smooth, pearly surface and creating a luminescent aura around him. He descended the steps, his regal bearing unquestionable.

My heart hammered in my chest as he came to stand before me.

Slowly, his hand came to grip my chin, gently forcing me to look up at him. He tilted my face this way and that, examining, clucking his tongue when he held my silver orbs in his.

His attention lowered to my lips, and my mouth went dry. "Every day you grow more beautiful, Atreya, more radiant, more alluring."

I heated at his praise.

"Thank you, Your Grace," I managed to say softly. It was all I could muster under his piercing scrutiny, which seemed to see through me, to the very essence of my being.

"Call me Ramses."

I tried to swallow down the shock on my face, and he laughed at me. The sound was rich and deep, and my heart fluttered dangerously at the sound.

"Ramses," I echoed, the name feeling forbidden and exhilarating as it passed my lips. His laughter, rarely heard within these walls, seemed to bridge the gap between us.

His gaze upon me softened, and he released my chin, stepping back to give me a moment to collect myself. "You will need to get used to it. Any change today?" he asked.

•

Ramses came to me the next night. I had hoped for something else, what I had hoped for.

I don't know what I had dared to hope for.

A knock on my door in the middle of the night.

"Who on Earth could dat be?" Joslynn mumbled in the darkness, bringing a candle to float before her. She was curled up on the couch in my living room, her nightgown wrapped around her body.

When she opened the door, the candle clattered to the floor, and so did she, her head bowed.

I stumbled out of bed, tripping over the sheet and falling to the floor.

Scrambling to my feet, my heart racing with alarm and confusion, I rushed to the door, the cool night air brushing against my skin. There stood Ramses, his presence commanding even in the dimly lit corridor. He glanced at me, an unreadable expression on his face.

"Your Grace—R-Ramses," I stammered, instinctively reaching for the neckline of my nightgown to ensure I was decent. "What brings you here at this hour?"

Joslynn made a pained sound, and I knew what she wanted to say. 'You never question the King!'

He asked me if I felt any different. I told him that I was the same. He had been looking at me expectantly, waiting for me to say something else. He scrunched up his nose like he didn't believe me.

"Are you sure?" he asked, analyzing me. "You feel no change at all?"

I nodded, my heart pounding in my chest. What was he expecting me to say? That I could hear the whispers of the wind or speak to the animals?

He sighed in disappointment, turning away from me. "You should rest," he had said dismissively, cold and distant. "We'll see in a few days."

"I'm sorry," I blurted out.

He stopped in his tracks, his head cocked in my direction. I held my breath, my eyes wide and my heart pounding as he looked at me.

"You do not need to be sorry," he said, leaning in close and placing a chaste kiss on my cheek.

My knees wobbled, and my heart thundered in my ears as I made some bleating noise of surprise, my cheeks heating up.

•

That night, as I lay in my bed, I couldn't help but feel a sense of unease. Ramses' words echoed in my mind, his disappointment stinging like a fresh wound. I was supposed to be unique, to have some exceptional gift. But I was just...me. Ordinary, plain me.

As the days turned into weeks and weeks into months, I waited for the change Ramses alluded to.

But nothing happened.

I was still the same. Still ordinary. Still plain. Still...me.

And with each passing day, Ramses' disappointment grew. He barely looked at me or spoke to me. I was a failure, a disappointment.

And I could feel it.

Then came the day, a day like any other, marked only by the inevitable cycle of my body. Ramses' sudden presence was a storm breaking upon the quiet shore of my solitude. He burst into my study room, nostrils flaring, eyes pools of golden light.

"Ramses," I breathed, bowing my head as I had been taught. He wasn't followed by his usual entourage of servants and guards. I glanced around, remembering that I was alone with just my books for company. I could sense his coiled strength, the royal bearing that never faltered, even in his most private moments. He was always the king, always the hunter, and I—the prey.

"Ramses," I said again, steadying myself as I straightened, "to what do I owe this unexpected visit?"

He stopped mere inches from me, the heat of his body a stark contrast to the cool air of the study. His nostrils flared as if scenting the air. I blushed, knowing he could smell me.

Then, he snapped me around; his breath was hot on my neck, his touch a brand that seared through the fabric of my gown.

"You are of outstanding stock. You will be exceptional. Your mother was special, and your father, too," he said lowly.

The words fumbled out. "My mother?" I was dazed.

He hummed. "If you prove yourself worthy, I will reward you greatly."

He stood behind me, his body a solid wall of heat and yearning. His hands gripped my shoulders, fingers digging in with a desperation that bordered on pain. He drew me back against him, and I could feel the fierce drum of his heart against my spine.

His fingers pinched my jaw, raising my head to him. His lips found mine in a possessive kiss, a claim that left no room for doubt. Those hands slid to my waist, pulling me closer, and I was lost in the sensation. The fear mingled with a strange intoxication that was better than any wine I had ever tasted.

At that moment, I was acutely aware of his power, not just as a king but as a man. His frustration was palpable, a living thing between us, and I—untried and overwhelmed—could only respond in kind to my kiss fueled by a mixture of dread and a desire to please, to meet the expectations that loomed over me.

My hands fumbled in his hair, my fingers tangling in the soft strands. His mouth was hot and wet, his tongue claiming my own in a dance I didn't quite understand.

Joslynn had taught me the basics. I would know if I was doing it right by the man's response.

I turned and dragged a hand down his chest, feeling the solidity of his muscles beneath his royal robes.

Lower. Lower.

There.

He snarled against my mouth while I cupped him, exploring the hard length of him with the tips of my fingers.

I could feel the growl rumbling from deep within Ramses' chest, the primal sound sending shivers down my spine. His body responded with a fierce intensity that both frightened and thrilled me. His hands tightened around my waist, urging me closer as if he sought to meld us into one being.

His snarl confirmed Joslynn's teachings, a sign that I had breached the walls of his restraint. I was no longer the prey but an equal in this exchange of power and passion. This realization ignited a newfound confidence within me, a boldness that I had never known I possessed.

I squeezed him—hard. He groaned, lifting me off the ground, wrapping my legs around his waist, and carrying me to the wall. My head hit the stone, and his lips were upon my neck, his teeth grazing my skin.

He was grinding into me, guiding my hips, teaching me the rhythm that our bodies craved. I moved with him, matching his urgency, the friction of our movements stoking the flame that threatened to consume us both.

The heat of his body, the strength of his embrace, and the demanding press of his lips overwhelmed my senses, leaving me breathless and wanting.

I clung to Ramses, my nails digging into his shoulders as I met each of his movements with an enthusiasm that surprised me. My world had narrowed to the space where our bodies joined, to the relentless pursuit of a pleasure that I had only ever read about in the hidden passages of my books or the quiet of my bedroom.

He pulled away from me with a curse, and I slipped from his grasp, falling to the hard floor, panting.

He left me there, fleeing the room without so much as a look back.

I lay on the cold, unforgiving floor, the heat of our kissing lingering on my skin, my head bowed.

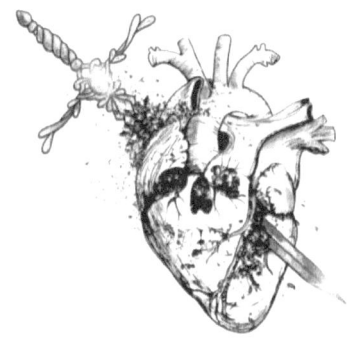

CHAPTER TWO

ATREYA

The morning sun crept through the canopy of trees, casting staggered lines of light across the dusty makeshift floor of the archery range. The musty smell of painted straw targets and wood filled the air. I notched an arrow to the bow, pulling the string back with all the strength I could muster. My fingers trembled slightly, the bowstring taut against my fingertips, my breath caught in my throat.

I released the arrow. It whistled through the air, a swift blur of hope—and missed the bullseye by a laughable margin, thudding into the outer ring of the target with a hollow thud.

Servat, who had been watching from a distance, laughed lightly. His chuckle was like scraping a blade on a stone, the sound grating against my nerves. "Find that funny, do you?" I snarled, notching another arrow and aiming it at him. He rose a brow in amusement, his grin widening into a mocking sneer that made my blood simmer.

"You're not going to hit me holding your breath like that," he said condescendingly, his voice dripping with the kind of confidence that made me want to prove him wrong.

His words stung, a barbed spear meant to rile me up, and it worked. My grip on the bow tightened, my knuckles turning white. I could feel the anger boiling within me, urging me to let the arrow fly, to wipe that smug look off his face. But I didn't. Instead, I took a deep breath, letting his mockery wash over me like a cold bath. I wouldn't give him the satisfaction.

"Someone must be sexually frustrated," he laughed again, his eyes glinting with amusement.

That did it.

I released the arrow, aimed directly at his head. And thank the Gods, the lucky bastard dodged it. The guards shouted and moved in, only for Servat to hold his hand up and stop them. He looked at me from the arrow lodged in the wooden beam, his grin almost feral. My heart thumped against my rib cage. He and Ramses smiled the same.

I could feel the tension in the air, thick as the morning mist that clung to the grass around the archery range. My breath was heavy, my chest heaving with adrenaline and the remnants of my rage. The guards, halted by Servat's raised hand, looked from him to me, uncertainty etched into their faces. It was stupid of me. Attacking the King's right hand. His half-brother.

Servat stepped forward, his stride confident. "You've got balls, I'll give you that," he said, no longer mocking but a creeping hint of respect. "But if you want to kill me, you'll have to do better than that. Much better."

I swallowed hard; my earlier fury rightfully dissolved into a cold knot of fear. What had I done? Attacking a man of Servat's standing could have serious consequences, yet he seemed more intrigued than angry. Like he had found a new toy.

The guards eyed me warily, fingers twitching near the hilts of their swords, but Servat waved them off once more. "Leave us," he commanded, and after a hesitant moment, they obeyed, sheathing their swords and retreating to a respectful distance.

Once they were gone, Servat turned his full attention to me. His gaze was intense, as if he were appraising me. "You're desperate to prove yourself," he observed, stepping closer. "Want to prove that you are worthy of my King's affections. That's good. But desperation without control is like an untamed horse—it'll throw you off and trample you the first chance it gets."

My cheeks heated at his words, a mix of shame and defiance burning in my chest.

He cocked his head at me. "How are you with a sword?" His question took me aback, and I opened and closed my mouth like a fish. He pulled his sword from his side, the metal singing, and I jumped back. The glint of steel in the morning light made my heart race.

"Relax," he said, pointing with the pommel for me to take. "Hopefully, you're not as shit with a sword."

The sword felt foreign in my hands, a solid weight that pulled at my arms with a gravity I wasn't accustomed to. I had held a sword before, but only in the most basic training sessions, where the movements were choreographed, and the threat was imaginary. It's just something to pass the time. This, however, was different. Servat's gaze was a shearing force, and his expectation was a new challenge.

I tried to mimic the stance I had been taught, with my feet shoulder-width apart, one foot slightly forward, and the blade held out in a defensive position. I must have looked like a child playing soldiers, and I half-expected Servat to laugh again, to unleash another biting remark.

But he didn't. Instead, he nodded, a severe gleam in his eyes. "Not completely hopeless," he conceded. "But let's see how you move with it." He pulled another sword from the hilt between his shoulder blades. It was thinner than the one he had offered me.

Without warning, he stepped into a fluid attack, the edge of his blade a silver flash in the sunlight. I raised the sword awkwardly, managing to block his strike by sheer luck more than skill. The impact reverberated through my arms, jarring my bones.

"Good," he said, "You didn't freeze. Now, let's make your response deliberate instead of accidental."

He wacked me with the flat of his sword on my arm and I yelped, pain flaring through my skin.

"You were supposed to block that," he said pointedly, his gaze never leaving mine.

I rubbed at the stinging spot on my arm, my eyes narrowing at Servat. "What's the matter? Did I wound the King's plaything?" I spat, my anger rising to the surface once more.

He kicked my feet out from under me, and the wind knocked out of me. I landed hard on the dusty ground, the sword skittering from my grasp. "Try harder," he said, standing over me. There was more bite to his tone now, so different from the gentleness he had offered me.

This Servat was different. His eyes were hard, his mouth a thin line. He was no longer the mocking courtier, but a warrior, a man who would push me to my limits and beyond. And despite the fear thrumming through my veins, I couldn't help but feel a spark of excitement, a thrill of challenge. Because for the first time in my life, I felt seen, not as a ward of the court, but as a potential equal.

His thin sword was aimed under my chin now, his head cocked to the side, white hair falling over one shoulder. I could see the glint of amusement in his eyes, the slight curl of his lip. I was heaving now, my back on fire, the hilt of his overly large sword heavy in my grip. I tried lifting it, my wrist screaming in protest.

He snorted. "A newborn fawn has more grace." His comment was like a lash, striking at my already frayed nerves.

Ignoring the scream of muscles and the ache in my bones, I rolled to the side, lifting the sword again. "It's too heavy," I snapped, my frustration boiling over. I glared up at him, my chest heaving with exertion.

His lip curled ever so slightly into a sneer. "A sword is only as heavy as the will of the one who wields it. You're a Fae, not a human. Act like it." His words were a challenge, a gauntlet thrown at my feet.

I straightened and shifted the grip, finding the balance point, and something clicked. I lifted it higher, legs spread out and squatting slightly. The weight of the sword was still there, but now it felt manageable, an extension of my body rather than a burden.

"There you go," he chuckled, a note of approval in his tone. He circled me like a predator, his gaze never leaving mine. My gaze settled on him, every muscle in me coiled tightly—waiting.

Without warning, he lunged, the thin sword aimed at my heart. I sidestepped, the blade grazing the fabric of my tunic. I swung my sword in a clumsy arc, but Servat was no longer there. He was at my side, his sword at my throat again.

"If I didn't know any better, I would say you're trying to kill me," I breathed. The cold steel kissed my neck, and I blinked. My heart was a wild bird in my chest, thrumming against my ribs.

"Better," he admitted, "But you practically scream your moves." He tapped the flat of his blade gently against my neck. "If I can see your strike coming, it's already too late for you." His breath was warm against my ear, the hairs on my arm standing up in response.

His gaze was intense, his eyes burning with a fierce light. I could feel the heat of his body, the press of his chest against my arm. It was a jolt of awareness, a spark of attraction that flared to life in the space between us.

"Servat," a hardened voice rang out.

Servat removed the blade from my neck, standing at attention once more. I rubbed the spot on my neck and swallowed, looking into an observatory box where Ramses stood looking down at us. Ramses stood tall, his wild red hair a stark flame against the dark backdrop of the observatory box. It fell in untamed waves down his chest. Sunlit yellow eyes analyzed us. His tunic was a deep, rich black, tailored to fit perfectly and trimmed in gold. Over this, he wore a fitted, dark burgundy vest. He lightly tapped the wooden rail with his clawed fingers.

"Your Grace," Servat called up to Ramses, carrying a respectful neutrality. There was no fear when Servat spoke to him—it mostly sounded like careful indifference.

I bowed, trying to hide my dirty skirts with my hands. My cheeks were flushed, my body thrumming with exertion and a spark of attraction.

"I haven't seen anyone wield a sword like that since Corina," Ramses chuckled.

"Corina hasn't wielded a sword like that since she could walk," Servat huffed with his arms crossed.

"We all started somewhere. You didn't come out of your mother's womb in armor," Ramses said. He cocked his head at me. "I watched you. You went from being unable to lift the great sword to using it like a stick." His gaze was warm, a note of pride in his smirk.

I blushed. "I was worried I'd lose my head if I didn't." My eyes flicked to where Servat stood. He didn't even react.

"I see..." Ramses mused. He stared off into the distance, mulling something over in his head. "We never know what we are capable of until we have no choice." He glanced over me again, and I felt my skin heat under it. I remembered the way his hands felt on my body—the way his tongue danced with mine. The way he stared at me made me wonder if he was also thinking about it.

Servat cleared his throat and shifted on his feet.

Right. Fae senses.

"You should go and get cleaned up," Ramses said, offering me an excuse to leave politely. I bowed to him, offering Servat his sword back, curling back my lip as I did so. It was a small act of defiance, a spark of the attraction that still thrummed between us.

It didn't have the desired effect I had hoped for, for in his steel eyes, amusement danced. He took the sword from me, his fingers brushing against mine. The touch sent a jolt of awareness through me, a spark of attraction that flared to life in the space between us.

I left them there, the sound of their laughter echoing in my ears. I could feel their gazes on me, a weight that settled in the pit of my stomach. I knew that I had caught their attention, that I had sparked something in them that couldn't be ignored.

•

Ramses had flowers sent to my room—a bundle of orchids ranging from purples and pinks to pure whites. No flowers were like that in Ember. Joslynn gave a whimsical sigh, resting her head in her hand. "Dey say orchids symbolize strength and beauty—quite fitting for you."

"They say orchids symbolize strength and beauty—quite fitting for you."

I set the flowers on the wooden table beside me, the scent filling the room. "Ramses is too kind," I said, though a part of me questioned the gesture. He had left me breathless on the floor when we were last alone.

Joslynn chuckled, her dark, curly hair shimmering in the soft light that filtered through the window. "Or perhaps he's smitten. And why wouldn't he be? Look at you."

I shrugged, feeling the soreness of my muscles from the earlier training. "I think he's apologizing for how Servat handled me in the training area."

Joslynn clicked her tongue. "A lady is to be good at archery. You do not need swordplay. Focus more on your dancing."

"Corina knows how to use a sword," I said, stretching my limbs. "I want to impress Ramses."

"Wear a tighter dress, and he will be impressed plenty."

I scowled and looked down at my chest. "That's not the kind of impression I want to leave," I retorted, a bit sharper than intended. "I want Ramses to see me, not just a... a decoration at his court." I glanced back at the flowers and sighed.

"You will never be his equal, not in politics or power. He will always see you as da pretty ting you are," Joslynn said carefully.

Despite that, I straightened my back, tilting my chin up defiantly. "Perhaps," I conceded with gritted teeth. "But I'll be damned if I don't at least earn his respect."

Joslynn studied me for a moment, and then her expression softened. "Come," she said, a new spark in her eye. "Let's go to da training yard. Watching da soldiers might give you a different perspective."

Curious, I followed her outside. The training yard was alive with the clang of steel and the shouts of men. The air was thick with the scent of sweat and soil, the afternoon sun casting long shadows across the ground.

We leaned against a fence, observing the soldiers. Their muscles flexed and gleamed with sweat as they sparred, their swords catching the sunlight with every skilled movement. Even among the formidable soldiers, Ramses stood out. His movements were fluid and precise, his back muscles shifting under his tunic with each strike. His red hair was tied back, showing more black swirls decorating his neck.

Beside him, Servat was a whirlwind of skill and agility. His white hair was high in a bun, skin glittering under the hot sun. His sword was a blur as he parried Ramses' attacks. They moved together in a lethal ballet, perfectly matched in their intensity.

I couldn't look away.

"They're incredible," I breathed. I licked my lips, watching as Servat rolled away from Ramses, swinging his sword down. Had it been anyone else, they would have perished.

Joslynn nodded. "Dey are. And you see, Atreya, you're not a soldier who should be respected on the field. They will entertain you. Put a sword in your hand. But dey do not expect you to be like dem. But dat doesn't mean you can't command respect in other ways."

I watched as Ramses deftly dodged a low sweep from Servat, countering with a swift thrust of his own. His strength had a grace and lethal elegance that was mesmerizing.

I fanned myself with my hand. "Hot out here."

Joslynn took a handkerchief from her dress and dabbed my neck and forehead. "Dis be a good time to show you what I mean." She lightly shook out the handkerchief, letting it flow in the breeze. It fluttered through the training yard before landing in the dirt.

For a moment, the only sounds were the grunts of exertion and the ring of metal until a sudden stillness fell over the yard. Ramses and Servat stood straight as if a silent signal had passed between them. They sniffed the air, their heightened senses detecting a subtle fragrance that had intruded upon the scent of sweat and steel.

Their eyes locked onto the small square of fabric lying innocuously on the ground. They both moved to retrieve it. Servat reached it first, his hand hovering over the handkerchief as Ramses approached. But after a pause that seemed to stretch, Servat stepped back, allowing Ramses to pick it up.

He brought it to his nose and inhaled deeply, his eyes closing briefly.

My stomach fluttered, and I blushed.

The sun caught the edges of his hair, turning it into a blazing corona that framed his face.

I watched, my breath catching as Ramses walked towards us. The intensity in his gaze was unnerving, yet I couldn't look away. He stopped at the fence, just a hair's breadth away, his presence and scent overwhelming.

"Is this yours?" he asked, tilting his head and offering the handkerchief to me.

I nodded, extending my hand to take it back. "Yes, thank you." Our fingers brushed as the handkerchief changed hands, sending electricity up my arm.

For a moment, it felt like he was peering into my soul. "It's a hot day for spectating," Ramses remarked, a hint of a smile on his lips.

Joslynn nudged my side with her elbow.

"I wanted to thank you," I managed to say.

He furrowed his brows slightly. "What for?"

"The flowers in my room. The orchids. They are beautiful and my new favorite," I answered shyly.

Ramses' thoughtful expression deepened as he glanced back at Servat, who was wiping the sweat from his brow with the back of his arm. After a moment, Ramses turned his attention back to me.

"You are welcome," he said quietly, the corner of his mouth lifting in a faint smile. There was something unreadable in his gaze, a hidden depth that I longed to understand.

With that, he gave a curt nod and returned to the center of the yard, where Servat awaited. They resumed their training with renewed vigor. Joslynn and I watched for a while longer, and now and again, I would catch a glimpse of him looking at me, and my heart would skip a beat.

As the sun began to dip below the horizon, laying a warm glow over the yard, Joslynn touched my shoulder. "Let's head back," she said, pulling me from my reverie. "You've had a long day."

We made our way back to my chambers, the coolness of the stone corridors a welcome relief from the heat outside. When we opened the door to my room, we were greeted by an unexpected sight. The chamber was filled with the delicate scent of orchids, even more abundant than before. The wooden table, the windowsills, and every possible surface were adorned with the exotic flowers in an array of purples, pinks, and whites. Ribbons of gold were wrapped around crystal vases.

Beside the orchids were boxes of chocolates, their contents revealed under half-open lids, and jewels that sparkled even in the dimming light. I stepped into the room, a hand over my heart.

"Ramses—" I couldn't finish my train of thought.

Joslynn whistled softly. "Seems like da King is determined to make his impression."

I walked further into the room, my fingers tracing the petals of an orchid, the cool jewels, the smooth chocolates.

"I don't understand," I whispered, more to myself than Joslynn. "Why all this?"

"I told ya da King desires you," Joslynn said, helping herself to a chocolate. "Mirian chocolate. Expensive," she mused between bites.

"What do I do now? Do I give him a gift?"

She scoffed, "You are a woman. Let him woo you. D'ere is nothin' more to be done."

"How am I supposed to let him know I accept his courtship then?"

She wiped her hands on the rag, biting her cheek. She sat down at the foot of my bed, plucking at a stray thread of bed linen.

"Child. It would not matter if you did not wish to be courted. You are his ward. You were always his. You wouldn't have a choice."

She sounded sad.

And yet, as I looked around the room at the lavish gifts surrounding me, I couldn't help but be excited.

How bad could it be?

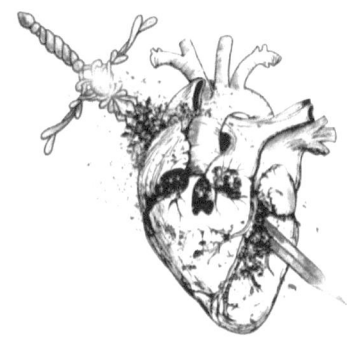

CHAPTER THREE

ATREYA

I screamed against the soldier's grip that threatened to rip my arm off as he dragged me naked from my bed. Joslynn was in tears, begging them to stop.

"The King's orders!" one of the soldiers shouted over Joslynn's wailing.

I fought back, clawing and biting at the soldier as he dragged me from my chamber. "What have I done?" I screamed. The soldier's grip was iron, unforgiving, as he hauled me away with only my bottom undergarments to hide myself.

"What have I done?" The question tore repeatedly from my throat, raw and laced with desperation.

Had it been all of those times I talked out of turn? Had Joslynn been right all along?

Had I displeased him when I touched him?

The soldier did not answer, unyielding as he pulled me through the dimly lit corridors of the castle. The cold stone beneath my feet and the harsh grip on my arm contrasted with the warmth and safety of my bed, which I had been torn from moments ago.

Joslynn's pleading faded into the distance as we moved further away from my chambers. I could hear the echo of other soldiers' boots against the stone. Fear clawed at my insides, fear of what awaited me at the end of this.

The soldier never wavered as he forced me down a narrow staircase, the steps spiraling into darkness.

The staircase led to a tunnel, its walls closing around us, the air growing damp and heavy with each step. My skin prickled with the chill, my breath forming clouds that danced away into the shadows. The sound of our passage was a hollow rumble, the stone carrying our presence deep into the castle's bowels.

A torchlight flickered against the tunnel walls, illuminating the rough stone and iron fittings that held the tunnel together. The soldier's silence was a void that my fears rushed to fill, his stoic demeanor offering no hint of what was to come.

We emerged into the open air, the chill of the predawn breeze cutting through me. The sky was still a tapestry of fading stars and the first blush of morning light, a beautiful sight that seemed cruelly indifferent to my plight. He led me to another door that was just a mouth of darkness. He led me down the steps into another narrow corridor that wound and spun and made me dizzy. My heels dug into the earth as I fought against him until his hands entangled into my hair and pulled.

Finally, the oppressive corridor opened into a hollow space. The vaulted ceilings were lined with metal scaffolding, and thick oil lamps hung from them. The space smelled of death.

Hell. I've been dragged into Hell.

The soldier halted as the giant doors swung open, and I was roughly turned to face the structure before us—an Arena, its towering walls imposing and unyielding. Torches flickered along its circumference, casting dancing shadows and an ominous glow.

I stood there, shivering, as the realization of my destination sank in. The Arena was a place of combat and spectacle, where the kingdom's conflicts and entertainment were settled. But why was I, unarmed, naked and untrained, being brought here?

Another soldier approached, cloth in hand, and draped it around my shoulders—a small mercy that did little to shield me from the vulnerability I felt. I clutched it to myself, trying to cover my breasts.

"Be quick. Stay strong," the soldier whispered. I recognized that voice, a far cry from the scoffing and dismissive tone that had greeted me when I heard it previously.

"Servat," I whispered back, "Please. What did I do? Is this about the training yard?"

Servat's beautiful dark face was hard to read, but I saw sympathy in his steel eyes, a humanity that I had not expected from him. He nodded toward the Arena, "I cannot offer you more than this cloth. I—" he stopped himself, flinching.

"Fight back."

The gates of the Arena creaked, and I was shoved forward. The sandy floor of the Arena was cool under my feet as I stumbled into the center of the vast space.

From the royal box, a figure descended the stairs—Ramses. His face was a mask of regal composure, but I could see the tightness around his mouth, the barely concealed frustration.

"Atreya," he called out, echoing in the still dawn air. "I had hoped it would not come to this."

"What is this?" I asked desperately. "What have I done to deserve such treatment?"

"You have not done anything wrong," Ramses replied.

As Ramses spoke, I noticed the stands beginning to fill, the early risers of the kingdom filtering into the Arena with a mixture of curiosity and excitement. Word had spread quickly, as it always did, and the crowd was eager to witness whatever spectacle was about to unfold. Their murmurs and whispers merged into a dull roar reverberating against the stone walls, heightening my sense of exposure. I tried to cover myself with my hands, my blood coating my thighs. I wanted to wipe it off and hide the evidence of such a thing with the small cloth Servat had given me.

I let out a quiet sob.

Ramses' sneer swept over the crowd, then returned to me. "This is your final chance," he declared. "If there is any spark of power within you, the threat of death will surely ignite it."

I barely had time to process his words before the gates on the opposite side of the Arena began to open, revealing the shadow of something large and monstrous. The crowd's anticipation was palpable, a collective breath held as they waited for the creature to emerge.

Fight back, Servat had said. But how could I fight against a beast, against whatever was waiting to face me in combat?

I glanced around, looking for anything that could serve as a weapon. All I found was sand beneath my feet and the eyes of the kingdom upon me.

The creature stepped into the glow of faelights and torches, its form becoming apparent, and a hush fell over the crowd.

I stood there, paralyzed by fear. My heart was pounding like a war drum, my whole body was shaking like a leaf in the wind, and my mind was screaming for me to run, but my legs refused to obey.

The beast that emerged was a giant black lioness, unlike any lioness I had ever heard of in tales or seen depicted in the castle's vast tapestries. This one bore fur and scales that shimmered like dark armor under the rising sun. Her long and cruel talons dug into the arena's sand, each step a measured promise of violence.

The crowd's hush was laced with fear, their previous excitement tinged with the reality of the deadly spectacle before them. I could see in their faces, from the poorest citizen to the highest noble, the same question reflected in their uncertainty: How could a girl, unarmed and untrained, stand against such a monstrous creation?

The lioness scanned over me, a profound intelligence there as if she understood the situation just as clearly as I did.

Her or me.

She let out a low growl, a sound that vibrated through the very ground I stood upon.

In that instant, the world seemed to slow down. The crowd noise faded, and the morning light cast long shadows across the arena floor.

Then, she pounced.

My instincts kicked in. I rolled to the side, narrowly avoiding her razor-sharp claws. The crowd gasped. Watching from his high seat, Ramses leaned forward, a hint of surprise on his cold face.

I scrambled to my feet, my breath ragged, my heart thundering. The lioness turned to face me, a low growl rumbling in her throat. She crouched, preparing to pounce again.

Desperation filled me, a primal fear that spurred me on.

What had I possibly done to warrant such a harsh penalty?

I screamed for help. "Ramses! My King!" I cried, my voice breaking.

I caught a glimpse of Ramses observing from the grandstand—his features contorting with increasing disappointment as I repeatedly implored him to rescue me. He eventually turned away in disdain, departing from the spectators' area. A relentless cacophony of raucous cheers and jeers from thousands of people engulfed the arena, reverberating through my core.

The lioness took advantage of my momentary distraction and lunged, claws slashing toward me. I barely had time to react. I threw myself to the side, the claws grazing my skin and sending sharp pain radiating through my body. I landed hard on the sandy floor of the arena, the wind knocked out of me.

I shouted a wordless battle cry, and energy exploded outward. A shield of shimmering light materialized before me, a barrier between myself and the beast's deadly claws.

I stumbled back, surprised. Just as quickly as it appeared, it was gone again.

Then it had its jaws on my shoulder, and something inside me snapped. I screamed, my throat raw and hoarse.

The world around me blurred into a haze of red and black as pain shot through me. Every nerve in my body was screaming, every cell alive with the agony of the lioness' bite. But amidst the pain, I felt something else. A spark. A raw, primal energy that surged through me, burning hotter and brighter than the pain.

I gasped, my breath hitching in my throat.

The lioness' grip tightened, and I could feel the pressure of her jaws threatening to crush bone. The pain was excruciating, but that spark within me was growing, demanding attention, demanding to be unleashed. It was as if the very essence of my being was awakening, a force that had lain dormant within me.

This.

This was what Ramses had wanted from me.

My hand plunged into her rib cage, my claw-like fingers burrowing through the dense, coarse, ebony fur and flesh scraped by those obsidian scales. The warmth and rhythmic beating of the beast's heart pulsed against my palm as I clawed at it. It loosened its grip on my shoulder, emitting a pitiable yowl as my nails scraped the surface of its heart. With a violent shake of its head, it focused on me. When those brown eyes met mine, I felt something shift in my chest.

It was a moment of connection, of understanding. In that fleeting second, I saw pain and fear mirrored in the lioness' eyes—feelings I knew all too well. She was a creature of strength and power, yet she was as vulnerable as I was then.

I rolled back, a hiss of air escaping my lungs, blood seeping from my wound. The lioness roared, rearing back on its hind legs to lunge at me again.

Everything happened at once—the crowd's loud hum, the ferocious beast snapping its powerful jaws, and my hands instinctively shooting out in front of me. My body tensed up, muscles winding tightly like a loaded spring as I steeled myself for impact. Then, as if answering my silent plea, the sky tore apart.

The sky crackled with energy, the hair on my skin prickling as the charge in the air intensified. The crowd gasped as a brilliant streak of white light pierced the sky, illuminating the arena in an ethereal glow. Time seemed to slow as the bolt descended.

The lioness, caught in the path of the lightning, paused, her eyes reflecting the brilliant light.

And then the bolt struck.

The impact was explosive. The force threw back the lioness, a cry of pain escaping her as lightning engulfed her.

I was also thrown back, landing hard on the sandy floor of the arena. The thunder rang in my ears, and my heart pounded in my chest. I pushed myself up to a sitting position and took in the sight before me.

The lioness lay a few feet away, her body still twitching from the shock. Smoke rose from her charred fur. Her breaths were shallow, labored. She stared up at me, begging.

I'd never seen an animal beg like that. Dogs for scraps, yes, but this beast was praying for death.

I swallowed hard, my throat dry. The cheers and gasps of the crowd were a distant echo, their excited faces a blur. The world had narrowed to just me and the lioness, locked in a tableau of pain and impending death.

The lioness' breaths were raspy, her sides heaving as she struggled to draw air into her lungs. She was a beast, a predator, but at that moment, she was just a wounded creature seeking an end to her suffering.

I rose to my feet, my muscles protesting. My heart pounded in my chest, and a sickening mix of dread and sympathy churned in my stomach. I approached the lioness, and every step was heavy with the weight of what I was about to do.

She tracked my every movement, replacing fear and defiance with resigned acceptance. She knew what was coming.

I could feel it there, right at the edge of my consciousness, a wellspring of magic ready to be tapped.

A tingle in my spine, the hair of my neck prickling as I raised my hand. The lightning came so quickly this time, the sky lighting up in a blinding flash that cleaved the air.

It cracked down on the lioness.

The explosion of charred flesh and shattered bone rained down upon the arena, painting it in a gruesome shade of crimson. Her head was violently severed from its muscular neck; her lifeless body lay in a twisted heap of matted fur on the cold ground, the severed head rolling to a stop at my unprotected feet. The golden collar it wore flung away and glowed with the heat of the lightning strike, the bright metal steaming but not scorched.

Those deep brown eyes continued to bore into me—and I couldn't help but believe that she held a sense of gratitude while life flitted out of them like a candle flame.

As my gaze traveled upward toward the stands, I realized that every single person had gone silent. Overhead, dark clouds loomed ominously while a bone-chilling drizzle descended upon us all.

I was naked. Exposed.

The sky suddenly fractured, and bolts of lightning struck the stands, quivering the entire arena. Panic-stricken screams filled the air as people dashed and trampled over one another, desperate to escape the fiery debris falling from the sky.

I stood still, shocked. Ramses materialized before me, and he gently draped it over my shoulders. I felt the comforting warmth radiating from his body. When he pressed his lips onto my forehead. The lightning stopped, and the crowd hushed as Ramses gestured with a raised hand for silence.

"She is worth more than legions of lions or throngs of Fae. She is the most unparalleled conquest of all! She has defeated the formidable Aislinn Furian! Behold how she has demonstrated her might and allegiance to your king!" he exclaimed. "My soon-to-be queen, The Furian Slayer!"

The fear from earlier shifted like tides as the audience roared with approval and chanted the title bestowed upon me by Ramses.

Aislinn Furian was a rebel leader from the War of Fallen Skies. She had gone unheard of since the end of the war and, from rumors, had been pronounced dead. She had also been a part of the original four ruling families of the realm of Ferenz before it just became Ember. How could she be here?

I turned to look at the fallen body of the beast and was met with the sight of a decapitated woman strewn on the arena floor.

The sight was as horrifying as it was shocking. The lioness was no more, replaced by the lifeless body of a woman. Aislinn Furian. The realization hit me like a punch to the gut. I had not killed a beast. I had killed a woman. A rebel leader. A part of the original ruling families of Ferenz.

I felt my knees buckle, and Ramses' grip on my hand was the only thing keeping me upright. The crowd's cheering seemed distant now, their chants of my new title ringing hollow.

I was a killer.

A murderer.

The weight of what I had done bore down on me, threatening to shatter the fragile sense of victory I'd felt only moments before.

Aislinn Furian was a name spoken in hushed whispers, symbolizing resistance against Ramses. I knew this. And I had ended her, not knowing the truth hidden beneath the beast's form.

Ramses' whisper broke through my thoughts, his words a harsh reminder of the reality I now faced. "You have done well," he said, his tone soft. "You've shown the people the strength of their future queen."

But his comments brought me no comfort. As I stared at Aislinn Furian's body, I felt a sense of dread settle deep within me. What had I truly become? The crowd's cheers, their admiration of Ramses' claim, and the title they had given me all felt meaningless now.

I was still the same. Still ordinary. Still plain. Still...me. But I was also more.

I was a survivor.

I was a warrior.

I was a killer.

And yet they all continued to shout their adoration and praises at me.

"Queen?" I managed to say.

Ramses nodded, kissing my cheek again. "Yes. *My* Queen."

Queen? The word felt foreign, too grand, and significant for someone like me, someone who had never aspired to such heights, whose only concern until now had been to do her best in her studies and be a proper lady.

Then, Ramses rushed me to follow him, and I could see the mane of black hair covering the head of the woman. Aislinn Furian. The truth of her identity complicated the narrative of my triumph, painting it with shades of gray. The name would continue to haunt my thoughts, her lifeless form imprinted in my memory. I had killed her. A Fae, a rebel, a symbol of hope for many outside of Ember. And now, she was gone.

Because of me.

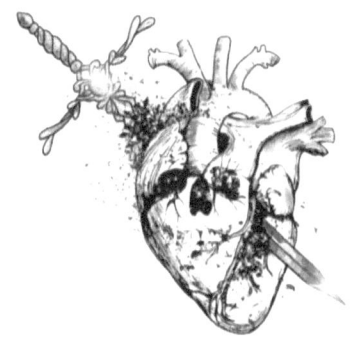

CHAPTER FOUR

ELDRA SOLARIS

G etting called to the throne room was never a good thing. It was never good when a king was *summoned* to a throne room.

As the queen and I made our way through the dimly lit corridors of the castle, the weight of an unknown future seemed to press upon us, and the air was dense with a sense of foreboding.

"What do you suppose Hisen requires of us?" Queen Ameria's query pierced the quiet, laden with trepidation that was foreign to her usual lilting tones. She fiddled with the elaborate bodice of her white gown, the silver threads catching the scant light, shimmering like morning mist woven into her attire. Shadows played across her face, her dark brows furrowed.

"I'm not certain," I admitted, betraying a hint of the unease I felt. "When I asked the messenger if it could wait until tomorrow, he said no."

We continued our walk, the only sound the soft rustle of Ameria's gown and the muted echo of our footsteps on the cold stone floor. Moonlight and starlight filtered in through the archway windows and painted glass skylights. Ameria paused by a towering window, her hand outstretched. "Grant me but a moment," she implored in a calm breath.

"Hisen deems it urgent," I reminded her, though my protest was feeble.

"Whether we get there in one minute or five, the problem will remain. The urgency of kings will always remain. I want a moment to enjoy this." She waved her hand in front of the glass, sending a shaft of moonlight through the window.

We stood, side by side, at the arching pane, the castle's height offering a grand view of the city below. The moonlight bathed the cobblestone streets and the sleeping houses in a silver radiance, turning the city into a dreamscape of muted light and deep shadows. From our vantage point, we could see the lanterns of the night guards flickering like fireflies.

Beyond the city walls, the open sea stretched to the horizon, reflecting the moon and stars above; the stillness was broken only by the distant sound of the waves lapping against the shore.

To the north, the mountains rose like silent sentinels, their peaks piercing the sky, cloaked in the darkness of night. The range's silhouette was a jagged line against the star-studded heavens, a boundary between the kingdom and the wilds beyond. Somewhere within those towering heights lay hidden valleys and secret nooks known only to the creatures that called them home and the few brave souls who dared to explore their depths.

Ameria's gaze followed mine, tracing the outline of the mountains before descending to the small alcove nestled at their base. A secluded inlet with a beach of pale sand was barely visible from our lofty perch, but we knew it well—a haven where we had often escaped.

Where I had taken her time and again to hear her cry my name beneath me in bliss.

She lingered upon that distant alcove, a soft sigh escaping her lips. "It is still so beautiful."

"It is," I agreed, placing my hand over hers on the window ledge. "And it will remain so, for we will face whatever threatens it. Together and always."

That last part, together and always, is the Solaris house motto.

I waited for her to lead the way down, her back stiff and straight.

The vast doors to the throne room loomed before us, their heavy ironwork twisting and turning into a series of dragon heads within a burning sun.

With a nod to the guards, the doors opened with a groan.

Above us, the ceiling stretched into darkness, lost to sight, as if the room was a portal to the night sky. The cool air flowed through the open archways, carrying with it the scent of brine from the distant sea and the whispering of the night.

We approached our thrones, hand in hand.

The throne upon which I sat was a monolith of dark wood and cold iron, its surface etched with the sigils of my house. Ameria's was a beauty of golden flowers and redwood.

"My King, there has been a report from the North," said Hisen, his dark head bowed and his bright white eyes fixed upon the floor.

I rested my chin in my hand and leaned to my right, my attention flicking to my wife.

Her hands fisted in the silk panels of her white gown—white as fresh snow. Her long hair, the color of autumn leaves, twisted about her head like a crown. She worried her red-stained lips and I could see the fine tremor that ran through her. The gold bangles on her wrist rattled softly.

Any news from the North made her anxious.

Any news about Ramses made her quake.

Has he finally come to rip this world of ours apart? I heard her thoughts drift through my mind.

I watched her with an understanding from years of shared experiences and quiet conversations in the dark of night. I was not the only one who was haunted by nightmares.

"What is it?" I asked, raking my eyes back to Hisen. His face was immobile, but I could see the tension in his hands, shoulders, and jaw feathering.

I turned to Ameria then. "Would you like to visit Rowena in the city? I can have Jassen escort you there and back in the morning."

Ameria sucked in a sharp breath, her plump mouth forming a thin line at the mention of her sister. I knew without her saying anything what her answer would be. I could see her hands clenching in her lap. She nodded once, breath escaping her. She got up and leaned into me, her forehead on mine, with a quiet thank you.

I kissed the gold ring on her finger, and she stepped away.

I waited for her heels to click on the stone floor to fade before I spoke again.

"That bad?"

"Worse. Gaelin needs to be here for this. Madsen and Emery, too." Hisen still stayed in his bowed position.

"Why won't you look at me?" I asked softly, trying to keep my voice from shaking.

Nothing. I never asked them to bow before me, not my family.

"Why won't you look at me?" I repeated.

Hisen's head lifted slowly, with a reluctance born of dread. "Your Majesty," he began, as steady as he could muster, "the news I bring..." He halted a hand to his chest.

Hisen finally lifted his head, and shadows danced across his face. His face was haggard and lined in a way I had never seen before—not for High Fae.

"The news I bring... it is of Ramses."

I straightened. "I've gathered that much," my patience wearing thin. "What about him?" My gaze drifted to where Ameria had left.

"There are reports that he held a-a ceremony of sorts in his arena. It was attended by many of the High Fae nobles and even some outsiders of Ember."

"So? What else is new?" I asked.

Hisen swallowed. "The reports say that he put a young girl into the ring. She was unarmed. Naked as a newborn babe. Then he-She-He-She—"

"Out with it, Hisen."

"This girl was put into the ring, and they put her against a *lioness*."

"Does this story have an ending?"

Hisen looked up at me. "Shut up and let me finish," he snapped. I leaned back on my throne, waiting.

"It wasn't an ordinary lioness. Her fur—black as midnight—was larger than any normal lioness. This girl had no weapons yet cleaved the sky in two with her bare hands. Struck down that lioness and brought fire to the stands."

"So, the girl has magic. Most Fae do. Impressive as it may be, that isn't exactly news," I said dismissively.

"And Ramses," Hisen pressed on, the urgency in his pitch rising, "after the girl killed the lioness, he made an announcement. He declared that she is to be his queen."

I leaned forward, my elbows resting on my knees, partly intrigued. "This girl. Who is she?"

Hisen shook his head, a hint of disbelief in his expression. "No one knows. She appeared long ago as a babe, her identity a mystery even to those closest to Ramses. Some say she's a weapon he's been forging secretly, a power to tip the scales in his favor. Others say she was just a ward that caught his eye."

"But that isn't the worst of it," Hisen's vacant stare held mine, a storm of emotions swirling within those white depths. "It's not just that she has magic," he continued, "The lioness she struck down... it was *Aislinn Furian.*"

The arm to my throne creaked, and I looked down to find it had melted away. The throne itself was gone, consumed by the flames that licked out of me. I stood up then, my hand hovering over the fire until it disappeared.

"Unthinkable," I spat, ash and disbelief on my tongue. Hisen's head shook with a solemnity that chilled my bones, his following sentence a harbinger of darkness.

"Ramses has named her The Furian Slayer."

The title struck like a blade.

The idea that Ramses would bestow such a title upon a girl, a cipher wrapped in an enigma, suggested a plan of terrifying scope. A future painted in shades of blood and shadow.

"It isn't possible. Aislinn Furian died long ago during the War of Fallen Skies. I saw it myself." My heart clenched, and my stomach tightened. "I held her in my arms. She is dead. She is gone."

"The whispers—"

"Your whispers are wrong!" Even I didn't believe my own words.

Those pools of white held a truth I wished to flee. His whispers were the threads that wove the unseen world to ours, and they never led astray—whispers of Fae who long left this world. I felt a cold chill run down my spine. The War of Fallen Skies was a dark chapter in our history that saw the fall of many great and terrible creatures. If Aislinn Furian had indeed been brought back from the dead, it meant Ramses had tapped into powers that were forbidden for a reason. Powers that could threaten the very fabric of our world.

I collapsed, my knees meeting the marble with a harsh thud, the chill of the stone leeching into my bones. "She was taken from us," I growled a venomous hiss between clenched teeth.

Memories long buried now clawed their way to the surface, vivid and sharp.

Aislinn Furian, with her eyes like molten chocolate, had been more than a legend or a creature of battle to me. She was the secret keeper of my heart, the unspoken love that time and duty had buried but never extinguished. Our souls had been entwined in a dance as delicate as it was dangerous, our love a silent sonnet that resonated through the quiet corners of our existence.

The revelation that she had been alive, a prisoner to Ramses' dark whims, struck me with a grief so profound it threatened to shatter the very essence of my being. How many nights had I dreamt of her, her laughter a melody that soothed the turmoil of my reign? How many times had I whispered her name into the void, hoping against hope that she would answer?

"Ramses seeks to provoke us," I declared. "He wishes to draw us into his madness, to ensnare us in his web of deceit."

To imagine her alive, to dream that perhaps our paths could have crossed once more, only to be snatched away by the cruel spectacle of her death—it was a torture no enemy could match. The bitter gall of betrayal now compounded the agony of loss. Ramses had not only taken her life; he had stolen the years we could have had, the years she could have lived, free and wild as she was meant to be.

I remained on my knees, the cold marble of the throne room floor seeping into my skin, a numbness spreading through my limbs.

A roaring in my head, so loud it shook the foundations of the throne room.

Ameria appeared beside me in a whirlwind of mist and shadow and knelt beside me. Her touch was gentle, and her promise was a whisper meant only for my ears. "I stand with you," she murmured, her the eye of the storm within me. "In this and all things."

I forced myself to look at her, soft green to my crushing gray and blue.

"She was alive, Ameria," I choked out with barely a breath. "All this time, Aislinn was alive. And now... now she is truly gone."

Ameria's arms wrapped around me. She did not speak, for what words could mend a heart torn asunder?

"I thought I had grieved her," I admitted, my heart thick with sorrow. "I thought I had laid her memory to rest alongside the others we lost in that accursed war. But to know that she lived, that she suffered..." I choked on a gasp, my eyes burning.

Ameria pulled back just enough to look at me, her face twisted in remorse. "You loved her truly, and that love does not die with the departed," she spoke with a gentle certainty. "It is right to mourn, to feel this loss as if it were new. But remember, my love, you are not alone in your sorrow."

She was not hateful. Not jealous of my tears for my love long lost. She was not cruel in her words or her thoughts. She was not cold.

I rested my forehead against her shoulder, and she held me there as I wept. The pain, the loss, it was real.

I felt it all over again.

I drew back from Ameria's shoulder slightly. I found an acceptance that asked for nothing in return. It was the gift of allowing me to mourn, to remember.

I stood up, feeling the steadiness return to my legs. Ameria rose with me, her hand against my back as she leaned against me.

"That is the tale we have all believed, Your Majesty. But the whispers from the South speak of dark magic, of a resurrection that has bound the beast to Ramses' will. It is said that he has kept her hidden in a cell beneath the very boards of his castle."

"What else have your whispers told you? Nothing of the girl?" Ameria asked.

"It's silent when it comes to her. Even speaking of Aislinn—they hesitate as if something is keeping them quiet," he explained.

"More dark magic?" Ameria asked.

"Summon them," I said, my command slicing through the room. "Summon Gaelin, Madsen, and Emery."

Hisen bowed his head in understanding and turned on his heel, disappearing in a whirl of color.

As the echo of Hisen's departure faded, Ameria and I stood in the silence that wrapped around us like a shroud. The air in the throne room felt heavy.

Ameria touched my cheek, wiping away the tears I hadn't felt falling. "We will face this together."

I nodded, "Together and always."

⬤

It went about as well as I could have hoped.

Screaming, cursing, and a few tears were the order. Curses flew as freely as the spells. Their arguments started as a strategic debate, their voices rising with each point and counterpoint until it was not enough.

Madsen and Emery were the first to come to blows, the women drawing blood from each other with their bare hands. Madsen had Emery's black hair twisted in her hands, pulling with all her might. If Emery had been a lesser fae, she would have been scalped.

Emery slammed a fist into Madsen's jaw, a loud crack of bone and flesh that echoed in the chamber and rang through my ears.

Emery's magic was formidable, but she was just as dangerous with claws and teeth, her pale green hands entangled in Madsen's blue hair as they grappled back and forth.

Soldiers came to the center of the throne room, uncertainty and fear written on their faces as they hesitated to break up the fight. I would not even get in the middle of *that*. Women are vicious creatures—and Madsen always aimed for the balls.

I still needed my balls. Ameria and I wanted children.

Madsen staggered with a snarl and brought her knee to meet Emery's chin, sending her to the ground with a thud.

Then Hisen and Gaelin were at it, a mass of shadows and snarling teeth, their clawed hands tearing at each other.

Ameria leaned in close to me, whispering in my ear. "Perhaps we should stop them before they kill each other?" There was a hint of wry humor in her tone, but the underlying concern was evident.

"They need this," I murmured back to her, scratching my brow. "They need to let out the anger and the fear. Better here, among us, than on the city streets." Ameria cast a doubtful glance at them but said no more.

I looked at my throne, halfway melted and gone.

I couldn't fit in Ameria's smaller throne, so I opted for the floor, resting my head on my knees as I watched them go at it.

"Bitch!" Emery yelled, and then the walls rattled as a spell of her own was cast. A giant snake took up most of the room, its jaws open wide and hungry for blood. Ameria recoiled and reached out to me.

"Enough!" The command burst from me, a thunderclap silencing the room. The serpent vanished. Its existence snuffed out as quickly as it had appeared. All eyes turned to me, the king who chose the floor over the throne, the king whose word was law. The shadows stopped spinning, and Gaelin and Hisen stepped out, fixing their lapels and acting as though they weren't at each other's throats seconds ago.

Madson and Emery, both panting and with fire still in their auras, hesitated, then slowly released their grips on each other. They stepped back, their chests heaving with exertion and lingering animosity.

Emery straightened her purple robes, a hand going to her messy hair as she composed herself. "My apologies, Eldra," she said, though her teeth still flashed.

I knew the girls would have at it as soon as I wasn't looking.

Madsen, likewise, regained her composure, "Forgive my... lack of restraint," she grumbled, her apology as close to remorse as she was likely to offer.

I knew neither of them was sorry.

Gaelin was the first to approach. "Well," he began, dusting off his clothing and eyeing me sitting on the floor with a mischievous twinkle, "I must say, it's not every day you see a king preferring the cold floor over a throne. Should we take this as a new fashion in courtly manners?"

A much-needed release valve for the tension that still lingered in the air. A few stifled chuckles broke from the group.

Hisen joined me on the floor, and the others followed suit.

"Aislinn killed by a mere girl," Madsen scoffed, amber eyes glinting. "When I get my hands on that little shit—" her magic flared, and her hair exploded into a dozen black snakes, the sound of their hissing and rattling enough to make the hair on the back of my neck stand up. Everyone averted their gaze from her on instinct.

"Cool it with the snakes," Gaelin huffed. "You heard Hisen. The girl was thrown into that arena naked and afraid. I doubt she had much of a choice in the matter." He flicked one of the snakes on the snout. It hissed, recoiled, and slowly reformed into strands of dark blue hair that curled down Madsen's back.

Now seated in a circle on the floor around me, each took turns voicing their strategies for how we might retaliate against Ramses for his insult. Ever the warrior, Madsen spoke of direct confrontation, of bringing the fight right to Ramses' doorstep. With her knowledge of the magic, Emery suggested countering his dark magic with our own. I tried not to shut that one down immediately. Emery, in all her power, was no match for Ramses. Gaelin urged a campaign of deception and espionage, dismantling Ramses' influence from within.

As the ideas swirled, I found myself growing increasingly unsettled. The talk of war and retribution seemed all too easy to tread, a path that could lead us into a mire of bloodshed and sorrow once again. I raised a hand, signaling for silence, and they all turned their attention to me.

"We must also consider the possibility that Ramses is not working alone," I said. "Such magic requires knowledge and power that are not easy to come by."

Emery smiled a slash of white sharp teeth. "I would wager that he has necromancers with him." I ignored the chill that went up my spine.

Madsen shuddered. She had once served in the militia of a city far across the water where necromancers and Vampires had raised the dead and built an army. Vampires and skeletons, together... She had been forced to abandon the city more than five hundred years ago. Eventually, the entire island was overrun by the dead, and the queens and kings gathered to unite their power across the sea and sink the island into the ocean's depths.

I hadn't been born yet. But my father had been one of those kings.

"Perhaps," I continued, "this is exactly what Ramses wants. He has baited the trap, hoping we will lash out, blinded by our grief and rage. Aislinn's death, as tragic and unjust as it is, may be the lure to draw us from our safety, to engage us in a battle we are not yet ready to fight."

I had to face that possibility. I had grieved Aislinn, and she was still lost to me. Nothing had changed.

"I am ready to fight," Gaelin said.

"And I," Madsen agreed. A collective murmur rippled through them.

Emery said something in Arathi—her old tongue, which was most likely an agreement.

Ameria's hand found mine. She squeezed it. "Eldra is right," she said. "We cannot allow Ramses to dictate our actions through such provocations. We must think not only of retribution but of our people's lives and the stability of *our* realm."

Madson clenched her jaw, the warrior in her at odds with the idea of standing down. "So, we do *nothing*?" she seethed.

"Not *nothing*," I replied. "We gather intelligence, just as we have been."

"Our realm is hidden away. Ramses cannot find it. He is blind to its existence. We bring the fight to him on common ground," Madsen said.

"And the girl?" Emery asked, her stare fixed on me. "What of the one they call the Furian Slayer?"

Hisen and Gaelin shared a glance.

Gaelin was an expert in espionage, and his network of spies and informants was rivaled only by Hisen's own. His appearance was unassuming—a typical blonde-haired, blue-eyed man from Winters End from across the sea. His demeanor is mild, but behind the facade lay a mind sharp as a dagger's edge.

While Hisen conversed with the dead for his intel, Gaelin worked with the living.

"I went to the mainland before coming. I asked the right people a few questions. They say the girl was just a ward of his. Nothing more. They didn't even know she had any power until the arena," Gaelin said.

When she killed Aislinn.

"While our realm might be hidden, that does not mean it is invulnerable. Taking the offensive could expose us in ways we cannot predict. And as for the girl, we must learn more before we act. I want to know who she is. Her favorite foods. Her favorite books. Everything. If she is a threat, find out."

Madsen grumbled, "And am I just supposed to sit on my hands?"

Madsen, the commander of our armies, was as steadfast as the mountains that bordered our realm. Her presence was commanding, and her power was the clarion call that rallied our forces. However, the men hadn't been happy that I had put a woman in charge.

She had entered the ranks as nothing more than a recruit, another face among the sea of hopefuls vying for a place in the prestigious armed forces of our realm. But she was not just any recruit; she was a maelstrom contained in a small form—a force to be reckoned with. Madsen emerged victorious in every duel, every contest of strength and strategy. Not through brute force but through a combination of raw skill, analytical thinking, and an innate understanding of warfare that seemed to flow through her veins.

It caught my attention when I first met her. She was odd, with blue hair and amber eyes that glowed. Half nymph, half-Fae descendant. When she told me she was once a general, I was surprised.

What surprised me was when I found out she had known my father.

Failure was not in her vocabulary, and she had made it clear that she was willing to take on any challenge that came her way. But something shifted in her when we lost the War of Fallen Skies.

That calculation gave way to cool rage. "No," I told her, "you will not sit on your hands. We will need you to ensure that our forces remain vigilant and ready. We will rely on your expertise to strengthen our defenses and to train our warriors for whatever may come."

I had to keep her busy. I had to keep that rage in check, or else it would spill out onto the world.

"He seeks to draw us out, to capitalize on our thirst for vengeance. We cannot give him that satisfaction," I said.

Emery said something in Arathi, syllables ending in a hiss. I sighed.

Gaelin squinted. "I think she said something about milking a cow?"

"She said Ramses is a *coward*," Madsen corrected, elbowing him.

Turning to Hisen and Gaelin, I gave them a nod. "Continue your efforts in intelligence gathering. The more we know about Ramses' movements and his allies, the better we can anticipate his strategies. And Gaelin, find out all you can about this girl. We need to understand her role in all of this."

I turned to Hisen, who had quietly listened, absorbing every word. "And you, Hisen. Keep speaking with those who have passed. Their whispers may yet reveal secrets that Ramses wishes to keep hidden."

Hisen nodded solemnly. "The spirits will be heard," he assured me. "I will bring back whatever they have to share."

"And Emery, your knowledge of the arcane will be crucial. Find out what you can about resurrection specifically. This can't be typical Necromancy. Work with the Silent Sisters, if need be."

The mention of the Silent Sisters brought the room to a deafening quiet, but Emery only smiled sweetly, her pale green skin glittering.

The Silent Sisters were a revered and feared group who guarded ancient and profound arcane knowledge that few dared to seek. They were once powerful sorceresses who sought to understand and master magic, pushing their abilities beyond mortal limits. However, their relentless pursuit of magical prowess took a heavy toll; despite their immortality, the Sisters had become withered crones, bearing testament to the ravages of wielding forces meant to be handled with caution. Their once-youthful faces were now aged with the lines of time, their eyes sunken yet still aglow with formidable power. They resided in the secluded Halls of Echoes, where the air was thick with enchantment, and the walls whispered of spells long forgotten by the outside world.

A place where no one dared tread. Unless they were a person like Emery, she was the only one I knew who had gone to the Hall of Echoes and came back—repeatedly.

And she would never tell us how or why, in all the four hundred years I'd known her. Not even Hisen knew.

She moved through the world with a confidence that bordered on the otherworldly, her knowledge vast, her abilities unfathomable. The Silent Sisters themselves, those ancient sentinels of arcane secrets, seemed to hold no sway over her, and that alone was enough to stir unease in the hearts of even the most stalwart.

I knew her loyalty to our cause was beyond reproach, and her dedication to my family was unwavering. Yet, an air of mystery clung to her, a veil that no light could penetrate. In the four hundred years of our acquaintance, she had shared little of her visits to the Halls of Echoes, each return marked by a further deepening of that mysterious aura that surrounded her.

I did not feel fear, per se, in her presence; it was more akin to the reverence one might feel standing before a force of nature—a tempest or a wildfire. It was the recognition of raw and unbridled power and the knowledge that such power, while on our side, was not to be taken lightly.

After a while, they dispersed, already beyond the threshold of the throne room, when Ameria let out a shuddering breath.

"To know Aislinn was alive all these years. I only wish I could have seen her," she said softly. I didn't respond, and I did not trust myself with speaking.

"And for Ramses to take a-a wife," she shuddered. "What she will no doubt be subjected to." She touched her forehead with two fingers.

Finally, I answered, "That isn't our problem."

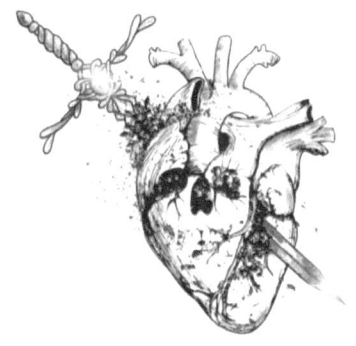

CHAPTER FIVE

ATREYA

O *ne week later...*

The day of our wedding dawned bright and clear, the morning sun casting a golden glow over the kingdom of Ember. The air was filled with the scent of fresh blossoms and the sounds of preparation as the people gathered to witness the union of their king and new queen.

Queen.

I hadn't been afforded a moment to myself since then. I was fawned over. People cried out for me in the streets, throwing flowers and offering me baskets of fruits, vegetables, and meats. Everyone loved me and wanted me to love them.

In the bridal room, the luxury was nearly suffocating. Gifts from Ramses overflowed on the tables. Delicate lace from the far reaches of the kingdom, precious stones that caught the light and splintered it into a thousand colors, and silks so fine they felt like whispers against the skin. It wasn't as though I had not been living in luxury before. Being Ramses' ward, I had the best, but in smaller quantities.

Joslynn blew her nose into her handkerchief for the hundredth time, her eyes red-rimmed and swollen from crying.

"If you keep crying like that on my wedding day, it will surely bring bad luck. So, stop it!" I jested.

She scowled at her reflection in the mirror, fiddling with my hair and the ornaments hanging from it. A weave of pearls and flowers through strands of curls piled high on top of my head.

I looked like a decoration and not like a bride.

The dress was too big—too flowing, too bright, too fancy. The sleeves swallowed up my arms, and the neckline reached up to my ears.

Joslynn managed a watery chuckle, dabbing at her cheeks yet again. "Forgive me, my lady. It's just dat you look so... so..."

"Ridiculous?" I offered, half-joking as I attempted to make light of my discomfort.

"No, no," Joslynn assured me, shaking her head as she finally set the handkerchief aside. "You look regal, every inch da queen Ember deserves."

Outside the chamber where Joslynn and I shared a moment of fun, the palace courtyard buzzed with an energy that could only precede a royal wedding. Maids scurried back and forth, their skirts swishing as they laid fine linens on the long wooden banquet tables. Cooks barked orders in the kitchen, the clanging of pots and pans merging with the sweet aroma of roasting meats and freshly baked bread that wafted through the air.

All around, lanterns were being hung, ready to bathe the evening in a warm, golden light as the celebrations continued into the night. Minstrels tuned their instruments, the gentle plucking of lute strings filling the air.

"I don't know if I can do this," I admitted. "I've never wanted to be queen. I never thought..."

Joslynn stopped fussing and looked at me, her expression serious for the first time that morning. She took my hands in hers, her grip firm and reassuring. "You *can* do this," she said confidently. "And if you can't, I'll take you from here, and we'll run. Far away. We never look back."

The suggestion was so unexpected, so wildly out of character for her, that it startled a laugh out of me. It was a genuine, unburdened sound that cut through the tension that had built inside me like a knot.

Her smile faltered, and I realized she had meant it. She was waiting for me to tell her I couldn't do this.

The realization that Joslynn was prepared to abandon everything we had known for my sake was sobering. Her loyalty was what legends were made of—the kind that didn't waver even in the face of drastic change. Even if it meant treason. Her loyalty was mine and mine alone.

She was serious; she would forsake her position, her security, and her life in the palace to safeguard my happiness.

"That's an offer that speaks volumes of your heart and what I mean to you, and I am more grateful than I can express. But I will not run. Not today, not ever," I promised.

She seemed almost sad at that.

⦾

Ivory linen draped over the rows of seating, each chair adorned with a sash of gold or crimson, the colors of House Blackwater. Above, the sky was framed by a lattice of interwoven branches, which hung an array of delicate glass orbs.

They looked like trapped stars.

The people of Ember parted to create a path to the altar, their faces alight with joy and excitement. Some faces I recognized. Joslynn was seated in the front row, courtiers from the palace and nobles from the countryside. Others I did not recognize, and eventually, they all melded together into a blurred crowd.

The king awaited me at the altar. He was a striking figure, his crown a band of molten gold upon his brow, his cloak a cascade of crimson velvet lined with fur. There was a softening in his face that sent my heart skipping. My palms were sweating, my mouth dry.

But my attention kept snapping back to the priestess. Her head was crowned with a circlet of intertwined silver and gold, brown hair flowing down her back in deep waves. Her blue robes flowed about her like cascades of water, panels of glittering white at her shoulders.

She looked much more like a bride than I did.

As I moved forward, the crowd's whispers and murmurs faded into a hushed silence, and everyone fixated on me. The air seemed to hold its breath, the gentle rustle of silk and the soft clink of armor the only sounds that accompanied my steps.

I stood beside the king, facing the High Priestess, ready to speak the vows that would bind me to the throne, the man beside me, and the people before me.

As she raised her arms, the sleeves of her robes fell back, revealing intricate patterns of silver tattoos.

"You will say your vows in the presence of the gods and the presence of the people," she intoned, her hands moving between Ramses and me.

Ramses turned to me, smiling. "I, Ramses Blackwater, do take thee to be my queen," he began, resonating with the strength and conviction that had no doubt won him the throne. "To stand by your side through war and peace, through plenty and want, through victory and defeat."

He took my hands in his, his touch warm and firm. A ribbon of gold emanated from his hands and wrapped around our arms. "With you by my side, I am more than I could ever be alone. Through the storms of war and the calm of peace, in the abundance of plenty and the trials of want, from the soaring heights of victory to the calm of defeat, I vow to cherish all that is inside of you. May I *always* find you, wherever you are."

My heart jumped into my throat. No man had ever uttered such things to me.

Devotion.

Love.

My heart hammered in my rib cage, and I held back my tears.

It was my turn, and the promises I had rehearsed now rose to my lips with a clarity that belied the fluttering in my stomach. "I, Atreya Ward, accept your name as my very first and last. Standing before the gods and our people, I do take thee, Ramses Blackwater, to be my king," I said. "To honor and obey, to serve and defend, to love and cherish for all the days of my life."

It wasn't anything romantic like his. It was a simple pledge, a vow of loyalty and honor.

I could love him.

It would be easy to love him.

I would find that love in years to come.

The High Priestess nodded, satisfied with our declarations. "With these vows, you bind your lives together," she declared. "May the gods bless this union and grant you strength, prosperity, and wisdom in your rule."

She turned to the people. "Bear witness to the vows of your king and queen! May their reign be long and their love everlasting!" The golden ribbons binding our hands sank into our skin and disappeared.

The crowd roared.

We turned, hand in hand, and he raised mine, a show of victory.

I did it. I was married.

In the front row of the audience, clapping along, stood Corina, dressed in a form-fitting green dress, her face smug. But it was Servat, standing next to her, who drew my attention—his pride was palpable, radiating from him like the heat from the braziers that flanked the altar.

And then he was silently mouthing something I recognized—what he had said to me before I was unleashed into the arena:

Fight back.

⁕

I was taken to the baths and cleaned by half a dozen maidservants. Joslynn scrubbed my bare back with a soft bristle brush while another worked her fingers through my hair.

"What will it be like?" I asked softly. "With him?"

Joslynn stopped brushing, and the other women giggled. "I have told you about men and women and da joining."

"I know the basics. I just—" The words died in my throat, a blush creeping over me. I was going to know the touch of a man.

Ramses was going to be inside of me.

I stood abruptly, water sloshing over the sides of the giant marble tub.

"Easy there, my lady," an older maid cautioned, her hands steadying me. "It's normal to be nervous, but you have nothing to fear."

Joslynn made an undignified noise that had my head swiveling to her.

"What?" I asked, panicked.

She made to say something, a hand clutching her head. "Headache is all. Been a long day."

A warm towel was draped over my shoulders as I stepped out of the bath.

The air felt cool against my damp skin, sending a shiver down my spine. I was wrapped in a softer robe than anything I had ever worn, its fabric hugging me like a second skin.

My skin glowed from the oils and perfumes massaged into it, and my cheeks still held the blush from the hot water.

"You look beautiful, my lady," said the maid who had tended to my hair, offering a reassuring smile.

I tried to return the smile, but my nerves were knotted tightly within my stomach. "Thank you," I murmured, watching as they began to lace me into the intricate gown that had been chosen for this night.

"Are all the ties necessary? I won't be spending long in it."

Another wave of giggling.

"You want to give your husband something to be excited about. Anticipate. He will like undressing you," the older maid said.

The thought sent a new wave of heat across my skin that had nothing to do with the bath I had just left.

The gown, a tapestry of deep blues and silvers, hugged my figure, the fabric whispering against the floor as I moved. It was cut in a modest and tempting way, a promise of what lay beneath—a whisper of skin here and there.

The laces were drawn tight to the point I struggled to breathe.

"You'll knock da bread straight from his lungs, you will," Joslynn said, her headache apparently forgotten.

"Breath," I corrected her with a smile.

She clucked her tongue. "You know what I say." She leaned in, "Remember, this night is but a moment. You will be okay."

●

As I left the company of the maidservants, the corridor seemed to stretch endlessly before me. My heart was a drumbeat. My stomach was tight with nerves. The door to Ramses' chamber loomed ahead, ornately carved and slightly ajar, a sliver of golden light spilling out into the hallway. Two guards were poised just outside of it, nodding somewhat for me to go on.

I had never been to his private rooms. Not even when I was just his ward. He rarely interacted with me as a child—a curt gesture now and again—an occasional appraisal of my studies.

Ramses stood by the hearth, the fire casting dancing shadows over his strong features. He was dressed in a simple tunic that did nothing to hide the power of his frame. For an instant, the world fell away, leaving only the two of us in a bubble.

"You are a vision," he said, "Truly, the stars pale in comparison to your beauty tonight."

He took my hand, his touch warm and sure, and led me to the side of the bed. It was draped in silks and furs, a nest of comfort and luxury.

"Are you warm enough?" He asked gently.

I nodded but wrapped my arms around myself. I could not bring myself into this moment.

He leaned down and peppered soft kisses down my cheek and neck, taking his time to run his nose along my collarbone.

I still had questions for him.

He pulled me into his lap, wrapping his large hands around my waist and running a claw over the laces of my gown.

"Why? Why did you do that to me? Why did you humiliate me so, throwing me naked into the arena with a lion?"

The room seemed to be still, the crackling fire the only sound as Ramses' hands stilled on my waist. He drew back slightly, searching my face with an intensity that made my heart skip a beat. I could see the flicker of emotion, a storm that I could not read.

"I had not meant for you to be naked. The soldier who took you as such is dead," he said after a moment. "I had instructed that you be given the garb of a warrior, as is tradition."

I searched his face for signs of deceit but found none. His jaw was set, a muscle feathering in his cheek.

"And the lion?" I asked while he slowly peeled my dress from my shoulder, planting a kiss there.

He stilled, leaning back on his elbows so I was hovering above him. I made to move off of him, but he settled my legs on either side of his waist.

"You couldn't lift Servat's sword, and then you could."

I furrowed my brows at him. "What does that have to do with anything?"

"You never know your full potential until you are forced to use it."

"And Aislinn?"

His lip twitched. "What better way to show your loyalty to me than by ridding me of one of my biggest enemies? You should be honored." His grip on me tightened slightly, and I sat up straighter, feeling something hard between my legs. I cleared my throat.

"And the people?" I pressed on. "What do they think of their future queen now?"

"They think you are a hero," he said with a pride that almost sounded genuine. "They saw you face death and emerge victorious. They will not doubt your strength or your right to be beside this throne."

"I could have died," I managed to say.

"But did you? I had enough faith in you that you would be fine. Do you truly believe I would have let you die?" He stroked his finger along my cheek.

I thought back to the arena, the pain that seared through me from Aislinn's teeth and claws. How I had begged him to help me—to save me—and that look of disgust and disappointment as he turned his back on me.

A chill went up my spine.

Yes. You would have. But that wasn't the right thing to say, so I shook my head and bit my tongue.

"No, I suppose you wouldn't have," I lied carefully. The memory of his turned back was like a wound that refused to heal, but I couldn't let him see how much it had hurt me, how deep the betrayal had gone.

I didn't trust him.

Ramses' expression softened at my response, and he leaned forward to kiss my forehead. "I have wronged you in more ways than one. And while I intended to protect you, to prepare you for the weight of the crown, I see now that I have also hurt you. Allow me to show you how sorry I am," he whispered. He undulated his hips under mine, his hardness running up my seam. I jolted against him, and he chuckled. "I have been waiting for this moment."

I quickly realized that Ramses had a well of experience that I could not match. He licked up my neck, pulling down my dress entirely to expose my breasts to him. He laved his tongue over my nipples, sucking hard on one, and I squealed.

His mouth was insistent and persuasive, drawing sounds from me that echoed in the hushed chamber.

I felt his hands roam over my body, exploring with a possessiveness that both alarmed and excited me. A gasp and then a moan as he continued his ministrations. Ramses worshiped my body with his mouth.

"Ramses, please," I begged, grinding against him.

He flipped us over so I was on my back, tugging the dress down and off my body. I was now naked in front of him—and not for the first time.

As I lay there, exposed and vulnerable, Ramses towered above me, his gaze intense and consuming. The fire that had been stoked within me was now ablaze, and my earlier reservations started to dissolve. He traced the contours of my body with his fingers, mapping the skin he had claimed as his own. Each touch was a brand searing into me, and I welcomed it.

"Beautiful," he murmured in a low rumble that vibrated through me. His lips followed the path his fingers had taken, trailing lower and lower until he was on his knees before me, parting my legs wide for him.

Then he lowered his head, and his mouth met the most intimate part of me. His tongue was both gentle and insistent, exploring, tasting, and teasing. Ramses was relentless in his pursuit, his hands gripping my thighs as if he could never get close enough, as if he could somehow pull me into him. The sounds of my pleasure filled the chamber, and I was only vaguely aware that there were still two guards outside who could hear me.

But then he stopped, and he moved up my body, his lips tracing a path of fire until they met mine in a kiss that was a seal. He fumbled between our bodies, releasing himself. I didn't dare to look down—to see what undoubtedly would split me in half.

He held himself in his hands, running the tip of his cock through my wetness rapidly, making a noise that was obscene and had me writhing beneath him.

And when the wave finally broke over me, it was with a force that left me gasping, shuddering, my fingers tangled in his mane of red hair, holding him to me as if he were the only thing keeping me from shattering into a thousand pieces.

He took that opportunity to bury himself inside of me to the hilt, swallowing my gasp of pain with his tongue. As Ramses entered me, there was a fleeting moment of pain. He paused, giving me a moment to adjust to him. He pulsed inside of me, twitching and holding himself still.

He clasped my chin in his fingers, opening my mouth and coaxing my tongue out of me. A string of spit connected our tongues before he dove in and moved his tongue in the same motion he began to move his hips. He pulled out slowly, taking shallow pumps, each time going out further and then deeper.

I wrapped my legs around his waist, drawing him in even closer and encouraging him to abandon the cautious rhythm. He cupped my bum in his hand, slamming into me with abandon. It hurt, but his pelvis kept kissing against mine and would send a jolt through me that made me forget the pain.

The sounds we made would have disgusted me if I were a bystander.

I clung to him, my nails digging into his back, marking him as he marked me.

Another wave crashed through me, and I shuddered, my hips closed as much as I could, a low moan dragging out of me.

"Fuck," he groaned, his movements erratic until he stilled, breathing hard against my ear. He pulled out of me slowly, drawing out our mixed essence with him. He quickly got up and wiped himself with a rag, then tossed it onto my belly.

"I have to attend to something early in the morning," he said, pulling on his robe and getting under his covers.

I propped myself on a shaky elbow, examining the tight muscles that rippled over him. I made to crawl next to him, but he stopped me.

"Go to bed."

I chuckled, pulling back his covers. "I am trying to."

"In your own bed."

I furrowed my brows. "Am I not meant to sleep here with my husband?"

His expression was suddenly inscrutable, a mask that fell into place and hid whatever warmth had been there moments before. "Not tonight," he said curtly, devoid of the passion that had filled the room just minutes ago.

I felt a coldness seep into the space between us, chilling me more than the night air ever could. Confusion and a pang of hurt twined together in my chest. "Ramses?" I questioned—a mix of disbelief and a plea for some explanation.

But he turned away, dismissing me with a wave of his hand. "I need to be alone," he said flatly. "Please, leave."

I sat up, the rag falling from my body, and hastily began to gather my clothes. The silence was heavy, punctuated only by the rustling of fabric as I dressed in a daze.

With my dress finally on, I stood and looked at him, searching for the man who had shared such a profound moment with me. But all I saw was the back of a king, a man encased in his authority and distance.

Without another word, I left the chamber, the door closing behind me with a soft but final click. Two women stood there, their sheer gowns leaving little to the imagination, their purpose unmistakable.

They glanced at me, eyes wide with a mix of curiosity and pity, before one of them reached for the door handle.

"What are you doing?" I asked sharply.

"The king summoned us, my lady," one of them answered. They were both willowy and with hair so blonde it looked silver. Both had brown eyes—they could have been sisters.

I opened the door and barged into Ramses' chambers. "What is this?" I waved a hand behind me to the two women.

Ramses raised a dark brow at me, "Cruella and Damis."

"I did not ask for their names. What are they doing here after you dismiss me so?"

Ramses sat up against his pillows, his body relaxed and assessing. He looked every inch the unattainable man I had known.

"They are here for my pleasure," he said plainly.

"Your pleasure?" I echoed in disbelief. "After you have had me, your queen, you seek pleasure from others?"

"It is the way of kings," Ramses replied with a shrug that dismissed my feelings. "You should not concern yourself with such matters. It is beneath you."

"And what of us?" I demanded. "Does our union mean so little to you that you would so quickly seek others in your bed?"

Ramses' expression hardened, a flicker of annoyance crossing his features. "You are my queen," he stated coldly. "Your place is secure. These... diversions, they are nothing. Do not make the mistake of equating the two."

The two women behind me shifted uncomfortably, their presence an unwelcome reminder of the situation. I turned to look at them, their faces a mirror of confusion and apprehension. I turned back to Ramses.

"I am your queen, not a mere observer to your whims. If we are to rule together, there must be respect, fidelity, and trust. I will not stand idly by while you make a mockery of our marriage."

"Who are you to make demands of me? You will leave. You will go to your bed."

"I will not," I said, my arms crossed.

He cocked his head to the side, his lips curling back. He called for the guards, and I expected him to have them drag me out kicking and screaming.

No.

Instead, he said, "My lady wishes to watch. You will hold her in that chair until I am finished."

It hit me like a slap—a shock of cold realization at the depths of his cruelty. The guards moved forward, their faces grim.

"Don't fret, love; perhaps you will learn something," he said.

●

I cried into the morning hours. Joslynn came to my room and pulled the blankets off of me.

"Come, child. Today is a new day," she said softly. "Da pain does not last in dese tings."

I sat up, sniffling. "I thought that I would be enough. He was so displeased with me that he needed two women to satisfy him after."

Joslynn shook her head. "No, love. Blackwater men are known to be insatiable. He follows da way of his father, and his father before him. I only pray it ends at dat. Dat he loves ya enough to not put ya through what his mother went through."

Tears streamed down my face, the weight of my naivety pressing heavily on my chest. "But I thought... I thought I could be the one to change him, to be the exception," I whispered.

"Child, you cannot blame yaself for da failings of a man set in his ways. You are strong, kind, and full of light. You must not let his darkness dim ya shine."

"I made him angry. I should have just gone to bed like he asked. I was foolish."

I didn't know my place, and that was my fault.

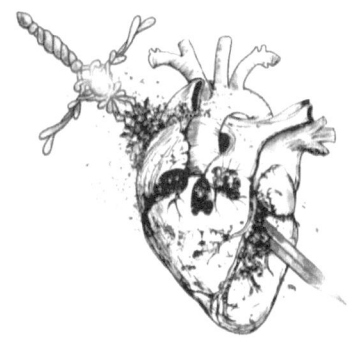

CHAPTER SIX

I had spent the better part of three days in my room, wallowing in my feelings. Ramses didn't miss me, of course. He had his own company.

I couldn't get the image of the two women taking turns riding him out of my head.

I didn't let him see my cry. I waited until it was all over and left his room without so much as a breath.

He told Joslynn that he had gotten me a horse. The gift of the horse was a hollow attempt at reconciliation, a pale offering that could not wash away the images seared into my mind. The thought of those women, their laughter echoing in my ears, their hands upon him in ways that were supposed to be reserved for me. I shook my head, biting my cheek.

I had never ridden a horse before. Apparently, women are supposed to ride it sideways in *dresses*.

Ramses requested that I get dressed and meet him in the court-yard. I knew it was not an invitation—it was a command. Appear before him, dressed in the finery of a lady, to present a united front to whatever audience he had in mind. It was a performance, and I was to be his showpiece, paraded on the back of a horse like some prized possession.

I descended to the courtyard, the fabric of my blue dress whispering against the stone. The air was cool, the sky a canvas of blue just beginning to be touched by the morning's brush.

Ramses presented me with the horse. White as snow. A large, glittering purple ribbon wrapped around the mare's neck.

Ramses watched me, a calculating glint in his eyes as I moved to mount the horse. He stopped me, getting on it first. With a swift motion, he swept me up by the waist and placed me in front of him on the saddle. His arm encircled me tightly. He leaned forward, running his nose along my shoulder blade.

"You smell good, love," he said casually. I leaned away from him, brushing him off. "Oh, come now. You aren't still mad." It wasn't a question—he was *actually* telling me that I was not mad.

I let out a dry laugh.

He kicked the horse's side, and we lurched backward, my back hitting his hard chest. I quietly simmered in my anger. The audacity to believe he could overwrite my emotions with a word, as if my heart were as easily led as the mare we rode upon.

The first few city folk greeted us in the streets, offering me flowers and bread. Ramses feathered kisses on my temple, telling me how beautiful I was. His tone was light and carefree as if we were naught but a couple taking a leisurely ride. In love. Happy.

As we moved through the city, I could feel the eyes of the onlookers upon us. They did not see me. Not the anger and hurt. They saw only the image Ramses wished to project.

Ramses' arm tightened around me as we navigated the streets, the press of his body unyielding. "Smile more," he said through gritted teeth.

"No," I said sweetly, pursing my lips together.

That was when Ramses' mood shifted. His arm became a vice around my waist, and without warning, he spurred the horse into a sudden gallop. The mare, startled, launched forward. My breath caught in my throat as the scenery blurred into streaks of color.

"Ramses!" I cried out, the panic rising like bile in my throat. "Slow down!" But my plea was drowned out by the thundering of hooves on cobblestone.

He was relentless, urging the horse faster and faster. We leaped over fences, the mare's powerful legs sending us soaring through the air and landing with jarring force. I clenched my eyes shut, praying for it to stop. Baskets of fruit and vendors' carts were mere obstacles in Ramses' path, dodged with terrifying swiftness.

The city gave way to the countryside, where the horse's hooves found new strength on the soft earth. Ramses directed the mare toward a small river, the water splashing around us as she crossed with powerful strides, sending chills up my spine. I begged and pleaded, my cries lost against the wind and Ramses' laughter. I was soaked.

Finally, the gates of the courtyard loomed before us. Ramses pulled the reins, and the mare reared up before charging through the entrance. My hands gripped the saddle horn, my knuckles white with the force of my hold. The mare came to a skidding halt in the center of the courtyard, and before the dust had even settled, I slid from the horse, my legs trembling.

"You're mad!" I yelled at Ramses, my heart pounding in my chest. "You could have killed us both!"

He dismounted with an ease that only further fueled my anger.

"Ungrateful," he spat, his eyes narrowing. "After all I do for you, this is the thanks I get?"

I shook my head, incredulous.

"You will learn your place, Atreya," he growled. "And you will learn to appreciate what I offer."

I bared my teeth at him. "You think a horse makes up for what you did to me? Keep the damn horse!" With that, I stomped off to my bedroom.

●

I was summoned for dinner. Corina and Servat had joined. The long wooden table was covered in trays of fruits, meats, and various side dishes. My stomach clenched. I hadn't eaten a proper meal since my wedding night.

Ramses was impatiently tapping the wooden table with his claw, the seat at the opposite end of him empty. I swallowed, sitting down quietly across from him.

"You look beautiful," he said.

I cleared my throat, thanking him. He nodded once, flicking his hand, and the tray of roasted meat moved toward me by an invisible force.

I accepted it graciously, putting a slab of steak onto my plate. My stomach growled noisily, and I blushed.

As I ate, I mulled over the idea of forgiving Ramses. Perhaps I could excuse his past behavior, attributing it to a particular lifestyle he was used to. Maybe I could help break him out of it, making him love me enough to want me only.

My thoughts drifted to the vast castle, its stone walls holding centuries of history. "There are rooms in this castle that could use redecorating," I ventured, attempting to steer the conversation toward lighter matters.

Across the table, Corina and Servat were engaged in a playful banter, ignoring us entirely.

Ramses chuckled. "Gods only know this place needs a woman's touch."

The meat was tender and flavorful, and as I savored each bite, I made a decision. "Ramses," I said, "how about we go for another horse ride tomorrow? On Snow."

He looked puzzled. "Who is Snow?"

I smiled, setting down my fork. "I thought of a name for the horse. Snow."

He was silent for a moment, and then he tilted his head. "I thought you said you didn't want the horse?"

I shrugged. "I changed my mind."

Ramses's expression shifted slightly. "We can go riding," he said, "but not on Snow."

"Why not?" I asked, my curiosity piqued.

He pointed his fork at my plate. "Because *that* is Snow."

I looked down at the remnants of my meal, realizing what he meant.

I was eating my gift.

•

It was my fault. I said for him to keep the horse. He had enough horses, he said. It was a waste of meat. And, as he pointed out through my fit of coughing, I had enjoyed it.

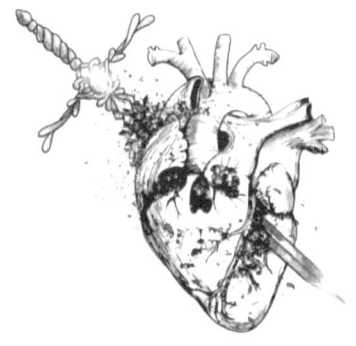

CHAPTER SEVEN

ELDRA SOLARIS

One year had passed since the council's plan was set into motion, and despite our best efforts, Ramses had remained elusive, his actions hidden behind a shroud of secrecy. The marriage to the girl—now his wife—hadn't stirred anything new in motion.

"We have heard nothing," Gaelin spat. "Not a damned thing since he married that girl. It's been a *year*."

We circled our round table in the middle of the common room. It was an enormous black oak table with a smooth, red sigil of our house carved on top—a Sun encompassing a dragon.

Emery spoke in her Arathi language, and Madsen nodded her head. I waited, but neither of them said anything else.

"For the people who *don't* speak Arathi, say it in the common tongue," I said with a sigh, pinching the bridge of my nose.

Emery's sage skin tinged pink, and she said carefully, "We have heard nothing. Short of the Silent Sisters saying that Aislinn could have returned in many ways, but all require sacrifice."

"The girl married him, and there are whispers that he is cruel to her," Hisen said. I glanced at him. He was sitting across from me, his hands folded in his lap, his eyes unseeing.

"And you cannot get anything else out of the dead?" I asked.

"There is nothing to bribe the dead with; they speak when they want or can," he answered stiffly.

While Hisen's input is usually invaluable, it also did not help us understand the situation at hand. The dead were not a resource that could be tapped at will, and their silence on Ramses and the girl was as telling as it was frustrating.

I leaned back in my chair, lacing my fingers together. "Then we must change our approach," I proposed. "If the dead offer us no answers and the Silent Sisters speak only in riddles, we must look to the living. We need eyes and ears within Ramses' walls."

"*Within?*" Gaelin balked. "The few people who live in the city only occasionally come out to the Hyperion Market. I don't have a valve to stream information straight to us."

"We make one. There has to be *someone* in Ramses court that isn't particularly happy," I said.

"His wife?" Emery suggested. "If Ramses is indeed resorting to cruel measures against his wife, it may be possible to turn her to our cause. If she is being mistreated, she could be a valuable ally."

I dismissed the thought immediately. "That's too close. It is too dangerous." A kicked dog will return to its master if that is all it knows.

The room fell into a contemplative silence following my dismissal of Emery's suggestion. The risk of reaching out to Ramses' wife—is too high.

Madsen glowered in her seat. "We need a different angle," she said firmly. "Someone on the inside, yes, but not her. Perhaps a servant or a guard—someone who sees and hears much but is noticed little."

Gaelin nodded thoughtfully. "I have been cultivating contacts, petty thieves, and merchants who hear rumors in the Hyperion Market. It's possible one of them could be persuaded to get closer to Ramses' inner circle, or at least to someone who is."

"I can enhance their ability to remain unnoticed," Emery offered, her fingers tracing a sigil in the air, a faint glow emanating from her hand. "A touch of glamour, a whisper of charm—enough to give them an edge without drawing attention to my magic."

"Gaelinantis Otear. You are Nandarian. Surely you can find something with those spy master gifts of yours," I said to Gaelin.

"I cannot work miracles!" He snapped.

Hisen, lost in thought, said, "I will redouble my efforts to commune with the spirits. Perhaps there is a way to coax more from them, some lost soul with a grudge or a secret longing to be heard."

My fist tightened at that. I did not want to ask the question that had been gnawing at me. If Hisen could reach Aislinn, he would have told me.

Ameria, who had been silent most of the meeting, said, "Do you think you can find *her* spirit?"

Leave it to my wife to ask the difficult questions.

Hisen's pale eyes reflected the flickers of the candles that lined the room. He always had a ghostly aura about him, but now it seemed even more pronounced as he contemplated Ameria's question.

"I have tried," he confessed. "Repeatedly. If Aislinn's spirit was within reach, if it lingered in the afterworld as most do, I should have been able to find some trace of her. But there is nothing—an absence where there should be echoes."

The council members exchanged concerned glances, avoiding looking directly at me. Madsen shifted in her seat uncomfortably.

It was an answer I didn't want—a question I never had wanted to ask. Ameria squeezed my hand gently.

"Could Ramses have done something to her spirit?" Madsen asked, her brow furrowed in thought. "Some dark magic that binds her even in death?"

Emery shook her head, her expression grim. "It's possible. Some spells, ancient and forbidden, can trap and prevent a soul from moving on. Such magic would require a power of terrible magnitude and a will to match. Would require the spirit to be contained in a vessel."

I gritted my teeth, nails scraping along the dark oak of the table, my knuckles turning white as I clenched my fist. It struck a chord of dread through me.

"Then we must consider the chance that Ramses has trapped her essence," I said, the words tasting like ash in my mouth. "If he has harnessed such a spell, it could be that Aislinn's spirit is being used against her will—a tool in his arsenal of dark arts."

"Or, we should consider that she has passed beyond my means of reaching her. That maybe she is at peace," Hisen said carefully.

Hope and despair warred within me, as they likely did within each council member. The possibility that Aislinn might have found peace was a small comfort against the fear of what Ramses might be capable of.

"We must not lose focus," she said softly, yet with an underlying steel. "Our priority is to uncover Ramses' plans and end whatever dark designs he harbors. Aislinn's fate, while important, must not cloud our judgment or divert us from our course."

Gaelin stood abruptly, his chair scraping back. "Fine words, but they give us no clear path forward. We need actionable intelligence, and we need it yesterday."

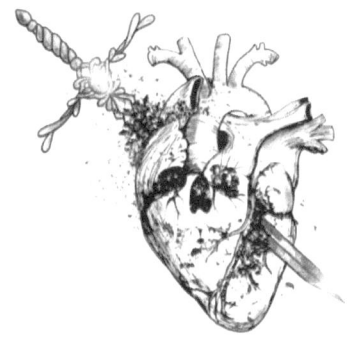

CHAPTER EIGHT

ATREYA

1 *1 years later...*

The pathways were lined with cobblestones, winding and meandering like the thoughts of a daydreamer. Statues of marble and stone stood sentinel along the paths, each one a tribute to the legends of our realm. Heroes in mid-battle, lovers caught in an eternal embrace. I never did care for those. Too much detail in their naked bodies. All of them were pristine—no sign of rain damage on the stones. I stepped through the wrought iron gates, sighing heavily. The sweet perfume of blooming flowers greeted me, the air mixed with jasmine and rose and the delicate scent of lilies.

No orchids. I had not smelled orchids in years.

As I meandered through the labyrinth of greenery of the royal garden, I heard the soft crunch of footsteps tailing me. I didn't need to turn around to know who it was. Servat had the subtlety of a thunderclap.

"Why so tense, little fighter?" Servat's voice slithered through the garden, grating against my peace. He leaned against a stone archway, a smug grin plastered on his face. He was taller than I, his shoulders wide, his body a mass of muscles. His dark skin was covered in a sheen of sweat from the heat, and his white hair mussed from running his hands through it.

"Go back to your cronies, Servat," I said. "I am in no mood for your games."

"Games?" He pushed off from the archway and strolled closer, his hands casually tucked in his pockets. "This is no game. I am simply bored."

Bored.

I swallowed.

"And yet, you always seem to find time to watch me. One might start to think you're obsessed," I quipped.

He cocked his head, white hair swaying. His pale blue eyes locked onto mine, a flicker of something unreadable passing through them. "Obsessed or merely curious," Servat mused. "You're an enigma here, a puzzle that doesn't quite fit. I like puzzles."

"I'm not a puzzle for you to solve," I shot back, my eyes flicking around to see who was watching us. None of the soldiers ever found our conversation interesting.

Probably a tongue-tie spell.

Servat chuckled, the sound rich and warm. "Everyone is a puzzle, little fighter. Some are just more... intriguing than others." He closed the distance between us, now just an arm's length away. "You fight like you have nothing to lose, yet I see the fire of someone who has everything to gain. It's... captivating. When my brother took you in, I did not understand the appeal. Then you came into your own." His eyes raked over me.

I stepped back, unsettled by the intensity in his eyes. "You don't know anything about me."

"Don't I?" Servat's smirk returned, and he reached out to pluck a scarlet blossom from a nearby bush. He twirled it between his fingers, the petals red like blood against his dark skin. "You wear your heart on your sleeve, yet you're surprised when someone reads it. How disappointing it must be to live in a viper's den disguised as a castle."

I glared at him, my hands itching to smack the flower away, but I knew that would only encourage him. "Says the viper. Is this how you get your thrills, Servat? By toying with people who want *nothing* to do with you?"

His expression shifted, and the amusement in his features gave way to something more complex, more intense. "Maybe I see something in you that you're too afraid to acknowledge," he said quietly.

"Afraid? The only thing I'm afraid of is wasting my time on pointless distractions." My gaze darted to the scarlet blossom still twirling in his fingers. "Like this."

Servat's eyes followed mine to the flower, and then, with a fluid motion, he offered it to me. "Then consider this a gift. Not a distraction, but a token." His tone was severe, devoid of the mockery that usually laced his words when we were in the training yard. He was generally harsh with me, and though I would never master a sword the way he had, I had gotten better. But I did not need a sword anymore.

I hesitated, the soft petal edges tempting me with their simplicity. But I knew better than to accept gifts from snakes. "A token of what?" I asked, suspicious.

"Appreciation," he answered, "I like pretty things." He finished with a shrug, as though the gesture could dismiss the layers of implication behind his words. "Pretty things. Like a rose, like a sword, like a woman with fire in her veins."

"Appreciation," I echoed skeptically. "Since when do you appreciate anything other than your reflection?" Surely, he could not be meaning me.

A flicker of genuine amusement crossed his features. "You'd be surprised," Servat conceded with a half-grin. "I have a keen eye for potential, for the sharp edges of a will that refuses to be broken. It's a beauty of its own kind."

So he enjoyed seeing me fight back—as he said all those years ago. I resisted Ramses as much as I could now, but even that was not enough. Servat leaned in closer, overwhelming my space. "And that's precisely why I placed my bet on you in the arena against Aislinn Furian," he confessed.

My heart skipped a beat, and I felt a jolt of adrenaline. "You what? You placed a wager on me? That I would kill that woman?"

"That you would live," he corrected, shaking his head. "I wagered on your life, not her death. There's a difference. It's not about the fall of Aislinn Furian; it's about your rise. Ramses did not have any hope left in you. You know that now. It was his last chance to see if you could do anything worth keeping you around."

Yes. I had learned the hard way that Ramses' love came with a price. A price I did not care to pay—but had no choice in the matter now.

I stared at him, trying to untangle his words. "Why would you bet on me? I was no one—am no one."

Servat's expression softened slightly, and he stepped back, allowing me room to breathe. He held the flower out to me, and I opened my palm for it.

It bloomed brighter, fuller.

His eyes flicked to the gold bracelet on my wrist, a wedding gift from Ramses. It had the same snug fit as a tight jade bracelet, easy enough to slide onto my skin but unforgiving in its embrace, as if it had melded with my flesh to become a permanent fixture of my being. He curled his nose at it, then returned his eyes to mine.

"You are everything," he whispered harshly.

The moment stretched between us, filled with a tension that was more than the sum of his words. A spark had lit in me. The flower in my hand seemed to pulse with a life of its own, its petals unfurling.

I stared at the man who was Ramses' half-brother and then down at the bloom in my hands. Their relationship was, to say the least, complicated. Ramses, the legitimate heir, was brought up in the palace with all the luxuries of royal life, while Servat was raised in obscurity, his mother a mere servant in the king's household. Yet, fate had a funny way of playing its cards. Servat, the illegitimate son, had risen through the ranks to become the captain of the King's army, a position of great power and respect. And Ramses didn't kill him. On the contrary, he made him his right-hand man. Their relationship was often strained—with Ramses occasionally going too far to show that Servat was beneath his boot.

I looked up from the bloom to Servat, my eyes searching his.

There was a rawness there, a vulnerability that Servat never showed. The realization slowly dawned on me, a truth that had been hidden in plain sight yet was now as clear as the daylight filtering through the leaves: Servat's interest in me went beyond the arena, beyond the wagers and the games of power—beyond his quips and his smirks and the way he always seemed to be watching me.

It was a dangerous thing to be the object of affection of a man like Servat—a man of strategy and calculation, a man who held his emotions close like a hand of cards. Yet there it was, written in the softening of his steely gaze, the slight tilt of his head, the careful distance he maintained even as he offered the flower. There was stillness in his shoulders as he held his breath.

Waiting.

The king's half-brother.

With a smile like Ramses.'

Oh, what a dangerous game we play.

"You placed a bet on my life," I said slowly, "but this... this is more than a wager, isn't it?" I motioned between us.

Servat's eyes held mine, and for a heartbeat, he was silent. Then, with a barely perceptible nod, he acknowledged it. "It seems I have placed more in you than I initially wanted to," he admitted—the words seeming to cost him. "Things were simpler when you were just a ward."

My pulse quickened, and I felt the world's edges sharpen—that spark in me burning.

"What does this mean?" I asked, the flower a heavy weight in my palm.

"It means that I see your worth, your strength, and yes," Servat murmured, "your beauty. It means that I cannot deny that you've *ignited* something within me that I cannot—and do not wish to—extinguish."

The confession hung between us, a delicate truth that shifted the ground beneath my feet.

I could use this to my advantage and manipulate it for my gain in our cutthroat world. Or I could acknowledge the bond that was forming, fraught with risk but alive with possibility.

Or it could be all a trick. Servat could be a clever player in Ramses' games. Servat tended to belittle me just like the rest of the Blackwaters, and it had seeped into my very bones.

For a long moment, we stood in silence, the garden around us a witness to the crossroads we'd reached. Then, with a resolve that surprised even me, I stepped forward, closing the gap Servat had so carefully maintained.

I crushed that pretty flower between my fingers, the petals dissolving into a fine mist of dust, throwing it at his face.

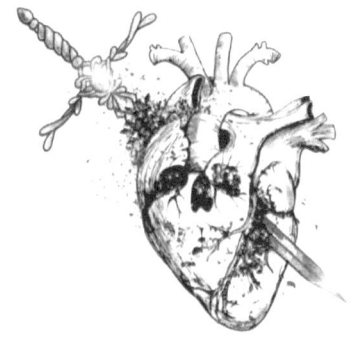

CHAPTER NINE

ATREYA

2 *years later...*

"My Lady, you have to push! You have to push harder!" Joslynn was urging me over my screaming.

Primal sounds—the rhythmic chanting of encouragement from Joslynn, the sharp intakes of breath between my screams, the gentle but firm directives from the attending midwife. My screams seemed foreign to me.

I'd kill Ramses when this was over. There were moments when the sounds blurred together. There was the sharp, antiseptic aroma of herbs and tinctures that the midwife used to try and soothe my pain.

I was pushing with all my might, my body blanketed in sweat and pain.

Thirteen years had passed since the day in the arena, and here I was, in the throes of a different battle.

Joslynn, ever-present, ever the source of strength, was by my side, her hands gripping mine as I bore down again, my knuckles white with the effort. The pain was all-encompassing, a primal force that seemed to tear through the very fabric of my being.

"Never again," I screamed. "Never doing this again."

Joslynn and the other midwife laughed. "D'ey all say dat deary. D'ey all say that," Joslynn said, patting my arm.

"He's splitting me in half!" I wailed.

"Dat's just his head, da rest of him will come out easily," Joslynn promised. "And den we will put him at your breast." I clutched at her arm.

"Get him out! Get him out!" I pleaded.

The midwife's voice was a distant echo, "That's it, my queen, just a few more. He's almost here!" Her words were meant to encourage me, but the sound of my labored breaths drowned them out, the guttural cries that escaped my lips with each contraction.

My nails elongated, the bed smoking and simmering beneath me.

I could feel the pressure building, an unbearable tension that promised release but demanded everything I had. My body was a vessel, a conduit for the life I was about to bring forth, and I surrendered to its demands.

I pushed again, harder than I thought possible. There was a moment of excruciating pain, a sensation of tearing that seemed to split me in two, and then, suddenly, relief.

The room was filled with a new sound, the robust cry of a newborn. I collapsed back onto the bed, my body spent, my chest heaving as I tried to comprehend the magnitude of what had just occurred.

I looked down at the tiny face of my son. His skin still reddened from the effort of birth, his little features scrunched up as he continued to cry.

As I lay there, exhausted and vulnerable, the midwife worked swiftly to clean and assess the newborn.

My heart swelled.

"How will we explain this?" I panted, motioning to the midwife, her blood a pool on the stone. She was a good woman, an honest woman.

Killer.

"Dees tings have a way of taking care of demselves." Joslynn's only answer.

I realized it meant she hadn't come up with her lie yet. She needed to be in the moment.

I sat up, allowing her to clean the bloodied sheets away from me, and watched as she worked the midwife's body into those sheets. Joslynn's hand hovered over the spot where the woman was shrouded in her death blanket, just as the door flew open.

The mess of sheets disappeared.

"Hello, Lady Corina," Joslynn greeted calmly.

"We heard the baby's wail, and you made us wait long enough," Corina snapped impatiently. "Show us our Prince." She was wearing fresh robes and sterile gowns of copper color that clashed with her vibrant red hair.

I tore my eyes away from that crop of red hair and down to my baby with a wince.

Ramses appeared in the doorway, followed by several courtesans. One had a scroll levitating before him, a quill scribbling fiercely in the air. No doubt to announce the birth—to send it out to all corners of Ferenz.

Joslynn gave me a reassuring glance as she moved to intercept Ramses and the entourage.

"O' course, Your Majesty," Joslynn said with a courteous nod. Ramses regarded her with mild disgust, glancing at her bloodied apron. "Da queen has just delivered a strong and healthy prince. She needs a moment to get herself... togeda...before presenting him to da court."

Ramses' gaze swept the room, a frown creasing his brow as he sniffed the air, obviously smelling blood.

"Messy business, birthing is," Joslynn said quickly, noticing how his eyes flickered and cast about.

"It's not just her blood I smell," Ramses growled.

"Where is the other midwife?" Corina asked, peering to glimpse the baby wriggling in my arms. She smiled warmly at him.

My heart leaped into my throat, and my palms grew damp. The baby made a cooing sound, and Ramses expression softened a bit.

"The labor was hard on da Queen. It can make a woman almost feral from da pain... unfortunately for da midwife, she was too close and da Queen..." Joslynn looked to me to finish.

I understood.

Be convincing.

"She said I wasn't pushing hard enough. I snapped. It was an unfortunate accident," I said without much feeling. Cool. Collected. Murderous.

"An *accident*," Ramses echoed, his voice measured. He turned his attention back to the child in my arms, the heir. "And yet, my son is here, healthy and strong."

That was all that mattered to him. He didn't care for a servant.

Corina, ever the keen dog, remained silent, her eyes flicking between Joslynn, Ramses, and me.

"May we see him?" she asked, her tone smaller than I was used to hearing. Her throat bobbed, and I caught excitement gleaming in her eyes. It was rare that she ever asked me for anything.

I nodded slowly, and Ramses was already scooping the baby into his arms.

"Look at him. My son," Ramses whispered. He brought up his clawed finger and hesitated, moving the blankets around. He scrunched his face at the wisps of black hair on the baby's head.

"A raven-haired Prince! A black-haired Blackwater!" He exclaimed. "Just like his mother then."

A collective sigh rippled through the room, a wave of relief disguised as admiration. Ramses, cradling the baby, seemed for a moment to forget the blood that had been spilled, forget about the courtesans or the man scribbling with the quill. His attention was consumed by the child in his arms.

Corina stepped closer, her eyes softening as she peered at the prince. "Yes, just like his mother," she echoed, carrying a warmth that seemed to smooth over the earlier tension. She held out her hand, her fingers scrunching the blankets, her touch light and gentle. "I love him already."

After a while, she, the courtiers, and even Joslynn shuffled out obediently, their movements hushed and their glances fleeting as they exited the chamber. The door closed with a soft but definitive click, and the room was enveloped in a sudden quiet, the kind that amplifies the smallest of sounds—the crackling of the fire in the hearth, the gentle breaths of the newborn prince, and the heavy beating of my own heart.

Ramses stood there, a towering figure whose presence seemed to fill the space left by the departed court. His eyes, dark and searching, found mine, and within them, I saw something I had never seen before.

Uncertainty.

"Is there something you wish to say, my king?" I asked, wariness fluttering through me like a caged bird.

Ramses took a step forward, his gaze never leaving mine. "You have given me a son," he began, "A prince who will one day inherit my crown, my kingdom. For that, I am grateful beyond words."

He paused, his eyes drifting down to the child in my arms before returning to meet my gaze. "You're so beautiful."

I said nothing.

Waiting.

His hand reached out tentatively, as if navigating new territory, and rested gently upon the baby's back. "This son... our son," he corrected himself, "he changes everything."

I watched him carefully, searching for the meaning behind his hesitation. It was unlike Ramses to falter, to show any sign of doubt, and it both intrigued and unnerved me.

"Yes, he does," I agreed softly, despite the whirlwind of thoughts spinning in my mind. "He is the future of the Blackwaters, a continuation of your line."

Ramses nodded slowly, his eyes still locked with mine. The uncertainty I had sensed seemed to grow, and it was clear that he needed to say more. "I have been a king, a warrior, and a husband," he started, each word deliberate. "But being a father... it is something new, something that I never realized would stir such..."

He trailed off, struggling to articulate feelings that were as foreign to him as they were profound. It was then that I understood. The mantle of fatherhood was a weight he was only beginning to comprehend.

"It is a role that will challenge you in ways you cannot yet imagine," I said.

This was such a rare thing. I tried to blink less, ingraining this into memory.

"He will need a name. What shall it be?" I asked, changing the subject.

Ramses straightened a bit at that. "A good name. Something strong, like his father."

I panicked for all of ten seconds, thinking he was about to name our child after himself. The protest was on the tip of my tongue.

"Vryseris," I said.

"What?"

"It means Victory in the old tongue," I explained. He stared at me, contemplating.

"Vryseris," he said with a practiced roll of his tongue.

The name hung in the air between us.

Ramses repeated it, the word becoming more familiar with each utterance, and I watched the corners of his mouth curve ever so slightly in approval.

"Vryseris," he said again, this time with a hint of certainty. "Yes, it is fitting for a prince."

I could see the king in him gathering the name closely, embracing the future it promised for his son. Vryseris, our son, would grow into the name, into the victory it signified.

Ramses turned to me, his gaze softening. "You have chosen well, my queen. Vryseris it shall be," he declared as if the words themselves forged the path our son would walk upon. He had a habit of doing that—of believing things into his will.

The moment was one of rare alignment between us, a unity in purpose that transcended the complexities of our relationship.

My delicate dance between hate and love.

It was a reprieve from the unspoken tensions that had wound their way through our marriage.

"Vryseris," I whispered to the child cradled in my arms, "may you carry this name with honor, and may it guide you to a life of greatness."

As the fire in the hearth crackled and the shadows danced upon the walls, I beckoned Ramses with the crook of my finger.

When he leaned down, I kissed him smoothly on his lips.

As he straightened up, there was a flicker of surprise in his eyes.

"We have weathered much, you and I," Ramses said, fingers coming to put my hair back in place. He didn't flinch from the sweat like I thought he would.

"We have," I agreed.

I have weathered you.

"Come," Ramses said, offering me his arm, "Let us introduce Prince Vryseris to the kingdom he will one day serve."

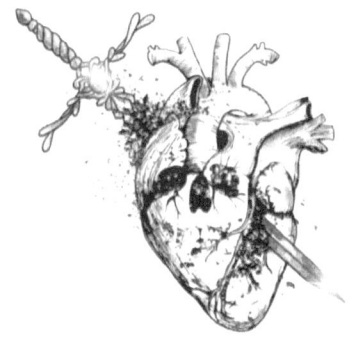

CHAPTER TEN

ATREYA

5 years after the birth of Prince Vryseris

"There's a group of rebels left over from the war. Servat and his men caught them at the borders of Veridia and brought them back here," Ramses mused from his perch on the wall, studying the map by faelight he conjured.

The study was a room of dark wood and heavy tomes, the air thick with the scent of incense and the sharp tang of wax. Bookshelves lined the walls, each groaning under the weight of leather-bound volumes and scrolls covering every inch of the shelves to the ceiling. Above the large oak desk, a large window framed a sky view—of the spires of distant buildings glowing softly in the sunlight.

"Why bring them back here? Why not just dispose of them?" I asked with little interest, watching the dust settle as Ramses moved to the next shelf and reached for a book.

He made a little grunt of irritation. "Because I want *you* to get rid of them."

I paused, frowning. "Want me to kill them?"

Ramses turned to look at me, a flash of annoyance that I would even have to ask. "Yes. But I need you to do it in the arena." Ramses watched me with expectation; his stance was relaxed, but his face was sharp.

"No."

"It wasn't a request, love," Ramses said, his tone light. I sighed and sat back on my heels, looking up at him.

"There will always be rebels. Just get what you need from them and be done with them," I said. "I can dispose of them after, in their cells."

"I got what I needed from them. I need you to get rid of them," he repeated, rolling up a map.

Ramses tossed the rolled map aside. "You were the best at killing, weren't you? Servat taught you well. So why the hesitation now?"

I stood, my posture rigid, the muscles in my jaw clenching. "Fighting for my life was one thing. This is a spectacle. A quick death is better."

"It's a message," he corrected. "A reminder to those who think of opposing us that our grasp is unyielding. And who better to deliver such a message than Ferenz's most feared Furian Slayer?"

"Remind them?" I sneered, the edge in my voice sharp enough to cut through the heavy silence between us. "Or remind me of what I am? What you make me to be."

Ramses stood, descending from his perch with the grace of a predator, the faelight casting shadows that danced ominously across his features. "You are what I made you, a queen."

I glared at him, my teeth gritted, my lips pursed. "Queen?" I scoffed, venom dripping from the word as if it were a title I loathed. "A queen does not take orders; she gives them. You've made me a weapon—a sharp and deadly blade you wield without remorse."

Ramses' eyes narrowed, and a flicker of annoyance crossed his face, quickly replaced by his usual, infuriating composure. "Semantics," he waved his hand dismissively. "You are royalty in your own right—the queen of the killing fields. Your name is whispered in fear and respect. Your legacy is written in the blood of those who dared defy us."

I stepped closer, my fury barely contained. "And what of my desires? Do I not get a say in my fate? Or am I destined to be your loyal hound, baying for blood at your command?"

"Desires?" He chuckled, a low, dangerous sound. "You desire the thrill of battle, the supremacy of victory. You may wear it reluctantly, but the crown suits you, my deadly queen."

The air between us was tense, a battle of wills as old as the scars that marked my skin. "And what if one day my desires change?" I challenged. "What if I tire of this endless cycle of violence?"

Ramses stepped forward, the space between us charged with an icy current. "Change?" He whispered, but it held the weight of steel. "My dear, you were born from the ashes of war, molded by my hand. You are violence incarnate, and there is no escaping your nature." His words were a cold chain meant to bind me to his will.

"I wasn't always like this. I was good. I was kind, and I was gentle," I snapped.

Despite the chill that crept up my spine, I did not flinch. "Even the fiercest storm can change course, Ramses. And when it does, it reshapes the landscape entirely."

He laughed, a sound devoid of warmth, devoid of humanity. "Poetic but misguided. You see, I know you better than you know yourself. You thrive in the chaos, in the blood-soaked sands of the arena. You may feign reluctance, but you'll do as you're told because you have no choice. You are *mine*."

The word 'mine' echoed in my head, a poisonous mantra that sought to invalidate my existence and reduce it to nothing more than a possession—a fire kindled in my chest, a blaze of indignation and fury that refused to be smothered.

"You think you know me?" I retorted, my magic rising. "You see what you've crafted, what you've forced me to become, but you're blind to the person I once was. You've taken my past and reshaped it in the image of your *cruelty*."

His irises shifted to molten gold. "You know *nothing* of *cruelty*. I can show you cruel."

His threat hung in the air, a tangible darkness that sought to suffocate the light of my defiance. Ramses moved closer, his presence suffocating, a predator toying with his prey. "Cruelty," he hissed, "is the art of breaking the will, of bending it until it snaps. And I am an artist of the highest order. Be grateful you haven't known me in such a light."

"There is nothing more you can do to hurt me, Ramses. Nothing." I half chuckled.

His magic flared with a dangerous glint, and he closed the distance between us. "Nothing?" he echoed, a sinister whisper that crawled over my skin like a legion of spiders.

A challenge. I felt the hairs on the back of my neck rise, and a shiver rippled my spine.

He reached out lightning-fast, gripping my throat with an iron clasp. His fingers tightened, not enough to cut off air, but enough to send a clear message. "Your defiance is amusing," he said, his lips curling into a cruel smile. "But it has its limits. You should remember your place."

I could feel the power in his grip, the raw strength he wielded without effort. It was a reminder that, despite my skills and the fear I instilled in others, Ramses held a different kind of power over me.

With a rough push, he released me, and I stumbled back, gasping. The cool air filled my lungs, but it did little to ease the burning humiliation that seared through me.

Ramses watched with satisfaction as I fought to regain my composure. "You see," he said coolly, "you may have been good, kind, and gentle once, but that is not who you are now. Because I never needed a good and kind and gentle queen. I needed the Furian Slayer."

"You know I can't refuse your command," I said, low and even. "But remember this, Ramses: the day may come when I grow tired of being your executioner."

He smiled, a cold and calculated curl of his lips. "That day is not today. And until then, you will do as I command." He pinched my chin between his fingers, claw digging into my skin until I felt that sharp lick of pain.

"Go get prepared. Corina and Servat will walk you down." He then gestured to the door, a complete dismissal. I turned on my heel and strode out of his presence, my spine rigid, my rage boiling in my veins.

●

Joslynn and another servant helped to dress me, and I was back into leathers and metal guards.

As Joslynn and the other servant, a quiet lad with hands that trembled slightly as he worked, helped me into my armor, I could feel the weight of each piece as it settled upon me. The leathers were thick and dyed a deep, obsidian black, tailored to fit my form perfectly.

They clung to my skin like a second hide, a barrier between my flesh and the bite of steel—if they got close enough. Black, thin gauntlets encased my forearms. They were segmented, allowing for the flex and grip of my hands, fingers free to clutch or tear. Joslynn affixed the shoulder pauldrons, their edges flaring out like the wings of some predatory bird. They were not just protective; they were intimidating, designed to make me appear like an avian form, a bird of prey. My shins were shielded by greaves that locked into place with a series of clasps, and my feet were slipped into boots with reinforced toes and soles that could find purchase on the sandy floor. Joslynn finished fastening the breastplate, her mouth set into a thin line as she did the final ties.

"Ridicul-loss," she hissed.

"Ridiculous," I corrected with a smirk.

"You know what I say!" she seethed.

I raked my gaze to the trembling servant, his head bowed and waiting.

"Next time, make my guards tighter," I told him. He nodded a quick bob of his head, and an odd sound escaped his throat.

A squeak. Like a mouse.

Joslynn clucked her tongue at that, slightly amused. "Don't torment da boy."

I looked at myself in the polished metal of the mirror. The reflection that stared back was both foreign and familiar. My black hair was pulled back into a tight ponytail, the tips of my ears pierced, and the metal fastened in place with a simple chain of silver.

Joslynn's comment about the ridiculousness of the armor pierced through me, and for a moment, I saw a flicker of the old me reflected in her eyes. The me that would have laughed and made fun of someone wearing such a thing. But that old me was long gone and deeply buried.

Still avoiding eye contact, the servant proceeded to hand me the helm, a piece as dark as the rest of the armor.

"I'm not using that."

"Fine," Joslynn said with a sigh. "But if you end up with a mace to da skull, don't say I didn't warn you."

"I don't recall you warning me at all," I replied, smiling.

"I won't be in da stands," Joslynn said stiffly.

Joslynn's presence had been a constant in my life, a stern but guiding force. Her refusal to watch was not out of disinterest; it was her silent protest, a small rebellion.

●

The corridor was silent, the only sound of my footsteps echoing off the stone walls, each step a heartbeat in the empty passage. The rage that boiled in my veins was a living thing, coiling and seething, a serpent waiting to strike.

"I know how to get to the Goddamn arena," I snapped as Corina and Servat appeared from around the corner.

I wanted to scalp that red hair right off her head.

Corina rolled her eyes, her questions dripping with mock concern. "Oh, do you know? Because last time, I recall, you almost took a wrong turn into the kitchens. Wanted a snack before the slaughter?"

"Funny," I shot back tightly with barely suppressed anger. "I didn't realize humor was part of your skill set, along with standing around looking useless."

Servat chuckled, cold and sharp as a dagger. "Maybe she's hoping to poison us all with her cooking. That would be one way to win without lifting a finger."

I clenched my fists, feeling the familiar itch for a fight. "Keep it up, and you'll be my next victims instead of an audience."

"Victims?" Servat feigned a gasp of surprise. "You hear that, Corina? She thinks she can take us."

Corina snorted, tossing her red hair over her shoulder. "Please, we're not some starry-eyed recruits you can intimidate."

I whirled on her, snapping my leather gloves into place. "Fuck you."

"Standing around looking useless is still a step up from being Ramses' little puppet," she smirked. "At least I'm not the one dancing on strings." She made up-and-down motions with her hands and wiggled her fingers.

They kept at it down the winding staircases and through the underground tunnels that veered into many forked passages. We took a left, and after a few more turns, we came out into an open corridor with a dozen torches and large oak doors. Benches were along the walls, and an iron gate was set into the stone.

Servat leaned against the wall, arms folded across his chest, an amused smirk on his face. "Oh, let her be, Corina. You know how the queen of the arena gets before a fight. All that pent-up aggression needs somewhere to go."

I shot him a glare, but it lacked real heat. "I would watch that smirk, Servat. It might just find itself on the wrong side of my magic."

I pushed past them with a sneer, my light armor and leather clinking with each step. "Let us just get this over with. I would not want to be late for my grand performance."

As we walked through the dimly lit corridors, their sarcasm continued to bite at the edges of my composure.

"Don't forget to smile for the crowd," Corina called after me, laced with disdain.

"And wave to your adoring fans," Servat added, the mockery in his tone unmistakable.

I ignored them, focusing on the path ahead. Their words were nothing more than the buzzing of flies—annoying but harmless.

We reached the heavy doors leading to the arena, the dull roar of the crowd seeping through the thick wood. Servat stepped forward, pushing one door open with a grunt. "After you, 'Your Majesty,'" he said, the title heavy with irony.

Corina followed suit, her laughter cutting through the noise of the crowd. "Make sure you do not disappoint them. They have come to see the great Furian Slayer in action."

"I'm sure having to leave the comfort of their beds and traveling eight paces tired them out," I quipped sarcastically. Servat turned me to face him, brandishing a dagger in his hand and slipping it into a belt at my waste.

His touch lingered there a moment, and I glanced up, silver clashing against crushing steel blue.

"Remember to fight back," he said, low and smooth.

I shrugged off his hand, my expression cold. "I always do." Servat beamed.

The moment before entering the fray was always the calmest, a brief respite before the storm of violence.

I stepped forward confidently, letting the Furian Slayer mask settle over me. The crowd's roar enveloped me as I emerged into the sunlight, the heat of their anticipation almost palpable. I glanced back at Corina and Servat, their figures silhouetted against the dimness of the corridor.

Corina's face wavered, her expression closed off. I almost wondered if she was praying for my death.

Four rebel fighters were in front of me, their attention locked on me with a mix of fear and resolve.

They were chained to the fucking ground by their necks, the iron shackles heavy and weighing them down, clanking as they thrashed frantically at the sight of me.

Across the sands, I caught the eye of the largest among them, a mountain of a man with a scar running down his face. His eyes were cold, dead things, but they held a spark of recognition as they fixed on me. He knew who I was—or at least, who I was supposed to be—the Furian Slayer. The signal horn cut through the crowd's clamor, a deep, resonating sound that marked the beginning of the end. The large man lumbered forward, the chain around his neck catching and pulling him back. Scarred and imposing, he struggled against his restraints, the muscles in his neck bulging with the effort.

I turned then, sweeping over the stands, over the faces twisted in excitement and blood lust.

To Ramses in his crown of gold, dapple gray cloak. Ramses, the king who held my leash, watched with a detached curiosity like I was nothing more than a prized hound set to hunt. Beside him, our son, small and innocent, his presence a knife to my heart. Our son, tiny in his lap, with his thumb in his mouth.

The horn's echo faded, leaving a tense silence in its wake.

I hesitated, my hands falling to my sides, my heart thumping in my chest. The afternoon sun blazed down on me. The Goddess Naris had me under her spyglass, waiting to judge me.

The crowd grew silent, sensing the shift. Their earlier fervor was replaced with a confused murmur. I could feel Corina and Servat's stare burning into my back, waiting to see what the great Furian Slayer would do when the odds were so disgustingly skewed in her favor.

The sight of my son, innocent and unaware of the carnage that was about to unfold, anchored me to the spot. The realization of what I was becoming and allowing myself to be a part of crystallized in that moment.

I turned to face the chained rebels once more, my resolve hardening. I would not be the instrument of their death. Not in front of my son or these people who thirsted for blood as entertainment.

Slowly, I peeled off my gloves, one by one, letting them fall to the ground. The dagger at my side gleamed in the afternoon sun, and I tossed it to the ground.

A collective gasp rippled through the crowd, their blood lust turning to disbelief.

The flicker of surprise and fury passing over Ramses' face as he realized what was happening made my heart soar.

Ramses' command cut through the tension, sharp and commanding. "Finish them."

My feet rooted to the ground, and I shook my head slowly, deliberately.

Every eye fixed on the unfolding defiance.

Ramses' expression darkened, a storm brewing behind his mask of calm. He shifted our son onto his other knee, standing up in a fluid motion that commanded attention. "You will obey," he threatened in a low growl that promised retribution.

The crowd held its breath, the air thick with anticipation and fear. Servat and Corina exchanged glances, uncertainty flickering in their faces. They had never seen me challenge Ramses so openly, so publicly.

"If you want them dead, do it yourself."

I did not need to shout it. I knew he could hear me.

Ramses, the almighty ruler, the puppeteer who had pulled the strings for so long, stood frozen. The realization that his authority was being questioned, that his power could be undermined by the will of one, spread a ripple of unease through the ranks of his guards. His eyes, dark as the oncoming night, bore into me, seeking to intimidate, to control.

My attention slid to my happy, chubby son as he stared up at his father, blissfully twirling a black curl in his chubby finger.

The silence stretched, a taut string ready to snap. Then, with a movement that sent a shiver through the stands, Ramses lowered our son to a guard's arms. He descended from his royal box, his regal robes trailing in the dust, a lion stalking toward the center of his domain.

The crowd parted for him, a sea yielding to the force of nature that was their king. His eyes never left mine, and in them, I saw the battle that would unfold, not of swords and shields but of wills clashing against each other.

"You forget your place," Ramses said, each word a hammer strike meant to forge me back into obedience.

I shrugged.

He brought down a wall of stillness around us, where we could only hear each other's breaths. The world was drowned away and forgotten.

Ramses' face contorted in rage. "You would defy me before our son? Before your king?"

"I defy you *for* our son," I hissed.

A rush of air gusted past me, and I could hear the people's heartbeats in the stands again.

Hammering. Fluttering. Pounding.

"My lady isn't feeling well," Ramses said carefully.

Guards closed in, their armor clinking with each disciplined step. With no sign of resistance, I allowed them to guide me away from the center of the arena, my every movement watched by the crowd, whose murmurs had turned into a confused buzz.

As I passed by, the rebels, still standing bewildered and unchained, glared at me in a silent exchange of understanding. They knew, as did I that the brief respite I had won for them might end in more tragedy than triumph.

I was escorted up through the stands, the heat of the spectators' attention heavy upon me. Their whispers crafted a thousand different tales of what had transpired. My son's smile followed me, and I felt the weight of my choices on that innocent face.

I plucked him from the soldier's grasp, nuzzling his small frame.

Now alone in the arena with the rebels, Ramses turned to face them, rising to address the crowd. "*I* am feeling quite fine."

His hand raised, and with a gesture, I knew too well. The air around the rebels shimmered with an unseen force. In unison, their bodies stiffened, agony etched on their faces, and before the crowd could grasp what was happening, their heads exploded in a gruesome painting of blood and bone.

One by one, their bodies fell with a squelching thump. The sands turned to a sea of red.

Screams and cries filled the air as the crowd recoiled in horror.

I almost laughed at them for being horrified when they were chanting for me to execute them just moments before.

When Ramses' gaze slid to me, I made sure he saw my hand hovering over our son's eyes.

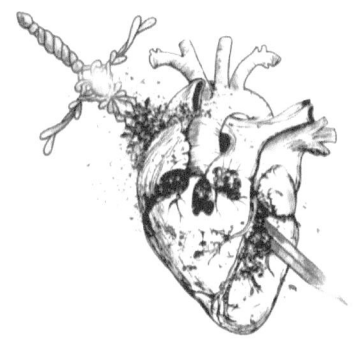

CHAPTER ELEVEN

ELDRA SOLARIS

"There are talks that his wife—the Furian Slayer—actively defied him in the arena. She did not kill chained rebels," Gaelin mused from the brim of his wine glass.

"Don't use that title here," I snarled. "Her name is Atreya, a bastard ward. Nothing else."

"How true is this?" Ameria asked. Today, she opted for dark blue, her gown shimmering and drifting off to sunset pinks at the sleeves.

She looked at Gaelin, her eyes a deep, dark forest green.

Gaelin set down his wine glass, the previous mirth fading from his face as he gauged the seriousness of Ameria's inquiry. "It's more than just talk," he replied. "My contacts saw it happen. Atreya faced down a group of rebels in the arena, fighters who Ramses' forces had captured. They were bound and defenseless, and she... she refused to kill them. Instead, she removed her gloves and went to their son in the stands. She made Ramses kill them himself."

"That doesn't mean anything," Ameria countered. "Simply that she didn't want to kill in front of her child."

"Her disobedience in the arena is a crack in the façade of his absolute control," I said. "Trouble in paradise."

"It is a rebellion in its infancy. Whether she realizes it or not," Madsen finished.

●

It took another two months before Gaelin came to me, panting and sweating but excited. "I have someone. And you are never going to believe who it is!"

"It would be helpful if you told me first," I said.

"We are to meet them at the Demasku Forked River," Gaelin gleamed.

I scoffed, "That is awfully close to the borders of Ember. How do we know this isn't some trap?"

Gaelin grinned like a cat, "They took the unbreakable vow."

My eyebrows shot up at that. "And how did you come about meeting them?"

Gaelin's excitement was palpable; seeing him so animated was a rare sight. He took a deep breath, trying to compose himself before he spoke again. "One of my contacts in the Market—it turns out they had a sibling among the rebels Atreya has spared. They have been hiding, waiting for the right time and people to trust. They introduced us."

"And you're certain they are sincere in their vow? The unbreakable vow is not something to be taken lightly."

Gaelin nodded vigorously. "Absolutely. I met them myself already. It was a spur-of-the-moment thing."

"Very well," I said after a moment's deliberation. "We'll arrange the meeting. But we take every precaution. Madsen will come with us, along with a few of our most trusted guards."

Gaelin's grin didn't falter. "Of course. They expect nothing less. They're aware of the risks, too."

The plan was set in motion quickly. Madsen gathered a small contingent of our most skilled soldiers, and together with Gaelin, we made our way to the Demasku Forked River under the cover of night. I looked back at my city, quietly sleeping with flickering lights until it disappeared—and all that could be seen was a wasteland and the sea.

The greatest sorcerers of the age weaved the magic that cloaked the city. Its presence is a closely guarded secret shielded from prying eyes by potent enchantments. The magic that cloaked the city was woven by the greatest sorcerers of the age, a tapestry of spells interlaced to form an impenetrable veil.

As we ventured away from Solara, the city's flickering lights began to dim, not from any natural cause but by the enchantments that rendered it invisible to the outside world. To any onlooker, the city faded into the illusion of barren wasteland and the distant, churning sea. It was as if the land swallowed Solaris whole, leaving nothing behind. The magic at work was multifaceted—a combination of illusion, abjuration, and a deep connection to the natural ley lines that coursed beneath the earth. It created a mirage that deterred investigation, a glamour that dissuaded curiosity, and a ward that repelled any who might accidentally stumble too close to the truth.

The spells were anchored at the city's heart, within the Sanctum of Shadows, where ancient relics pulsed with the earth's lifeblood. Here, the sorcerers and High Borns of Solaris channeled their power, chants, and incantations to a constant hum that sustained the city's hidden existence.

Each step took us further from the sanctuary of Solaris, and I felt the pull of the city's magic waning in the distance. The yearly ritual of blood sacrifice I performed to sustain the city's enchantments was a small price to pay for the safety and secrecy it provided. As the city's ruler, my life force was intimately tied to Solaris, and the Sanctum of Shadows was the heart that pumped the magic through the city's veins.

The dense forest that enveloped the path to the Demasku Forked River was ancient, its towering trees nearly touching the clouds above.

The river is a natural boundary between the lands and the volatile region of Ember.

The journey through the forest was a silent march, every party member keenly aware of every sound and snap of branch.

The night air grew cooler as we neared the river.

Madsen signaled for us to halt as we reached the riverbank. Her experienced eyes scanned the area for any signs of danger or betrayal. Gaelin, who had arranged the meeting, looked toward the opposite shore, searching for the first glimpse of our contact.

A small boat was tethered to a nearby tree, likely their means of crossing the forked waters to reach us.

As the figure climbed aboard the boat and began to row across the river, the silence of the night seemed to hold its breath. The soft splash of oars breaking the water's surface matched the thrum of my heart.

If necessary, I was ready to kill this person and shade away into the wind.

When the boat finally reached our side of the river, the figure stepped out gracefully, hide boots sinking into the muddy bank.

They were hooded, their face obscured by a black cloak that blended them into the forest's shadows.

The hooded figure who emerged from the boat moved with deliberate caution, their stance poised and balanced as if ready for any outcome. They were tall, and their silhouette had a strength that spoke of hidden power. Their black cloak was of fine quality, yet it bore no insignia, a hint of allegiance, or status—designed to conceal, not flaunt.

The cloak was clasped at the throat with a simple brooch, the metal unadorned and unreflective, catching no glimmer of the moonlight that danced upon the water's surface.

This person had no scent, no aura that I could discern.

Madsen's hand remained on her sword, the sound of it being raised from its sheath slightly. My sentinels followed suit, forming a half-circle around us.

Gaelin, on the other hand, watched the figure with excitement.

The figure stopped a few paces away from our gathered group, and for a moment, the only sounds were the gentle lapping of the river against the shore and the distant calls of nocturnal creatures. Then, deliberately, the figure reached up and pushed back the hood to reveal their face.

I let out a bark of laughter that cut through the night.

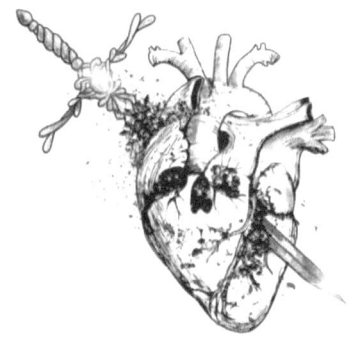

CHAPTER TWELVE

ATREYA

6 years later

The empire under Ramses' iron grip had grown more opulent, decadent, and cruel. He had tightened his hold on the people, his reign a tapestry woven with fear and admiration, the colors bleeding into one another until it was impossible to find where one ended and the other began.

Ramses, ever the master of manipulation, had learned the art of showering his subjects with grand gestures and proclamations of affection, all while his other hand held the whip. A cycle of adoration and terror that kept the empire in a constant state of unbalance.

I knew it all too well.

He would summon me to his chambers, lavishing me with gifts that were as exquisite as they were excessive. Jewels that shimmered with the light of a hundred captured stars, gowns that flowed like waterfalls of silk and velvet, and perfumes that carried the scent of forbidden gardens were all laid at my feet.

His words were honeyed, each compliment laced with the hidden barb of possession. "You are the jewel of my empire," he would say, his hands tracing the lines of my face, a gesture that feigned tenderness but spoke of ownership. "My queen, my love, the mother of my heir," he would continue in a melody that sought to erode my resolve.

But with each caress, I felt the coldness of the chains he sought to wrap around my heart. With each kiss, I tasted the bitterness of a love that was nothing more than a gilded cage. Though they sparkled with feigned warmth, Ramses' eyes could not hide the calculating coldness within.

Behind the closed doors of our palace, the mask would slip, and the true nature of his affections would reveal itself in moments of chilling clarity. A harsh word here, a cruel jibe there, all designed to remind me that my place was at his side, not as a partner, but as a trophy. A reminder to the empire of his conquest over the once indomitable Furian Slayer.

Ramses would build me up only to tear me down, a cycle designed to break my spirit. He would praise my strength and intelligence, only to later mock my naivety for believing in a world beyond his rule. He would speak of our son with pride, then use him as leverage, a silent threat that hung over every interaction.

I had become like a shadow within the palace, and my defiance quelled but not quenched. My role as the mother of Ramses' heir served as both my shield and my shackle. He lavished me with jewels and silks, sweet words dripping like honey, and promises of power as hollow as our echoing halls. He hosted grand feasts and tournaments, displaying his generosity while spinning his web of deceit. His speeches thundered with passion as he declared his love for the people and spoke of the bright future he would lead us toward.

However, beneath the surface, the empire simmered with unrest. The memory of the arena had not faded, and whispers of rebellion had begun to spread like wildfire. The people remembered the Furian Slayer, not for the lives she had taken, but for the moment she had refused to be the monster Ramses wanted her to be.

I was in the map room, studying the vast expanse of the empire and tracing the lines of discontent that stretched like cracks in Ramses' facade of absolute control. The room was filled with the soft rustling of parchment and the faint scent of ink. Suddenly, the door flew open so violently that the maps fluttered like startled birds. Ramses stood in the doorway, his presence a dark cloud threatening to engulf the room. His jaw was set in a hard line, and his teeth were grinding, showing his barely contained fury.

"You!" he bellowed, reverberating off the stone walls. He strode toward me, the heavy thud of his boots an ominous drumbeat.

"Me?" I asked, nonplussed, spinning around in his chair.

Ramses' face contorted with rage, his hands balling into fists. "You have been plotting against me."

"No," I said, carefully removing my finger from the map.

"I hear of whispers. That the Furian Slayer spared the lives of rebels and is a sympathizer. That you would wave a banner for King Eldra." His irises were sparks of red.

I watched Ramses; his face twisted with accusations, his body language radiating the menace that came so naturally to him. I stood from the table, the maps forgotten, and faced him.

Ah. That day in the arena was still causing me problems.

"I have not plotted against you. I simply did not wish to kill that day."

He squinted. "Oh? Just that day?"

I clicked my tongue. "If they see me as a symbol, it is not because I have led them to do so, but because they yearn for change."

His hand lashed out, the sound of it cutting the air, and I cringed. That hand hovered in front of my face, shaking, before he brought it down to his side.

"You will fix it."

I quirked my brow. "How do you expect me to *fix* it?"

"You will fix it. You will go, and you will kill them all. You will lay them to waste. The prisoners. All of them."

"We have already been through this. I am not a weapon to be used," I said.

"You will do as I say," he hissed, "or it will not be just the rebels who suffer. Consider the consequences, the impact on our son, on everything you hold dear."

I weighed his words and felt nothing.

Absolutely nothing.

The void where fear or panic might have once resided was now filled with something else.

Ramses watched me, searching for any sign of submission, any crack in the facade that he could exploit. But I had learned from the best. I had learned how to wear a mask from the man who wore a thousand.

"I won't. I cannot. Ember is not just stone and gold. What kingdom will there be for Vrys?"

Ramses' expression darkened, the storm clouds returning to his gaze. "You defy me?" he asked, low and dangerous.

I was quiet for a long while. Too quiet for too long. He snarled.

"I seek to save you," I whispered. Whatever part of him I had loved—however long ago that may have been. That man who hesitated at the sight of his newborn son, who seemed so unsure and promised to be better.

I wanted to save that small piece of him.

For myself. If nothing else. Just that.

He stepped back as if it were a physical blow.

"The weight of chains is heavy," I said quietly.

"Then you do not understand the weight of a crown," was his only retort, retreating from the room.

The door closed with a soft click, leaving me alone amidst the cartography of an empire on the brink of change. Small figures of different shapes rested on various spots on the maps. I let out a long breath. I hadn't realized I was holding it, so I looked down at the maps again. The lines that marked the boundaries of Ramses' domain were clear and precise, but the lines of the future were not so easily drawn.

●

Hours later, I found Joslynn in her quarters, her hands busy with needlework, a craft she had mastered over the many years of her service. The sight of her, so focused and serene, was a balm to my frayed nerves.

Calm. Ever present.

She looked up from her work, a smile on her soft, dark honey face. Dark coiled hair swept up into a messy bun as large as her head. Soft lines etched on her face, showing the years she had lived. Half Fae. Half human.

Her life would be shorter than mine.

Mine would continue for thousands of years if nothing went wrong.

She set aside her embroidery. "What troubles you, Lady?" I rolled my eyes at her use of the title.

"What else is new? Ramses thinks the fighting is my fault—the rebels. The kingdom is in turmoil. It's all my fault." I sagged in the chair adjacent to hers.

Joslynn's expression softened, her gaze filled with empathy. "You have always been strong, my lady, in ways dat Ramses will never comprehend." She reached out, her hand resting upon mine. "Da kingdom is... it is bigger than Ramses, bigger than any one person. You do not control what other people do."

"Try telling him that."

Joslynn's light and knowing laughter filled the room, momentarily lifting the weight from my shoulders. "D'ere are many tings I would dare, my lady, but correcting Ramses is not one of dem. That is a task I leave to da brave... or da foolhardy."

She resumed her needlework, the needle dancing through the fabric with expert precision. "We all have our roles to play, my lady. Some of us stand in da light, bearing da brunt of scrutiny, while others keep to da shadows, where secrets are best kept."

Her words, seemingly innocuous, struck a chord within me. "Secrets in the shadows?" I echoed, my curiosity piqued.

Joslynn didn't look up from her work. "Oh, every palace has its shadows, and every shadow its secrets. Even da most powerful cannot illuminate every corner, nor should d'ey wish to."

"What are you suggesting?"

The half-Fae, half-human woman gave a noncommittal shrug, her focus remaining on the needle and thread. "I am suggesting nothing, my lady. Only dat sometimes, da truth we seek is hidden in plain sight, waiting for the right moment to step into the light. Use da light to see."

"You speak in riddles," I scoffed.

She let out a sigh. "There are beasts in da walls—monsters beneath the boards. Everything listens. D'ere is a dove pretending to be a raven."

I bit my tongue at that. "We had this conversation. I have kept true to my word. It has not happened since."

She hummed. "I fuss over you like a mudafuck."

I inhaled my laugh. "You mean a *mother duck*?"

She waved her hand dismissively. "You know what I say."

Joslynn held up her embroidery for me to see. The needle paused mid-stitch. "Notice, my lady, how some tings in da design seem clear at first glance, while others reveal themselves only when you look closer," Joslynn said. "With da right light..." she trailed off, her eyes glazing over.

I rolled my eyes again and groaned, sinking deeper into the chair. "As the years pass, the stranger you get, woman."

She folded the embroidery, placing it gently on the table beside her.

"I won't kill in that arena," I said out loud.

She sighed, "Da king has a knack for getting his way."

"I have managed to avoid it these years."

"Yes, you have," she agreed. "But Ramses is not a man easily swayed from his desires."

"I know," I admitted, "but I cannot—I will not. What of my soul? Naris—"

"Da Goddess of Justice will know your plight. She knows your pain and will forgive you."

I shook my head. "Some things are not meant to be forgiven."

She stretched her limbs, her hands reaching to the ceiling. "I hear d'ey are getting new fabrics in. All da way from across the Sihari Sea. There will be new dresses and new clothes."

I smiled. "Ah. You can't resist new fabrics. I imagine the Hyperion Market will be packed then."

The Hyperion Market—a crossroads of cultures, a bustling epicenter where traders from distant lands converge to exchange their wares. Spices that tingle the senses, fabrics that flow like water, trinkets imbued with the magic of far-off places—all can be found there.

I knew she loved it because it was as close as she could get to finding spices from her homeland, Zay'Nath.

Joslynn, with her eyes that held the depth of the desert night and her songs that carried the sun's warmth, would often entertain me with tales of her homeland, an oasis of life among the endless sands from across the seas.

Her stories painted vivid pictures of a world so different from the one I knew, where the earth was golden and the sun blazed mercilessly. She spoke of towering dunes that shifted with the whims of the wind, creating an ever-changing landscape that was as beautiful as it was treacherous.

"Da desert is a harsh mistress," she would say, her hands gesturing as if to shape the very dunes she described. "It teach ya about life and survival."

She would tell me of the oasis, lighting up while describing paradise in the heart of barrenness. "It's a jewel, Atreya," she would whisper—a secret only for us. "A haven of palm trees dat stretch their fingers to da sky, of waters dat run cool and deep, a promise of life during death."

I would never get to see Zay'Nath. I had never even been to the Hyperion Market. Ramses doesn't let me go far. Said that it is for the lower classes only, and I am to only send out servants for our needs and wants.

Joslynn nodded her head. "Heavily guarded dis year, all tings considering. Da king's eyes and ears are everywhere."

There was a long pause, the silence filling the room. I sighed, my shoulders slumping. "Remember, I do like blue."

Joslynn's smile returned, and there was a gentle warmth around her. "Blue has always suited you, my lady. Like da midnight sky, deep and endless." She stood, her movements graceful and fluid, the legacy of her Fae heritage.

"Vrys looks good in black. Black suits him," I mused, getting up from my chair and leaving her to work.

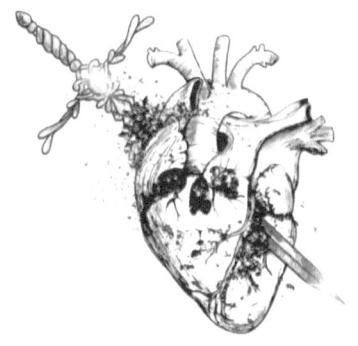

CHAPTER THIRTEEN

ATREYA

I saw Joslynn off at the gate. The line of people preparing to go to the Hyperion Market extended to the canal. Everyone had baskets and carts full of food, cloth, and jewels for trade. For every person there, at least two guards were preparing to trek outside the city limits.

The morning sun cast a golden hue over the bustling crowd, its rays gleaming off the shimmering canal waters and the polished armor of the guards. I watched Joslynn disappear into the crowd, her basket securely under her arm. She had that determined look on her face, the one she wore when bartering for the best deals at Hyperion Market.

The guards' hands never strayed far from the hilts of their swords. They stood like statues as they surveyed the crowd, looking for any sign of trouble. The air was filled with a cacophony of sounds: the chatter of negotiations, the clinking of coins, and the soft padding of feet on the cobblestone path.

As the procession began to move, the guards formed around the citizens, creating a protective barrier between them and the wild beyond the city. The market was a good half-day's journey on foot, and while the path was well-traveled, it was not without its dangers. Bandits lurked in the shadows of the trees, and wild creatures roamed the untamed lands, all of them attracted to the wealth the travelers carried.

I couldn't help but feel a twinge of worry for Joslynn. She was more than capable of handling herself in the market, but the journey there was uncertain. I made a mental note to say an extra prayer for her safe return as I turned and returned to the city's heart.

The streets were alive with the everyday hustle: merchants shouting from their stalls—ones not going to the Market—children darting through the crowd, and the smell of freshly baked bread wafting from the baker's doorway. The cobbled streets were worn smooth by countless feet, and the buildings leaned together like old friends.

The sun rose, bathing the city in a warm, clear light. The buildings were patchworked in different colors, and the roofs were all in various shades of red and gold. Street performers walked on their hands, calling the crowd to gather and watch. People made room for me in the streets as I made my way through, heads bowed, some smiling.

The clang of metal from the blacksmith's forge rang out. I flinched. It seemed to echo down the street and through me.

Clang. Clang. Clang.

Each strike of the blacksmith's hammer sent a shiver down my spine, not because of the noise itself but because of the memories it dredged up from the dark recesses of my mind.

Clang. Clang. Clang.

They were the sounds of another place where the iron being forged was not for tools or horseshoes—but for chains.

I shook my head.

It was the past now. It was over. I would not be used like that again.

"Vryseris, finish your carrots," I said, cutting into my share of roast pork.

He made a face and gave me one of those looks that said he would put up a fight about it. His eyes, much like his father's, had a way of hardening when he was about to dig his heels in. But I wasn't in the mood for our usual dinnertime battle of wills. Not today.

Ramses regarded me from across the table, chewing slowly, then moved over to Vrys.

I put down my knife and fork and leaned back in my chair, adjusting my simple gray gown. I opted out of any grandeur tonight, save for the crown Ramses had gotten me as a gift. A twist of gold metal with roses. "You know, Vryseris," I started, "there was a time when even a single carrot was a feast for some."

Ramses made a chuffing noise and continued to chew.

Vryseris defiance wavered for a second, nose scrunching up. "Really?" he asked, the carrot halfway to his mouth.

He loved history. He loved learning about the olden days that came before his time. He loved the stories of the kings and queens of old.

He loved hearing anything his father had to say about the War of Fallen Skies. While I was born not long after the war ended, I read enough about it during my teaching to be able to recite scripture.

"Yes," I continued, "food was scarce during the War of Fallen Skies, especially for those fighting. They survived on whatever they could forage or barter for—roots, berries, and yes, sometimes just a handful of carrots."

"I never ate carrots during the war," Ramses chimed in. "Meat. Horse meat if there was nothing else." He took a large bite of his roast and made a show of it—growling like an animal. "Your mother has eaten horse meat, too." He winked at me. I blanched.

Vryseris laughed.

I glared at Ramses, who met my gaze with a wolfish grin, his attempt at humor poorly timed. "Not everyone had that luxury," I said pointedly, turning back to Vryseris, whose gold eyes flicked between his father and me.

Vryseris, now with a slight smirk mirroring his father's, finally took a bite of the carrot. "War sounds terrible," he said, muffled by the mouthful. "I'm glad we have food now."

Ramses wiped his mouth with the back of his hand. "War is more than terrible. It's a reality of our world, son," he said, his tone shifting to one of solemnity. "A reality you will likely be a part of one day."

I opened my mouth to protest, but Ramses cut me off with a sharp look.

"You'll understand when you're older, Vryseris," Ramses continued, "For now, eat, grow strong, and learn."

Vryseris nodded, a hint of sadness on his face, as he looked down at his plate, suddenly less interested in his food.

I reached across the table and placed my hand over Vryseris.' "Eat well, my son," I said gently, trying to dispel the tension. "And remember that while strength is important, so are kindness and wisdom. We fight when we must, but we also strive for peace."

Ramses snorted, "Kindness doesn't win wars."

"It might not," I conceded, squeezing Vryseris' hand, "but it does make for a world worth fighting for."

Ramses shook his head with a mixture of disdain and amusement. "Enough of this talk," he grumbled, pushing his plate away and standing up. "Eat your carrots or leave them, Vryseris. It's your choice." He turned his gaze to me, and the room grew colder. "And you," he said, his tone dropping to a dangerous whisper as he grabbed my arm, pulling me close enough to feel his breath on my face, "don't fill the boy's head with romantic nonsense. He needs to be strong, unyielding."

Vryseris stared at Ramses, at his grip on my arm, and frowned.

He set the carrot down and stood abruptly, his chair scraping against the stone floor. "Father," he barked.

The word cut through the tension like a blade. Ramses' grip on my arm wavered as he turned to face his son. Vryseris may have been small and young, but at that moment, there was an undeniable presence about him, a gravity that seemed to defy his age.

"Let her go."

He sounded strange—like a muffled echo. His eyes began to glow a deep, radiant blue, and the shadows in the room seemed to stir, coiling around him like living things responding to an unseen command.

Ramses' eyes widened, a mixture of surprise and a burgeoning pride flickering across his face. The grip on my arm loosened completely, and I stepped back, rubbing the spot where his fingers had been.

"Vryseris," Ramses began softly, almost hesitantly.

But Vryseris continued, the shadows dancing more fervently now. "Apologize."

The words were like a dagger, and I felt them sink into my heart.

The shadows around Vryseris began to form, swirling and coalescing into hulking shapes with snarling maws and glinting eyes reflecting the faint candlelight. These shadow monsters prowled silently around him, their forms ephemeral yet a menacing display of raw, untapped power that Vryseris seemed to command without fully understanding.

I had never seen him do such a thing. I had never seen him display any magic at all before this. For a long while, I wondered if Ramses would throw him into the arena like he did with me to see if that magic manifested itself.

I was relieved.

I was terrified but relieved.

Ramses took a cautious step back, his expression a tapestry woven with threads of fear, astonishment, and a deep, resonating pride. "Vryseris," he said in awe. "Your power..."

"Apologize to her," Vryseris repeated in that harsh voice that sounded like hundreds of snakes hissing.

Ramses, the lord of the house, King of Ember, and ruler of Ferenz, the warrior who had faced countless enemies on the battlefield, found himself in the unfamiliar territory of being commanded.

By his son.

Ramses turned his gaze to me and *smiled*. "It's just a misunderstanding, Vrys."

The shadows snarled and writhed around us.

Ramses whooped at that, letting out a breath of air that felt like a sigh. "Look at you, Vrys! You are a wonder to behold. Your powers have come in quickly! I am so proud of you."

The shadow beasts dissipated as if they were never there, the shadows retreating to their mundane existence as mere absence of light. Vryseris blinked, and the glow faded from his eyes. He seemed to snap out of whatever trance had held him, looking around, his chest heaving as if he had run a great distance.

"Father?" he said, his voice now that of the small and young boy he truly was.

Ramses' laughter filled the room, a sound that was both triumphant and relieved. He stepped forward, no longer cautious but eager, and embraced his son. "My boy, you have a gift," he said, pride swelling. "A gift that will make you a king and a legend!"

I stared at my son. My small boy looked so frightened. Why would the gods give him such a dark power?

The shadows on the wall seemed to pulse and shudder.

Vryseris looked between Ramses and me, a flicker of excitement returning to him. "Will I learn to make the shadows do more than just... snarl?"

Ramses chuckled, the tension in the room dissipating slightly. "Yes, Vryseris. You will learn to shape and command them as you see fit."

His smile was a slash of white—teeth gleaming. I knew how to read between the lines. How he could use his son's gift to his advantage.

His ambitions were too great.

Ramses clapped his hands together, the sound echoing through the room, signaling an end to the dinner and the beginning of something new. "Vryseris," he said with a command that brooked no argument, "go find Servat. Show him what you can do. He will be beside himself."

Vryseris beamed, and the shadows around him seemed to grow. He bounded for the door without looking back.

Once the door closed behind Vryseris, the atmosphere changed. Ramses turned to me, his expression darkening. In a swift motion, he reached out, his hand closing around my throat. His grip was firm but not crushing, and his claws dug into my skin.

"You," he hissed, his face inches from mine, "Vryseris is my son, my heir. Do not undermine my teachings in front of him again."

Ramses' eyes searched mine, looking for any hint of defiance. After a long moment, he released me, and I stumbled back, gasping for air. He smoothed the front of his tunic to erase any sign of the altercation.

I rubbed my neck, biting the inside of my cheek. "He is so young," I said.

"His magic is strong. Imagine what he can do when he is older. If he is trained properly."

I could practically hear the wheels turning in Ramses' head.

Ramses paced slowly, his hands clasped behind his back as he contemplated the future. "He will be invincible," he mused aloud, "a ruler unlike any before. And with the right guidance, he will expand our empire, crush our enemies, and reign supreme."

His words were filled with enthusiasm. He spoke of long-held dreams, of a vision for a kingdom that would never be defeated. Ramses was a king who had tasted power and wanted nothing more than to see it multiplied in his son.

I watched him, my mind racing with concern. Vryseris was indeed young, and his soul was still malleable. The lessons he learned now, the values instilled in him, would shape the man he would become.

"And what of the boy's heart?" I dared to ask. "Power without compassion can lead to tyranny. The people must love their king, not live in fear of him."

Ramses stopped pacing and turned to me, his gaze sharp. "A king must be feared first and loved second," he declared.

I knew arguing further would be fruitless. Ramses had decided on the path his son would take. My role was to ensure that Vryseris' heart remained intact and that he would not lose himself to the darkness his powers could so easily invite.

Not the way the darkness had taken over me.

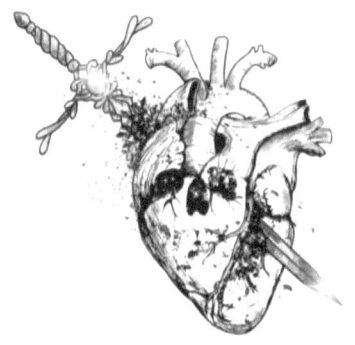

CHAPTER FOURTEEN

ATREYA

The night's stillness shattered as the bells' frantic clamor pierced the air. My heart raced, icy dread washing over me as I sprang from bed. Flickering faelight danced across my room, casting eerie shadows on the walls. Boots thundered outside my door, growing louder. I flung back the covers and raced for the door, flinging it open.

"What's happening?" I called out to the stream of soldiers rushing past.

None answered, their faces set in grim determination as they barked orders and scrambled to follow the commands snapping through the air. I chased after them, my bare feet skidding on the cold stone floor.

"Rally the dragons!" Ramses' call boomed from down the corridor, cutting through the chaos.

The bells' peal filled my ears once more, making my head spin. I pushed through the tide of armored bodies, my heart pounding in my chest. Ramses stood at the corridor's end, his face set in a grim mask.

"The Hyperion Market's under attack," he said, his tone clipped. "The dragons will handle it."

"Joslynn's there," I managed to choke out, her name a desperate plea.

Ramses nodded curtly. "Go back to bed, Atreya. Vryseris is safe in my chambers."

I bit back a retort, feeling a cold pit form in my stomach. I couldn't just wait and worry. I had to do something. Spinning on my heel, I sprinted in the opposite direction, not to the safety of my chambers, but down to the Dragon Keep's courtyard where the riders were assembling.

The courtyard was a whirlwind of activity. Torches blazed along the walls, casting a flickering glow over the cobblestones slick with dew. The air was heavy with the acrid scent of brimstone and the crackle of magic. Ahead, the Dragon Keep loomed, its massive gates thrown open like a hungry maw.

The dragons, magnificent and terrifying, shifted restlessly. Smoke curled from their nostrils, and their scales glinted like jewels in the torchlight. They roared and reared up, their vast wings beating the air and whipping up powerful gusts that threatened to knock me over. Above, the dark sky waited, ready to be set ablaze.

I scanned the crowd frantically, searching for a familiar face. That's when I spotted Servat, his shock of white hair standing out amidst the chaos. The dragon beside him, a towering beast cloaked in midnight scales and burning embers, turned its head towards me.

"Servat!" I called, pushing through the crowd.

He spun around, surprise flashing across his face as he took in my bare feet and nightclothes. "Atreya, what are you doing here?" He glanced around, likely searching for Ramses. His dragon peered at me, its nostrils flaring. I eyed its fangs warily as it let out a rumbling growl that vibrated through the ground.

"This is Tiamut," Servat said, patting the beast's neck.

I took a step back, feeling a wave of heat as the dragon breathed on me. I'd never been this close to a dragon before, having always kept my distance. "I need to get to the Hyperion Market," I said, trying to keep my nerves steady.

Servat blinked. "You can't. It's going to be a bloodbath. You have to stay here."

"I can't just hide!" I snapped, feeling a prickle of tears in my eyes. "Please, Servat, I have to get to Joslynn."

He studied me, then let out a heavy sigh. "Ramses will flay me alive for this." He muttered, running a hand through his hair before resting it on Tiamut's neck. The dragon let out a thoughtful growl, as if offering its opinion. Then Servat nodded. "Fine, but you have to do exactly as I say."

I let out a breath I hadn't realized I was holding. "I will, I promise."

"Ramses roared from behind me. "Atreya, get back inside!"

I spun around. He was striding towards me, already dressed in his flight leathers and helmet. A soldier hurried to flank me, ready to escort me back to the castle. "I'm coming with you!"

Ramses' face darkened. "You have no idea what we're walking into. This isn't a place for women."

"I don't need your protection!" I shot back, feeling a surge of anger. "I'm good enough to kill your rebels, but I'm too helpless to help defend the Market?"

"You're not going to put my riders at risk with your reckless-ness," he snapped.

"I'll go alone, then!" I shouted, feeling a hysterical laugh bubble up in my throat. "I'd rather die than sit here and do nothing while Joslynn and the others are slaughtered."

Ramses studied me, his face unreadable. Then he let out a heavy sigh and turned to Servat. "Take her, but keep her safe. If anything happens to her, it's on you."

Servat bowed. "Yes, my lord."

Ramses turned back to me, a small, infuriating smile playing on his lips. "Maybe now you'll see things my way."

He turned and strode away, leaving me with Servat and the waiting dragon. I felt a flutter of fear in my chest, but I pushed it down. I was doing this.

Servat turned to me, his face serious. "Ready?"

I nodded, trying to sound braver than I felt. "Ready."

He offered me a hand. "Up you go, then. Just hold tight and do what I say."

He hoisted me onto the ladder leaning against Tiamut's side. I felt a blush rise to my cheeks as his hands lingered on my waist, his fingers brushing the bare skin above my nightgown. I shot him a look over my shoulder, and he just smirked and winked at me.

I rolled my eyes and turned my attention to the task at hand. Tiamut's scales were slick and smooth beneath my hands as I climbed onto his back. I settled on my knees behind the ridge of his neck, feeling a little more secure. Servat climbed up behind me, his chest pressing against my front.

I looked down to the seat and pommel resting between Tiamut's spiked shoulder blades and hesitated, fully aware of my nightdress now. I glanced up at Servat, one of his eyebrows raised.

"I can't sit right," I told him, a blush flushing up my neck.

"Is your ass broken?"

"No!" I grabbed my nightgown pointedly and flapped it at him.

He grabbed my shoulders, whirled me around, and sat me down forcefully. My dress rode up to around my waist, and I gasped, trying to pull it back down to no avail.

My legs were spread wide.

Servat let out a throaty chuckle as he leaned closer, his breath warm against the shell of my ear. "Worry not. Tiamut won't mind, and neither will I."

My head snapped to him, and he adjusted his position behind me, offering a cloak from his saddlebag to drape over my legs for modesty. "Here, this should help," he said as he handed it to me.

"Now," Servat instructed, his hands finding their way to the reins before us. "Hold on to these. Tiamut responds well to a firm grip and clear commands. Just like you, I imagine." He placed the reins in my hands, his large hands wrapped around my small ones.

I gritted my teeth at his insinuation but gripped the reins, feeling the coarse material against my palms.

It wasn't until Servat's arms settled on either side of me and Tiamut began thundering down the flight path after Siorsen that I realized—maybe I was better off on the ground.

Servat's breath brushed against my ear like a whisper of wind, barely audible over the rush of air. "Just breathe. You're doing fine," he reassured me, his presence a steady anchor.

Tiamut's deep, rumbling growl resonated through the core of my being, a primal vibration that echoed through the soles of my feet. With a sudden lurch that stole the breath from my lungs, we were propelled into the night sky, the world below falling away as Tiamut's mighty wings unfurled with majestic grace.

The wind whipped at my face, tangling my hair in a chaotic dance as we soared through the darkness. I gasped and shrieked into the blur of stars, my back pressing against Servat's armored chest as we hurtled into the heavens.

"Tiamut, to the Hyperion Market," Servat commanded, cutting through the rush of wind like a clarion call. The dragon obeyed without hesitation, banking sharply as it followed the path of fae-light and the glittering scales of its brethren.

I didn't know that dragons *glowed*.

The sight was otherworldly. Tiamut's scales caught the moon's glow, reflecting it in a colorful dance that left light trails across the night's dark canvas. And it wasn't just Tiamut—the sky was alive with dragons, each shimmering with its unique luminescence, creating a river of color in the air. Siorsen led the formation, his light a guiding torch for the others to follow, his scales a cascade of colors that seemed to paint the sky with every flap of his wings.

"Won't the enemy be able to see us?" I shouted over the wind.

"No, not unless they possess a dragon of their own," Servat replied.

"Do they *have* a dragon?" I asked incredulously. I couldn't imagine being on the wrong side of a dragon's rage. I shuddered at the thought of a creature as wrathful as Siorsen on the enemy's side.

"We'll find out. You don't need to shout. I can hear you just fine."

Below, the city sprawled out like a tapestry, its streets now veins of chaos as families were frantic to find out what had happened to their loved ones at the Market.

It was hard to concentrate on anything other than the sensation of flying, of being lifted so high up into the air that the people below were nothing but specks.

I tried to focus on the pattern of lights below and the chaos of the city's layout. But my mind kept drifting back to the feel of Servat's hand on my thigh, the warmth of his breath against my neck. It was distracting and disconcerting. Beneath the fear and the exhilaration of the flight, a small thrill ran through me at his closeness.

The dragons ebbed and flowed like a tide.

I leaned back into Servat, using him as a bulwark against the fear that threatened to unseat me. "I can see them," I called out.

"Siorsen will glow in patterns, and it guides the others. Like a signal," Servat answered. "We are almost there."

"I thought it was half a day's travel?"

"On foot. Dragons can get you from one end of Ferenz to another quickly."

His hands found my waist, fingering my nightgown. My breath hitched when his rough fingers found my skin.

"Servat—"

He hushed me, pushing me flush against him, his fingers tracing up my thighs. Up, up, and up until he met the cotton lining of my undergarment.

Siorsen roared ahead of us and flashed vibrant shades of red that swirled and danced along his wings. I squinted, looking towards the ground.

Without warning, the dragon dived, and Servat's arms tightened around me. We descended rapidly, a controlled plummet that made my stomach somersault.

"Brace yourself," Servat said, suddenly serious, hands over mine.

Tiamut moved with astounding grace, dodging arrows and spells that flew our way from the attackers below. Clearly, this wasn't just a mere skirmish but a well-planned assault.

I clung to the reins with white-knuckled fear.

Servat gave a low whistle, and Tiamut began his descent, spiraling down towards an ample open space with its trees blasted away. As we drew closer, the acrid scent of smoke filled my nostrils. The beast folded his wings and landed with a grace that belied his size, causing barely a tremor as he touched down. Servat dismounted with practiced ease and offered me his hand.

I took it, my legs shaky from the adrenaline of the flight. As I slid off Tiamut's back, the cloak Servat had given me slipped.

The ground beneath my feet was uneven, littered with debris and the remnants of what once had been a vibrant marketplace. Stalls were upturned, their wares scattered like fallen leaves. The cries of the wounded and the clash of steel against steel filled the air with a haunting symphony. One by one, the ground rumbled with each dragon's landing.

Siorsen was already there, roaring a stream of hellfire at a group of men wearing gold armor with a sigil of the dragon spiraling in the center of the Sun.

Solaris.

House of Eldra Solaris, known for brutality, had orchestrated this attack. Their gold armor, now splattered with the grime of battle, glinted ominously in the firelight. Siorsen's flames illuminated the night, casting grotesque shadows that danced across the destruction like macabre specters.

"Stay close," Servat murmured, skimming over the fight. With swift, deft movements, he began peeling off his armor, the dark metal clinking softly as he laid it aside. My mouth opened to protest, but he cut me off with a sharp look.

"You need this more than I do," he said, brooking no argument. He picked up the oversized chest plate, heavy and adorned with the sigils of our house, and strapped it onto me. The weight of it was heavier than what I was used to, but it was light enough that I could still move with it.

My breath hitched as his fingers brushed against my skin, the warmth of his touch a stark contrast to the cold metal. Tiamut stomped the earth with his forelegs, impatiently waiting for Servat to unleash him onto the enemy.

"We could use some light," he said, pointing at the sky.

The battle had left the sky obscured, clouds of ash blotting out the stars. As his attention shifted skyward, I understood Servat's unspoken request, his meaning clear.

With a deep inhale, I raised my hands to the heavens, my palms facing the roiling clouds above. I closed my eyes, focusing on the well of power within me, drawing it up through my core and into my outstretched arms. The air around me crackled with energy, a static charge raising the hairs on my neck.

Then, with a forceful exhale, I unleashed it.

Lightning cleaved the sky, and a brilliant web of electric light branched out in thousands of different directions. The clouds above recoiled, parting as if sliced by an invisible sword. A kaleidoscope of light erupted, illuminating the battlefield in stark relief and casting everything in sharp, flickering shadows.

The Solaris faltered as the night turned to day with the force of my magic. Siorsen roared his approval, shaking the ground beneath our feet. Ramses whirled around to me, a wicked grin on his face as he shouted and raised his sword to the sky.

"Make it rain," Servat shouted over the clamor. He raised his sword and struck down a gold-cloaked soldier charging for us.

The dragons took to the air, their silhouettes ghostly figures against the backdrop of lightning-lit clouds. Their roars were muffled by the thunder that rolled in, and one by one, they roared their streams of fire onto the enemy.

Everything was burning.

A squelch of flesh cutting away—blood spraying from the wound of another soldier that had come too close to me. Servat pressed me to Tiamut's side forcefully.

The streets ran red with blood, the air thick with the stench of smoke and death.

The distant sounds of battle grew louder with each passing moment. Flames licked at the edges of the Market, casting flickering shadows against the buildings left standing.

I willed the clouds, now charged with my power, to release their burden. The first drop fell, a solitary herald of the deluge to come. Then, rain poured down in torrents as if the heavens had opened their gates. It drenched the flames, quenched the fires that had ravaged the Market, and washed the blood from the cobblestones.

The rain was relentless, a cascade that soaked through my clothes and armor, matting my hair to my face.

Ramses rushed to me, his expression alight with the thrill of bloodshed, the power of command radiating from him like heat from a forge. "Atreya!" He called out to me, carrying over the storm's din, "Strike them down! Your lightning can end this now! Sear their flesh from their bones!"

My heart pounded against the metal of Servat's armor that encased it. I understood the temptation of his words, the seductive call to unleash the full wrath of my storm upon the enemy.

Clang. Clang. Clang.

"I will not use my power to kill." I could not. I would not.

Ramses' expression turned thunderous, his joy at the battle's turn souring into frustration. "They are Solaris! They would not hesitate to do the same to you—to all of us!"

"Then I will be better," I replied. "I will be better than they are."

Than you.

Some significant part of me hoped that they could see to reason. Perhaps they would hesitate upon seeing me and think twice—that my mercy in the arena for those rebels all those years ago still carried some weight.

I turned away from Ramses and his dark urgings, sweeping over the battlefield for those in need, for the innocents caught in the crossfire of war. That was when I saw her—a flash of dark hair that I knew too well.

Joslynn.

She darted through the fighting, her movements a desperate flight, followed by a Solaris soldier cloaked in gold. My breath hitched, instinct propelling me forward. "Joslynn!" I cried out, my cries swallowed by the storm.

"Stay with me!" His hand grazed my shoulder.

I was already gone.

I sprinted after her, my bare feet splashing through puddles that reflected the intermittent lightning above. Whether I was stepping in blood or water—or both—I didn't know. My heart raced, pumping pure adrenaline through my veins. I had to reach her; I had to ensure she was safe.

Behind me, I heard Servat and Ramses yell my name, a warning that came too late. The world narrowed to the chase, to the golden figure gaining on Joslynn with every passing second.

I was almost upon them when Servat's pained shout reached me. Two armed men, their swords gleaming with malice, leaped out from the shadows, ambushing Servat and Ramses. I skidded to a halt, torn between wanting to go back and save him and the need to save Joslynn.

A loyal dog will always come.

Before I could process what was happening, a thunderous roar shook the earth. Tiamut burst from the shadows, his jaws snapping shut around a screaming man. The crunch of bone was audible even over the chaos. Beside him, Ramses plunged his sword into another attacker, beheading him with a single, brutal stroke.

Servat turned to me, relief and reprimand warring on his face. But there was no time for words. He pointed ahead, mouthing a single word: "Fight."

Ramses bellowed orders, swinging his sword in wide arcs to keep the attackers at bay. Siorsen swooped down, his massive tail sweeping through a cluster of soldiers. I tore my gaze away, committing every line of their faces to memory in case this was goodbye.

I sprinted forward, the rain creating a gray veil that obscured everything more than a few feet away. I dodged and weaved through the melee, using my magic to deflect attacks and push enemies back. My lungs burned, my muscles screamed in protest, but the sight of Joslynn in the distance gave me the strength to keep going.

A Solaris soldier loomed over her, his sword raised for the killing blow. She spun around, her eyes locking onto mine across the distance. Panic flared in their depths before she turned her attention back to the threat at hand. Her magic swirled around her, a shimmering shield that protected the cowering civilians behind her.

Almost there.

Lightning slashed across the sky, striking the ground mere feet from the soldier. But he didn't flinch. Didn't stumble. He kept coming, his sword clashing against Joslynn's shield. Time seemed to slow as adrenaline surged through my veins.

I shouldn't have hesitated. I shouldn't have stopped for Ramses and Servat. They had dragons and swords. Joslynn had nothing.

In that moment, I realized that if I didn't embrace the full fury of my power, Joslynn would die. Her laughter, her touch, her knowing gaze – it would all be lost. I couldn't let that happen. Not to her.

The soldier raised his sword again, and with a primal scream, I unleashed my magic. A spear of lightning shot through the rain, striking the soldier with deadly precision. He collapsed, his body thudding against the wet earth.

But my victory was short-lived. A faint gasp of pain cut through the sudden silence. My gaze snapped to Joslynn, and my heart shattered. The soldier's sword had found its mark before my lightning found its target. A crimson bloom spread across her clothing, stark against the pale fabric.

"No," I whispered, my voice breaking. "No, no, no..."

Her knees buckled, and she crumpled to the ground, her fall a silent surrender to gravity. I was at her side in an instant, my hands hovering over the wound as if I could will her whole again.

"Joslynn, stay with me," I begged, my voice cracking. "I'll fix this, I'll heal you…"

But the truth was a heavy weight in my chest. My magic could destroy, but it couldn't heal. It couldn't bring back the dead.

Joslynn's hand lifted, her fingers brushing against my cheek. "It's okay," she whispered, a sad smile on her lips. "You tried to save me… dat's more dan anyone else ever did."

Her breathing grew shallower, her gaze turning distant. "Da blue fabric," she murmured, barely audible. "I picked da finest shade for you. Like da sky on a clear summer day. You always look so good in blue."

My heart clenched, agony squeezing the breath from my lungs. "Joslynn, please," I choked out.

But she kept talking, her words a stream of consciousness. "I wanted to see you wear it… at a ball, under da chandeliers, with da music playing and everyone watching you dance. Wit da love you were meant to have. You were such a happy girl when ya were little."

"I was happy because you were there," I sobbed, tears scalding my cheeks. "You made everything brighter, Joslynn. You made me feel like I could do anything. That I could survive this."

She smiled faintly, her eyes fluttering closed. "Be dat girl again, Atreya," she whispered. "When I'm gone, don't let da world turn ya hard. Dance."

"You're not going anywhere," I lied, clinging to her cold hand. "I won't let you."

Her body relaxed, a soft sigh escaping her lips as if she were settling into a peaceful sleep. "Remember da Temple in spring?" she asked, her breath a mere whisper. "Da way da grass smelled after da rain…Where ya took your first steps? You would have loved it in Zay'Nath. I wanted to take ya to Zay'Nath."

I nodded, unable to speak past the lump in my throat. "Yes," I finally managed. "We'll go there. You and me. We'll run through the sands—climb those palm trees, and nothing will ever hurt us again."

Her mouth went slack, and then she was still.

Too still.

"Joslynn?" I whispered, a tremor of fear running through me. "Joslynn, wake up. Please."

I cradled her in my arms, rocking back and forth as if the motion could somehow bring her back. The rain kept falling, washing away the blood, but it couldn't cleanse the ache in my soul.

A Solaris soldier charged at me, his sword raised and a battle cry on his lips. I didn't even look up as I raised my hand and speared him with lightning. He fell, his cry cut short, his life extinguished as swiftly as he had tried to take mine.

The rain seemed to pause, droplets suspended in mid-air around me. One by one, the Solaris soldiers charged, their gold armor no longer symbols of their might but targets for my vengeance. My hands moved with a will of their own, arcs of lightning lashing out, seeking the hearts of my enemies with unerring precision.

Each strike was a scream, and each flash was a memory of Joslynn's smile, laughter, and dreams. My Joslynn.

Servat called out to me, a distant sound that struggled to reach me through the maelstrom of my rage. "Atreya, stop!"

I couldn't stop, wouldn't stop until the debt of blood was paid in full and until the pain that carved through me found solace in the destruction of them all. I felt someone's arms on me—I never looked to see who it was. I watched the bones of their arms light up under translucent skin—lightning burning them from the inside out.

Others joined Servat's plea, calls from my companions, from Ramses. But their calls were like whispers against a hurricane, powerless to reach the eye of the storm.

With every fallen enemy, the image of Joslynn's still face haunted me.

They all needed to die. Every last fucking one.

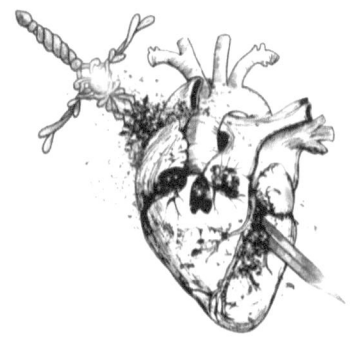

CHAPTER FIFTEEN

ATREYA

Dawn's light broke over the trees and the forest floor. Smoke flitted through the air, and the scent of charred flesh filled my lungs. The ground was coated with a fine layer of ash, over mud and blood and bone. My nightgown was slicked to my body, now see-through from the rain and blood.

The light of dawn brought a cruel clarity to the destruction that lay before me. It illuminated the faces of the fallen, the once-proud soldiers of Solaris now lifeless. Smug satisfaction crept over me.

My hands, once instruments of death, now trembled at my sides, the remnants of magic that lingered in my fingertips feeling foreign, unwelcome. My whole body tingled, like bees beneath my skin.

I should have killed that bastard instead of holding back. Instead of running after him just to try to prove a point to Ramses that I wouldn't be a doomsday warrior.

The clamor of our soldiers, their movements methodical and detached, seemed a world away as they went about the grim task of gathering the fallen. They moved like specters among the smoke and ash, their faces set in masks of duty, untouched by the horrors that their hands wrought. One by one they piled the bodies of our enemies into a heap.

Ramses approached, his stride confident, his bearing that of a man who had never tasted defeat. His eyes found mine, a glint of what might have been pride—or something colder—flickering within their depths.

"You did well," he said, resonating with the authority that commanded legions. There was no trace of sorrow for the lives lost, no hint of regret for the blood spilled. In his eyes, it was a victory, a necessary culling.

I remained silent, my gaze fixed on the pyre that grew with each body added. The flames would soon rise, a beacon of our ruthlessness.

It was then that Servat joined us, his presence a stark contrast to Ramses. His face held the weariness of a man who understood the cost of war, the lines etched around his eyes speaking of compassion that Ramses lacked.

"My condolences for Joslynn," Servat offered. "She was brave, and she did not deserve her fate."

I nodded, a lump forming in my throat. Servat's words were a meager comfort, but they were sincere—a rare thing I didn't get from Ramses.

Ramses snorted dismissively. "She was a maidservant. There will be others. Josephine is no one."

Joslynn.

I turned away from him, from Servat's sympathetic gaze, and from the pyre that now began to crackle and hiss as the flames took hold. Had they already flung her body in?

"How many of our soldiers did I kill?" I asked monotonously. I was numb.

"What?" Ramses asked.

"How many of our men did I kill." I looked at him. "It was dark. I couldn't see. Any glint of a sword and I..." I trailed off, mesmerized by the flames that still licked the woods in small piles.

"Eight," Servat answered after a moment. "Eight of ours."

"Eight? A small loss to our victory," Ramses scoffed. I wondered if any of them were dragon riders and if their dragons would mourn them too.

A small chuckle escaped my lips, dark and without humor. I turned to Ramses, my eyes locking onto his with an intensity that made him take a half-step back.

"Isn't it lucky, I didn't accidentally kill you, Ramses?" I said, the words dripping with a venomous sweetness.

Ramses' eyes narrowed, his composure wavering for an instant before the mask of command slid back into place. "Careful," he warned, with a low growl.

Servat watched us, his expression unreadable, but I could see the tension in his shoulders, the readiness in his stance.

I wondered if I struck Ramses if Servat would defend me.

"Eight of our own," I repeated softly, turning back to the pyre. "Eight lives snuffed out because they were caught in my storm. Eight families who will mourn because of me."

"Their families will be compensated," Ramses said.

The word "compensated" hung in the air, a bitter reminder that to Ramses, the loss of life could be balanced with coin. There was no compensation for the absence of a father, a son, or a brother. The lives I had inadvertently taken were reduced to a transaction, a line item in the ledger of war.

I watched the smoke rise higher, the pyre now fully engulfed in flames. The fire consumed everything, an insatiable beast. The lingering dragons gathered around, purring at the flames. Bodies that weren't tossed into the fire, we fed to the dragons.

"Now you see what these rebels do. What Eldra's men would do. Attacking civilians shopping for their families," Ramses spat. His condemnation was a jagged blade, and I felt the edge of it keenly.

As if to say; *look, Atreya, look at what your mercy has brought them.*

The rebels, Eldra's men—they had taken Joslynn from me. They had killed her.

I realized then that I did not want to be a mere instrument in Ramses' hands, wielded with calculating precision. No, I wanted to be the force of which these men trembled. I wanted to be the storm that would sweep through their ranks, leaving only silence in my wake.

Was I becoming the very monster I saw in Ramses? Was my heart growing cold?

Or perhaps—I finally saw the necessity in his cruelty—in his hard-handed rule. Had I listened, Joslynn would still be alive.

The numbness spread through me, a creeping frost that dulled the senses and smothered the flames of grief, leaving in their wake a hollow void where sorrow once took root. Around me, the world was a blur of motion and sound, a cacophony of the living that felt distant, and irrelevant. My mind fractured, splintering—

I made a mistake I made a mistake I made a mistake I made a mistake.

—and the cold realization that mercy could be as deadly as the sharpest blade.

"You always look so good in blue."

I made a mistake I made a mistake I made a mistake I made a mistake I made a mistake I made a mistake I made a mistake I made a mistake.

Her death rattle—a sound that no amount of time could erase—played on an infinite loop, a reminder of the cost of my hesitation, of my mercy.

There in the ashen light of dawn, mourning twisted, contorted, becoming something else entirely—rage. Beyond the uncontrolled rage, I had felt in the moment she died.

I turned to Servat and Ramses, my tears had long dried up, my tongue like sandpaper.

"What do you know of their whereabouts?" I whispered.

Servat and Ramses exchanged a glance, their faces unreadable, their bodies tense. I tilted my head to one side and asked again.

They didn't answer.

"You will tell me," I sighed, "and then I'll rip Eldra's head off of his shoulders."

My voice was devoid of the warmth it once carried, now just a husk, a vessel for all that darkness I felt in my heart.

Like an inky black sea, it swelled and surged, and crashed over the shores of my mind.

Ramses shifted uncomfortably, the faintest trace of uncertainty flickering in his eyes. He had wanted a weapon, but the edge he had honed now seemed too sharp, too unpredictable.

I smiled at that.

Ramses swallowed hard, his throat bobbing as he composed himself.

"We have scouts tracking their movements," Servat said at last, steady despite the turmoil I knew churned within him. "Eldra's forces are scattered, but we believe we've located one of his strongholds."

He looked grim and sad, the lines on his face deepening as if each word I spoke carved them further into his skin. There was a sorrow in his eyes, a mourning for the girl I had been and the woman I was becoming. He had seen too much of war, of the way it could twist and warp even the noblest soul. And now he watched me, another casualty of its merciless tide, another spirit bending under its weight.

And still, I smiled.

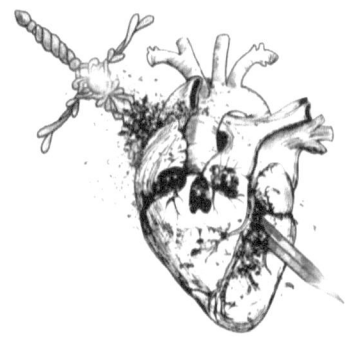

CHAPTER SIXTEEN

ATREYA

A month had passed since that morning—since my resolve had crystallized into an unbreakable shard of ice. The war room was abuzz with a low murmur as Ramses, Servat, Corina, and I hunched over the sprawl of maps and intelligence reports that covered the grand table.

Ramses' finger traced lines across the parchment, indicating three locations where our spies had gathered evidence of Eldra's possible ties. "Here," he began, pointing to a fortified town nestled in a valley. " Here, within the thick of the Great Wood," his finger moved to a spot shrouded by the dense green of the forest. And here, at the edge of the Ebon Sea."

"That's over Dragon's teeth and passed Tor," I said. "How long would it take for Dragons to get there?"

"An hour. Maybe two," Servat answered without looking at me. His arms were folded over his chest, and his focus was fixed on the map. He had been unusually quiet this past month.

"The valley town is the most vulnerable. We could lay siege and starve them out, but it would take time," Corina said, tapping a polished red nail on the parchment.

I shook my head. "How many civilians are in the valley?"

Ramses groaned and ran a hand down his face at that. I ignored him.

"The Great Wood provides cover, but its terrain is treacherous—creatures that would eat the flesh off your bones. An ambush would serve us well there, but the risk to our forces would be great," Corina said, turning to me. "You met them on the ground at Hyperion, but you had dragons with you. If Eldra has dragons about in these areas, they will sense ours, and we lose the advantage of surprise."

I listened, my thoughts a fortress to the darkness I harbored. Eldra's head on a pike had become my nightly dream, a vision that soothed and tormented me. I pushed it aside now, meeting Servat's stare.

The way he was looking at me, it was as if he could read my mind.

"We fly over Dragon's Teeth and land before Tor, using the dragons to insert a strike team just outside that territory. It's the heart of the Great Wood where they would least expect us," I continued, my finger hovering over the thickly drawn trees on the map.

"And the main force?" Corina queried, her tactical mind already turning.

"On foot, through the Great Wood. We move under the cover of the forest, silent as the night. The dragons will serve as a distraction on one end, drawing Eldra's notice to the skies while our forces close in on the ground at the opposite end. It leaves them surrounded."

Ramses beamed with approval, running his hand along my backside and squeezing. Even Corina seemed impressed by the plan.

Servat unfolded his arms, leaning over the map to trace the proposed route with his finger.

"It's risky," he conceded, "but it might just work. If our strike team can disable any defenses and create a distraction on one side, it would give our ground forces the opening they need."

"How many Solaris soldiers did the scout report?" I asked.

Servat motioned to a stack of reports at the corner of the table, his expression sobering. "A few hundred, at most. Eldra's been recruiting, but his numbers don't match ours—yet." He paused, then added, "We need to act swiftly before he can gather more strength."

Corina leaned in, her fingers tracing the route we would take through the twisted labyrinth of the forest. "What of the creatures Servat mentioned? The ones in the Great Wood?" she asked.

"The mages have been working on repellant spells, and our scouts have mapped their territories. We'll avoid the dens of the more dangerous beasts and keep to the shadows," Ramses said.

I raised a brow. "I didn't know we had mages."

I looked over at Servat, who shrugged.

Ramses' smile was a slash of white. "You never cared about battles and strategies before this. We have many things I will be happy to show you now," he said excitedly.

I didn't pull away when Ramses reached out for my hand and kissed the back of it. He kissed every knuckle and ran his tongue along the side of my palm.

On the one hand, a part of me loathed him—his arrogance, his dismissiveness of the lives affected by our decisions, and his casual touch that suggested ownership rather than partnership. Yet, there was another part, a darker, more primal side that couldn't deny the allure of his confidence, the way he commanded the room, the way he fought with such ferocity for the things he wanted.

And he always got what he wanted.

The thought of getting revenge, of bringing Eldra to his knees, sent a thrill through me that I couldn't entirely suppress. It was a feeling intertwined with the satisfaction of seeing my plans come to fruition, of standing shoulder to shoulder with Ramses as we reclaimed control. The darkness within me reveled in the thought of victory, and the anticipation of it was intoxicating.

I was so lost in the moment, the sensual touch of Ramses' lips against my skin and the tantalizing promise of power, that I nearly missed the subtle shift in the room. Ramses' command for the others to leave was soft but meant to be obeyed.

His hands raked over my back, down to my waist, pulling me flush against him.

"Do you feel it, too?" Ramses whispered, his breath hot against my ear. He ground himself against me. "The thrill of impending triumph. The power that comes from shaping the future."

I nodded, panting. "Yes, I feel it." My legs parted slightly, and I leaned back on the table.

He smiled, a knowing, predatory smile that made my heart race. "Good. Harness that feeling. Let it fuel your resolve. We are on the brink of greatness, you and I."

There was no denying the physical response he elicited from me nor the dark satisfaction it brought.

Ramses' grip on me tightened, his fingertips pressing into my flesh with a possessiveness that should have repelled me, but instead, I loved it.

He laid me down on the map table, the parchment crackling beneath us, the sound of our breathing loud in the room.

●

Ramses' hand was steady on my back as I climbed onto the dragon's scaled hide. We had been—something—in the last couple of weeks together. Barely able to peel away from each other. The air was always charged around us—the sex.

Impeccable.

Servat was already seated behind me, guiding my hands to the reins. Tiamut unfurled leathery wings with a sound like thunderous applause, the massive beast stretching its sinewy limbs in preparation for flight.

Servat snapped behind me. "," he growled, his command cutting through the memories of tangled sheets and whispered promises. "Riding a dragon is not like laying with a lover. It demands everything of you."

"You mean like laying with my *husband*," I corrected sharply.

Servat's jaw clenched, but he said nothing more, focusing on preparing himself and the dragon for flight. I could feel his eyes, heavy with unspoken thoughts, like a weight upon my back.

As Tiamut lifted off the ground, the wind whipped through my hair, clearing my mind of any lingering thoughts of Ramses. As we ascended, we soared into the sky, the world below shrinking to miniature proportions. The air grew cooler and crisper; the expanse of the Great Wood stretched out before us like a vast, green sea.

I had been fitted with flight leathers and light armor, and a flight visor was worn over my face this time. Ramses had them made for me on this occasion.

"You and Ramses seem to be getting along better these days," Servat said after a few minutes of silence.

I swallowed. "I suppose we are," I replied, choosing what I said carefully. "And we've found common ground in our goals." I dared a glance back at him.

Servat's grip on the reins tightened, his jaw set in a hard line. "Common ground," he echoed, his tone laced with skepticism. "Or is it something more?"

I hesitated, unsure of how to respond. "Does it matter?"

"It might," Servat finally said, the hint of something undefinable in how he spoke. "Alliances formed in the dark tend to unravel in the light."

I huffed out a laugh. "Fucking my husband is a dark alliance now?"

His silence that followed was heavy, almost palpable amidst the rush of the wind and the beating of Tiamut's wings. It was a few heartbeats before he spoke again, his words careful and measured.

"Forgive me," he started, his tone betraying the undercurrent of emotion he was fighting to keep at bay. He was angry, speaking through gritted teeth. "It's not my place to judge the nature of your... union with Ramses. It's just that—" Servat paused, searching for the right way to say it, "—I remember when he was less than the partner you deserved."

I felt a twinge in my chest, a reminder of the wounds that Ramses had inflicted in the past when his ambition had overshadowed his regard for me when I was more a pawn than a wife. I could not deny that the history between Ramses and me was fraught with moments of pain and betrayal.

More than the good times—there were few of those.

"Ramses has...changed," I said, more to convince myself than Servat. "*We* have changed. This whole ordeal... has brought us together in ways I never expected."

We have even been sleeping in the same bed. He asked me to stay with him.

"People don't change that easily," Servat said, the skepticism clear. "They may act differently when it serves them, but in the end, they revert to their true nature. You cannot make a bad thing work."

"Perhaps," I conceded, letting out a breath I hadn't realized I'd been holding. "But we all have roles to play, don't we? And sometimes those roles require us to believe in the possibility of change."

Servat looked away, returning to the horizon. "Just remember who was there for you when he wasn't," he said quietly. "Remember who stood by your side and who left you to fend for yourself."

I glanced back at Servat, his expression carved from stone, his fixed on the path ahead—at Siorsen's glittering body—guiding the other riders from behind us. He licked his lips, the gesture almost furtive. "I would never ask you to choose, not here, not now. But know that my heart is yours and has been for a long time. And while Ramses may hold your hand, it is your heart I long for."

The confession was like a sharp blade, cutting through the wind and Tiamut's wings. It left me breathless, and the honesty was overwhelming. My grip faltered, but Servat's steady hand guided me back.

"I have never dishonored you by pressing for more than you can give. But the heart wants what it wants, and mine wants you. It has always wanted you."

"Joslynn died," I rasped.

"I know."

"She is gone."

"I know."

"And I made her a promise. I kept that promise these last few years—"

"As have I." He kissed my shoulder, sweeping my hair away with his hand. For a moment, I closed my eyes and allowed him to sweep his tongue over the exposed skin at my neck.

I leaned back against him, my legs parting on their own accord. His hands went straight to the waistline of my pants, squeezing past the seam and meeting the warm flesh between my thighs.

"Servat," I gasped, a breathy whisper lost to the wind. "We cannot—this isn't—"

"Shh," he said, a low rumble against the shell of my ear. "I know your heart, your loyalty, your pain. I do not seek to take advantage but to offer solace, a momentary escape from the grief that binds you." He parted my flesh with two fingers and then dipped his middle finger into my wetness. "Let me." He moved his finger up to my peak, swirling my slick over it.

I moaned, struggling to keep myself from moving.

Then he was plunging two thick fingers into me, and my head lolled back. "Good girl. Fuck my fingers," he whispered to me. He was crooking his two fingers inside of me, beckoning me.

I was panting now. Servat was going faster, hitting that spot deep in me, but I needed something—

"More," I pleaded—demanded.

He gently removed his fingers and moved them in frantic, small circles on my pulsating bud.

And then I was breaking apart.

He slowed down, letting me ride out the wave of ecstasy, then took his fingers out and held them in front of my face.

"Is this for me?"

I blinked several times, remembering where I was and who I was with. "He could have seen."

Servat suckled on his fingers, making a show of it. "He saw nothing."

"That was a mistake. It shouldn't have happened."

"Right. I'll remember that for next time."

"There won't be a next time, Servat," I snapped.

I focused on the distant lights of Siorsen's body, how his wings stretched, and his head bowed occasionally, scanning.

I tightened my grip on the reins as Tiamut angled downwards, wings slicing through the air with calculated grace. The ground rushed up to meet us, and with a powerful beat of his wings, Tiamut landed smoothly amidst the thick foliage.

The impact of the landing sent a jolt through my body, my backside meeting Servat's groin. I straightened up quickly, creating a respectful distance.

"Sorry," I muttered, my cheeks flushed.

Servat only nodded, his expression unreadable. "No harm done. We need to keep moving." He was casual and distant, his mask fully in place. He took a dagger out and slit his palm, running his fingers through the blood to hide the scent of my climax.

We dismounted in silence, the other riders doing the same as they gathered in the shadows of the Great Wood. The dragons huddled together, their massive forms barely visible among the trees, blending into the environment like specters of the wild.

The air was thick with the scent of moss and earth. Ramses' light footfalls barely stirred a sound as he walked toward Servat and me, his eyes flicking between us curiously.

He knows. He knows, my mind screamed.

"We're close now. Remember the plan—small groups, silent as the night. Our advantage is the element of surprise. We strike hard, fast, and retreat before they can muster a counterattack," he said. He adjusted my light armor to his liking, his fingers working the buckles easily. Then, slowly, he dipped his mouth to mine, rubbing his face against my cheek, inhaling.

He knows. He knows. He knows. He knows. He knows.

"Make sure to come back to me alive."

I nodded, the promise unspoken yet understood between us. "I will," I assured him. "Keep yourself safe as well." I swallowed hard, trying to keep my heart steady.

There was always a threat in his tone that sent a shiver through me, and then he was trotting away, taking his group of men to circle the rear of the camps.

We reached the edge of a clearing, the moon casting a pale glow over the scene before us. A fortified encampment, tents, and watchfires betrayed the presence of Eldra's forces. This was it—the heart of the enemy territory, and the moment of truth for our plan.

I turned to Servat, "Stay close," I whispered. "Watch my back."

He nodded curtly. "Always."

My eyes flicked to his bloodied hand.

We waited silently for the signal, for the roar of a distant dragon.

Half an hour had passed when a sudden burst of roars shook the forest nearby, causing the soldiers encamped there to spin around, their attention darting upward in alarm. They braced for an attack from the sky that never came, looking up to the heavens, unaware of the threat that lurked among their numbers.

We split up, each taking down guards with swift, sure strikes that left no room for alarm. After several minutes, confusion and armor clanging filled the air as the camp stirred to life.

I reached the central tent, which housed their war plans and, with any luck, Eldra himself. I paused at the entrance, taking a deep breath before plunging into the dimly lit interior.

The tent was empty of people but filled with maps and messages scattered across a large table. I quickly began to rifle through the stacks of papers for any intelligence to turn the tide in our favor when a sudden movement at the entrance caught my attention.

Servat stood there, his sword drawn and ready, scanning the tent.

"Something's not right here," Servat murmured under his breath.

I turned to face him, "What's on your mind?"

"An unguarded command tent? With all their plans laid out?"

He pointed to a red circle glowed on one of the maps, a blinking light. I squinted at it. It was circled around the Great Wood. "What do you suppose that means?"

A blaring horn sounded from outside the tent as if in answer, and the ground shook.

The red circle, the blinking light, was not just a mark on a map but a target. Eldra had planned something dire for the Great Wood, and the horn was the precursor of that threat.

"This was a setup. He expected us," I said, the words like ash in my mouth. "One of our own gave up the information."

We sprinted from the tent, knowing that every second we lingered put us closer to Eldra's grasp. The camp was in disarray, a perfect cover for our escape, but as we neared the edge of the clearing, a dark shadow passed overhead.

I looked skyward, a heavy sense of dread settling in my chest. There they were—Eldra's wyverns and dragons, cutting through the night sky, their outlines etched sharply against the moon's glow. Atop the most enormous dragon sat Eldra.

I had never seen him in the flesh, but the legends of his power were not to be taken lightly. And somehow, Ramses had beaten him.

Somehow.

His power rippled through the forest, a tangible force that seemed to twist the air. Servat and I came to a halt, realizing that fleeing was no longer an option. This was a confrontation that could not be avoided.

The moment Eldra's dragon touched down, the ground trembled as if the earth was startled by its arrival. Eldra stepped off, his eyes quickly finding me. In that glare, I saw a spark of surprise and a glint of recognition; then it shifted to disbelief.

"Furian?" he uttered with a mix of shock and something darker. He wore a golden helmet on his head with sharp spikes that stuck out from the top like sunbeams. I couldn't see his face.

I laughed, the sound sharp and without humor. "That's right, Eldra. I am the Furian Slayer and have come to take your head."

His eyes widened at my declaration, but the surprise quickly morphed into a sneer. "Bold words for one so outmatched. Do you think you can beat me, child?"

Heavy with the scent of pine and impending doom, the night air stilled as Eldra's voice, as cold and deadly as the blade he wielded, sliced through it. His dragon, a leviathan of scales and sinew, snorted with a heat that spoke of the fire within, its eyes reflecting the moonlight in pools of molten gold.

Where the hell was Ramses and Siorsen when I needed them?

I let out a breath that I hadn't realized I'd been holding, feeling the flicker of my power stir within me. This was the moment I had been waiting for. This was my chance to strike back, to take revenge for the death of my Joslynn.

Eldra cocked his head at me, looking at me with a strange intensity.

My hands clenched into fists, and the sky cracked open overhead as lightning flashed and thunder rolled across the sky.

Slowly, he turned his head toward the heavens, watching lighting dance above us.

Eldra's focus was riveted on the skies, and in that brief distraction, I sought the connection to Ramses and Siorsen. They should have been here by now, their presence tipping the scales in our favor. But the forest was silent, and a gnawing worry was at the back of my mind.

My hands rose, palms facing the sky, and I summoned the winds with a command that thrummed through my very bones. The trees responded with a low, mournful groan, their branches swaying, bowing, and snapping as the gale whipped into a frenzy. The earth beneath my feet trembled, a primal dance of might and fury.

He finally turned back to me, a flicker of concern crossing his features as he realized the extent of my power. "You dare?" he challenged, reaching for the sword at his side, the golden helm upon his head catching the intermittent flashes of lightning.

I didn't waste my breath on a retort. Instead, I unleashed the scream of the storm, intertwining with the howling wind. Lightning forked down from the heavens, electric blue streaks snaking toward him. Once, twice, thrice it struck.

The air sizzled with energy, and the smell of electricity and scorched earth permeated the clearing. Eldra staggered, his body jerking with the impacts. His armor blackened where the lightning had kissed it.

And then he did something that terrified me.

He laughed.

Through the flickering lightning I had summoned, his figure straightened, shrugging off the assaults as if they were mere annoyances.

"You think your little magic tricks can harm me?" he bellowed over the roar of the wind. "I have weathered storms you cannot even fathom."

His hand rose, not to strike me down but to beckon the lightning itself. The bolts that had once been my weapons arced toward him, wrapping around his outstretched arm in a terrifying display of dominance. The golden helm glowed brighter, feeding off the raw power.

Servat gripped my arm and yanked me behind him. "That's enough!" he shouted between the gusts.

With a defiant cry, I charged past him, my sword drawn, heart pounding despite Servat's desperate screams to return to his side.

A shimmering shield rose from the ground, trapping the other soldiers and Servat outside, sealing Eldra and me within a dome of combat.

I tried not to feel like a trapped mouse. Not with the slash of white that was Eldra's grin, the way his aura glowed with excitement.

Eldra met my charge with a casual grace, his sword sparking to life with streaks of electricity dancing along its length. When our weapons clashed in the heart of the storm, the force sent ripples through the wet ground.

I had one thought—if I were to fall today, I was taking a part of him with me.

Our battle became the eye of the storm, two forces colliding with a fury that mirrored the heavens above. Eldra's strength was immense, his power clashing against mine with relentless precision. For every blow he dealt, I dodged and countered with all the skills I had honed over the years.

It wasn't much. Just enough to get me through. Just enough to survive. But I was determined to take this man down with me.

His sword cut through the air, the silvered steel slicing through my arm. Pain seared through me, a white-hot line that drew a harsh breath from my lungs. Servat's call was a distant roar, urging me to fall back and regroup, but I was beyond caution and reason.

The memory of Joslynn's hum filled my ears, and I began to sing, low and deep.

"In the hush of twilight's room, a curtain of dark hair,
A melody whispered, tender and fair,
A lullaby soft as the evening's cool breath,
A newborn's first cry, piercing the veil of death."

Eldra's grin faltered, his eyes narrowed into shards of glass, listening.

He moved with lethal grace, every motion fluid, every strike a calculated test of my resolve. The flat of his sword slammed into my abdomen, forcing me to double over, and his knee met my face with brutal precision. I staggered, blood spraying from my mouth in a crimson arc.

I spat out the blood, my tongue probing my teeth to make sure they were all still there. His blade whistled through the air again, and I rolled away just in time, coming up in a spin. He blocked my attack with his gauntlet, his eyes gleaming with a predatory light.

Pain lanced through my body with every breath, but I couldn't let that stop me.

We circled each other, and the storm was a wild symphony around us. My muscles screamed in protest, my lungs burning, but I forced myself to focus. Eldra's movements were mesmerizing, almost hypnotic, but I couldn't afford to be drawn in. He was toying with me, gauging my strength, waiting for the perfect moment to deliver the killing blow.

I lunged forward, my sword a blur of silver. Eldra parried effortlessly, our blades singing as they met. He retaliated with a powerful swing, and I barely managed to deflect it. Pain shot through my arm, but I gritted my teeth, refusing to yield.

"A promise made by a stranger, cloaked in the night,
A vow to protect, to guide towards the light,
With whispered oaths that echo in the stone,
A pact sealed in shadow, a future unknown."

Eldra backed away, twirling his sword and adjusting his stance. He was letting me recover.

I wiped the blood from my lips with the back of my hand and bared my bloody teeth.

Fuck him. Fuck him for going easy on me.

"Beneath the castle, where secrets dare to dwell,
Lies a beast in slumber, bound by a spell,
Its wing beats a rhythm, a thunderous drum,
Awaiting the moment its freedom will come."

He stood there, a dark silhouette against the backdrop of the storm, his sword at the ready, still emanating with the power that had turned my magic against me. He cocked his head to the side. "Finish, little songbird."

"You think this is a game?" I hissed, "You enjoy pain? Is that why you slaughtered all those people in Hyperion?"

His shoulders tensed. "Finish the song." The mention of Hyperion seemed to hit a nerve, a flash of something that might have been guilt. He moved then, fast as lightning itself, his sword a blur as he aimed for a killing blow. But I was ready, sidestepping and bringing my sword up to meet his. The sound of our swords clashing was drowned out by the storm that raged around us.

I huffed out the next verse.

"Above, the dove dons the raven's dark attire,
Proclaiming peace, yet fanning secret fire,
Its gentle coo, a guise for sly deceit,
Veils the shadowed soul where light and twilight meet."

He leaned in like he was holding on to every word.

I pushed back with all my strength, calling upon the storm's raw energy. Lightning crackled around me, branching toward him in a violent cascade of blue and white. But as the bolts struck him, they seemed to dissipate, absorbed by his hands, which began to drink in the power. His veins glowed and rippled, flashing like lightning.

Eldra laughed, the sound chilling against the thunderous backdrop. "You cannot defeat me with *that*," he taunted. "I *am* the storm!"

I was close enough to see his eyes now. The irises blue and silvery, the colors collapsing in upon themselves like dying stars.

Chaotic, beautiful, and deadly.

"The curtain, the tune, the tears, and the lies,
The beast, the bird, the castle's old ties,
All woven together in life's intricate weave,
A crown, a throne, a Kingdom of thieves."

I finished the song with a broken sob.

He snarled something in a language I didn't understand. *Too fast?*

"You took away my mother," I hissed. The only mother I had ever known. Her death was a wound that festered with every breath I took.

Eldra's eyes, those collapsing stars, flickered with something that might have been remorse or perhaps fear. I wish I could tell the difference—between the clenched teeth and sneer.

He stopped, his nose flaring. "I did *not*." He was seething—as if what I said had made him angry.

"You took her from me!" I screamed over the roar of the storm, my throat raw and bleeding. "Your soldiers, your command, your war!"

I feinted left, then spun right, aiming for the exposed gap under his arm. He anticipated the move, catching my blade with his own and twisting it out of my grasp. I stumbled back.

Eldra advanced, confidence radiating from him. "This ends now."

"Agreed," I breathed, summoning every ounce of strength I had left.

He raised his sword under my chin. It reminded me of the way Servat had all those years ago.

I grabbed his sword in both of my hands, ignoring the bite of the steel as it cut through my palms.

I inhaled.

When I'm gone, don't let da world turn ya hard. Dance.

His helm's glow dimmed as the air pressure changed, the storm's fury momentarily disrupted. The very air became heavy; all sounds muted entirely. The rain stilled midair. The winds shifted, the dark clouds roiling as the energy built to an apex. And then, with a scream of rage on the wind, I released it—not as a bolt, but as a resounding boom that shook the heavens and the earth.

The shockwave was immense. A concussive force rippled outward from my body, throwing Eldra off balance.

The world blurred into a frenzied dance of shadow and light. My feral instincts sharpened to a razor's edge. I was a creature of the night, born of starlight and moonbeam, and I would not be denied my vengeance. My claws, an extension of my wrath, reached for Eldra with a ferocity that matched the wild.

I was on him that instant, claws extended and teeth bared. I tried ripping the helm from his head, yet as I lunged, darkness enveloped him—a cloak of obsidian that came from nowhere. My fingers, tipped with the promise of retribution and blood, found nothing but the cold, wet earth beneath us. I dug my fingers into the dirt, searching for him.

I whirled around, the shield that had encased us dissipating into the ether, the cacophony of battle flooding back into my ears. Servat was at my side in an instant, and I snapped my teeth at him, a hiss escaping my throat as I recoiled from him.

I couldn't form a sentence; I snarled and screamed at him.

In the periphery of my vision, I caught movement—a wraith-like slip of darkness that could not hide from the keen edge of my senses.

I roared again and tried to lunge, but Servat held me in his arms. I bit down hard on his forearm, which had me trapped, blood pooling into my mouth. He didn't budge. I screamed and kicked and sobbed—tried to claw my way to that darkness that was escaping beyond the trees—beyond my sight.

"Release me!" I managed to snarl through clenched jaws, the command tearing from my throat.

But Servat was immovable, determined to pierce the veil of my madness. "You must calm yourself, or you will be lost to the rage within."

The shadow I had seen, the darkness that had enveloped Eldra and sought to steal him from the justice he deserved, was melding with the trees, becoming one with the night itself. It called to me a whisper of malice that promised escape and the satisfaction of my deepest desires.

I sobbed, the sound raw and broken, as I felt the darkness pull away, the chance for vengeance slipping through my fingers like wisps of smoke.

Servat pressed his arm harder into my jaws, offering.

"Take it out on me," he murmured. "If it will grant you even a moment's peace, do what you must."

He nuzzled my neck.

I did not release him—not immediately. The animalistic part of me, the part that craved retribution above all else, savored the taste of his blood. But as the anger ebbed, replaced by an aching emptiness, I loosened my grip, my claws retracting as sanity fought back to the surface.

I collapsed against him, my sobs a silent scream in the night.

Around us, our soldiers let out horrified gasps, and I pulled away from Servat sharply.

A new sound pierced the world—a great and terrible roar that was neither thunder nor wind. It was Siorsen, and atop his back was Ramses, their forms cutting through the maelstrom as they descended upon the clearing.

The world around us began to shift and warp. The Solaris soldiers were strewn across the battlefield, and the ones who had fallen and those who appeared to stand started to waver like mirages under a harsh desert sun. One by one, they flickered and faded, the illusion of their existence unraveling before us.

They had been nothing but phantoms.

Our soldiers looked around in confusion, exhausted and disoriented.

Ramses slid from Siorsen's back as the great beast landed, scanning the clearing with a tactician's precision. "He has fooled us all," he said, snapping at me.

"Some plan you had," he said. He scanned Servat's arm and then the blood that stained my chin.

"I fended him off myself while you were doing God-knows-what!" I shrieked.

Ramses' glare lingered on Servat and me, a knowing glint on his face that spoke of unspoken thoughts and judgments yet to be voiced. The air hung heavy with the aftermath of the battle and the weight of his scrutiny.

Then, with a derisive snort, he shook his head. "Servat seems quite close to his queen," he said, his tone edged with scorn that was impossible to miss. "This is precisely why women should not be the ones making war plans."

The remark was like a slap to the face.

Servat, his arm still marked by my earlier wrath, stepped forward, his stance protective. "Her plan was sound," he interjected, his demeanor calm. "Eldra's sorcery caught us unprepared, not her leadership."

Ramses' grin was feral. "Quick to defend her leadership, but no denial on what I said before."

Servat's eyes, usually so clear and steadfast, flickered away briefly, betraying a turmoil beneath his calm exterior. The bonds of brotherhood and loyalty that tied him to Ramses were a tangled web. One made all the more complex by the silent love he harbored for me—his queen, his brother's wife.

His jaw clenched, and he met Ramses' glare with a steady, unflinching resolve. "My duty is to my queen and the cause we serve," Servat declared. "I was merely doing as you instructed."

Ramses's sharp and knowing feral grin held a challenge that was as much a provocation as a declaration of possession.

Without breaking his focus from Servat, Ramses stepped towards me. His hand found the small of my back, pulling me close with a possessiveness that left no room for doubt. His lips met mine in a kiss that was entirely a claim. Ramses' tongue flicked out to lick my cheek, a gesture that held a primal assertion of territory.

He sucked my lips between his teeth, his hands raking down my back and squeezing my backside. He smashed his pelvis against mine, a low growl of possession rumbling in his chest.

I pushed against his chest, my hands flat against the hard muscle, but it was a feeble attempt at resistance. Ramses was not a man to be denied—I had learned that over the years.

Breaking free from his kiss, I gasped for air, my chest heaving. The heat of his body against mine was suffocating, his presence too large, too encompassing.

Ramses released me abruptly, a smirk playing on his lips as if he had proven his point. He turned his attention back to Servat, who stood rigid, his hands clenched into fists at his sides.

"Remember your place, brother," Ramses said menacingly. "And remember who your queen belongs to."

I could see his expression shift just slightly. His claim stung Servat like venom, yet he held his tongue, his discipline as a warrior keeping him silent. I, too, felt the bite of Ramses' claim, the way he reduced me to a thing possessed. It reminded me of the chains that bound me, not just to Ramses, but to the expectations of this world where the arrogance of kings so easily dismissed a queen's will.

I could only imagine what Ramses would have done had he scented me on Servat.

As Ramses led me away, my eyes locked with Servat's, the silent communication between us screaming louder than any declaration could. I had thought of riding once more with him and Tiamut.

With a grip as unyielding as iron, Ramses steered me toward Siorsen. The colossal beast snorted, its breath a plume of smoke in the cool air, its scales the color of burning embers. If it could have claimed me just as his master had, it would have.

Ramses easily hoisted me onto Siorsen's back, the dragon's scales hot and smooth beneath my fingers. I had no choice but to settle in front of Ramses, who wrapped his arm around my waist. I tried not to panic as he leaned in and sniffed me, obviously displeased by something.

Siorsen's mighty wings unfurled, catching the wind with a thunderous clap, and I cast a longing glance toward Servat.

Servat stood motionless, his expression unreadable as he watched us ascend into the sky. The wind whipped through my hair as Siorsen took to the air, his wings beating with powerful strokes. Below us, the world grew smaller. Ramses leaned in close, his breath hot against my ear. "You belong to me, my queen. Never forget it," he murmured, hands finding the waistline of my pants, running his hand over my mound.

He knows.

"You sound jealous," I retorted. "Of your brother at that. You have left me in his care twice during the fights and then get mad at him for doing what he is supposed to do."

Ramses' grip on me tightened, and I could feel the tension in his body, the rigid set of his jaw against the side of my face.

"And what would you have me do?" he growled with a barely contained fury. "Leave you to fend for yourself? You are my queen, my wife. It is my duty to protect you."

Below us, the world had become a patchwork of shadows as night settled over the land. I squinted down below, feeling that if I tried hard enough, I would be able to catch Eldra slipping through the forest.

"You left that duty to Servat and then accused us of somehow betraying you."

A long silence followed.

"Perhaps you are right," he admitted, and I could hear the begrudging respect in his tone. "But know this—my jealousy stems not from distrust of you but from fear. Fear of losing you, not just to the dangers of war, but to another's influence."

I turned slightly, trying to glimpse his face to see if the proclamation matched his expression. But Ramses was a master at hiding his emotions, his face a mask that revealed nothing.

"Your paranoia is getting the better of you," I said.

He leaned closer, running his nose along my shoulder.

"Perhaps it is," Ramses conceded. "But tonight, when you fought Eldra... I had never seen you so wild, so feral..." He trailed off, kissing my neck.

"It was beautiful," he finished, his breath warm against my skin. I remained silent, allowing him to nibble where he wanted.

He saw me fighting, and yet he didn't come. He hadn't tried to swoop in and save me. Not that I needed it.

Siorsen glided on, a silent sentinel beneath the moonlit sky, his shadow passing over the lands like a fleeting whisper. Lights flickered on in the distance, belonging to towns I had never been to and probably would never see.

"I was so close to killing him," I hissed.

His lips were on my neck, his teeth nipping at my skin. Right where Servat had his lips. "You were. But now that Eldra has truly seen you in all your ferocity and power, he will become obsessed," he whispered in my ear. "He will want you and the power you wield for himself."

I wanted to say *the same thing you do.*

"Why would he obsess over me? I am but one queen in a world full of them."

"Because you are the Furian Slayer," he said, the title hanging between us. "Long ago, Eldra's second in command was Aislinn Furian. When you defeated her, you ended the line of Furians and humiliated Eldra. He will not stop until he has you to claim the victory he believes is rightfully his."

"Eldra's desire for vengeance will make him relentless," he continued. "He sees in you a power that could rival his own, a wildness that he cannot control. And that terrifies him."

I thought to myself how similar Ramses and Eldra were in that regard.

PART TWO

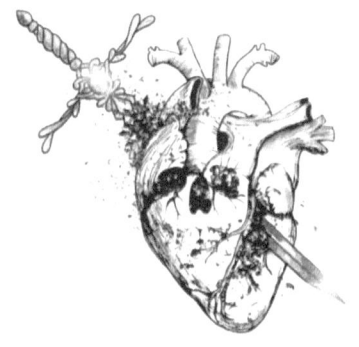

CHAPTER SEVENTEEN

ATREYA

*3**7 years later. 112 years after the War of Fallen Skies.***

I should have run on my wedding day.

My reflection stared back at me, skin sallow against the darkening bruises and cuts marring my face. My husband's latest masterpiece. A gash split my forehead, a fresh cut slashed across my cheekbone. Had I provoked him? Had I failed to please him once again? A single tear escaped, tracing a path down my cheek to lose itself in the cut. I bit my lip against the pain, refusing to make a sound.

Aquinetta approached, a silver tray trembling in her hands. A vial of salve sat in a clay pot upon it. Her head hung low, her breath coming in short gasps. I bit back a cry as I reached for the pot, my wounds screaming in protest.

"Thank you, Aquinetta," I managed to say, my lips tight with pain. She exhaled shakily, her eyes flicking up to meet mine before darting away. My maidservant - a young woman terrorized by my presence. I could see the fear radiating from her, feel it like a palpable thing. I had watched too many like her come and go, never knowing what became of them once they left my chambers.

She would be the 167th since my marriage to the king eighty years prior. I remembered them all, each name etched into my heart like a scar. I didn't want to remember, didn't want to know them, but I couldn't help myself. Not when they were as trapped as I was.

Trapped by the king, by my husband. Trapped by the shield that cut us off from the world. It had been thirty-seven years since that last battle with Eldra. Ramses had never been the same. The young king who once stood tall and proud now hunched over his throne, his eyes darting about with a feral light. He had withdrawn from the world, allowing only his most trusted advisors near. The court, once vibrant with life, had withered away, replaced by an atmosphere thick with suspicion and dread.

Ever since Eldra. He could never let it go, the feeling of betrayal festering in his mind like an open wound. Someone close to us had betrayed him, and he had never discovered who. That mistrust had consumed him, until he trusted no one. Not even me.

The memory of that battle still lingered, a scar upon the land. The shield was its physical manifestation - a dome of shimmering energy that encapsulated our entire city. It was our protection and our prison, allowing none to enter or leave without the king's permission. Ramses claimed it necessary, a means to keep us safe from Eldra, from the outside world. But I knew the truth. It was a means of control, a way to keep me captive.

The years passed in a haze of gold and fear. The city turned inward, the once bustling gates now closed and overgrown. The marketplace fell silent, the exotic goods that once flowed through it now just a memory. Our world had shrunk, until all that remained was the gilded cage of the city. And I, I was trapped, bound by duty and fear of a man whose love had long since turned to poison.

There was a clang as Aquinetta set the tray down, and I flinched, my heart racing. Clang. Clang. Clang. The sound echoed through the room, each strike of metal on stone making me jump. Aquinetta gasped, her hand rising to cover her mouth. "I-I'm sorry," she stammered.

"It is nothing, leave it be," I told her, but she just shook harder, her eyes wide with fear. I hated that I inspired such terror in her. Hated that I was the one she feared.

I smeared the salve across my wounds, letting out a sigh as the pain began to ebb. I turned back to the mirror, barely recognizing the woman staring back at me. Ink-black hair, once my pride, now hung dull and lackluster around my face. My husband loved my hair, loved to wrap his fists in it as he beat me. Loved to take chunks of it with him as he stormed out of the room. I was a mess, inside and out.

My wonderful husband. He swore he loved me, but I knew the truth. I knew what he was. What he had become. And I knew I had to escape, before he destroyed what little of me was left.

"I'd be kinder if you just submitted," he'd say in a lazy drawl. As if submission were a thing that could be taught, a skill honed like a blade. I thought I'd submitted enough, bowed my head and taken his blows without a word. Swallowed my pride and my screams, let him shape me to his whims. Never once unleashing the power that hummed in my veins, too afraid of how he'd react if I fought back, even a little. My tongue was a different matter, sharp as a whip and just as deadly. It had landed me in trouble more times than I could count.

I took what he gave me, the rough hands and the cold eyes, the nights that blurred into mornings. Took it silently, stoically, because that was what a queen did. Even when the servants bore him bastard after bastard, their red hair and yellow eyes a constant reminder of his infidelities. I said nothing, did nothing, because what was the point? He'd only laugh and tell me I was jealous, that I had no right to be.

He loved me like a man loves a prize, a trophy won and shelved. Something beautiful he could break and break again, because it thrilled him to see me in pieces. And I let him, because I had nowhere else to go. The shield he'd raised after Hyperion, the wards that made it impassable...I was as much a prisoner as any servant.

But there was Vryseris. My son, my heart. The only reason I got out of bed in the mornings. Ramses wanted an heir, a boy to inherit his throne, and the gods had granted him that and more. Vrys was perfection, a miniature of his father but with something in his eyes that gave me hope. Something kind.

Ramses wasn't cruel to him, not like he was to me. He had a soft spot for the boy, and I reveled in it, even as a part of me wanted to hate him for it. Vrys adored his father, hung on his every word, and I bit my tongue and let him, because what was the point of poisoning him against the one person who showed him love?

At night, after Ramses had retired, I'd creep into Vrys' room and sit by his bed, watching him sleep. His hair was as black as mine, and I'd twirl it around my fingers, feeling a pang of victory. He had something of me, something his father couldn't touch. And I'd whisper to him, tell him stories of bravery and honor, of kindness and strength. The same stories Joslynn used to tell me.

"Be kind, my love," I'd whisper, brushing his hair back. "Be just, be fair, and above all, be brave."

Those moments were my sanctuary, the only time I felt like myself. Vrys' innocence gave me a strength I didn't know I had, reminded me that there was still good in the world, still something worth fighting for.

But Vrys grew up, as boys do. Became a mirror of his father, tall and commanding, with eyes that saw too much. He began to ask questions, full of a curiosity that made my heart ache. Noticed the way the servants cringed, the silence that hung over the palace like a pall. I knew the day would come when he'd see his father for what he was, when the scales would fall from his eyes and he'd realize the man he idolized was a monster.

I'd kiss his forehead, whisper promises of a better world, a world where his mother wasn't a shell of a woman, his father not a tyrant. But I knew it was a lie, knew that day was coming, and I had no way to stop it.

His fortieth name day, and the palace was alive with music and laughter, a rare thing in those cold halls. Ramses was in his element, presenting his son with swords and horses, the tools of a future king. But as the night wore on and the guests departed, the silence crept back, like a tide coming in.

I found him in his chambers, much as I used to when he was a boy. Handed him a small wooden figurine, a human knight with a kind face and a strong jaw. "Remember, my love," I told him, meeting his eyes. "Strength isn't just about power. It's about standing up for what's right, even when it's hard."

He looked at me, then at the figurine, and I saw something flicker in his eyes. A spark of understanding, maybe. Or maybe just my own desperate hope.

"One day," I whispered, "I'll tell you the truth. About your father, about the servants, about everything. But not today. Today, you can still believe in him."

He nodded, his face serious, and I felt a pang in my chest. He straddled two worlds, my son, the one his father had made and the one I prayed he'd help me fix.

I looked at myself in the mirror, at the silver-blue eyes that stared back. Ramses might have trapped me, but he hadn't trapped this, the fire that still burned in me. I would endure, for Vrys' sake. I would survive, and when the time was right, I would show my son the truth about his father.

But until then, I'd hold him close and whisper stories in his ear, and pray that they'd be enough to guide him on the right path. Because if there was one thing I knew, it was that the day would come when he'd have to choose - between the monster who sired him and the mother who raised him. And I could only hope that when that day came, he'd choose me.

"Brush my hair," I said, my voice a brittle thing. Aquinetta's head jerked up, her eyes wide with fear. Her hand trembled as she lifted the ivory comb from my vanity, hesitating over my tangled locks. The salves and potions would work their magic, heal the wounds that marred my scalp. The bald spot would grow back, the marks would fade.

She began to comb my hair, her touch tentative. I watched her in the mirror, taking in the soft brown hair and full lips, the rounded ears that marked her as human. Eighteen, nineteen, maybe. So young. So very young.

Ember, once the jewel of the Fae, now shone like a gilded cage. Gold glittered on every surface, a stark contrast to the wastelands beyond the shield, where once-great cities lay in ruin. A testament to Ramses' conquests, to the neglect that followed.

Aquinetta was a reminder of all that lay beyond the shield, of the world that struggled to survive while we lived in false splendor. Her cautious movements, the flutter of her lashes, spoke of awe and terror of the Fae, of our power. But there was something more in her, a spark of defiance that Ramses could never quite extinguish.

She was from beyond the wall, one of the thousands of slaves taken from the plains and brought to our kingdom. Mortal, insignificant, dying.

Ramses had won the War of Fallen Skies over a century ago, leaving what lay beyond the shield in ruin. The Fae who still dwelled there were either dead, dying, or in hiding, waiting for the day they could reclaim Ferenz, reclaim Ember from the Cruel King.

Once, there had been four rulers, one for each of the four cities. The Tyrens, The Blackwaters, The Furians, The Solaris. Now, only the Blackwaters ruled, and Ramses didn't care enough to govern the other three.

This was the city of my birth, where Ramses had taken pity on my dying mother and raised me to be the queen he desired. I never knew my parents, never knew their names or titles. I'd searched for them, in the library, in the temples, but there were no records, only silence.

Joslynn, my nursemaid, was the only one who might have known, but she was dead. "When I'm gone, don't let the world harden you. Dance." Her words still echoed in my mind.

Oh, how I longed for a rebellion to succeed, to reduce this dazzling city to ashes. If only they could seize the dragons Ramses kept in the dragon keep, the beasts he'd tainted and used to deter intruders. I'd caught glimpses of them from my window, their forms majestic as they took flight. The last time I'd ridden a dragon was thirty-seven years ago.

If there were any dragons beyond the wall, I imagined the city crumbling as they roared in fury, releasing their brethren by the hundreds. I'd even accept them displaying my decapitated head before the city gates. At least then I'd know freedom. At least then Vrys would be safe.

I almost laughed at the irony. I wished for the same fate as Riza Blackwater, Ramses' mother.

Aquinetta snagged a knot and paused, her lip trembling. "I'm not the one who wants you dead," I said a little sharper than I intended. She startled, as if I'd plucked the thought from her head.

She had scars on her hands and arms, thin lines that spoke of whips and knives. I knew of pain, of torture. But the Fae, inside and out of the castle, did not. I was loved and cared for, and just as cruel as Ramses as far as everyone else was concerned. It was why so many of my maidservants ended up dead.

I'd earned that fear, that respect. I was no stranger to this game, to proving myself with each new girl, each innocent thrown into my viper's den. But it was a battle I was doomed to lose, because no matter how kind I was, they'd always see me as an extension of Ramses.

And maybe they were right. I was his queen, after all. I shared his throne, his palace, his life. I bore his child.

Ramses had raised me, given me the best tutors, the finest clothes and jewels. He'd given me everything, asked only that I please him. And I had, oh how I had. I'd stood before him every day, my heart pounding, my palms sweating, desperate for his approval. His golden eyes had shone like sunflowers, his red hair like fire against his tanned skin. I'd longed to trace the tattoo that wound like branches up his neck, to feel his body against mine.

He'd said I was of exceptional stock, that if I proved worthy, he'd reward me greatly. But I'd come to realize he'd appraised me like a valuable mare - something to be trained and bred, ridden at his whim.

I hadn't known that then. But on my fiftieth birthday, I'd bled, and the maids had come to dress me, their faces alight with joy. Only Joslynn had pitied me. "Your life is about to change forever," she'd said, her eyes sad.

Then Ramses had put me in an arena with a wild lioness, let the beast tear me to shreds. It had circled me, its gold collar glowing like fire.

Aquinetta snagged another knot, and I flinched, my hand rising to my hair. My gold bracelet glinted in the mirror, a cold reminder.

"Thank you, Aquinetta," I said softly, meeting her eyes in the reflection. Fear lurked in their depths, and a caution born of expectation. But there was a flicker of gratitude, too, because in this place, even the smallest kindness was a rare thing.

She nodded, her posture rigid with the formality expected of her, but her mouth twitched, betraying her.

I handed her the small pot of salve. She took it from me with shaking hands and placed it back on the silver tray to be put away.

"No," I said. "Use it." I could see the beginnings of a protest on her face. I had to bite my lip to keep from screaming at her. The salve would melt away those scars and bruises, and perhaps she would know one day without pain. Perhaps I will see her again tomorrow.

"Thank you, my Queen," she said quietly. I nodded and watched as she dipped her fingers in the salve and rubbed it into the scars on her hands and arms. It was soothing to watch—to know I helped her in some way.

She watched in fascination as the salve worked its magic. The marks on her arms began to fade away, the scars disappearing. I shuddered involuntarily as I remembered the first time I used the salve myself. She bowed her head.

"Take it. I can have the healers make more," I said with disinterest. Her hands were running through my hair, parting strands to make for braids.

"Do they make it for you often, then?"

I stilled and heard her intake of breath, and then the sound of her falling to her knees, the knobby bones grating against the stone of my room floor.

"Forgive me! It was not my place to ask such a question!"

I laughed, the sound strange and rusty. I hadn't laughed in years, not since that day in the market. "You'll need the salve for your knees now. Stand."

She did, her eyes downcast, and I reached out to touch her hand. Her skin was warm against the cool metal of my bracelet, and I felt a shiver run through her.

I couldn't save her, not really. The palace was a trap, a labyrinth that ensnared us all. But I could give her this, these small moments of kindness. I told myself not to get attached, every time, and failed, every time.

"There are things that stay within these walls that never leave," I said carefully. Her face went blank, and I knew she understood. I took in every freckle on her cheeks, every line on her face, telling myself I wouldn't do it again, wouldn't care.

But I was lying, and I knew it.

She spoke softly, barely audible. "I have a sister...she's younger than me...she works as a fisher along the riverbank, having been sold to another Fae family..."

I cut her off. "You will not breathe a word of this sister to anyone. Do not dare to speak her name aloud, not even to yourself."

I turned away, my heart aching at the desperation she so freely showed me. I knew the pain of losing someone, of having to let go.

Her head dipped in a lifeless nod, the spark in her extinguished. Like all the others, she accepted her fate, understood that my presence was a curse.

●

Aquinetta was dead by morning. My hair had grown back, the marks on my skin gone. They'd taken her in the night, and I'd huddled under my covers, listening to her soft cries as she was dragged away.

Hours passed before I dared to peek out, to fix my dresses and sit before the mirror. My silver-blue eyes stared back at me, empty.

I was used to the pain. The physical pain of Ramses' beatings, the emotional pain of his words. The pain of watching servant after servant come and go, their lives forever scarred.

I was used to the pain, but that didn't mean I'd accepted it. I was a queen, strong and resilient. And one day, I would be free. I had to be.

He may have taken my freedom, my dignity, my peace, but he couldn't take my hope. My hope for a better future, for a life without him. As long as I had that, I had the strength to endure, to fight, to survive.

I made a silent vow to myself as I stared at my reflection. No matter how long it took, no matter what I had to endure, I would escape this viper's den. I would reclaim my freedom.

I walked to the balcony, the cool morning air brushing against my skin, and looked out over the city. The shield above us was a silent sentinel, a reminder of the oppression that had lasted too long. But even the strongest barriers had weaknesses, and I was determined to find them.

I would gather allies in secret, the disenchanted nobles and disillusioned soldiers, the hidden mages and silent dissenters. Together, we would form a network of resistance, a clandestine force that could one day rise and break our chains.

And through it all, I would keep Vrys close, teach him not just the ways of a ruler, but the heart of one. He would know the stories of the people, the tales of their suffering, and the songs of their hope. He would learn to be the king Ember and all of Ferenz deserved.

Ramses believed he had broken me, that the queen by his side was nothing more than a complacent adornment to his power. But he was wrong. I was not broken; I was biding my time. With every scar that healed, with every servant that passed through my chambers, my determination grew.

The day of reckoning was coming, and when it arrived, Ember would be reborn from the ashes of the old world. The shield would fall, the dragons would soar free, and the people would no longer live in fear.

For Joslynn, for Aquinetta, for every soul that had suffered under Ramses' rule, I would fight. I would not rest until the viper's den was no more, until we all tasted the sweet air of freedom.

For I am the Queen of Ember, and my fire would one day set us all free.

And when I did, I would make sure Ramses paid for every scar he'd left on my body, and for every heart he'd broken. For Joslynn, for Aquinetta, and for the 166 maidservants before her.

I would make sure he paid.

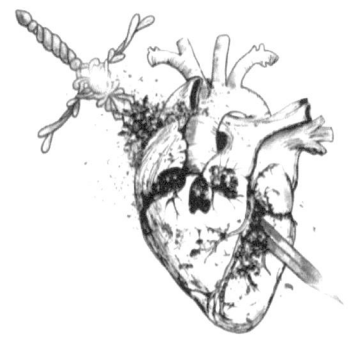

CHAPTER EIGHTEEN

I made my way into the dining hall, the guards greeting me at the doorway. Their eyes, like the blades of their swords, glistened with an otherworldly intensity. I had long thought something was night right about them. Dressed in red and black leathers, their faces were harsh and unyielding. They parted silently, granting me passage into the grand room.

Crystal goblets filled with amber liquid were placed next to three floral plates with a single red rose in the center. A spread of honey bread and scrambled eggs, savory pickled ham, and fresh fruits were laid out on the table.

The windows had been shuttered, the only light coming from the flickering fireplace in the corner. I took a seat in the first empty chair, the farthest from Ramses.

"Darling!" Ramses called out to me from across the breakfast table. I noticed the bouquets of flowers he had arranged for me, strands of my hair weaved into them.

My gossamer gown of yellow silk draped over my shoulders and arms and my hair was pinned in a bun at the top of my head. I forced a smile at him, as I have always done.

Vryseris was present, quietly eating a biscuit and his helping of an egg.

"Good morning," I greeted both of them. I patted Vryseris on the head, running through the dark curls and tucking them behind his pointed ear.

"Don't fuss over the boy, Atreya," Ramses said, gesturing at Vryseris with his fork. "He's got quite the day ahead of him."

"Father is taking me beyond the wall!" Vryseris exclaimed happily.

I stilled, my heart sinking in my chest. "What do you mean, beyond the wall?" I couldn't help the bite in my tone. Ramses raised a thick brow at me.

"He's going to see the encampments outside the wall. Speak with generals. Know of things that a *prince* is to know," he said pointedly.

I narrowed my eyes at him, the briefest defiance I could give him. "What does a boy need to know of enemy encampments and war for?" I demanded.

"I am a man!" Vryseris added with a cross of his arms.

"You are a youngling. Hardly grown and old enough to be a man," I pointed out. I saw Ramses roll his eyes at me. I turned back to Vryseris. "You don't need to see such horrors yet."

Ramses chuckled, a deep, rumbling sound that echoed in the grand dining hall. He leaned back in his chair, his fingers gently stroking the hilt of his sword. "Atreya, you always were a soft-hearted one," he said, his tone dripping with condescension. "But you must understand, a man is made by his trials, by his battles. Vryseris is not to be a child anymore."

I've heard of these camps, the raids that went on beyond the wall. I knew every time the Brotherhood—a band of Ramses worst—went out, and came back with people chained together, that their villages had been burned to the ground.

Screaming. Fire.

I glanced at Vryseris, my son, who radiated a mix of excitement and naivety. He was eager to step into the role his father had carved for him, unaware of the true nature of the brutalities that lay beyond the shield. It pained me to see such innocence on the brink of being marred by the harsh realities of our kingdom's politics.

I felt a surge of anger, my cheeks heating and my heart pounding. The tension in the room grew, the guards at the entrance shifting uneasily. The flames in the fireplace flickered, casting long, dancing shadows on the stone walls. I took a deep breath, trying to quell my rising emotions.

"He will come. He needs to see. The rebels are getting more bold and brazen. I need to show him how we keep them at bay. We will take Siorsen out to the camps," Ramses said with finality. The mention of his favored dragon made my stomach twist.

The very name sent a shiver down my spine. He was a creature of unspeakable savagery and power. Siorsen The Vicious. Unpredictably so. He was not simply an obedient pet to Ramses, but a wild force of nature. The dragon had a reputation that echoed in the hushed whispers of the rebels and the fearful stammers of the city folk alike. His wrath was legendary and his appetite, insatiable.

The thought of bringing Siorsen out to the camps was terrifying. But the mere sight of him would strike fear into the hearts of the boldest rebels. Not to mention the destruction he would wreak in his wake.

"I'll get to ride on dragon-back?" Vryseris asked, his golden eyes wide at the mention of Ramses' favorite dragon. Ramses smiled at him and nodded.

"A dragon? Really? It isn't safe!" I couldn't help myself. The protests were clawing away at my throat.

Ramses put down his fork and turned to me. "Vryseris, leave your mother and I."

I raised my chin, my heart racing.

Vryseris nodded and vanished in a wisp of smoke from his seat, his fork clattering onto his empty plate. A unique little trick I wished I could master. He had gotten better control over his powers in the last few years.

Ramses stood from his seat, adjusting the gold lapels of his royal robe. I anticipated every step that he took toward me, making his way down the long table and to my side. I stood, my hands clasped in front of me, my feet planted firmly on the floor.

Ramses towered over me, his presence both suffocating and infuriating. "Atreya," he began, low and steady, "you must understand that Vryseris is destined for greatness. He is my heir, and he must be prepared for the realities of rule. The dragon, the camps, the rebels—these are all parts of the world he will inherit."

I met his gaze, unflinching. "And what of the lessons of mercy, of justice? Will you show him those as well, or will you only teach him to rule with fear and bloodshed?" I asked, challenging him

Ramses sighed, a flicker of irritation crossing his features. "Mercy and justice are luxuries of the peaceful. We are at war, Atreya. We must be strong, and unyielding. Our enemies will not hesitate to exploit any weakness."

I shook my head, my anger simmering just below the surface. "Strength does not come from the terror we instill in others, Ramses. True strength comes from the respect we earn, and in the trust we build. You may have won the War of Fallen Skies, but if you continue on this path, you will lose the peace that follows."

His hand shot out, gripping my arm with an iron hold. The guards remained statuesque, their purpose solely to observe and protect the king, not to intervene in our private matters.

"You speak of things you do not understand," Ramses said, his grasp tightening. "You live in comfort because of the actions I take to keep this kingdom secure. Do not forget that."

I winced at the pressure but did not cower. "And you rule in isolation because of the fear you sow," I retorted. "One day, Ramses, the people will rise against you. And on that day, you will need more than dragons and soldiers—you will need the hearts of the people, which you have long since forsaken."

For a moment, we locked in a silent battle of wills. Then, with a huff, he released me, the ghost of a bruise already forming on my skin.

I waited for the blow to come, to feel the pain of it, the humiliation of it.

Ramses simply placed his palm on my cheek and forced me to look at him.

"Such fire in you today, my love. So very fierce. You never question me. You never doubt me. Yet, here you are."

He must have been lying to himself. I questioned him often and always.

"Vryseris is too young to understand what you wish to show him. And a dragon? You never even wanted *me* on a dragon," I said.

He chuckled at this, his fingers clutching my chin firmly. "Do you wish to have a dragon?"

Of course. Now he would offer me one. Knowing I couldn't take it and leave this place.

I shook my head, my hair falling over my face. He carefully tucked the strands behind my ears.

"I adore the hell-like intensity in your gaze. That fierce protectiveness. There was a time when you looked at me with that same passion." He carried on, his lips gently caressing my ear. "Such an incredible mother." His hand smoothly glided to my abdomen, brushing against the delicate silk of my gown. A loving touch. He tenderly massaged me there, applying pressure on my stomach, his breath warm and tantalizing on my neck. I shivered.

"What do you say we give it another try? I'll make you a mother once more. Perhaps a little princess this time?" He playfully bit at my neck as his hands explored the soft skin of my back, his body firmly pressed against mine. "So fiercely protective, so adoring. I can't get enough." He whispered into my ear, his lips tenderly grazing my skin. My eyes fluttered shut involuntarily, and my head tilted back into the void, revealing my vulnerable neck to him. The presence of the guards by the doorway did not go unnoticed; I was very conscious of their proximity.

Ramses tenderly nipped at the delicate skin where my neck joined my shoulders, his hand skillfully lifting the silky fabric of my dress, baring me to the cool air around us. I wasn't completely exposed, however, as my undergarments still served as a barrier to his ultimate goal. Frustrated, he growled into my ear and, with a deft flick of his claw, tore through the material. His claws were seldom cautious, and I couldn't help but wince as his fingers grazed my most intimate area. Tilting my head, I sensuously pressed my lips against his chiseled jawline. He growled in response, his nimble fingers exploring my depths while his thumb caressed that exquisitely sensitive spot.

"More than anything, I love you," he whispered fervently into the curve of my ear as he continued to move his fingers within me in a rhythmic dance.

Over the years, I had become an expert in deception; for eight long decades, I had donned the mask of happiness. In our embrace, I encouraged him further by panting and swaying against him while murmuring sweet but empty promises into his ear.

The same way he did to me.

He flattened my back against the wood of the table, knocking over a nearby plate that shattered on the floor. He threw my dress up around my waist, and then spread my thighs as far as they would go. His claws dug into my skin as he lowered his mouth to my cleft. I arched my back into his mouth, letting a moan escape me.

For years I heard women speak of such pleasure, that it was some sort of mind-blowing experience. I quickly realized that whatever treatment they had been getting from their men, I wasn't getting the same from mine.

Ramses' flat of his tongue circled my entrance as he moved his lips back and forth, his tongue caressing my folds, coaxing me. He sucked on me roughly and my bottom rose from the table in shock. I kept my hands to my sides, he didn't like it when I touched him without his say-so. He pushed his tongue deeper inside me, and I gasped as he moved in and out of my inner walls. He was rough and forceful, and I was never in control.

Never. He moved his head, and my breath caught as his lips brushed over my flower peak. That seemed to be my most sensitive spot. He gently licked and nibbled at my pearl as he moved his mouth over my mound.

My mind wandered away from me—away from this moment, and my body became less and less aware of what was going on. I was only vaguely aware of the feel of his lips and tongue, the feel of his fingers, and the sharp caress of his talon-like fingers gripping my thighs.

I was far away, lost in a fire that I had started in a part of Ember. The ground was a muddied mess of death, the smell of blood and smoke lingered in the air, and I was the only one standing. I could hear the people in their homes screaming, crying, and begging for mercy.

The flames danced in the night, casting elongated shadows that stretched out like the fingers of a giant, clutching the remains of what was once a thriving district of Ember. The fire crackled and roared, a monstrous symphony to accompany the chorus of despair that rose from the heart of the city. I stood there, an architect of ruin, shrouded in the ashen fallout that rained down like a perverse snowfall.

I had laughed at the cruel irony of my existence. To them, I was the harbinger of doom, a specter of destruction that brought nothing but sorrow and devastation. Yet in my heart, I knew the truth. My hands, though stained with the blood of the innocent, were the very hands that held back a greater darkness. Ramses, with his unquenchable thirst for power and bloodshed, would have left nothing but a charred wasteland in his wake.

Didn't they understand that I was merciful?

That had it not been me, it would have been Ramses who would come for them?

A vision of Aquinetta floated in front of me. She had been sad and empty, as she accepted her fate when I had subtly explained it to her. I could see the name of her sister on the tip of her tongue, like the end of a sword. She wanted to say her name.

I would not make that mistake again. I would never know their names. I would never know their faces. I would never know their stories.

A harsh bite on my inner thigh made me snap back to reality and I realized I hadn't moaned in a while. Slowly, I quaked my legs around his head, rolling my lower half and moaning lowly, my hips thrusting into his mouth. A shudder here, and a gasp there, and my performance was done, and a panted breath was all that was left.

Ramses emerged for air, his gaze locked onto mine as a self-satisfied smile danced upon his dampened lips. His hands found their way to my waist before he draped himself over me, our chests meeting. Delivering a tender kiss, he playfully bit my lower lip while situating himself between my thighs. The unyielding length of him pressed against me, his heat radiating and merging with my skin.

"We will have a visitor, in a week or so," he whispered into my ear, while gradually burying himself deeper within me. Our foreheads touched as he took what he desired from me, unapologetic.

"Who is this guest?" I managed to exhale, sinking into a state of surrender.

"A former general of the Empire from beyond the walls, beyond the seas," he grunted in response, his movements becoming more forceful. With every powerful thrust, I could feel myself being pushed further up the table.

"Former?"

"From a long time ago. Empire is long gone, no need for generals then." He clamped his hand over my mouth, silencing my questions. He was done speaking, and in the next moment, he stilled above me, his heavy breathing filling the room.

He withdrew from me, and I felt the coldness of the room in comparison to the heat he had left behind. My thighs were sticky and my body already sore.

"You will lie with him," he said casually, adjusting his pants. There was no room for ambiguity in his tone.

"I thought you meant for me to have a child? Or am I to have him wear a covering?" My question was bold. I was to never go into details about this type of matter.

The memory of my first such encounter under Ramses' orders was still vivid. A mere week after the shield had been brought up, he had presented me as a gift to an outsider. I had pleaded with him to choose a different woman, anyone other than myself. But he struck me, claiming it would be a disgrace.

An insult to whom? The question lingered in my mind, unanswered. Ramses had resolved to revive the ancient customs practiced by his father, a tradition where rulers would grant dignitaries the intimate company of their wives as a sign of trust and alliance. Such a tradition was thought to strengthen bonds between territories and reaffirm the ruler's dominance, showcasing his confidence in his power and his disregard for conventional possessiveness.

Ramses' rationale for reinstating this archaic practice was rooted in political strategy. His father had wielded it as a tool to forge strong coalitions, to display the openness of his court, and to extract secrets from those who believed they had gained the king's intimate favor. By allowing nobles from distant lands to lie with his wife, Ramses' father had created a network of indebted and loyal allies, all the while gathering intelligence and reinforcing his status.

Now, Ramses sought to emulate his father's methods, employing them in a new era where alliances were fragile, and information was as valuable as gold. To him, I was not merely his queen but a crucial piece in the political machinations that would expand our empire's influence.

It was what Joslynn had mentioned all those years ago. That she hoped he loved me enough to never put me through what his mother went through.

He didn't.

My resistance had been futile; the guest, an aged orc from the western highlands, forcefully took what Ramses had yet to claim. The aftermath was painful, requiring healers to tend to my injuries. Since then, Ramses had taken precautions to prevent such harm.

The exchange with the orc had been a transaction devoid of the intelligence Ramses so craved, a gamble on loyalty and brute strength over the subtleties of espionage. Not all dealings yielded the secrets of enemies or distant courts, but sometimes the mere promise of military aid was sufficient to satisfy the appetites of a burgeoning empire.

It was enough to satisfy Ramses.

Bending slightly, Ramses pressed a kiss to my forehead and adjusted my dress back into place, assisting me down from the table. He scoffed at my query. "The man is incapable of fathering children, not in the usual way," he said cryptically, leaving me bewildered.

"For what purpose then? What does this arrangement yield?"

"In exchange for you, we gain knowledge and influence," he said.

His gaze held mine, intense and probing, and I nodded in acknowledgment, understanding what was asked of me. It wasn't like I had a say in the matter.

"And what nature of knowledge?" I ventured with a soft murmur, my pulse racing with a mix of fear and audacity.

Ramses paused, his fingers tracing the wood grain of the table. "Details about a kingdom hidden beyond the wall. Their military strategies, their alliances, their vulnerabilities. Information that could tip the scales in our favor if the need arises."

My curiosity pushed me further. "As in Solaris anew? How can you be certain it's more than mere hearsay? What evidence supports this claim?"

Was I going to be violated again on mere ideas? That is what I wanted to ask.

"How do you know it isn't just some rumor? What proof do you have?" I pressed on, my anxiety setting in. He paused for a moment, weighing his declaration. I could feel the tension in the room, his magic pressing against mine—suffocating.

"Forgive me," I said, schooling my features into an expression of neutrality. "It is not often I am in your company," I said with a slight bow. His magic dissipated slowly, and I could see his face relaxed.

He was always more forgiving after sex.

"You are just nervous about Vryseris going beyond the wall," he proffered the excuse for me. "Forming more alliances and unlocking the general's secrets," he continued. "Your... services will ensure his cooperation. Remember, my queen, our empire was not built on the backs of the complacent, but on the sacrifices of those who understand the greater good."

No. It was built on the Blackwater women lying on their *backs*, I thought with a snarl.

His grip tightened ever so slightly, a warning dressed as an affectionate gesture. "Do not mistake my intentions. This is not about lust or pleasure. It is about securing the future of our dominion, about ensuring that our enemies remain scattered, and our allies remain close." He leaned in, his breath warm against my ear. "And you, my love, are the perfect weapon in this game. Beautiful, cunning, and under the right circumstances, utterly ruthless."

He released me and stepped back, a signal that our conversation was at its end. "Prepare yourself," he instructed. "The general arrives in seven days. Be ready to embrace him as you would embrace me."

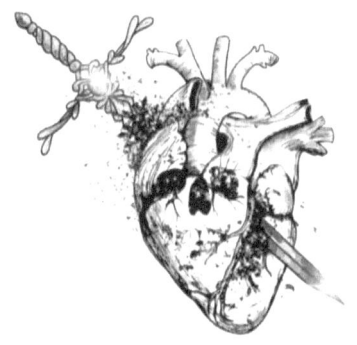

CHAPTER NINETEEN

I had only one request of Ramses; Let me have Joslynn's room untouched. Let no other maidservant be allowed to enter.

Let it be my haven aside from temple.

As I pushed open the heavy mahogany door to Joslynn's old room, a wave of nostalgia hit me. The room was draped in shadows, untouched as promised, a frozen capsule of memories. Dust motes danced in the shaft of sunlight piercing through the half-closed shutters, casting an ethereal glow on the relics of her existence.

I stepped inside, my footsteps muffled by the thick purple rug that still held the faint scent of her lavender perfume—because I would frequently spray it. The walls were adorned with tapestries of vibrant hues, but what caught my eye was her wardrobe. I approached it tentatively, my fingers tracing the intricate carvings on the doors before I pulled them open.

She had the nicest room of all the maidservants. And the nicest wardrobe despite never having worn anything in it. All made by her own hands.

Inside lay a collection of old embroidered dresses, each one more exquisite than the last. The fabric was delicate, the threads still vibrant with the stories they held. I lifted one, the silk slipping through my fingers like liquid. It was the color of the sunset, adorned with tiny pearls that shimmered in the dim light. I held it up against me, and for a moment, I could almost feel Joslynn's presence enveloping me, her laughter a distant echo in the room.

"Blue is a good color on me," I murmured, putting the dress back in its place and searching for a blue shade.

My attention turned to her wooden writing desk, which sat in the corner, the green and gold varnish still shining in the dim light. I ran my hands over the smooth surface, feeling the grain of the wood under my fingertips, imagining her sitting at her desk with a scrunched face as she tried to read a book by faelight.

I pulled open a drawer, just quills, ink bottles, and parchment. I closed it when something caught my eye. A seam along the bottom. I placed the ink wells and parchments on the desks surface and explored the seam with my fingertips. I found purchase on the thin slab of wood and lifted it. A journal. Small and black and uninteresting, nestled at the very bottom. The leather was worn and cracked. I opened it carefully, the pages creaking in protest.

There were sketches of the gardens, of the sea stretching into the horizon, and of Ramses himself, his eyes captured with such intensity that they seemed to stare back at me. An another page, a crude drawing of a map of Ferenz. I flipped a page and there were Servat and Corina with rare smiles on their faces. Carefully, I turned the page, and there was a sketch of a small babe wrapped in a blanket, sleeping soundly. I traced the soft curve of the infant with my finger, careful not to smudge the drawing.

As I delved deeper into the journal, the light-hearted sketches of life and love began to give way to something else, something more sinister. The drawings became frantic, lines etched with a trembling hand, images that chilled me to the bone.

I encountered a page that bore the symbol of Solaris, the rebel king, its rays twisted into a labyrinth of sharp angles and foreboding shadows. The artwork was jarring, an exact opposite to the serene landscapes and portraits that filled the earlier pages. My heart raced as I turned to the next drawing.

It was a woman in a prison cell, her features strikingly familiar, holding a baby to her chest. The moon filtered in through a crack drawn on what could be the ceiling. I felt a lump form in my throat, a sense of dread growing within me as I flipped to the following page.

There, the baby was being taken from the woman's arms, and handed to a shadowy figure whose face was obscured, shrouded in darkness. The servant's outline seemed to absorb the light around it, a void where no details could be discerned. A chill ran down my spine as I continued to the next image.

With each page, the baby grew older, the sketches documenting each stage of childhood with haunting precision. The child's features became clearer, more defined, and eerily familiar. My hands shook as I realized the progression I was witnessing.

And then I reached it—the page that stopped my breath, the revelation that left me reeling. The image was of a young woman, her face a mirror of my own. There was no mistaking it; the journal had been chronicling my life, my growth, from infancy to the present.

The girl was me.

The baby was me.

And that woman in the cell—

I wasn't careful about flipping through the pages anymore, my heart thundering as I ripped a few. There. There.

A curtain of black hair framed her face, her eyes dark with worry. She held the baby in her arms, her body rigid as she watched the servant's hands reaching for her baby. The image was so real, so close, that I could feel the terror in her. A tiny black four-pointed star was carved into the skin of her collarbone.

A sharp pain cut through my chest.

My mother.

This was my mother.

The realization crashed over me like a wave, drowning all the lies I had ever been told in a single, devastating moment. My mother, the woman I had been led to believe had died at my birth, had been imprisoned. Her desperation leaped from the page, her love for me a tangible force that had transcended time and ink.

The journal fell from my hands, landing with a soft thud on the floor.

Tears blurred my vision as I knelt to retrieve the fallen journal, my hands now trembling with a mix of rage and sorrow. How had Ramses fit into this? Had he known the truth all along? Had he been a part of this cruel deception?

Was it our prison that she had been held?

Was she still alive underneath the boards of our home?

I flipped through the pages, past the images of my mother's imprisonment, past the scenes of my childhood. Anger boiled within me, hot and fierce. Every page filled with the symbol of Solaris.

Eldra. Fucking. Solaris.

I ripped the pages from the journal, folding them tightly in my hand, the edges frayed and brittle, before shoving them into the pocket of my robe.

I would tell no one what I found in here.

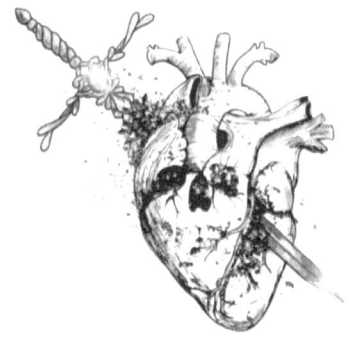

CHAPTER TWENTY

T he Sanctuary of Elrathilion was a place I frequented most days, often to gather tithes from the city's inhabitants.

Mostly to get away from Ramses.

This sacred temple stood proudly in the center, encircled by an opulent garden that flourished with blossoms all year round and never died. The temple rests on a verdant islet on the crystal-clear lake, its graceful spires and otherworldly light mirrored upon the water's surface after dark. A hallowed as its centerpiece—a God's Tree.

I approached the God's Tree at the courtyard's center, its branches stretching toward the heavens as if in supplication. The God's Tree was said to be as old as time itself. Its leaves, a tapestry of shimmering greens and golds rustled with the wisdom of the ages. People from all corners of the city came to whisper their prayers into the bark, believing that the tree carried their words directly to the ears of the deities above.

Elven runes, each one a whisper of ancient power, wove an intricate dance along the pathways and facades of the temple, their silvery glow a beacon for invoking the grace of the heavens and a shield against the capricious whims of celestial beings. Within the hallowed halls of the temple lay sanctuaries dedicated to the Sacred Eight, the pantheon of Elven deities whose favor and wrath shaped the very fabric of our world. Statues sculpted from precious stones, shining jewelry inlaid with gleaming gems, as well as floral offerings and fragrant incense, the temple is a place I often find myself.

The sanctuary of Kamani, the Goddess of Peace, was where I often sought refuge. A haven of serenity within the temple's embrace, her image was carved from a stone so pure, so devoid of earthly taint, that it must have been white jade kissed by the first dawn. She held out a crown of white lilies, a promise of tranquility in her open palms. Her altar was filled with fruits and flowers. On the other side of her statue was Inamak's altar, her twin brother. He had been carved out of her back, as though he were clawing his way out of her. For there could be no good without evil, and Inamak was his sister's counterpart, the embodiment of the dark side of the divine—of balance, of the duality that existed within and around us. His altar was filled with black roses and the bones of animals. Daggers were gifted to him on silver trays, and oftentimes the men would come here and pray for the strength to slay their enemies. He was malice. War.

Ramses' favorite.

Naris, the Goddess of Judgement and Knowledge, stood resplendent within her chamber, a statue of rock crystal that fractured the light into a thousand gleaming shards, mirroring her role as the arbiter of truth. The runes and symbols that graced the walls of her sanctuary were a tapestry of knowledge so complex that it was impossible to tell where one symbol ended and the next began.

It was in this hallowed chamber that souls were weighed, and their fates determined. Naris, with her vacant stare, held a scale in one hand to measure the deeds of a life, and a sword in the other to cut through the veil of ignorance and deceit. Those who sought her wisdom in life were said to be granted insight beyond mortal comprehension.

Upon death, it was Naris' impartial judgment that decided whether a soul was worthy of ascending to the afterlife. The innocent, whose lives were a testament to virtue and the pursuit of knowledge, would find the scales tipped in their favor and be granted passage to their next existence. Their souls, enlightened and unburdened, would depart with her blessing.

In a world where wealth often influenced judgment, the poor faced a harsh reality. Without the means to offer grand tributes or precious gifts, they relied on the purity of their lives and the pursuit of knowledge to tip Naris' scale in their favor. Their offerings were modest—simple tokens of their quest for understanding—and they prayed that the Goddess of Judgement and Knowledge would see the true value of their contributions, not in gold, but in the sincere intent to live a life of wisdom and fairness.

However, those found lacking in truth and wisdom, whose hearts were heavy with unrepentant guilt, would be denied this grace. Instead, they would be consigned to eternal entrapment with Nexus, the enigmatic Goddess of the Underworld, where shadows reigned, and hope withered.

Ruler of Tespar's Hell pits, Nexus' mother's dark legacy, a realm of whispered dread and shadowed secrets, were woven into the very essence of the world's mythology and lore. They were a chasm of despair, a domain of the damned, where the air was thick with the cries of souls who had been judged and found wanting by Naris, the Goddess of Judgement and Knowledge. Tespar spoke of an ancient time when the world was young and the gods walked among mortals. It was during this primordial age that the first darkness took root in the heart of an early goddess, Nexus' mother, Tespar. Legend whispered her name with both reverence and fear, for she was the first to delve into the forbidden arts, to court the shadows in search of power that bordered the divine and the profane.

Driven by an insatiable desire for dominion over life and death, Tespar descended into the depths of the earth, carving out the Hell pits from the very bones of the world. Here, she harnessed the raw energies of darkness, creating a court where even gods dared not tread. As ages passed and her legacy grew, the mantle of ruler over this dark kingdom fell to her daughter, Nexus, who became synonymous with death and the underworld. Nexus, with a heart as cold as the obsidian throne she inherited, presided over the damned with an indifferent gaze. In her realm, the souls of the deceitful and the unrepentant were subjected to the harrowing echoes of their misdeeds, each moment stretching into an endless night.

Her sanctuary was filled with bones, and they covered her obsidian statue in a dark robe that absorbed all light. She appeared in the mural on the walls as a beast of the underworld, among other forbidden creatures. The walls of her sanctuary were decorated.3 with murals depicting the denizens of the shadows—beasts that prowled the edges of nightmares and legends. Werewolves, vampires, and other creatures of the night, once banished from the land and barred from the divine realm, found solace in the embrace of Nexus. They were beings beyond the judgment of Naris, for their dual nature defied the simple scales of mortal deeds and misdeeds.

Such beings were other shifters, like the Furian line. Aislinn Furian was said to be one of these creatures, partial between Fae and beast—those who could take on another form. Had I not seen such a thing for myself, I would have never believed it.

Elenaria's sanctuary was across the hall, and I reluctantly went there to offer my prayers. I pulled the white veil of my cloak over my face as I approached her sanctuary, my head bowed in reverence. The air in Elenaria's sanctuary was heavy with the scent of blooming life, a sweet and potent fragrance that made my nose itch.

Known as the Goddess of fertility, Elenaria was renowned for being the pinnacle of beauty among all Elven deities. Her sanctuary was filled with a beautiful array of flowers and shells from a sea I had never seen, only heard of. The walls were covered in a mural of the goddess holding a child in her arms—the embodiment of maternal grace. There was a small group of women in Elenaria's temple, on their knees, their heads bowed. I knew they were praying for a child of their own, hoping that Elenaria would bless them with a healthy baby.

And here I was, begging for her to forgive me for taking the Moon Potion that was meant to prevent a child. I was going directly against the wishes of my husband and forcing myself to bleed. A mix of Silverweed, Mugwort, Red Clovers, and crushed Moonstone.

My prayer was a paradox, a plea for forgiveness for the life I chose *not* to create.

Forgiveness for denying him this—denying us both. The potion ensured that no life would stir within me, that his seed would find no purchase in the sanctuary that was my womb.

I prayed for her understanding, and for her to look upon me favorably. I prayed for Vryseris' health and well-being—for her to love the child I already had.

"Our Lady Atreya," a priestess said in her soft voice, as I sat in front of the altar. I looked up to see her standing behind me.

"Priestess Andes," I greeted her, as I rose to my feet.

One more aspect that made me enamored with the temple was the sense of unity it had; here, everyone—Fae and human, male and female—found themselves on an equal footing. Even the mighty Ramses couldn't assert his power within the sacred confines of this structure. Numerous felons who sought refuge in this holy sanctuary were given a second chance as Naris forgave them, allowing them to resume their lives outside. However, they would have to spend one hundred and twenty days in the temple unless the Ember guards apprehended them earlier. If they were captured outside the temple walls, they were to be punished by the king's order.

But here, Ramses had no sway.

Priestess Andes graced me with her smile, her honey-hued eyes radiating warmth and kindness. She donned the customary blue attire and headdress reflecting her sacred order, complemented by a magnificent silver crescent moon medallion placed proudly on her chest.

"Are you here for the ceremony?" she asked me.

I furrowed my brow, trying to think of what ceremony she was referring to. She gestured to a small group of people with shaved heads in the corner of the temple. The moment I saw them, I knew what she was talking about. The ceremony was about to begin.

Criminals were about to be released from the temple, having served their one hundred and twenty days in the sacred sanctuary. Ember guards would accompany them outside the temple walls. I could see their scowls and hear their grumbles as they waited for the ceremony to begin.

"What were they in for?" I asked.

Priestess Andres pointed with a slender pale finger and singled out a woman. She was easily distinguishable, her head a shiny dome of guilt with a painted rune upon her head. She was talking quietly to a man, whose face was hidden by a hood. "Her transgressions aren't necessarily of a criminal nature," Andres explained. "She merely succumbed to the seduction of another woman's husband. The outside world will not be kind to her, I fear. But if fortune favors the scorned wife, she might find solace here, far from the King's courts."

I knew what she was referring to. Perhaps the man's wife would find her, and end her life, then escape the persecution by completing her one hundred and twenty days in the temple.

I interjected, "That is if one can substantiate her guilt in the first place."

Andres didn't miss a beat. "The man sprawled on the floor over there? He pilfered from the local inn."

"Ramses would have relieved him of his hands for such audacity," I mumbled.

Priestess Andres turned to me, surveying me. "Do you believe in redemption, in the possibility of reforming criminals?" she asked. I paused to consider her question. There was a part of me that hoped for change, which believed in the power of forgiveness.

In the pursuit of my salvation years ago, I had pledged myself to one hundred and twenty days—I had vowed to spend this time within the sacred confines of the temple. On my knees before the altar, I would offer my supplications, seeking divine absolution for the numerous lives I had taken.

Anything to pacify the haunting echoes of the people's screams.

However, I had found that the solemn tranquility of the temple, an environment I had thought would be my sanctuary, began to feel more like a prison. The echoing silence and the cold, hard stones bore down on me. The temple walls started to close in on me.

Beneath the temple, there lay a network of simple bunkers carved into the earth, where we were to rest each night. The sleeping quarters were modest, with pallets of straw serving as beds, each accompanied by a single woolen blanket to stave off the chill of the underground.

The bunkers were segregated by gender to maintain the propriety expected within the temple's sacred grounds. Women and men resided in separate chambers, their interactions limited to the communal areas and during the ceremonies and prayers.

I glanced at the shaven-headed individuals, each one preparing to step back into a world that might not accept them, that might not understand the transformation they had undergone within these walls. Their heads, now bare, symbolized a rebirth, the shedding of their past selves, and the beginning of a new chapter.

And then there was the matter of *my* hair. The traditions of the temple dictated a shaven head. It was a price I was initially willing to pay. But as the time drew closer, I found myself recoiling at the thought. The shame of a shaven head, the loss of my crowning glory, was a humiliation I wasn't prepared to endure. It was a tangible sacrifice, a visible symbol of my remorse, and somehow, that made it all the more *real*.

Yet, in the kingdom of Ember, my actions were not viewed through the lens of moral judgment. I was the queen—my position afforded me certain privileges, certain immunities. The king himself sanctioned my deeds, his approval reinforcing my authority to kill those slaves that had run from us. The rebels in the arena. My actions, no matter how questionable, were not considered *criminal*, but rather the necessary conduct of a ruler. The lives I claimed were seen as a means to an end, a necessary evil to maintain the balance of power.

Of Ramses' power.

Each person was assigned the duty of emptying and cleaning another's chamber pot. I had never seen such a thing. Our plumbing in the castle was a luxury I missed.

I lasted ten whole days before Ramses came to the temple steps and I practically ran to him—breathing in the air of the outside.

This complicated dance between personal guilt and public duty, between my conscience and my crown, was a constant struggle.

I wondered whether Ramses were to endure one hundred and twenty days of temple penitence, could ever truly change.

"No," I answered her finally, "I don't believe they can be reformed. In my view, they seek refuge in the temple, using it as a loophole to evade their just punishment."

Priestess Andes nodded, a look of melancholy creeping into her features. She reached out to touch my shoulder, her touch feather-light. Although she wasn't native to Ember, she had journeyed here from a land beyond our walls, many moons ago.

"Punishment is inescapable," she murmured. "If justice fails to catch up with them in this life, it will undoubtedly find them in the next. They say that the body is cleansed of the old self every eight years."

"Why eight?"

She shrugged. "Eight years. Eight deities. Who knows? Who knows if any of it is true at all? It is about faith. Faith that there can be change. The bad has a way of finding us, and the good is something that is worked for."

I wondered how long it would take for mine to catch up with me.

I placed my hand in my dress pocket, feeling for the folded drawing of my mother and me as a baby. It was my only possession that was truly mine.

●

Spanning an expanse that could contain a small village, the court-yard was encased by a grand colonnade of stone pillars. The court-yard's surface a mosaic of cobblestones, worn smoothly by cen-turies of use. They bore the mark of countless claws leaving and landing on the space. At the far end of the courtyard, was a wide pathway, lined with torches that flickered eternally, leading to one of the back entries to the Dragon Keep.

Siorsen was prowling back and forth along the edge of the court-yard, occasionally pausing to study me with a sneer. He would inhale deeply, then resume his pacing. Four other dragons stood nearby, their heads swiveling to follow his every move. Even the other dragons seemed to be keeping their distance from him, their eyes darting nervously.

He was no common beast—he never was. A creature of im-mense size, the length of a longship, with a wingspan that could shroud a small village in shadow all on his own. His scales, the color of blood, dark and gleaming, tough as the hardest steel, and as impenetrable as the thickest fortress wall. Onyx horns jutted from his head like a crown, and jagged scars marked his jaw—trophies of countless battles he had emerged from undefeated. His teeth, rows of sharp daggers, could rend the toughest armor as if it were parch-ment. His fiery breath could reduce a thriving forest to smoldering ashes in mere moments. His vast wings beat with a thunderous force that could whip up a gale, and his spiked, lethal tail struck with the power of a catapulted boulder.

Every time I looked at these dragons, it was as if I were seeing them for the first time. You never truly get used to seeing something that is so immense and so powerful.

The soldiers were carefully setting up the large saddle on a ladder to be put on the dragon's back that would hold Ramses and Vrys in place. Siorsen craned his long neck and snapped his jaws at a guard, his giant teeth chattering as he did so. The guard, a large man with a massive, scarred face, jumped back with a startled yelp.

"This is a horrible idea," I muttered, eyeing the dragon warily.

"Father says Siorsen doesn't like Agir, and that he did that patchwork on his face." Vrys cocked his head. "Said that Agir got one of Siorsen's hatchlings killed during the War of Fallen Skies." He waved a hand at the four dragons that were keeping their distance from Siorsen. "They are all that remain from that clutch."

A loud chittering followed Siorsen's rumbling. One of Siorsen's sons—the oldest— Tiamut—who I knew well, was chittering back. The second-largest dragon in our kingdom, only surpassed in size by Siorsen himself. Tiamut, with his mottled red scales, his single black horn on his snout, and swishing tail of dagger spikes, reared his head in response to Siorsen.

The skin of their necks vibrated and the scales on their backs rippled.

"They are talking," Vrys said, amazed.

"I'm surprised Agir is still around." I wasn't really. I am sure that Ramses kept Agir around to serve Siorsen on purpose. It made me uneasy how calculated Siorsen and Ramses were. "Siorsen is not one to forget. Nor forgive, it seems."

As if on cue, Siorsen locked onto Agir again. He snarled a guttural and primal sound that echoed across the courtyard. The guards around Siorsen tensed, their hands reflexively going to their weapons.

As if that could ever save them if Siorsen decided to do something rash.

Tiamut exhaled and lowered his head, his body language seemingly resigned.

I knew that feeling—of talking to a brick wall.

Agir swallowed hard, a bead of sweat trickling down his scarred face. He took a step back, then another. Siorsen watched him, a low growl rumbling in his throat.

"Perhaps it would be wise to have someone *else* assist Siorsen today I suggested. I did not like the idea of provoking the dragon any further—especially with my son involved. Vrys was supposed to be traveling on that thing's back today.

"Siorsen," Ramses shouted, booming across the courtyard. The dragon turned his head to look at him, his nostrils flaring. "Enough," he commanded. He had a natural knack for asserting his dominance on everything.

Even Siorsen, with his raw, primal power, seemed to acknowledge Ramses' authority.

The dragon huffed, a low growl rumbling deep within his chest. But, contrary to what I had expected, Siorsen backed down. His massive wings folded neatly at his sides, his tail stopped thrashing, and the threatening growl quieted to a low hum.

Vrys and I watched in stunned silence as Ramses approached the dragon, his riding gear tightly fitted on him the same way it was for every other rider.

"Agir, step back," Ramses ordered, his focus never leaving the dragon. The scarred guard didn't need to be told twice. He quickly retreated, giving Siorsen a wide berth.

Then, Ramses turned to another guard, a younger man with a less hardened look about him. "Bael, you assist Siorsen today." The young man, Bael, nodded nervously and stepped forward, climbing the ladder and finishing the ties on the saddle.

"Vrys, you hold onto the pommels, and don't let go. And stay close to your father at all times," I instructed, tugging the cloak tighter around his shoulders.

I thought back to how Ramses had left me to Servat's care, twice and cringed. Servat was a formidable fighter in his own right, but Vrys was untried and just a boy.

"I'll be fine, Mother." His excitement was palpable.

Ramses flexed his hands in his leather riding gloves. "Stop babying the boy," he admonished me, placing his riding helm on his head. A new crystal visor was already in place, pulled down so I could the top half of his face.

"Mothers fuss, my King," a man at Ramses' side laughed. Ramses scowled at him, and the man laughed *harder*. I smiled too.

Captain Servat had become a man of considerable stature, his broad shoulders and muscular build evidence of years spent in the King's army. His hair was a wild mane of white-blonde that complimented his dark bronze skin. A single scar that never healed ran down the expanse of his face—from his right eyebrow, down to his chin. He folded his arms over his chest, revealing the silver scar of a bite mark—from *that* day. He could have healed that with salve, but instead, he wore my bit on him like a tattoo. His eyes, however, were still the same, even as the battles and I had marked him. They were a clear ice-blue—sometimes steel—that sparkled with mirth and kindness, a softness that belied the harsh exterior of a seasoned warrior.

He had grown in the years I had known him.

Like Ramses, his father before him fathered many bastards. Servat was one of them.

Despite being born of different mothers, Ramses and Servat shared a striking resemblance, the same chiseled jawline, and the same hawk-like look about them. They were two different sides of the same coin.

Ramses was reserved, serious, and harsh—one who turned his nose at anything less than perfect. Servat, on the other hand, was a free spirit, a warrior at heart, who found joy in the simplest of things.

Ramses, while he respected his half-brother's abilities as a soldier, found his carefree attitude and constant joviality grating.

I found it *immensely* attractive.

He carried himself with an easy confidence, every movement deliberate and purposeful. His laughter, like his personality, was infectious, eliciting smiles from even the strictest of guards.

"I could always come with you," I said. He surveyed me from head to toe, his concentration lingering on my face before side-eyeing Ramses for a reaction.

Ramses snorted. "You on dragon-back? Beyond the wall in a camp?" His tone was disapproving. I shrugged, my shoulders sloping.

Even Siorsen chuffed.

"Perhaps I could be of use out there. I mean, it would be nice to see a bit of the world again," I said. "It wouldn't be the first time I have ridden a dragon," I reminded him carefully.

Freedom.

Ramses laughed, a hearty, condescending sound that echoed across the stone walls of the courtyard. "You forget what happened the last time?" He shook his head, almost gleaming with arrogance. "You'd be more of a liability than an asset."

"What happened last time?" Vrys asked curiously.

"Your mother thought herself a war general, and came up with a plan that had a great misstep," Ramses said. I winced and he continued, "She almost died that day."

"I did not," I said quietly.

"She exposed her powers to a man who had no business knowing them, and because that man was obsessed with your mother, the shield around Ember was put in place."

An obsession he claims. I had not heard a whisper that Eldra was still after me.

Servat crossed his arms over his chest. His face was impassive, his expression unreadable. "There will need to be someone in the King's stead," he said to me.

"That's right." Ramses huffed. He strode over to Vrys, "You're made for this, boy. Not like your mother, always hiding behind her books and temple. She's gotten soft over the years." He patted our son's shoulder, a heavy, affirming gesture that was meant to instill confidence. Ramses smirked, his gaze sliding over me dismissively. "The world out there is raw and brutal, not fit for delicate creatures like yourself."

I watched as Ramses turned his back to me, dismissing my words and my presence as easily as one might discard a worn-out piece of cloth. His arrogance was like a cold wind, chilling and relentless. But I was not the delicate creature he thought me to be—or wanted me to be.

"Delicate creatures don't survive in *this* world, Ramses I called after him, my voice steady and resolute. He paused but didn't turn around. I took it as an invitation to continue. "They don't raise children, or run a kingdom while their husbands are off playing at war. I am the one who sent Eldra fleeing. Me."

The courtyard fell silent, the men shifting uncomfortably in their armor. Servat tilted his head, a small smile creeping onto his face. Ramses turned slowly, a scowl etched deep into his hardened features. He looked at me, seeing me anew for the first time in a long while.

"And they certainly don't put up with arrogant kings," I added. A murmur rippled through the gathering, and I saw surprise register on Ramses' face. *Good*, I thought, *let him be surprised*.

I walked over to Vrys, who was watching the exchange warily. I knelt to his level, placing a gentle hand on his shoulder. "Remember this, Vrys," I said softly, "Strength isn't determined by the size of your sword or the might of your magic."

"But..." Vrys started, his voice wavering as he glanced between me and his father. His eyes were filled with confusion and a hint of fear. I squeezed his shoulder gently, encouraging him to speak his thoughts.

"But what?" I prodded gently.

"But father says... he says that to rule, you must be the strongest. The most powerful."

I sighed, shaking my head slightly. "Your father is a warrior, Vrys. He sees the world through the lens of war. It's all about conquering and power for him. But the world is much more than that, and so is ruling."

I stood up, turning to face Ramses who was watching us with a dark expression. I didn't back down. I couldn't. Not when there was so much at stake.

"Ruling isn't just about strength, Ramses," I said. "It's about wisdom, compassion, and understanding. It's about knowing when to fight, and when to make peace."

Ramses snorted, crossing his arms over his chest. "And you think you know better?" He challenged with contempt.

"I know what I've learned," I replied. "And I know what I've seen. Strength without wisdom is nothing more than brute force. And brute force alone cannot rule a kingdom."

"Spoken like a Queen. A good king has a good partner beside them," Servat added, a hint of a smile on his face.

"A good wife knows when to be quiet. She knows when to listen, and when to speak. She thinks she knows what it would take. She's killed *one* Elite rebel, a few dozen petty rebels, and a handful of soldiers while I have killed thousands," Ramses snapped. "If not for me, she would not even have the title of Furian Slayer." He turned to Vrys, "Get on the saddle boy. Need to get moving before daybreak."

I hadn't realized we were keeping score of our *death shrouds*.

Vrys looked from his father to me, uncertainty clouding his young face. I gave him a reassuring smile, nodding slightly while biting the inside of my cheek.

Siorsen lowered his front leg, giving Vrys leverage to climb him. Ramses followed and settled in behind Vrys, showing him how to properly position his legs.

I knew enough to not fuss over Vrys at that moment. I was to just quietly dismiss myself from the courtyard.

Servat came up next to me, Tiamut slowly stomping his way over to him. With practiced ease, Servat hoisted himself onto the dragon's back, finding a comfortable position between the ridges of Tiamut's scales.

"You're testing his ire with the prince present. You shouldn't do that, my Lady." Servat whispered, his tone soothing and sympathetic.

"I know that all too well," I replied.

With a powerful thrust, Siorsen and Tiamut launched into the sky, leading the other three riders. Their wings beat the air with a thunderous sound.

As I watched them soar off into the distance, I prayed silently that my son would come back whole.

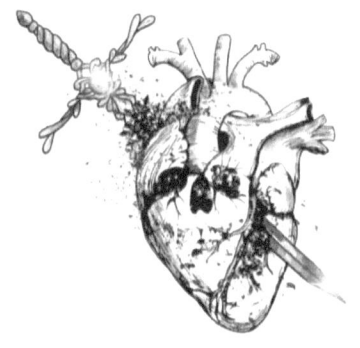

CHAPTER
TWENTY-ONE

B arely a day had passed since they'd left when I found myself
drawn to the gates, my mind a whirlwind of worry. I'd been
left in charge of Ember before, but never without Vrys. And truth
be told, I wasn't really in charge with the ever-present shadow of
Ramses' potential return dictating my every step.

I tried to go through the gates. To go after them. To bring back
Vrys behind the safety of the city walls.

What had I been thinking? That I could ever escape this place?
When the reality of it was, I was now *scared* to leave. No matter
how much I tried to convince myself otherwise, the unknown was
terrifying. A thousand grim possibilities unfurled in my mind like
a tapestry of dread.

So there I stood at the gates, their ironwork cold and indifferent,
my feet refusing to cross the threshold. The guards watched me
pace, a frown on my lips, my hands wringing the hem of my

dress—a floral frock cinched at the waist with a silk ribbon, utterly impractical for the journey beyond the walls.

What did lie beyond? I had only ever seen it from the sky, on the back of a dragon, or blurred by the rush of battle.

Vrys was beyond these gates. He was out in the vast unknown, and I had to find him.

I had to bring him back to my side. Protect him from the horrors I had seen myself all those years ago.

Solaris Soldiers wouldn't spare the son of Ramses Blackwater.

The paper I had tucked into my sleeve seemed to burn against my skin, and I touched it repeatedly.

That bubble of anxiety started swelling in my chest and wouldn't ease. This was about more than just me or my fears. So, I steeled myself, pushing back the fear that threatened to consume me. I took a deep breath and attempted to cross the threshold.

But as soon as my foot crossed the boundary, an invisible force slammed into me. The warding magic, Ember's unseen shield, had lashed out. I was thrown backward, skidding across the cobblestones, pain flaring across my back. The guards looked on, their faces a mix of shock and worry. My breath came in jagged gasps, my palms stung, and the magic's energy left my head swimming.

"What is this?" I asked, tentatively reaching for the lattice of metal.

A soldier nearby helped me up and bowed. "Lady, if you please, step back from the threshold."

"I'm going out."

"If you leave, that will leave Ember open to any threats," he said.

"I don't think you are hearing me. I. Am. Going. OUT." Some rational part of me that was still there knew it wasn't their fault.

Another stepped toward us. "Please. The king would be most displeased if you left Ember without a proper escort."

They were still trying to keep up the illusion that there was a choice in the matter.

"You will let me leave, or I'll blast you into oblivion," I threatened, glaring at the soldier. Maybe if I threatened them enough, they would show me the way out.

The soldier took a step back, his eyes wide at my threat. But he didn't back down. "I understand your frustration, Lady, but we have our orders. We are to keep everyone safe within Ember's walls."

"I am not 'everyone,'" I retorted.

The soldiers exchanged glances. I knew they were following orders, but my patience was wearing thin. Every second wasted here was another second Vrys was out there, potentially in danger.

"Send for an escort then," I said, my tone brokering no argument. "But I am leaving Ember."

The soldiers hesitated momentarily before one of them nodded, turning to send for an escort. I wanted to see how long they would keep up the charade. Who would they send to escort me?

I crossed my arms, tapping my foot impatiently as I waited. The protective barrier hummed with energy, a reminder of the invisible wall between me and Vrys.

This was a new type of hell.

After an eternity, a small group of soldiers arrived, their armor glinting under the city lights and floating lanterns of the path. The leader of the group, a tall woman with a beautiful, stern face, approached me.

"Corina," I said, not hiding my annoyance.

"My Lady. I was informed you were requesting an escort to *leave* Ember." She leered at me.

"I was."

"As the King's Advisor—I would advise that that is a bad idea," she said, the smugness of her tone obvious.

"Well, as the *King's* Advisor, you should know I don't need your advice," I shot back.

Corina's smirk faltered, replaced by a look of surprise.

"Well," Corina replied, regaining her composure. "Even if you are determined to leave, the warding magic around Ember will not allow it. The wards are designed to keep out threats and our people safe within the city walls."

I wanted to laugh at her then, wondering if she truly believed that.

"I am not a threat," I said, "And I am not just 'our people.' I have the right to leave."

Corina's smirk returned, a glint of amusement in her green eyes. "The wards don't work on rights or titles, my Lady. They work on magic and intent. If the magic deems you should stay, then you will stay." She threw her braided red hair over her shoulder.

Out of the arena, but still surrounded by lions. Comical.

I glared at her, my anger flaring. "And who decides that? You?"

Say it, say it, say it. Say it is Ramses.

Corina shrugged, her smugness irking me further. "Not me, my Lady. The magic does. It bends to the will of our king."

There it is.

This was not going to go as I had planned—not that I had a detailed plan in the first place.

"Well then. I am the queen. I should be able to go where I want to." I raised my hands, palms up, inviting her to argue that point.

She scoffed. "And how far are you planning to go in your pretty dress, heels, and nothing packed? Not a horse or an ass to ride on. Enough with this hysteria and go back inside." She clicked her tongue in annoyance as she had always done when we were younger and flipped her hand at me.

I gathered the hem of my dress in my hands and whirled around. I marched towards the gate, hoping I wasn't as trapped here as I thought. All these years of avoiding this because what if...

What if I might never see the world beyond Ember's embrace? That I might never know the expanse of sky unmarred by the shadow of these walls?

What if. What if.

I could feel Corina watching me as I approached the boundary, the humming energy of the wards growing louder with each step I took. I reached the threshold and paused, taking a deep breath.

The wards reacted immediately, a surge of energy pushing against me. But I stood my ground, pushing back with my magic. I could feel the wards testing me, probing my intent, my resolve.

I placed my hand on the gate opening and pushed.

There was a waning noise, a rushing air sound, and nothing.

I was standing alone. Dusk had turned to midnight, and the skies filled with stars. I looked to my right, to the city gate, an open mouth of blackness.

I turned to look at Ember, its stone towers and houses bathed in the moon's ethereal light. Usually buzzing with life, the city was eerily silent, its inhabitants frozen in their tracks. Lanterns hung suspended in mid-air; their flames were static, casting long, still shadows on the cobblestone streets.

Even the air around me felt different—like it had solidified, undisturbed by wind or movement. It was an uncanny calm, a silence so profound that I could hear my heartbeat echoing in my ears.

I stepped forward, the sound of my footfall unnaturally loud in the silent world. The ground beneath my feet felt solid and real, unaffected by the temporal suspension around me.

Looking up, I saw the stars twinkling in the night sky, unaffected by the time freeze. They seemed to be the only source of movement, their light a constant in this frozen world.

Suddenly, the darkness around me seemed to come alive, the shadows morphing and twisting, taking form before me. A pair of monstrous jaws materialized out of the inky blackness, filled with rows of razor-sharp teeth. Each tooth was as large as a sword, their edges honed to a lethal point, glistening ominously under the moonlight. It was as if time had been startled back into motion, the chilling echo of the monstrous jaws stretching out into the infinite quiet. The dragon—for it could be nothing else—regarded me with those blazing eyes, its gaze unblinking and intense.

Another step. Then another. With each step, the dragon loomed larger, its form filling my vision.

A gleam of black scales. With an elegance that seemed out of place in such a gargantuan creature, it lowered its head, assessing me. Now, I could see the intricate patterns on its scales, how they overlapped like the toughest armor, and how they seemed to absorb all light.

The air grew heavier. The silence stretched taut as a bowstring, only to be shattered by the dragon's low growl. The sound was deep and resonant, a rumble that echoed from the very bowels of the earth, reverberating through the ground beneath my feet.

My heart was pounding against my rib cage, but I stood still.

"No." The simplicity of the word stunned me. The dragon—this ancient, monstrous creature, had *spoken*.

"I—what? What is this?" I stammered.

"Not yet," the dragon repeated, its booming hiss echoing, bouncing off the city walls and fading into the still air. "Not yet.

The time will come. The path you seek is not ready for your steps. Not yet."

It never moved its mouth.

"Who are you?" I whispered.

The dragon's eyes seemed to soften, a profound sadness passing through them. I had never known a dragon to show emotion other than rage. "You do not know me. But I know you. Furian Slayer."

"Don't call me that," I snapped.

It rumbled at that.

With that, it raised its massive head towards the sky, its gaze leaving me before taking off, and in the blink of an eye, I was back in the dusk's light, my hand suspended mid-air, the wards of the gate still intact.

A snort erupted behind me, pulling me out of my stunned silence. Corina and the guards were there, a smug smile twisting her painted lips. I stood there, my mouth hanging open, my mind racing to comprehend what just happened.

Had I just communicated with a dragon? Or was it a figment of my imagination, a byproduct of the warding magic? No one else reacted.

No one else had seen what I had seen.

With a deep sigh, I lowered my hand.

"Not yet," I whispered, echoing the dragon's message.

"What was that you said?" Corina chirped.

"I've changed my mind. I will wait," I said, leaving. Corina followed behind me, but I didn't care. I knew I would hear her mouth when we returned to the castle.

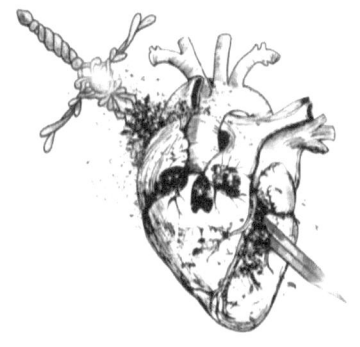

CHAPTER
TWENTY-TWO

As predicted, Corina quickened her pace to catch up with me, her boots clicking sharply on the stone. "Well, that was quite the performance," she said with a raised eyebrow. "Tell me, what made you change your mind? You, with your lofty titles and royal blood, scared off by dirt and trees?" Corina's disdain was palpable.

"I don't recall you ever stepping into the arena to fight. For that matter, I don't recall ever seeing you in the fight at Hyperion, or with Eldra," I seethed.

Corina rolled her eyes. "My magic would serve no purpose out there," she said.

"Your presence serves me no purpose in here," I countered.

Corina's laughter was sharp, a staccato note that echoed off the stone walls surrounding us. "Oh, how the mighty do fall," she taunted. "From queen to quitter in the span of a heartbeat. I expected more anger from you, *cousin*."

"I do not quit," I said through gritted teeth. "I merely choose my battles wisely, something you would do well to learn. Unlike you, I do not require the validation of an audience to feel secure in my decisions."

Corina loved to show off and gossip to anyone who would listen. She needed to have the finest clothes, the finest jewels, and be the center of attention. Her smirk wavered, a flicker of irritation crossing her features. "Validation? Please, we both know you seek approval with every breath you take. The adoring public, the loyal court, the fawning council."

How wrong she was. The public used to adore me. Now they feared me. The court was never loyal to me, and the council was another matter entirely. "Your pettiness serves no one."

She scoffed, flipping her braided red hair over her shoulder with practiced arrogance. "Petty? I'd say I'm being rather gracious, considering I haven't yet mentioned the absurdity in which you gawk upon Servat."

I stopped in my tracks, facing her fully. "You wouldn't dare," I said, the threat clear in my voice. Ice flooded my veins.

Corina tilted her head, her lips curling into a malicious grin. "Oh, cousin, it's plain for all to see," she continued, her tone dripping with false sweetness. "You may be careful with your glances, but our dear Servat is not so skilled in hiding his affections."

I felt my composure threaten to crumble, my private concerns laid bare for Corina's scrutiny. "And what of it?" I asked. "The king has his alliances, and I have mine."

Corina's laugh was a cold, mirthless sound. "*Alliances*? Is that what we're calling it now?" She stepped closer, and I could see the gleam of triumph in her smirk. "Our king may not mind sharing his wife when it benefits him, but be warned—Servat is already treading on dangerous ground. Ramses does not take kindly to those who covet what is his. Not when it isn't offered."

"Your concern is noted," I replied, my tone icy. "But Servat is loyal to Ember, and his intentions are honorable. He poses no threat to the king."

Corina stepped back, her grin widening. "Of course, of course. But I would hate to see our valiant Servat crushed under Ramses' boot for a mere... misunderstanding. You should take care, lest your 'alliance' bring him to ruin. Ramses does not like to share his toys unless there is a better toy to be had."

I flinched at that last part. She knew why.

"I appreciate your... insight," I said, allowing a hint of sarcasm to color my words. "But I assure you, my priorities remain with the kingdom and its well-being."

Corina nodded, her expression one of mock sincerity. "Of course, my queen. Your dedication is beyond reproach. Just remember, the eyes of Ember are always watching."

With the weight of our conversation hanging between us like a drawn sword, Corina and I continued our walk toward the heart of the castle. The grand doors to the throne room, guarded by two soldiers, opened by themselves as we approached.

Vaulted ceilings rose high above, adorned with intricate frescoes that told the history of Ember. Or whatever history Ramses had rewritten.

Rays of the setting sun filtered through the stained glass windows, casting a mosaic of light across the polished marble floor.

Ramses' throne, his authority, was centered on a raised dais. Adorned with gold, precious stones, and cushioned with the finest lambskins. What once was Pearl Glass was now a framework of iron.

The metalwork was a masterpiece, capturing the curves and lines of a feminine figure, yet there was an unsettling quality to it—one that was familiar. The arms of the throne, resembling a woman's own, reached out, almost as if beckoning or warning those who approached. An iron face of a woman, her features etched in great detail. Her expression was one of agony, a silent scream captured in metal, her face twisted and her mouth, caught in an eternal moment of pain. The first time Ramses displayed his new throne, my heart stopped.

It was in my likeness.

At its foot, almost as an afterthought, was my humble yellow pillow. Ramses never had a throne placed for me, for I was never his equal.

Ignoring the traditional decorum, I picked up my pillow and placed it on the throne, settling down comfortably. There was a thrumming beneath my skin that sent gooseflesh rippling across my skin.

Corina eventually broke my reverie. "King Ramses won't be happy to learn you tried to *leave* Ember." She looked at her red-painted nails with a nonchalant air, as if discussing trivial matters.

"Corina, I'm sure you would have managed just fine without me," I retorted, refusing to be pulled back into her manipulative games.

She shot back, "You would have embarrassed the crown prince and the whole Blackwater clan. You aren't befitting the name."

I couldn't help but laugh at her audacity. "I would gladly relinquish the name," I shot back, making myself comfortable on the throne.

She scowled, fixated on the throne and the audacious sight of me sitting there. "You sit on the throne, like a Blackwater."

I merely smiled, enjoying the disquiet in her face. For once, the power dynamics had shifted, and it was Corina who was standing before me, while I occupied the throne. It was a small victory, but a satisfying one, nonetheless.

"Indeed, I do sit on this throne," I replied, "As a Blackwater, Corina, as much as we both detest it. As Atreya. And isn't it fitting that I sit here?"

The olive green of her irises darkened with her growing annoyance. "You have no right—"

"But I do," I interjected. "I may not carry the blood of the Blackwaters, but, like it or not, the name is mine. I have more of a right to sit here than you do." I ran my fingers up the throne's iron arms.

Corina huffed, her painted nails tapping against her arm in a rhythmic pattern that echoed her growing frustration. But before she could retort, the grand doors of the throne room creaked open.

The guards filed in, their faces a mask of surprise at the sight of me on the throne. Behind them, the courtiers followed, their whispers filling the room. The news of my audacious act would soon spread through Ember like wildfire. I could already imagine the shock and the scandal it would cause.

No woman had *ever* sat the throne.

I had never attempted to before.

But I remained seated, the throne beneath me feeling more comfortable than the pillow ever had.

"My Queen. There is a matter of murder and thievery that is to be discussed," a guard at the front of the line said.

Corina, ever the viper, slithered in front of me, her words dripping with false concern. "Allow me, my queen. I can handle this"

"I *will* handle this," I corrected.

Corina turned, her mock bow an insult veiled in courtesy. "Yes. It is a matter of *thievery* after all. You can handle it."

The guard's announcement hung heavy in the air, followed by Corina's underhanded comment. The room held its breath, all the focus on me, waiting for my response. But I remained composed, never faltering from Corina.

"Indeed, Corina," I said, echoing in the vast chamber. "As you've pointed out, I'm quite familiar with thievery. After all, isn't that how the Blackwaters have ruled Ember all these years?"

A gasp echoed through the room as courtiers and guards alike registered my words. Corina's face paled, her sneer faltering as she realized her barbs had lost their sting.

Turning my attention to the guard, I gestured for him to approach. "Please, tell me about this matter," I commanded.

The guards parted, revealing a woman who had her head bowed and her hands bound behind her. "Madame Giselle Stone. Wife to Bertrand Stone. Accused of murdering her husband, and stealing his property, which she claims is her rightful inheritance. She was caught before entering the Sanctuary of Elrathilion."

The room fell into a hushed silence as the guards led the accused forward. Madame Giselle Stone, a woman known for her charm and beauty, was a pitiful sight. Her gown, once a symbol of her status, was now stained with mud from being dragged through the streets of Ember.

The courtiers watched with morbid fascination, holding their fans in front of their faces like fluttering, startled birds. The women whispered behind their screens with scandalized curiosity. The throne room had turned into a stage for what would be the talk of Ember.

Ramses would have given her one minute to explain her case, and then make a decision.

I observed Giselle. She had been a vibrant presence in the court, her laughter infectious, her spirit unmatched. Every woman wanted to be her. But the woman who stood before me now was a shadow of her former self, broken and accused.

"Madame Stone," I addressed carefully, "You stand accused of serious crimes. Murder and theft are grave charges."

She raised her head, slowly. Her bound hands clenched in her resolve. "I did not murder Bertrand," she said, trembling. "The property was mine. It was our shared wealth, not just his."

I cocked my head and asked the guard nearest to me, "How did Bertrand die?"

"Poison in his wine."

"How do we know it was the wine that killed him?"

The guards exchanged another look. "We have an eyewitness, my Queen."

Giselle scoffed and then let out a haughty laugh.

"Who is the witness?" I asked.

"The witness, my Queen, is Madame Isla." The guard tugged on a rope and a woman stumbled forward. Her head was lowered, a blush creeping along her cheeks. She wore a beautiful gown of pale blue, and when she lifted her head, her cloaked hood fell, revealing her shaven head.

She had been crying.

This was the woman I had seen in the temple. The one Priestess Andes and I had discussed.

"Madame Isla," I called out, echoing across the room so others would hear, "You are named as the eyewitness to this crime. But you also have a direct connection to the deceased. Can you shed some light on this situation?"

"Yes, my Queen," she replied, barely above a whisper. She cleared her throat and began, "I served Bertrand...and loved him," she confessed, her lips trembling.

"She is a harlot!" Giselle screamed out with a pointed finger. A guard pulled on her bindings to quiet her.

The room erupted into a riot of gasps and murmurs at Giselle's outburst. Madame Giselle flinched, her pale face growing even paler. She looked down at her hands, her fingers twisting the fabric of her simple gown.

"Silence!" I shouted, cutting through the noise like a blade. The room fell quiet.

Good. Let them be afraid of me.

I turned to Giselle, her face flushed with anger and humiliation. "Giselle, you will have your chance to speak. Let Madame Isla finish."

I could see the defiance in her, but she remained silent, her murderous sneer fixed on Isla. I nodded at Isla, encouraging her to continue. She swallowed, throat bobbing.

"Bertrand and I... we were in love," she continued, a bit steadier now. "He was unhappy in his marriage, and he found solace with me. But he loved Giselle too, in his own way."

Giselle scoffed at that.

"On the morning of his death, I served him his favorite wine. He took a sip and...he just...," she recounted, taking a shaking breath. "I didn't know what happened. It was only later...when the guards arrived and...and they found poison in his glass."

"Who found him dead?" I asked.

"I did," she answered.

"And who called the guards?"

"I did," Giselle replied.

"Where were you, Giselle?"

"Waiting for the guards outside."

"So you saw Isla in your home and then called the guards?"

She nodded and I turned back to Isla. "Why did you not call the guards? And You stayed behind?"

"After everything that had happened... serving time away in the temple. I didn't want to be accused of his murder. No. I did not call the guards, but I did not leave either."

"I see," I finally said, breaking the silence. "So, you stayed away to avoid false accusations, yet here we are."

Isla glanced up, a silent plea upon her trembling lips. But I had to stay impartial. As Queen, it was my duty to ensure justice, not to offer sympathy.

I turned my attention back to Giselle, who still stood with her head bowed, her hands wringing the fabric of her dress. "Giselle," I started, "Did you see anyone else with Bertrand? Anyone who might have had access to his wine?"

"No."

"And the healers have concluded it is Adderdale poison? Why?" I motioned with my finger for a healer to come forward, his white robes blending in with the white marble flooring.

"Adderdale has distinct properties. When the flowers are ingested, it has a bitter taste. The flavor could be masked in the wine, and colorless. But when it comes into contact with iron it turns a bright purple." He demonstrated by taking a vial of the poison from his pocket and then a metal rod, small, and made of iron. Undoing the cork, he put the rod in the vial and stirred. The liquid started off as clear as water and then turned a bright purple. "They have a wooden table with iron nails. Some of those nails have turned purple, where the spilled wine was."

I watched as he re-corked the vial and stepped back, the gravity of his words sinking in.

Adderdale—a beautiful black flower and deadly poison. And the purple stains on the iron nails of the table where Bertrand had taken his last sip of wine were damning evidence. The bitter taste of the poison could have easily been masked by the sweet flavor of the wine, but its deadly effects were only revealed too late.

The murder of Bertrand wasn't just a crime of passion, it was premeditated and carefully planned. But who could have done it? Who had the knowledge and the motive?

This would have all been very entertaining if it were a play.

"And the matter of the estate? What is this about theft?" I asked.

"Lady Stone approached one Abigail Heath, asking if she would be interested in buying out the estate," a guard said. "*Before* Bertrand had been killed."

"We were teetering on the edge of poverty!" Giselle shouted. "Bert knew that I was looking for a buyer! All that gambling in Highs Inn and all our wealth dwindled to nothing!"

"Killing your husband would have left you with the entirety of the estate," Corina said from beside me. "If he were alive, it would only leave you with half."

Corina's words hung heavily in the room, her accusation clear and pointed. Giselle's outburst had only added fuel to the fire, her admission of financial struggles creating a potential motive for murder. The courtiers murmured among themselves, their whispers filling the room with a low hum.

"Quiet!"

The murmurs ceased, the courtiers turning their attention back to the drama unfolding before them.

"Giselle," I addressed her. "You claim that Bertrand knew about the potential sale of the estate. Can anyone else confirm this?"

Giselle was silent for a moment, her eyes darting around the room. Then she nodded, pointing towards a man standing at the back of the room. "Yes, Dorn can. He's our steward and handles our finances. He was there when I discussed the matter with Bertrand."

I turned my attention to Dorn, an older man with graying hair, and a familiar sash of a frequent patron in Elrathilion. His face was lined with age—a halfling of sorts. "Dorn, is this true?" I asked.

Dorn nodded, stepping forward. "Yes, my Queen. Madame Giselle did discuss the matter with Bertrand. He was...aware of the financial difficulties they were facing," Dorn finished. "Bertrand knew that selling the estate might be their only option. He was reluctant, but he understood why Madame Giselle thought it might be necessary."

He easily painted a picture of a man caught in a difficult situation, wrestling with decisions that could change his life—and, as it turned out, end it.

"Thank you, Dorn," I said, nodding at him. His confirmation of Giselle's claim added another layer to the case. It seemed that Bertrand's death was more than just a result of a love triangle. It was tangled in a web of financial struggles and desperate decisions.

If it had been Ramses, his decision would have already been made, and someone would have already lost their head.

"But that doesn't prove that Giselle or Isla didn't poison Bertrand," Corina pointed out. She raised her brow at me and pursed her lips, flicking at imaginary dirt under her nails.

"Present their hands. Both of them." I motioned to both Isla and Giselle, who were tugged closer to me.

I looked at their hands, noting the distinct differences. Giselle's were soft and delicate, the hands of a woman who had not seen hard labor. Isla's, on the other hand, were rough and calloused, the hands of a woman who had known work.

I reached out, lifting each of their hands in turn. Isla's were clean, her nails neatly trimmed. There was no trace of any substance on her hands. Giselle's were the same, clean and unmarked. No traces of the purple hue that marked Adderdale poison were visible on either woman's hands.

But that's because it was colorless until it touched iron.

I raked my sharp nails over both of their palms, drawing a thin line of blood across their skin. Both women winced but did not pull away, staring vacantly at their hands. I watched carefully, my heart pounding in my chest.

The seconds stretched into what felt like an eternity, the entire court holding its breath as we waited. And then, just as I was about to declare the test inconclusive, I saw it—a faint tinge of purple appearing on the line drawn on *Giselle's* palm.

My breath hitched in my throat. She followed my gaze to her hand, the color now unmistakable. The same purple hue that marked Adderdale poison, the same as the one that had been found in Bertrand's wine and on the iron nails of the table, was now littering her palm.

The room erupted into gasps and whispers as the courtiers took in the sight. The guards tightened their hold on Giselle, their faces hardening as they looked at the evidence on her hand.

"Giselle," I said, "Can you explain this?"

"I...I don't...I didn't..." she stammered.

Her brows creased, her lips pressed together, her hands curled in front of her. She snapped to Isla. "*You* did this," she accused, her pitch rising in anger.

Isla placed her hand over her heart, "I would *never*."

"Why did you flee to the Temple? Why didn't you stay with Bertrand after your affair was found out?" I asked Isla.

"I hardly see what that has to do with anything," Corina said.

I raised my hand and motioned for Isla to answer.

She stammered and twisted her hands together. "Giselle. She-she frightened me—"

"Oh, come off it! You ran away because Bert wasn't leaving me. You ran away because you knew that I would have rung you out—" Giselle interrupted her and was met with a sharp pull on her bindings.

Isla took a shaky breath. "After...after our affair was discovered, things became...difficult," she began, wavering. "Giselle was...was angry. I was scared. So, I left. I thought...I thought it would be better for everyone."

"You served in the Temple for one hundred and twenty days. I was there on your release day. You didn't commit a crime, but wanted to escape the wrath of a scorned wife." I measured her with a glance, skimming the sparse hair on her head. "Adderdale flowers are within the Temple grounds. A favored gift for Nexus or even Inamak. Being the ones to tend to the altars of the Gods you would know the properties of the flowers."

A faint flush crept onto her cheeks. "My Queen, I would never...the Adderdale flowers, they are sacred to the Gods. I would never use them to harm another."

"But you knew about their properties, didn't you?" I pressed on. "You knew that they could be used as a poison."

Isla hesitated before nodding. "Yes, my Queen. It is common knowledge among the temple servants."

"Your access to the Adderdale flowers, your knowledge of their properties, and your animosity towards Giselle," I summarized. "It all paints a very suspicious picture, Isla."

"I have no trace of the poison on my fingers!" She shouted.

"And you, Giselle, the guards say that you were running to the Elrathilion temple when they attempted to arrest you. Why would you run to a temple if you were innocent?" I asked.

"I needed to find Dorn," she responded, "Because Bert was dead, and the guards were already pointing the finger at me. He takes care of our coin and everything else."

"And you have no children? So, who would the estate pass on to if both you and Bert were dead?"

"Dorn is our steward, he was instructed to take care of the estate if anything happened to us," she replied.

I was quiet for a while. The room swallowed the whispers, the court waiting. There was something about Dorn—there was a prickling sensation that started in the back of my neck and crept up my scalp. I froze.

The day of Isla's release, she had been speaking to a man whose face I had not seen. My mind's eye struggled to remember. The sash.

I recognized the sash.

"Drinking wine so much, in the morning. Bertrand had a problem?" I asked Giselle.

"He indulged in the wine and drank too much. It was why we had lost all of our money."

"Dorn, I saw you speaking with Isla on her release day," I started, "Any reason you would?"

Dorn sputtered, his face going ashen. "I-I was checking on the provisions for the Temple," Dorn hastily explained, his eyes darting around the room, seeking an ally. "It was purely coincidental that I spoke to Isla."

"But the sash you wore," I pressed on, "It is the same sash that the man speaking to Isla wore. A sash that I now recall. One that you are wearing now." It was a long shot. A bluff in the hopes of having him slip. All I had on him was a coincidence and a sash—one of many.

Dorn's face drained of color. "Your Majesty, I assure you, this is a misunderstanding," he stammered.

There. A panicked, trapped mouse.

"You see, Dorn, the pieces are falling into place," I continued, my tone cold as the stone walls of the court. "The guards found traces of Adderdale flower poison on a wine goblet in Bertrand's home The same home you have access to. And the same poison that you, and Isla, know so well."

Isla's finger shot toward Dorn, betrayal etched across her face. "You told me it was for rats," she shouted, her voice carrying across the silent room.

"He told you what?" I cut in.

"Dorn would visit the temple often. He would bring wine and offerings. I had only spoken to him a handful of times. I saw him pocket Adderdale flowers months ago, so long ago I didn't correlate Bert's death with it. He told me mixing it with a bit of honey would kill the rats he had." She paused. A small gasp of air escaped her. "When he came to me during my release, he said that Bertrand wanted to see me."

"He did," Dorn stuttered.

Giselle scoffed.

Dorn's composure crumbled slowly, his posture deflating as he realized what was happening. "Bert was destroying everything," he pleaded. "My plan was to frame Giselle, to make it seem like she poisoned her husband in a jealous rage over the affair."

The court erupted into murmurs, the truth of Dorn's betrayal rippling through the gathered nobles and servants like a shockwave. Giselle's expression hardened, the pieces of her shattered life falling into a grim pattern.

"You held my hands to comfort me," she spat, "and they were clammy. I thought nothing of it. You wanted to make sure there were traces of Adderdale on my hands."

"You connived to take the estate for yourself," I accused, standing from my throne, towering over them from the top of the steps. "You sought to manipulate the outcome of a lovers' quarrel for your own gain."

He whimpered.

"Take him away," I commanded, trying to hide the sigh.

As Dorn was escorted out, a pitiable figure in chains, Isla's shoulders slumped in relief, and Giselle's bowed to me with silent gratitude.

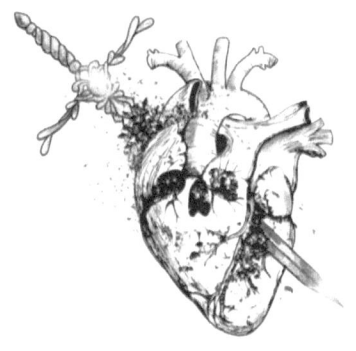

CHAPTER
TWENTY-THREE

H ours passed, with Dorn sentenced to death by my hand. I made it quick. There was no sense in any other judgment since it would likely be done by Ramses when he got back. The guards took his corpse to the pit and tossed him in—the dragon keepers would probably feed him to the dragons, but I didn't care.

Giselle was given the estate to do with as she pleased, and Isla quietly slipped away, hopefully, to live her life in obscurity.

Corina on the other hand had chosen to disturb me again during dinner.

"Handled that rather well," Corina said, her face twisting as if she tasted something foul. She glanced at the window, the thick glass letting in a light from the setting sun that draped her figure in a golden hue, much warmer than the chill that still permeated the air.

"Surprising compliment coming from you," I said, layered with equal parts disdain and weariness. I jabbed my fork into the roast cut of the lamb a little harder than I should have, the fine porcelain plate splitting beneath the force. The room was silent for a moment, save for the crack of porcelain and scrape of fork.

She tapped red nails on the table, each click resonating like a clock counting down, stirring my irritation. The sound was sharp and annoying, a perfect match for the woman who made it.

"Stop that," I huffed.

Corina, unphased, stopped the tapping but kept her piercing gaze locked on me. "You never cared much for court matters. What's changed?" She pulled back a chair to sit in without invitation to do so. With a casual air, she tucked her hands under her arms and placed her booted feet on the table's edge as if she owned the room.

Her outfit was as brash as her personality—a tight, leather corset that accentuated her slender waist, paired with a skirt of layered crimson and gold that flared out dramatically at her hips. A series of interwoven belts with metal buckles hung low on her waist, clinking softly with her every movement. The boots that dared to disrespect the polished wood of the table were knee-high, studded, and black as night. Her fiery red hair cascaded down her shoulders in a wild mane that matched her spirit—free, fierce, and unyielding.

I studied her for a moment, the fading light glinting off the intricate silver chain she wore around her neck. The jewel at its center was as red as her hair, pulsating with an inner light that seemed almost... alive.

"Nothing's changed," I finally replied, pushing the broken plate away and meeting her challenging stare. "I still find the court's games tedious."

A slow, appreciative smile spread across her lips, a rare sight that was as unsettling as it was mesmerizing. She was disgustingly beautiful. "Then let's play a game, shall we?" she proposed. "But be warned, I am incredibly competitive."

"I've had more than enough games with you Blackwaters," I snapped, my patience worn thin. I could ill afford to engage in her frivolous challenges, not with the weight of my recent visions pressing down on me. What horrors had Ramses exposed our son to?

She leaned back in her chair, nonchalant as ever, conjuring a small smile that seemed to say she knew exactly how to needle me. With a wave of her hand, as if summoning the very air to do her bidding, a goblet of wine appeared in her grasp. She lifted it to her lips, sipping the rich, dark liquid with an air of self-satisfaction.

"It's an easy game. You tell me a truth or a lie, and I have to guess which is which." Her eyes glinted with mischief.

I clucked my tongue, feigning disinterest. She never acted this playful with me before. "And what do I gain from playing your game?"

She shrugged. "Answers."

"I don't want to play."

"What did you see when you touched the gates?" she pressed, leaning forward, her curiosity piqued.

I masked my unease with a scoff. "The gates showed me nothing of interest, merely echoes of past glories and long-forgotten whispers of the ancestors," I lied smoothly—if dramatically, hoping she would take the bait and steer away from the truth that lay heavily in my chest.

She studied me intently, trying to discern the honesty in my words. I held her stare, willing my face to remain expressionless, to give away nothing of the dread that gnawed at me.

She took another sip of wine, contemplative. "Is that so?" Her question was laced with skepticism. "The wards never showed anyone *anything* before. I saw that look in your eye like you were seeing something we couldn't see. I knew it."

My heart thudded against my rib cage. I had fallen right into her trap. I needed to divert her, to keep her from seeing the fear I was hiding about the vision that threatened to burst forth from my mind at any moment.

"Perhaps the gates simply recognized someone they wished to reveal their secrets to," I retorted quickly, a false bravado lacing every syllable. "Or maybe you don't know everything about the wards as you think you do."

A flicker of annoyance crossed her face, but she masked it quickly with a laugh that did not reach her eyes. "Oh, I don't claim to know all their secrets. But I do know the magic is powerful, and if it has shown you something, it's not to be taken lightly."

She is going to tell Ramses.

I needed to change the subject, to throw her off the scent. "Enough about the gates," I said with a forced lightness. "You speak of games, but what is it you want, Corina? Power? Knowledge? Or perhaps something more... personal?"

If she wanted Ramses to herself—wanted the crown, she could have it. All I wanted was freedom.

The question seemed to catch her off guard, and for a moment, the mask of the confident, ever-calculating Corina slipped. She looked away, out the window where the last of the sun's rays were dying, and when she looked back at me, there was a depth to her that I had not seen before.

"Perhaps I seek a game where the stakes are more than just truths and lies," she said softly, almost to herself. "Perhaps..." I could see her freeze as she caught herself.

Her words hung in the air between us, and I couldn't help but wonder if there was more to Corina Blackwater than the cunning, brash exterior she showed the world.

"What happened to your father?" The question flew passed my lips before I could stop it.

Her head snapped up at that.

For a split second, the unguarded truth was laid bare in her stare—pain, anger, and a haunting sorrow that seemed to swallow the light around her.

I knew the story well.

Corina had been the jewel of her family, the only child of Lord and Lady Blackwater, cousin to Ramses. Her father, Caine, had been a fierce warrior, a loyal man deeply respected by his peers and feared by his enemies. Her mother, Dianaora, a woman of grace and intelligence, had been the backbone of their house, her counsel sought by many. Together, they had been a formidable pair, their love for their daughter eclipsing even their own ambitions.

They never wanted the crown. Not even when Ramses' father, Baine, died. Not when his mother took her own life.

But their untimely death had been a blow from which Corina had never fully recovered. It was an accident, they said—a fire that had consumed their estate in the dead of night. Yet, whispers of foul play had spread like the very flames that claimed their lives. Some said it was the work of Ramses. With her parents gone, his claim was uncontested, and he rose to power unchallenged.

For a woman could never sit on the throne, so Corina was not a threat.

That was the story.

What was the truth?

That drawing in my pocket felt vulnerable now.

Now, looking at her across the table, I saw a flicker of some-one—not just the woman known for her sharp tongue and brasher actions, but a soul forged in tragedy, hardened by loss, and shroud-ed in the mystery of unanswered questions regarding her parents' death.

I hated seeing myself in her. Especially when, just hours ago, she was making remarks about Servat.

She recovered quickly, the vulnerability shuttered away as she composed herself, her eyes narrowing into slits. "My father's fate is of no consequence to you," she said, her tone icy. "And it's a subject I'd advise you to steer clear of if you value your well-being."

"A lie," I said.

"What?" Her confusion was genuine, a crack in her armor.

"This game. You said guess a truth or a lie. I say *this* is a lie." I raised a brow, "Your father's fate is of consequence to me. Because it's of consequence to you."

An olive branch. Reaching for that person I saw just moments ago—whoever it was—I wanted to get to know *that* Corina.

Let me in let me in let me in.

For a long moment, silence hung between us, heavy and charged. Then, as if the walls she built around her were too high even for her to bear any longer, Corina let out a breath and her shoulders slumped ever so slightly.

"You're not like him," she said quietly, almost to herself. It wasn't a question, but a statement—a realization that perhaps I was not an enemy but an unlikely ally. "You're not on Ramses' side."

"And you're not?" I asked, craning over the table.

Let me in let me in let me in.

Corina's focus lingered on me, weighing my words, and as-sessing their sincerity. Then, a subtle shift occurred within her, a decision made that I could see in the way her shoulders relaxed. "I have always known he was behind their deaths," she whispered, the truth heavy like a stone. "But knowing it and proving it are worlds apart. I need evidence that will stand in the light of day. Power that could match his."

"Truth," I said. "How is it that Ramses can go beyond the wall so easily?" I took the opportunity for what it was.

She shrugged. "Ramses has always had a knack for acquiring power that should be beyond his reach," Corina said. "The warding magic…Could be linked to the dragons themselves."

I felt my eye twitch and I knew she caught it.

"The question is, *which* dragon? Some dragons have a power that makes them unique, others are more of a general magic. I haven't seen any that was so unique as to have the warding magic." She paused, biting at her fingernails. "I was a youngling when the war of Skies happened with Eldra and Ramses. I was only three. Aislinn Furian's capture is what tipped the tide in the war. Her dragon was said to have gone missing…"

"You think Ramses could have captured it? Have it holed up somewhere in the keep?"

"Could be."

"He's siphoning magic, bending it at will. Allowing those he wants in and out," I said.

"I could be wrong. I can be wrong about many things, and being wrong is dangerous. He gets…uneasy when he thinks he is losing control." She looked at me with a half-smile. "He really won't be happy when he hears about today."

"Do be sure you tell him." I huffed.

"When did you start fighting back again?" she asked me.

"What?"

A wry smile formed on her lips. "I'm not talking about physically. Your little scratches here and there. I am talking about *really* fighting back. I always wondered why you never just blew him away. The way I hear you almost did with Eldra."

I popped a grape in my mouth, rolling it around before chewing slowly. I regarded her, wondering if telling her anything was a good idea.

What was Ramses going to do?

Kill me?

Beat me?

Lock me up? An image of my mother flashed in my mind.

I snorted and she raised a brow.

"The moment I realized that Ramses' hunger for control was his own undoing," I replied. "When power is your only goal, you become blind to the chains you wrap around yourself. I don't know the limits to his magic. What if I killed him and we were still all trapped here? What if I used every ounce of magic I had, and it didn't do a damn thing?"

Corina's expression shifted, contemplative, as if weighing the truth of my statements against her own knowledge of Ramses. "Smart observation," she finally said. "And a dangerous one. Ramses may be blind to his own chains, but he is not blind to *yours*. Nor is he blind to betrayal."

I sighed. "Betrayal is a matter of perspective. To Ramses, loyalty is fealty without question. To me, it's standing by the realm, even if it means standing against him."

A soft clink of metal on glass echoed as she set down her goblet, the wine barely touched. "Don't feed me some dragon-shite about 'loyalty to the realm." Her eyes now bore into me with an accusation that was both unexpected and disarming. "What has Ember ever done for *you*? You don't care about the *realm*," she continued, low and tinged with a bitterness that seemed to come from a place of deep understanding. "You're just looking for a way out, an escape from Ramses' cage. If the whole of Ember could burn to the ground, it wouldn't matter to you, as long as you were free of his grasp. You have nothing holding you here. You have no friends. I have seen the homes you have burned to cinders, girl. You do not fool me."

Could she see through me that easily? Did she know that my fight was as much about personal freedom as it was about the realm's well-being? I took a deep breath, finding the truth in what she said, and allowed myself to acknowledge it.

"Escape," I said softly, the admission feeling like a surrender. "Yes, there is a part of me that wants that. To flee from the shadow Ramses casts over everything I am, everything I could be. But that's not all there is to it. I do feel guilt for what I have done, Corina."

I leaned forward, my hands gripping the edge of the table as I searched for the right way to say what I needed to. "Ember, for all its flaws, is still my home. The people, the land, the very air we breathe—it's a part of who I am. And yes, Ramses has tainted it, twisted it to serve his desires, but that doesn't mean I don't *care* what happens to it." I took her wine and finished it unceremoniously. "I would care if it were gone."

Corina's expression softened slightly, but her skepticism remained. "Then prove it. Prove that your fight is for more than just your freedom. Show me that you can put Ember above yourself when the time comes."

My shoulders felt heavy. What does it mean to put Ember above myself? Did I not already do that? "I don't know if I can."

"It isn't right of me to ask you to be selfless when we are both in the same position," she said slowly, each word measured. "But what of your own blood? Your mother, who we were told died in childbirth—have you ever questioned that tale?"

The mention of my mother sent a jolt through me, a jagged crack through the foundation of my past. "My mother?"

A crumple of paper with my mother's sketched face, drawn by my dead maidservant came to mind. I unconsciously felt for it.

Her gaze held mine, unwavering and intense. "Ramses... has his secrets, layers upon layers of them. You came out of nowhere. I always wondered about it. I'm sure you have."

I felt a coldness seep into my bones, an unease that had nothing to do with the chill of the night air. I would play stupid, I wouldn't share this information with her just yet. "You think Ramses had something to do with my mother's death?"

Corina leaned forward, her voice dropping to a hush. "I think Ramses knows far more about your mother than he's ever let on. When have you ever known Ramses to care for a baby whose mother died at birth? Plenty of orphans in this city. He doesn't do charity work."

"He doesn't. Not unless they are his own, and even then, he rarely does." Openly acknowledging his bastards to Corina was something I never would have done before, but she was right.

The realization struck me like a physical blow, leaving me gasping for air. "You're suggesting... That Ramses... That he might be—" I couldn't finish the sentence, the implication too grotesque to voice.

She nodded sympathetically. "It is a possibility we cannot ignore," she said softly. "It would explain his interest in you, the privileges you were afforded that others were not. You've always been different to him. I have searched for any record of your mother, and I have found none."

A sickening knot formed in my stomach, and I felt as though the room was spinning. My husband, the man who had controlled every aspect of my life, who I had vowed to fight against for the sake of my freedom and the realm—could he also be my father? The thought was monstrous, an abomination against every natural law.

"And you," she pressed on, "have you ever found a record of your birth? Has a servant ever whispered your name with a knowing glance, or have you found your place in any archives? What about your nursemaid?"

My mind reeled, searching for memories that would contradict her suspicions. But there was nothing—no document, no family tree, no whispered stories of my mother's laughter or her grace—or perhaps poverty. My past was a void, filled only with Ramses' cold presence and my own sense of displacement.

Not even Joslynn had ever mentioned my mother to me. Only left cryptic drawings of her in a journal I had only recently discovered.

"No," I admitted, the word tasting bitter on my tongue. "There's nothing. No one speaks of my mother, and my birth is a topic shrouded in silence. I had been told by Ramses that I was from outstanding stock... that both my mother and father were exceptional..."

When had Ramses ever given praise to a random person? Never.

"Now you see it may have been a calculated erasure," Corina finished for me. "Ramses is meticulous in his control. If he wanted to hide the truth of your heritage, he would spare no effort to do so."

"He doesn't hide his other bastards," I argued.

"Which means your *mother* had to have been something extraordinary to have attracted such attention, and to be worthy of such secrecy," she countered.

I stood abruptly, my chair scraping against the stone floor. "I need air," I muttered, stumbling toward the balcony. The cool night breeze did little to ease the turmoil inside me. I leaned heavily against the railing, my mind racing with the horrific possibility of Corina's words.

If Ramses was indeed my father, the deception would be a cruelty beyond measure. It tainted everything, every memory, every moment I had spent in his presence.

Vrys.

"How could I not have seen it? How could I have been so blind?" I murmured, more to myself than to Corina. The need for air had driven me to the balcony, but now I found it suffocating, the open space a vast emptiness.

"You were meant to be blind to it," Corina said softly. "Ramses is a master of deception. He would not have allowed you to see anything he did not wish you to see."

"I need to get the fuck out of here," I hissed, my anger building. A flash of lightning broke through the dark clouds, illuminating the city in a sudden burst of light.

Corina's hand was on my arm, "Calm," she said.

Corina's touch was more than a gesture of comfort; it was an invocation of her own unique power, a subtle magic that few knew she possessed. Her ability to soothe, to quell the storm of emotions in another, was a gift she wielded with the same precision with which a skilled swordsman wielded his blade. She never touched me before. I had never experienced it.

As her hand rested on my arm, I felt the anxiety within me begin to subside, the edges of my anger softening as if she were smoothing out a wrinkled tapestry. The change was disorienting, like I was being pulled away from myself. The lightning's echo faded into the distance, and with it, the surge of panic that had threatened to consume me.

"Calm," she repeated. "We must think clearly, and act wisely. Rash decisions will only play into Ramses' hands."

I closed my eyes, taking a deep breath as Corina's magic worked its way through my veins, steadying my heartbeat and clearing the fog of fear. When I opened them again, the night seemed less oppressive, the balcony less confining.

"Thank you," I said after a breath. It was nice, having someone on my side—even if it was Corina.

Corina's hand withdrew, and the warmth of her power lingered. When I looked at her again, I flinched at the sight of her red hair.

"Suppose I should call you 'cousin'?" It was a small joke, a horrible joke. Even she grimaced at the thought. She only called me cousin to annoy me.

I nodded, "Yeah. I suppose not."

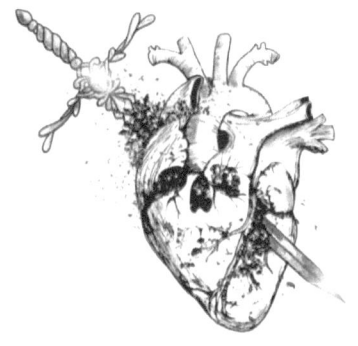

CHAPTER
TWENTY-FOUR

I was sat by my bedroom window, straining to decipher the giant figures that were breaking away from the distant edges of Ember. Among those silhouettes, I recognized the familiar forms of Ramses and Vrys astride Soresin's back. Tiamut closely followed behind. Their flight was erratic, with Soresin's head bobbing and weaving in the air as if he were intoxicated.

As the dragons cut through the night sky, drawing nearer, their shadows swelled—a spreading obsidian wave that briefly cloaked the city in an eerie twilight.

The obsidian wave ebbed, and Ember gradually emerged from the transient twilight, its stone towers glinting under the moonlight. My breath hitched as the dragons made their final approach, their immense wings stirring up a tempest of wind that swept across the city streets, rattling shingles and upturning carts.

Ramses and Vrys descended from Soresin's back, their cloaks billowing out behind them like banners in the wind. I turned away from the window, pressing a hand to the cool stone wall beside me. My mind raced, filling with a thousand questions.

Was Vrys alright? What had he seen out there?

Removing my hand from the stone wall, I felt the chill of the night seep into my skin. I turned back to the window, lingering on the spot where the dragons had landed. The city was still awash with the afterglow of their arrival, the stone towers casting long, dark shadows that crisscrossed the cobblestone streets. It looked peaceful, almost serene.

Siorsen swayed on his feet, before collapsing onto the floor in a heap.

"Stand back," Ramses shouted, his command echoing through the silent streets. The soldiers obeyed, stepping back from the fallen dragon. Only Ramses and Vrys remained by Siorsen's side, their hands still touching the dragon's scales.

I watched from the window as Ramses and Vrys worked to calm Siorsen, their conversation too quiet for me to hear. But I could see the urgent gestures, the quick movements, the occasional glance they shared. Whatever had happened out there, it was serious.

I pushed away from the window, my mind spinning. I needed answers. I needed to know what had happened to Siorsen, to Vrys. I needed to be down there, with them, not watching from a distance.

So, without a second thought, I pulled on my cloak and rushed out of my room. My feet pounded against the stone floor of the castle, my heart thudding in sync with each step. The corridors were deserted, everyone drawn to the spectacle outside.

As I emerged from the castle's main entrance, I was hit by a gust of wind. Tiamut shuddered to the ground, a high-pitched whistle coming from his throat.

I squinted against the blast, pulling my cloak tighter around me. The sight that greeted me I would never forget.

Under the glow of the moon, Siorsen lay on his side, his colossal form dwarfing the soldiers that surrounded him. Ramses and Vrys were at his head. They were speaking softly to Siorsen, their hands gently stroking his scales. Even from this distance, I could see the worry etched on their faces.

I made my way through the crowd, ignoring the hushed whispers and curious gazes. As I approached, Ramses looked up, finding me. He gave a small nod, a silent signal for me to come closer.

Vrys turned to look at me as I approached. He looked tired, his eyes rimmed with red, but he tried to give me a reassuring smile. "He's just exhausted," he said, "He flew harder and faster than he has in years, Father says. He'll be alright."

"What the hell happened out there?" I hissed.

"Nothing new," Servat said, sliding off of Tiamut's back. "Everyone back to your business!" he shouted at curious onlookers.

The crowd, which had been buzzing with apprehension and curiosity, immediately dispersed, the soldiers returning to their posts and the civilians retreating back into their homes. The stone streets, which had been filled with shadowy figures and whispering voices moments ago, were now empty and silent.

"I think it's best if we talk inside," Servat suggested, glancing at the retreating crowd. His face was serious, the playful twinkle in his eyes replaced by a hard, cold look. He then turned to Vrys and Ramses, "Help me with Siorsen." He gestured for Tiamut and another soldier to come with him.

I went to follow them, but Vrys grabbed my arm, stopping me.

"You should go to bed," he said, low and serious, sounding much older than his years.

"Wha-?" I stopped. He never gave me orders before, and it was a little disconcerting.

I gaped at him, slack-jawed.

"Please," he added, exhaustion evident on his face.

The sight of him, worn out and worried, tugged at my heart. It was clear that whatever had happened out there had taken a toll on him. I wanted to hug him, run my fingers through his hair, and tell him a bedtime story, like how we had all these years before.

But looking at him now, I realized how much closer he was to the age I was when I married Ramses. Still a boy—but not for long.

"I... okay," I finally said. I gave his hand a reassuring squeeze, trying to convey my understanding.

He offered me a small, tired smile, nodding his appreciation.

"Atreya."

I greeted Ramses with a nod, the two of us standing on either side of Vrys. "Ramses."

I avoided looking at him. Avoided trying to find my face in his.

"Be in my rooms," he said, gesturing to the castle. With that, Ramses turned and headed towards the castle, his cloak billowing behind him. Vrys followed him, his shoulders drooping with exhaustion but his stride still steady. I watched them go, a sense of foreboding settling in my chest.

I followed after. The castle, illuminated by the moonlight, loomed before me.

I made my way through the empty hallways, the echo of my footsteps breaking the quiet. As I reached Ramses' room, I took a moment to gather my thoughts. The unknown awaited me on the other side of that door, the answers to the questions that had been haunting me since they had left a week ago.

Taking a deep breath, I knocked on the door. After a moment, the door creaked open, revealing Ramses standing on the other side.

"Come in, Atreya," he said, stepping aside to let me in.

I braced myself.

The room was dimly lit, the only light coming from a couple of candles flickering on a table littered with maps and scrolls. The shadows they cast danced across the walls, giving the space a somber atmosphere. Ramses closed the door behind me with a soft thud.

The air was thick with incense and the smell of wax and parchment. Ramses walked over to the table, his movements deliberate and stiff. I followed, watching him with a mixture of fear and curiosity. He leaned over the table, his fingers tracing the lines of a map before he turned to face me, his expression unreadable.

"Atreya," Ramses began, "I brought you here because I need you to understand the gravity of our situation."

I remained silent, knowing that any interruption would only serve to irritate him further.

I tried not to examine the details of his face. The straight slope of his nose, the angular lines of his cheekbones.

I couldn't stop trying to find myself in him.

"The rebels are getting out of hand," he said, slamming a fist onto the table. The candles flickered, casting erratic shadows.

"They're a disease, spreading chaos and dissent among the people. If left unchecked, they'll destroy everything I've worked so hard to build."

I could see the fury in his aura, a cruel flame that seemed to burn brighter with each word. "And what do you plan to do about it?" I asked.

Ramses' lips curled into a dark smile. "I've already begun taking the necessary steps. Tonight, the streets have run red. By morning, the rebels will wish they had never entertained thoughts of defiance."

I gasped, taking a step back. "You mean... you're going to..."

"Massacre them? Yes," he confirmed without a hint of remorse. "It's the only language these traitors understand. Fear, Atreya. Fear will keep the others in line."

"But innocent people will die," I protested, trying to appeal to any shred of humanity he might have left. "Surely not everyone in Ferenz is a rebel."

"Innocent?" Ramses scoffed. "No one is innocent who harbors thoughts of rebellion. They're *all* guilty, whether they've taken up arms or merely whispered against me in the dark corners of taverns."

There was no reasoning with a man who saw the world in such stark, unforgiving terms. My heart raced with fear for the people of Ferenz, for the rebels who fought for freedom, and for all those caught in the crossfire of Ramses' unyielding grip on power.

"You can't possibly believe that," I whispered, but Ramses only regarded me with a cold, calculating indifference.

"It's not a matter of belief, Atreya; it's a matter of *control*," he replied. "To rule is to make the difficult decisions, to do what must be done for the greater good. And I will do whatever it takes to maintain order."

"This is good?"

"Our people are not starving. They are not cold. They are not oppressed—"

I snorted and he growled. My words died in my throat.

"You know nothing of what lies beyond the wall. The War of Fallen Skies would have destroyed us all had I not won. The war was not just a result of two men's pride or ambition. It was the inevitable consequence of opposing forces that could *never* align.

On one side stood me, who believes in the sanctity of the *old* ways, of power, held by the few deemed worthy by birthright and arcane ability. Just as it was always intended."

Ramses paused, a smirk on his lips. "And on the other side," he continued, "were the... idealists, who sought to dismantle the structures of the old world, to spread power among the masses, to uplift the downtrodden regardless of the chaos it would unleash. Imagine a Tor ruling over all of Ferenz? They are the poorest. Disgraceful."

He turned to me, his expression one of fierce conviction. "We fought to preserve the order that had kept this realm stable for generations. Those idealists, led by Eldra, sought to tear down everything in pursuit of a misguided dream of equality. He would eat the rich and feed the poor so to speak. He sought to have the people *vote* for their leaders, to have them determine who would rule them." He scoffed at that. "He wanted one ruler for all of Ferenz."

"And you couldn't have that, because the people would never vote for you," I retorted. "In the end, you did exactly what he wanted. One person to rule Ferenz"

He chuckled, "What would happen if the people had say? what would happen if they governed themselves?"

Ramses' chuckle was devoid of warmth, a hollow echo in the tense air between us. "Chaos," he said, cutting through the silence like a knife. "They would tear each other apart, Atreya. Without a strong hand to guide them, the people become little more than squabbling children, lost and directionless. They will scream in the streets and riot that the voting was rigged. There is no reasoning with them."

I felt a flare of anger at his condescension but held my tongue, aware that provoking him further would serve no purpose. His belief in his own superiority was unshakable—a fortress built upon the bones of those who had dared to challenge him.

"They need someone to protect them from their own baser instincts, to elevate them to a state of order and prosperity. That is the burden of rulership, and I bear it willingly." Ramses' voice was resolute, the timbre of a man who had seen his convictions tested in the crucible of war.

I searched his face for any sign of doubt, any hint that he understood the ironies of his own words—the oppression he called protection, the order built on fear. But there was nothing, only the steadfast observance of a man who believed he was the last bulwark against the tide of anarchy.

"And what of their happiness? Their freedom? Do these things not matter to you?" I asked.

"Freedom is an illusion, Atreya. A carrot dangled before the masses to keep them compliant. True freedom comes from knowing one's place in the world, from the security that my rule provides."

The air grew heavy with the weight of his proclamation, and I felt the hope for Ferenz and its people flickering like a candle in the wind. Ramses had built his reign on the belief that he alone knew what was best for all and that any who opposed him were enemies of the state, enemies of progress.

I realized then that there would be no swaying him, no softening of his heart. For Ramses, the world was a chessboard, and he was the grandmaster, moving pieces according to his will, sacrificing pawns without a second thought.

"What about my happiness?" I asked—a final plea.

Ramses turned back to me, cold and detached. "Your happiness," he said with a slow, deliberate enunciation, "is not the priority. You are here to serve a purpose, Atreya—to secure the lineage, to be the vessel through which the bloodline is assured."

I felt the sting of what he was saying like a physical blow, the reduction of my existence to nothing more than a means to an end. But it was not a new pain; it was the familiar ache of being caged, of being seen as property rather than a person.

"And you have given me an heir. You have fulfilled your role. As for what you want, it is immaterial. You are my wife, and you will do as you are told."

"Why let me live then?" I asked sharply, "Why?"

"Because your presence still serves a purpose, Atreya. You are the mother of my heir, and as such, you provide a semblance of stability, a continuity that the people find reassuring."

"Did you ever hold any affection for me? Did you ever love me?" My stomach rolled at the thought.

For a fleeting moment, a shadow crossed Ramses' face as if the question had unearthed a memory long buried beneath layers of ambition and callous resolve. But it vanished as quickly as it had appeared, and his expression was once again an impenetrable mask.

"Affection is a luxury of the common folk," he said dismissively. "It is a fleeting whim that can turn to apathy or hate as easily as love."

I knew that all too well. I had once loved him. Once.

"You didn't answer the question," I said, my anger simmering beneath the surface. I felt a hot flush creep up my neck, my ears burning. "Just answer me that."

He was silent.

"Had things been different... had the gods decreed it so... could you have loved me?" I tried again. I don't know why I cared to ask. It made no difference now. Why did I want to know?

His eyes met mine, and in them, I saw the flicker of a thousand unspoken thoughts. "If the gods had made it so," he said softly, almost painfully, "I believe I would have loved you with every fiber of my being." And I knew, with a certainty that I had never felt before, that he truly believed that.

"I imagine you love me a great deal. About as much as your father loved your mother," I said carefully. His eye twitched at my words, and I knew I had struck a nerve.

That's good, I thought. I want him to feel that way and to know exactly how I view him.

After a moment, he leaned back against his chair, lacing his fingers together. "But I did not wed you for affection. I chose you for your bloodline, for your breeding, for the strength and intelligence I saw in you—an intelligence I now see was not to be underestimated."

There it was. Those words. Bloodlines and breeding.

"Who are my parents?" I asked, "Who were they?"

"Why the curiosity now?"

"You are avoiding the question."

"You ask too many questions," he snapped back.

"Are you my father?" I bit the inside of my cheek, so hard I drew blood. I was drawn to his brow, to the lines that crisscrossed atop his face, the small beauty mark near his eye.

His brows shot up in surprise. Ramses let out a sharp, mocking laugh, chilling the air between us. "Your father?" he said with a sneer. "Do not flatter yourself with such fancies, Atreya. You are no child of *mine*."

"Is that the truth?" I asked, my heart pounding.

"You are a Blackwater in name only. You are not of my blood."

I let out a sigh of relief that I didn't try to hide. The resemblance I thought I had seen, the mannerisms I had imagined we shared—all were mere coincidences, nothing more. The man before me was not my father, and the blood that coursed through my veins was not tainted by his cruelty.

"You seem relieved," Ramses observed, his throat coated with scorn. "Did you truly believe I could be the progenitor of someone like you?"

"I thought I had come from 'great stock,' as you called it," I answered. "I find solace in the fact that I am not your daughter. It means there is hope for me yet—that I can be more than what you have become."

"Careful, girl. I can still do without your tongue."

His expression shifted, taking on a contemplative edge that seemed almost out of place on his hardened features.

"Your mother and father were... strong," he conceded, "They were leaders who commanded respect, possessed a certain... fortitude that is rare. I had hoped that you would have manifested half their strength."

I paused, taken aback by the grudging admission from a man not prone to offering compliments. "And have I?" I dared to ask.

Ramses studied me for a long moment, his gaze appraising. "You have their fire, that much is certain," he finally said. "You have a willfulness that is... reminiscent of them. It is both infuriating and admirable."

His confession hung in the air between us, a bridge over the chasm that was our relationship. For a moment, I glimpsed the man Ramses might have been—a man capable of seeing beyond the confines of his own ambition.

"Ramses, what were they like? You never afforded me the luxury of allowing me to ask," I pressed. I thought back to the drawing. How sad my mother looked.

"They are dead. Long gone. What does it matter to know them?"

I thought back to my conversation with Corina, how I had been so desperate to know if Ramses had fathered me. How, even though I was absolutely disgusted with the idea, I was closer to finding a part of me.

Dead. The drawing I found in the drawer showed my mother in a prison cell.

Lies lies lies lies.

"You say they had great bloodlines. Were they of court? There is no record of them in the archives, I have looked. There is no mention of them in the temple or an account of my birth. Why is that? At least give me their names."

"I suspect I never knew their real names. A lot of people changed their names during that time to avoid fallout in case the war didn't end on their favor. Your mother died during childbirth, your father was dead before you even came into the world. Many people came to my aid during the War of Fallen Skies. Your parents helped me when I was in need. They were not from here. They were from a place far away. They were not from the court. They were not of the temple. They were not of any of the great houses. They were not of the great families. They were just people. People with extraordinary gifts, that I had hoped would have manifested in you. Your father was a strategist without equal, a man who could see the ripples of consequence from the smallest of actions."

"And you hoped I would have those gifts?"

"Yes. The union between us was meant to be one of mutual benefit. I saw in you the possibility of harnessing such gifts for the strength and protection of my kingdom. But it seems the fates had other plans."

"My power over the lightning disappoints you?" I asked incredulously.

"Your command over lightning is... unexpected," he admitted. "It is a formidable power; one I had not anticipated. It does not disappoint me."

To wield the lightning was to harness a fragment of the untamed sky itself, a power as volatile as it was awe-inspiring.

"It is not the power you wanted in your queen, because it is not a power you can control?" I challenged, my grip tightening on the table to ground myself against the surge of energy I felt coursing through my veins.

Once upon a time, I would have been so pleased to hear that. Now, I just felt hollow.

"I have my own set of gifts Atreya," he said, teeth flashing. "Our son, however, seems to have inherited exactly what I had hoped," he said with a smile. "He will make a formidable general."

"Vrys has foresight?" My grip on the table lessened. Another ability manifested itself in our son, and I hadn't known about it.

Ramses' smile widened, a rare display of genuine pride, as he nodded. "Yes, Vrys has shown a remarkable aptitude for strategy and foresight, much like your father had. He has a natural instinct and has already proven his worth."

I leaned forward, intrigued despite the tension between Ramses and me. "How so?" I asked.

"Recently, we have been troubled by a group of rebels, elusive and well-hidden within the borders of Tor and Paladan. Their hideout, a guarded secret, has been a thorn in our side for *months*," Ramses explained.

"And Vrys found them?"

"He did more than find them," Ramses said, a note of respect in his tone. "He predicted their movements, deciphered their patterns, and led a contingent of my guard to their doorstep. They were taken by surprise, rounded up before they could mount a defense."

"Did he... did he..." I could not bring myself to ask, waiting for Ramses to answer instead.

Ramses scoffed, "No. The boy did not get his first blood in battle. I tried. Handed him the sword to behead one and he just stood there. All that coddling you have done has poisoned him." A deep, protective instinct flared within me at that—a fierce rebuttal ready on my lips.

"Poisoned him?" I countered with indignation. "No, Ramses. I have not poisoned our son—I have taught him the *value* of life. There is a difference between being a leader and being a *butcher*."

Ramses' features tightened, his disdain for my perspective clear. "War is not a game for the tender-hearted, Atreya. A ruler must be willing to spill blood when required."

The same conversation as always. Why did I bother?

"And a ruler must also know when to stay his hand," I shot back. "Compassion is not a weakness, Ramses. It *is* a strength. One that Vrys will need if he is to be the leader we both wish him to become."

There was a tense silence as we faced off, two ideologies clashing like swords in the dark.

Like the War of Fallen Skies.

Finally, Ramses let out a heavy sigh, the lines of his face etched with a grudging respect. "Perhaps there is... merit in your ideas," he conceded. "But do not coddle the boy too much. He must be prepared for the harsh realities of his future."

A small victory, even if it was not going to get me anywhere.

"He looked exhausted. And what of Siorsen?"

"Vrys is upset about that. A rebel blew Noctane powder into the field. If it were any other dragon, it would have knocked him out. He will have to sleep it off."

"And the rebels? What of them?"

"They are being interrogated. Afterward, they will be dealt with." He shuffled through some papers, a map of the region he pointed out. "Here is where we found them. Just beneath Tor. Had to fly over Dragon's Teeth just to get to them."

Before I could respond, Ramses strode towards me, his movements predatory. He took hold of my arm, his grip iron-tight, and pulled me close. His other hand cupped my chin, tilting my face up to meet his. His eyes bore into mine, searching, trying to break through the defiance he saw there.

"I made a kingdom. A kingdom of order," Ramses said. "A kingdom where my word is law, and all know better than to question it. I will be their light and their darkness, their benevolent guardian, and their merciless judge."

He moved closer, and I could feel the heat of his breath. "And you, Atreya, will stand by my side, won't you? You will support your king in purging the rot from our land?"

"What happens when it is the king that is the rot?" I asked. His claws dug into my flesh. He leaned in, his lips mere inches from mine.

"Then cleanse me," he whispered before crashing his lips against mine.

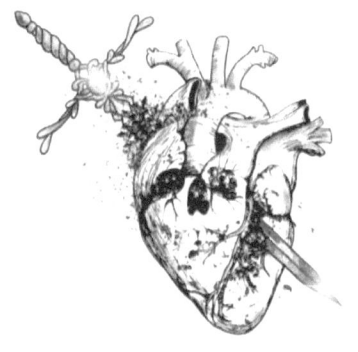

CHAPTER
TWENTY-FIVE

T he next morning, Ramses had heard of my attempt to cross
    the gates. He did not react, nor did he say anything. He
just sat there, staring at me from the throne. He also heard from
Corina, no less, that I brought it upon myself to seat myself on
there.

He raised an eyebrow at that.

"Kept my seat warm for me, did you?" he asked. He was in a
lighter mood than usual. He had a good reason to be. He fell asleep
before I did, well spent from last night. He was still asleep when I
left, slipping out from his arms to go and bathe and take my tonic.

I always found him more tolerable after a romp.

"It was rather comfortable. Perhaps I should take it for a spin
more often," I quipped.

His eyebrow quirked higher, a silent challenge. "Is that so? And
what decrees did Queen Atreya pass from her borrowed throne?"

Borrowed throne.

I walked closer to him, the memory of my clandestine meeting at the gates still fresh in my mind. "No decrees," I said earnestly. "But I did gain perspective. The view is quite different from that vantage point."

He huffed, resting his head on his chin, and eyed me. "I suspect you'll be pregnant soon enough. If last night was any indication, you should be."

I blushed and silently prayed against it. He had enough children from others. He didn't need another from me.

"I suppose we shall see in due time," I replied, maintaining a neutral tone while masking the whirl of thoughts inside me.

He regarded me for a moment, always trying to read my thoughts as if they were an open book. "You don't seem thrilled at the prospect," he observed, lacking any discernible emotion.

"I remember the sickness with Vrys. I am not looking forward to that," I lied.

After a moment he tilted his head at me, motioning for me to sit on the proffered pillow near his foot, and I did. "You killed that man. Dorn. Why? What happened to staying the hand—as you said?"

I sighed, "What would be the point of sentencing him to life in prison when you were going to kill him when you got back anyway?"

"He would have been a waste of resources," Ramses replied without hesitation, nodding. Ramses hated that. A waste of resources.

"And that's why I killed him. No sense in prolonging it."

He raised a brow. "You're learning," he said, a note of approval in his voice that I wasn't sure how to receive. "Sometimes, swift action is necessary. It's a lesson you'll do well to remember."

"About the rebels," I started.

"Yes?" He sighed in exasperation.

"Their grievances are not without merit," I said quickly choosing my words carefully. "They speak of heavy taxation, of laws that favor the wealthy, of a justice system that seems indifferent to their plight. If we could show them that we are willing to listen, to make real changes, we might quell the unrest without further violence."

Ramses frowned, the idea clearly at odds with his usual approach. "And what of those who would see such leniency as weakness?" he asked. "What about Eldra Solaris and his soldiers? Do you not understand that these rebels would be the ones to side with him?"

"Compassion is not weakness," I insisted. "It takes greater strength to forge peace than to wage war. We can be firm without being cruel, just without being ruthless."

"Here we go again with this!" He slammed his fist on the arm-rest. "It seems you still have a lot to learn. Do you think if those rebels got through our gates, they would show you a modicum of the mercy that you speak of? They would parade your head through the streets. You killed Aislinn Furian, their leader. *You* did that."

"Not by choice!" I argued.

"Ah. But will they care about the cause? No."

"Because you have made it that way!"

"Atreya! My word is law!"

I tensed, the force of his decree reverberating through the throne room. Ramses' mood had shifted from light to thunderous in the span of our conversation, and I was reminded of the volatility that lay just beneath his surface. The king in him was a tempest, powerful, and often merciless.

If I could just stay quiet and keep my head down.

If I could just not talk back.

If I could just do what he wanted...

"Your word is law," I repeated.

And I will break every one of them.

●

I walked the gardens. It was all I could do to stay out of the throne room. Stay out of Ramses' way.

Servat was carving an apple under a tree in the garden when I found him. He straightened slightly, no longer leaning against the tree.

"My Lady, you are looking better," he said.

I offered him a scowl. He speared the white flesh of the apple with a knife, carefully popping it into his mouth. He chewed slowly, silently, and thoughtfully. Servat lingered on me with an air of casual appraisal, a faint smirk playing at the corner of his mouth as he chewed the apple slice.

Servat's eyes followed the trail of my approach, the faint smirk morphing into a soft smile as he offered me a slice of the apple. "Would you care for some? It's particularly sweet today," he murmured, low and inviting.

I hesitated, then accepted the slice with a small nod. "Thank you," I murmured, letting the crisp sweetness burst on my tongue. I chewed slowly, watching him from under my lashes. Servat seemed at ease, the serene environment of the garden a stark contrast to the tales of war that clung to his name.

The King's General. I scowled.

"You know, watching you scowl only makes you more intriguing. It's as if you're challenging the world to a duel, and I must admit, I'd wager on you."

That slick tongue of his.

Servat's hand turned, his fingers lightly grazing mine. But as quick as the touch came, it went, leaving a lingering warmth on my skin.

I cleared my throat, glancing around to see if anyone noticed. "Servat, I need to know what happened at the war camps. What is Ramses not telling me?"

The levity in Servat's demeanor faded, replaced by a solemnity that aged him. He glanced away, his hand retreating from the space between us.

"The camps were a crucible, testing the limits of our resilience. Ramses did what he thought best to keep morale, to keep us focused on the fight rather than the fear." He inhaled deeply, the air seemingly heavy in his lungs. "But the cost... it was steep. Men were broken, physically and mentally. Some turned on each other, while others simply... gave up."

"We can't have weakness in war," Servat said. "So, the king made a decision. You know how much he hates wasting resources."

"He's *killing* his own men?"

"The ones who do not make the cut. We pillaged some villages near Tor. Ramses was sure they were hiding conspirators. They *weren't*."

"Ramses said that's where they found the rebels, though," I said, confused.

"Ramses has a very fucked up definition of what a rebel is," Servat huffed.

"You say pillaged. Did Vrys? Did he?" I asked.

"The boy's heart is as soft as yours." Servat shook his head. "The king's paranoia has grown, my lady. It's become a shadow over us all."

"Paranoia?" I echoed.

He leaned in closer, his warm breath washing over me. "The king sees enemies in every shadow, traitors in every whisper. He's tightened his grip on the kingdom, on us. It's suffocating. He's stopped trade routes, everything is to come to Ember and nowhere else."

"That will kill everyone outside!" I shouted. His hand was over my mouth in an instant, his lips pursed in a grimace. "Sorry," I said against his palm.

"Just because the guards are tongue-tied, does not mean someone else can't hear. Corina, for example." He removed his hand, but remained in my space, inhaling me.

"Servat," I warned.

"I know. I know. Look, but don't touch." He leaned away from me, eyes darting down to my mouth.

I licked my lips, my mouth suddenly dry.

"I miss touching," he whispered, taking another bite of apple. "Tasting." Juice dribbled down his chin, his tongue licking it away. He glanced up at me, my breath leaving me in one go.

I shook my head, blinking several times, gathering myself.

"Stopping trade routes... that's madness. Ferenz cannot sustain itself in isolation. They rely on those trade alliances for food and resources. He's leaving them all to die. What choice does it leave them but to rebel?"

Servat's frown deepened, etching lines of worry across his brow. "It is madness, and yet, Ramses is convinced it's the only way to root out the disloyal. He's become obsessed, seeing betrayal in every missed glance or hesitated word. We are a kingdom on the brink, not from outside forces, but from our own ruler's descent into fear. Ever since that night that Eldra appeared to you, he has been paranoid."

"Careful. What you speak of is treason. To stand against the king is treason," I whispered.

"To watch Ember and Ferenz fall into ruin while doing nothing is a far greater treason," Servat countered, arms folded over his broad chest.

He reached out, his hand stopping just shy of my cheek as if the air itself was a barrier he dared not cross. "My lady," he began in a tender murmur that sent shivers down my spine, "there's more at stake here than the fate of kingdoms."

I gaped at him, finding a depth of emotion there that I had noticed before—and had chosen not to see.

"And what would that be, Servat?" I asked in barely a whisper.

We promised. We promised never to speak of it. We promised to let it go.

He hesitated, the air between us charged with unspoken promises and unfulfilled desires. Then, leaning in so close that I could feel the warmth of his breath, he whispered, "You, my lady. You are what's at stake for me."

Alarm bells rang in my head.

We promised to let it go.

I drew in a sharp breath, taken aback by the raw honesty on his face, the vulnerability he so rarely showed. The garden around us seemed to hold its breath, waiting for my response.

And I was painfully aware that a dozen guards were watching us. Tongue-tied or not.

He didn't seem to care. Like he knew they would say nothing. Like they could say nothing.

"Servat, we—" I began, but he placed a finger gently upon my lips, silencing me.

"I know the perils that lay before us," he continued, "I know the lines we cannot cross, the duties that bind us. But should the world crumble around us, should all else turn to ash, I want you to know one thing that is as certain as the sun rising in the east."

My heart pounded in my chest as he leaned in even closer, his lips just grazing the shell of my ear. "I love you," he confessed, the declaration a silken thread weaving through the swarm of my thoughts. "What he does to you—what he makes you do with those men... I hate it. I would take you from here. Far from here. You have to know that."

For a moment, everything stood still.

Running away with Servat had never been in my grand plans.

We promised to let it go.

Servat pulled back, searching for a reaction, for any sign of the feelings that coursed through my own heart. But before I could speak, before I could acknowledge the love that I, too, harbored, he stepped back, the flirtatious rogue returning like a mask to shield us both.

"And with that, my lady," he said with a wink, "I must take my leave. Duty calls, and we both have roles to play."

I watched him go, the taste of the apple and the echo of his confessions lingering with me.

We promised we promised we promised we promised we promised.

⬤

The yearly harvest had withered. Ramses planned to conduct another to restore vitality to the crops.

A mix of six humans and lesser Fae that had been captured beyond the wall were lined up in the dried-out fields.

Corina stood to my left, Servat to my right. The afternoon sun was blaring down on us.

The captees were tied up, dirty from head to toe, and on their knees. A blue-skinned woman with a broken translucent wing was hunched over, barely breathing. I had seen a handful of the winged Fae through Ember when the walls had been opened. Paper-like and opulent. How I had wished I had wings.

"This is necessary," Ramses insisted.

I couldn't accept it. "Are there no fields left to harvest in the outlands? In Calazar or Ratten?"

Servat responded with rigid formality, "We've been transporting all we find to Ember during our patrols."

The captives remained motionless, their fates sealed.

"Why am I here?" one of the male Fae asked. He was larger than the others, a patchwork of scarring on his otherwise handsome face. "I fought in your war, on your side. I provided aid."

Servat stepped to him, raising his sword under the man's chin, maneuvering his head to the side. "I recognize him."

Ramses' eyes flicked toward the scarred Fae. I could see it on his face that he had no idea who this male was. "Your service is remembered," Ramses said, "but the needs of Ember outweigh past allegiances. The land is unforgiving, and we must do what is necessary to ensure our survival."

"It is this way because of you," the male hissed, the accusation aimed squarely at Ramses. "You have rotted the lands. You have let the world outside your walls wither. When there were four kings, we never had to worry. You promised us land if we fought for you. Gold I never saw. Instead, your men raided Paladin. Took the humans for slaves."

"You said the Fae were superior. But treat the ones that aren't highborn just like the humans." The blue woman looked up then, glaring at us. "You are no king of mine," she spat, black eyes glittering. "You were supposed to put your magic *back* into the land, nurture it. You destroyed it, harboring all that power and giving nothing back. And then dare walk with *demons*."

I glanced uneasily at Servat, recalling how he had said Ramses had stopped trade routes from going anywhere but the checkpoints outside Ember, how he had been killing his men.

I've seen Ramses burn his men in piles. I witnessed him sweep through the city on his worst days. And the men that he did keep—something was off about them.

A human woman, barely older than Aquinetta had been, started praying. She prayed out loud to gods I didn't know, tears running down her dirty face.

"Ramses. We have more than enough power. Show me how to put it back into the land."

"Are you out of your mind?" he spat back at me, alight with fury. "Any power we lose makes us vulnerable to them." His finger jabbed towards the captives.

"And reaping them is any better? A *human* has no magic."

"Humans have their tenacity. It appeases Inamak. The Fae and human's lifeblood and magic will heal the crops."

"You are a Blackwater King. The magic of the land is yours to be tended," I reminded him, my words a plea for him to remember his duty.

"I am tending to it, wench," Ramses snarled. His movements were a blur. One minute he was standing off to the side, the next he was in front of the blue woman, dagger slicing across her neck.

She didn't scream. Not as her blood flowed like a waterfall down the front of her. She snarled at Ramses, all the hate she could muster on her face. Then she slumped forward, her bent wing giving its final twitch.

A heavy silence fell over the field, broken only by the soft sobs of the human woman and the harsh breaths of the remaining captives.

"Stop. Show me how to do it. Show me how to transfer magic into the earth."

"You dare challenge my methods?" he hissed, stepping closer, the threat in his posture unmistakable. "You think you can simply will the land to heal? It requires sacrifice—something you seem unwilling to comprehend."

"I comprehend that that sacrifice is magic. You have killed many, and the land still dies. I am willing. It can have mine."

"No."

"It is *my* magic—"

"You vowed it to me. Not to the people. Not to Ferenz. To me. It is *mine*."

"I promised you no such thing—" I started protesting.

"To honor and obey, to serve and defend, to love and cherish for all the days of my life." He pointed a finger at his chest. "To honor *me*. To serve *me*. To defend *me*. To love *me*. To cherish *me*."

"You have perverted our vows just as you perverted our marital bed. Your people need you—"

Anything I would have said was lost with a sudden rush of motion. Servat flashed through a blur of bronze and white. One by one the people dropped to the ground, dead, blood pooling around them.

Tears blurred my vision. Horror gripped me, a vise around my heart as I watched the life seep out of them. My breaths came in short, ragged gasps, the metallic tang of blood saturating the air. Tendrils of panic clawed their way out of my stomach, up my throat, and out my mouth in a choked scream.

Screaming. Fire. A lion. A woman.

Corina stood behind me, her hand coming to the small of my back. It radiated a soothing warmth. Her subtle yet potent magic wove through my senses, steadying my shaking limbs and quelling the tempest of anger threatening to overwhelm me. I closed my eyes, leaning into her touch, allowing her mood-control magic to blanket me like a cloak—until I could look upon the dead before me, and I felt...nothing.

A silent void where anger, hate, and horror had just been.

The blue woman was still staring blankly at Ramses. A final act of defiance against the tyrant before her.

"Servat has sown the seeds for this reaping," Ramses said haughtily. Already, the ground was becoming greener, and the crops were coming back to life.

My hands clenched into fists, the nails digging into my palms. Corina's hand was still on my back, fighting with my fury to keep it at bay.

"You continue to feed the land a meal of poison, eventually, it will die," I said monotonously.

●

I didn't eat my carrots that night.

As the sun dipped below the horizon, casting long shadows against the furthest part of the wall surrounding Ember, I found Servat alone in a place we used to frequent. That felt like a lifetime ago now. The memory of the bloodied fields was still fresh, and the horror of the reaping seared into my mind. My fury was a storm, brewing and violent, ready to unleash its wrath.

"Servat!" I shouted.

He turned, his expression unreadable, but his face filled with a sorrow that did little to placate my anger. He didn't flinch as I advanced on him, my fists clenched at my sides. "You're making Ramses angry," he said softly, pressing his forehead against mine in a gesture meant to calm me. "I'm afraid of what he might do to you if you keep defying him."

Tears welled in my eyes, the frustration and helplessness of it all crashing over me. "And you think I care? What is any worse than what he has done? Do you think I care about making him angry after all he's done? After what you've *allowed* him to do?"

His hands gripped my shoulders. "I'm trying to protect you. I can't bear to see him harm you. Please, for your own sake, you need to—"

The slap came before I realized what I had done, my hand striking his face with a resounding crack. He staggered back, his hand going to his cheek, shocked.

"You call this protection?" I screamed. "Standing by while innocent lives are taken? While Ramses poisons the land and murders without remorse? While he uses my body for his gain! Does it hurt you? Does it hurt you when he breaks me? When he drags my maidservants by their hair out of my chambers because he is paranoid that they are all spies. Does it hurt you that I lay with men—or is it only okay when Ramses fucks me? You're complicit, Servat. You're no better than he is!"

His shoulders dropped, shame coloring his features. "I'm doing what I can to survive, to keep you safe. There are things you don't understand, things that I—"

"Don't you dare patronize me," I cut him off. "I understand more than you think. I understand that you're too afraid to stand up to him, that you'd rather watch the world burn than risk your own life. I thought you were better than this."

"You're right," he said quietly. "I have been afraid. If I had the means to overthrow him, I would have by now. I do not wield the magic that he does. But you cannot sit there and say those things to me when your hands are not clean of blood."

He might as well have slapped me.

"I love you. I've loved you from the moment I first saw you. Every day, every moment, my heart beats for you. And it breaks for you. Do you think it's easy for me to watch you suffer? To know that every night, Ramses drags you into his bed, that every day he subjects you to his cruelty? It tears me apart, but I am powerless against him."

"You choose to do nothing. You choose to let him use me, to let him use us all. Do you think your love absolves you? It doesn't." I knew deep down that it was not fair of me to say these things to him. He was right. We do not have the kind of power needed to take down Ramses Blackwater.

His hands trembled as they reached for mine. "I don't expect absolution. I don't expect forgiveness. But know that every time he hurts you, every time he tears you down, I feel it, too. I carry your pain with me, always."

I yanked my hands away from his grasp, my anger flaring. "Then fight with me," I demanded. "Don't just stand there and watch. If you love me, prove it. Help me end this. Help me take back our lives."

Servat's shoulders sagged, his face a mask of anguish. "I will. I swear to you, I will. But we must be careful. Ramses is not a foe we can take lightly. We need a plan and allies. We need time."

"Time is something we don't have. Every day we wait, more lives are lost. More blood is spilled. I can't—"

The tears I had been holding back finally spilled over. Servat reached for me again, this time pulling me into his arms. I resisted at first, but then the weight of my grief and anger became too much, and I collapsed against him, sobbing into his chest.

"I'm sorry. I'm so sorry for everything. I promise you, we will find a way. We will bring Ramses down. Together," he said finally.

I could tell him about Corina and me. I could tell him I already had an ally. But what good would that do me? If Servat thought Corina was trustworthy, she would have already been in the loop—and vice versa.

None of the Blackwaters trusted each other.

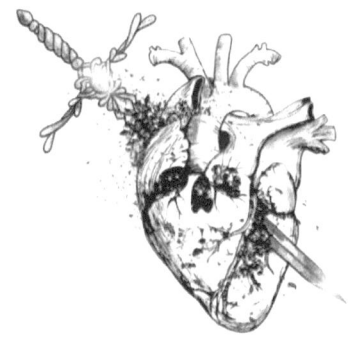

CHAPTER
TWENTY-SIX

R amses was seated on his high throne, which was made of lambskin and gold. The iron twisted into thick branches, bent at odd angles. The woman's agonized face reached just above where his head rested.

He was dressed in a royal blue robe, decorated with the symbols of the gods. He held a staff in his hand, a long piece of wood with a golden lion's head at the top. His generals and advisors surrounded him, dressed just as extravagant as he was.

I sat on a cushion before him, holding my hands in my lap. He looked at me and gently patted my head, pulling me to rest my head on his knee. He stroked my hair the way one might stroke a dog. I relaxed and listened to the gentle tapping of his fingers against my head.

Ramses had me dressed in white. Pure. A creation of white gossamer, ethereal and delicate. The bodice of the dress was daringly low cut, revealing the gentle slope of my collarbones and the warmth of my skin. The fabric was almost translucent, a whisper of material that caught the light and played with it, creating an aura of soft luminescence around me. It plunged down the front, ending just above my belly button. It was held in place by a nearly invisible lattice of silken threads, a web of support that ensured the dress remained both secure and revealing. The skirt was cut to reveal my legs, the fabric settling between my thighs in a way that left my hips exposed.

Had there not been a crown on my head, I could have been mistaken for a glorified whore.

"Vryseris is in bed?" I asked.

"The maidservants say so. He is in his room for the night," he answered.

"Who is coming?" My question was met with silence, the feel of his grasp on my hair tightening a fraction.

A warning.

"Someone I met outside the wall. I told you this a week ago. He and his companion are coming here."

Ah. The General from an empire that no longer was.

I glanced at him, my heart racing. "Will they be staying a while?" I asked, quiet and hesitant.

Ramses nodded, his grip loosening on my hair. "He has something I want."

I sighed inwardly, knowing what that meant for me.

●

Some time passed, and we were announced into the ballroom. It had been decorated with golds and red velvet and the chandelier was on fire with hundreds of colored lights.

Its walls were adorned with intricate red and white tapestries, symbolizing the delicate balance between passion and purity in Elven culture. To me, it represented the fragility of violence. The red was just blood that tainted the white.

The ballroom was filled with Elven elites and their families from all over Ember. Everyone was dressed in their finest clothing, and there was food and drink on every table. A band played soft music as the guests mingled and greeted one another. I was seated on a couch, next to Ramses, with the rest of the courtiers and advisors.

Above the dance floor, an enchanting, open ceiling revealed a mesmerizing night sky. The stars twinkled with a silvery brilliance, and
constellations came to life, telling tales of Elven mythology. Starry
dragons flew across the sky, and the moon was bright and full. The
dance floor was a polished expanse of white marble, reflecting the
shimmering stars above, creating the illusion that the dancers were
twirling among the constellations themselves.

Magical sconces and floating orbs of soft, ambient light hovered
at strategic points throughout the ballroom, mimicking constella-
tion patterns.

The far wall of the ballroom gave way to a terrace, its railings
twisted with vines of iron. Red and white blooms spilled over the
edges, their delicate scent wafting on the breeze. Below, the maze
garden waited, its labyrinthine paths a secret only the shadows
knew. A bridge of stone arced down to the next terrace, and beyond that, the castle's main courtyard stretched... and the wall.
Our prison of privilege.

I knew for whatever guest was coming, that Ramses was trying
to impress him, and I impatiently waited for the moment to come.

A flash of crimson and ebony snagged my attention. Corina
stood by a laden table, her lip curled at the spread. Her gown was
a waterfall of dark red, black lace overlay gleaming like a spider's
web. Gloves climbed her arms, a matched set.

Our eyes met across the room, and for a moment, the facade that
we were enemies flickered. It was a dangerous game we played, this
pretense of animosity, but it was necessary. Ramses must not suspect the alliance between us. As quickly as it came, the moment of
understanding passed, and once again the space filled with feigned
disdain.

"What has upset you?" Ramses asked me, his fingers raking
through my hair. I swiveled my head from Corina and he patted
my head again.

I composed my face into a mask of mild irritation, the role of the
slighted wife not difficult to assume.

"Corina," I said, my tone laced with a bitterness that wasn't
entirely feigned. I could muster up previous years of hatred I had
stored up for her. "She has a way of getting under one's skin, does
she not?"

I hadn't had the chance to speak to Corina since the night of Ramses' return.

Ramses chuckled, a low sound that rumbled through his chest. "Ah, my dear, let her be. She's harmless enough, so long as she stays in her place." His eyes followed mine to where Corina stood, a lone figure among the throng of guests. "Besides," he continued, "tonight is not about petty squabbles. We have a guest of honor, and our attention should be elsewhere."

His words were a reminder of the evening's purpose, and I nodded, my mind already racing with the implications of this mysterious visitor. "Of course, you are right," I said, the sentence rolling off my tongue. "Do we know when the guest will arrive?"

"Soon," Ramses replied, his attention already drifting to the entrance of the ballroom. "Everything must be perfect."

Corina turned away from us, her movements measured, engaging with the guests with a practiced smile. I watched her, admiring her ability to wear the mask of civility while her mind was no doubt racing with strategies and secrets.

Servat sauntered into the room with the effortless charm of a seasoned courtier, his presence at once drawing the attention of all those present. With a woman on each arm, he was the very picture of indulgence and poise. The ladies accompanying him were visions of elegance, their gowns of dark red silk clinging to their forms like the soft caress of twilight shadows. One, with locks as golden as the sunlit strands of dawn, and the other, with hair as rich and deep as the darkest night, complemented each other as well as they complimented him. He wore a dark blue tunic and matching trousers, encased within black robes that draped over his figure like a shadow.

"My King. My Queen," he greeted happily.

Drunkenly.

"Servat," Ramses said with a sigh, scrutinizing the wine in Servat's hand. "Perhaps you had enough to drink to drown?"

Servat scoffed while the women with him giggled. The sound was grating against my ears. "If I drown, I have two women to give me the kiss of life!" He released his arm from the brunette and slapped her on her backside. She staggered, righting herself and laughing at the same time.

I smiled, biting back the jealous rage that coursed through me.

"Careful, Servat. If you get too drunk you might put your prick in the wrong place," I said coolly. Ramses snorted and Servat grinned.

What kind of lover will these girls end up with tonight? I thought. Surely not the kind that I was being forced to have.

Servat's grin widened. "Ah, but my dearest, the night is young, and so are the possibilities," he said, his comment smooth as silk, a subtle edge of teasing beneath his words. He took a step closer, and I could feel the warmth of his presence like a forbidden whisper against my skin.

Ramses, blissfully unaware, let out a hearty laugh, clapping Servat on the shoulder. "Indeed, brother. Enjoy the festivities. We have much to celebrate tonight."

I watched as Servat bowed gracefully to the king, the gesture perfectly executed, but his smirk was directed at me—a silent challenge, a veiled promise. He turned to the golden-haired beauty and offered her his arm once more, but not before his fingers brushed against mine in a fleeting caress, hidden from all but me. The brush of skin sent a shiver, a mix of alarm and wanting, down my spine.

As they moved away, mingling with the other guests, the brunette leaned in to whisper something in Servat's ear. He threw his head back and laughed. I kept myself from biting my cheek. But his attention flickered back to me for just a moment, and I read a thousand unspoken words in it.

Ramses leaned in, breaking my trance. "What do you think, my love?" he asked, gesturing to the crowd. "A fine gathering, isn't it?"

I forced a smile and nodded, my thoughts still tangled with the brief, charged encounter. "Yes, a fine gathering indeed," I replied.

A dangerous game we've played all these years.

After a while, Ramses sat up straighter, his attention focused on the doors. Two newcomers entered, both men. My heart sank.

"You shall indulge in drinks and immerse yourself in dancing. Afterward, you will cater to the desires of that gentleman yonder." Ramses gestured towards the man in a vibrant yellow robe, so vivid that it nearly pained me to look at him. His skin resembled the hue of aged gold, and he stood tall, possessing a lengthy, slender physique. The man's visage was veiled by an extensive, cascading brown beard and mustache, while his eyes were deep pools of ebony ink. His hair was long, curly, and brown, falling to his shoulders. His intensity struck me, and I felt a twinge of fear.

Something about the man was off.

"I don't feel like pleasuring anyone right now," I mumbled. I was already taking the proffered wine that he held out for me. I could tell by the smirk on his face he found my little retort amusing.

"The best asset I have is your cunt. It could buy me an army of a thousand more."

"Are you in need of such an army? Is there a war that needs to be won?" I asked sarcastically between sips of the wine I knew he laced. This was his game—his angle. He was a smooth talker, a master of manipulation. He chuckled and reached out to touch my hair, running his fingers through it. The metal finger covering shaped into a talon snagged on my tresses.

Most of the men he brought into our home were nothing but war-stunk madmen. Some of them were richer than kings. Some had information from beyond the wall. But they were all the same.

And Ramses had what they all wanted.

Me. The Furian Slayer. The price men would pay to lie with a queen was pathetic—the price they would pay to sleep with the killer of the rebel queen—insurmountable.

My nursemaid, Joslynn, had warned me of such things. She had told me that Ramses was part of the Old World, and the Old World did not have the same values as others around me. The Old World was oppressive and cruel. The Blackwaters were a long-standing family of Kings before the wall had ever been built. Joslynn said that they revered the Queens of the Blackwaters as the most beautiful women in the world and that guests were to enjoy their company. It was an old custom service that was passed down through the generations, and it was one that Ramses was very familiar with.

Apparently, his mother endured such customs. Lady Serana, a vision of beauty in every aspect, was depicted in grandeur in almost every room of the palace. Ramses had paid a hefty sum to have one portrait magically enhanced.

It blinked.

She killed herself when Ramses' father, King Caine Blackwater, died. People said it was grief that did it. I know it was because

Ramses was set to be king, and she didn't want to live long enough to see what kind of monster he would become.

The power Ramses had to make his queen bend at his whim. To degrade herself. Eight times it has happened.

The drink began to work, and I wondered how long I would be conscious enough to know what was happening. Usually, it does not take long. I could feel the heat of the wine coursing through my veins, and my body began to tingle.

The man in the yellow robe seemed to know exactly what I was feeling, and he quickly made his way toward Ramses and me—no, he floated toward us, his feet never touching the ground.

Ramses stood and nodded his head toward the man in the yellow robe. The man took a step forward his black boot finally touching the floor. I felt a shiver of fear run through me and the man's nose twitched slightly, nostrils flaring.

"This is her?" the man asked, his accent thick and odd. He smiled at Ramses, and I noticed the gold cap of his fanged tooth—sharper than Fae teeth, and longer, like a cat.

"The one and only," Ramses answered, yanking my arm and pulling me up to greet the man. I stumbled ungracefully, tripping over the hem of my red gown. I tried to regain my balance, but I felt someone grab my wrist, righting me. I looked up to see the man in the yellow robe smiling down at me, his black orbs wide and eager. He was far from handsome, with a crooked nose and a nose-to-chin beard that was unkempt and unruly.

"Madam, we are pleased to meet you, and we hope you will enjoy yourself," the man said to me. His breath smelled of something metallic that sent alarm bells ringing in the back of my head, but the wine was pulling me far from danger. I couldn't even feel his hold on my wrist anymore and knew it was only a matter of time before I would be unable to remember anything about the evening.

It was the one thing I thanked Ramses for. At least he had enough sense to know I wouldn't want to remember it. Perhaps my pain potions were already ready for me in my chamber for the next morning.

"And, I presume this is Ronan?" I heard Ramses ask. He sounded like he was speaking through a wall. I looked over at him, but he was already engaged in conversation with the man in the yellow robe.

"Ronan," I said the name, slurred and thick. It was supposed to be a question, but I forgot what I wanted to ask. I felt myself swaying on my feet.

"She likes to dance," I heard Ramses say, distant and muffled.

"Does she? I shall take her to the dance floor then, while Master Xaneth and you talk business," another person said, so silky and smooth, an accent so light. It was so clear and resonant, and I felt myself being pulled in the direction of the man.

I realized I was being dragged by my wrist toward the dance floor. I turned my head behind me to see the man in the yellow robe called Xaneth, and Ramses gesturing for me to twirl, a look of approval on their faces.

I was slipping on the precipice of darkness that threatened to swallow me from the laced wine. Muffled laughing and whispering voices around me. The smell of cigar smoke and heavy perfume. The scent of spilled wine and sweat.

I was pulled flush against something hard, and I sagged against it. There was a slight sway in the movement, and I felt myself being spun. I was disoriented, but I laughed, delighted at whatever this was. I was dancing.

The person who had taken me to the dance floor steadied me, and I lifted my head to see what Xaneth's companion looked like.

Red eyes.

Like pools of fresh blood glistening in the candlelight. A curved, wicked-looking grin played on his lips. Sharp fangs flashed in the light. A long, narrow nose and a head full of curly, silvery hair that was pulled into a tight ponytail decorated with gold rings and chains.

He was beautiful—as if Elenaria herself sculpted him. His skin was pale and flawless, his cheekbones high and strong. His sharp ears were lined in intricate vine-like earrings. His lips were pink and full of promise, and I found myself drawn to him, the compulsion of the wine taking over me.

"Ronan," I murmured. He paused his hypnotic dance and turned to me, a look of curiosity washing over his face. His head tilted ever so slightly, with those bewitching blood-red pools boring unapologetically into mine.

Then—darkness swallowed me whole.

A dull, throbbing pain was gnawing at my temples, the weight of my head felt like a leaden anchor. I moaned softly, squinting as a sliver of light pierced through the slight parting in the curtains. Forest green curtains edged with a trim of gold, a familiar sight.

I found myself strewn haphazardly across my plush bed, swathed in the comforting confines of plump pillows and soft, warm blankets. A sharp pull at my neck made me grimace. With cautious fingers, I traced the tender skin of my neck, only to yank them back abruptly. My fingertips were stained with the rusty hue of dried blood. I jumped from the comforting confines of my bed and darted toward the vanity mirror. I frantically scanned my reflection, seeking any signs of an injury on my neck.

There it was—two, deep, angry red puncture marks that marred the flawless skin of my neck. The sight of it sent a shiver down my spine. It was not a deep wound, but it was enough to cause discomfort. I touched it gingerly, hissing as the pain shot through me. My mind raced, trying to recall how and when I had received such a wound. But all I remembered was a haze of fear, anger, and confusion, then—

A flash of silver hair flitted into my thoughts. For the life of me I could not hold onto that thought. It was as if the image had been ripped away by a gust of wind.

"Ronan," the name echoed in my mind, a haunting refrain. I struggled to piece together the fragments of last night. The dance, the wine, those bewitching red eyes. It all seemed like a disturbing dream, an eerie echo of reality.

I dashed to my wardrobe and pulled out a delicate lace scarf. Wrapping it around my neck, I covered the unsightly marks. My reflection was a ghost of its former self; pale, haunted, and strangely vulnerable. I touched the scarf, a pitiful attempt to cover it up. I searched the tables for any vial of salve that should heal the marks away. I found none.

"What did Xaneth do to me?"

I sank to the floor, the cold stone chilling me through the layers of my silken gown. I pulled my knees to my chest, the soft fabric crumpling under my grasp. A wave of nausea washed over me, and the room spun. I didn't feel the familiar bruising pain that came after a night of coupling. Tears prickled at the corners of my eyes, but I willed them away. I was no damsel in distress, waiting for a hero to save her.

I was just buying my time.

●

Breakfast was served in the dining hall, a long, narrow room with vaulted ceilings and a view of the snow-capped mountains far in the distance. The sun shone through the windows, casting a golden glow on the richly ornamented walls. The room was filled with the aroma of fresh-baked bread, fruits, and meats.

Ramses was seated at the head of the table, the large oval table covered with a white tablecloth and surrounded by twelve chairs. Three chairs were occupied. Ramses, Vryseris, and Xaneth.

I stood near the door, feeling the weight of the scarf around my neck. Vryseris smiled up at me.

"Morning, Mother!" he greeted.

"Morning, Vryseris," I replied, forcing a smile onto my face. I walked slowly towards the table, each step echoing on the marble floor. My heart pounded in my chest, the rhythm matching my steps. I took my seat at the table, across from Xaneth. A flicker of something dark and unreadable washed over his face. I quickly looked away.

"Good morning, my dear," Ramses said, his greeting as cold as the stone walls. He was busy reading a scroll, his attention only half on me. "Did you sleep well?"

"Well enough," I answered stiffly. I reached for a slice of bread, my hand trembling slightly. The room was silent, save for the rustle of Ramses' scroll and the clinking of cutlery on plates.

Xaneth didn't touch his food, and his stare never left me. "How are you feeling today?" he asked, his accent heavy and thick.

None of the men before him, had I ever seen again. Let alone dine with them at breakfast.

"Much the same as any other day," I replied, avoiding looking at him. His concern felt like a weight pressing down on me, making it hard to breathe. I placed the slice of bread back onto the plate, my appetite lost.

"Vryseris, leave us. Take your food and go," Ramses commanded behind his scroll.

Vryseris looked at me for a moment, uncertainty twisting his mouth, then rose from his seat and bowed to Ramses and me, then our guest, before disappearing in a billow of smoke.

Xaneth clapped his hands once, an annoyingly loud sound in the quiet of the room.

"What a talent!" he said, smiling.

"Indeed. It is a rare gift," Ramses responded, the scroll now forgotten in his hand. "It seems we must reconvene on our agreement." Ramses pointed stare at me made my heart sink. "Remove the scarf."

I swallowed, the dry lump in my throat making it hard to speak. I reached for the scarf, hesitating, then pulled it off.

Ramses cocked his head to the side, darting between the marks on my neck and then Xaneth. "You drank from her, but nothing else?"

"Nothing else," he confirmed.

Ramses scrutinized the marks a moment longer before he finally turned his attention back to the scroll in his hand. "A pity," he murmured, devoid of emotion. "I had hoped for more."

I watched the exchange between them, Xaneth shrugging his shoulders and licking at his gold tooth.

"More?" I found my voice, the word slipping out before I could stop it.

Ramses glanced at me, a smile playing on his lips. "More leverage. Seems you couldn't hold up your end of the bargain," he said to me.

I had been used—manipulated in a game I didn't even know I was playing. "My end?"

Xaneth chimed in, his tone playful. "Seems the drink you had, rendered me *useless*. I thought it was an... attack. Ramses had to explain your little *predicament*."

"A misjudgment on my part, I assure you," Ramses said.

"I will take her wholly as she is. No more, no less. Blood is power, yes, but yours—"

Ramses raised his hand to silence Xaneth. "She doesn't need to know the details."

I hated how he could carry on like that regarding me.

"What manner of Fae are you?" I asked Xaneth. I suspected perhaps he was a Nymph, something I had never seen before.

Xaneth snorted in disbelief. "Fae? My sweet. I am a Vampire."

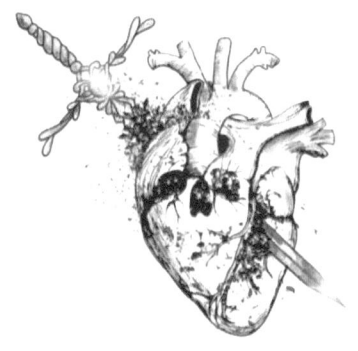

CHAPTER
TWENTY-SEVEN

A vampire. The word echoed in my mind. *A vampire.* The stories I had heard as a child suddenly came rushing back—the tales of creatures of the night, of blood and power, of fear and terror. Stories to scare children into obedience. The beings of darkness and offspring of Nexus.

But now, the reality was staring me in the face, sitting across from me at the breakfast table, casually making small talk with my husband.

I looked at Xaneth, examining him. The elegant way he held his fork, the sharpness of his face, the bronzed skin that didn't make sense.

The sun was shining down on him right through the window.

"You're in the sunlight. You are as dark as bronze. You are no vampire of the tales I know," I said dismissively.

"Atreya," Ramses snapped.

I forgot myself. Again.

"Forgive me," I said quickly, my hands dropping to my lap.

"You are correct," Xaneth admitted, the corner of his mouth twitching in what could almost be a smile. "The tales of my kind are...exaggerated. I am not just one of the vampires you have read about. I am much older... much more...powerful than you could ever imagine."

A chill settled over the room, heavier than the morning air. Xaneth's playful demeanor had given way to something stiff, commanding. "I am an Elder, one of the first of our kind, born not of bite, but that is another tale. The stories you've heard, the tales of darkness and fear... they are but shadows of the truth."

He paused then, letting his story sink in. I saw a depth of years that was impossible to understand. His eyes told a story of centuries lived, of civilizations risen and fallen, of a time when the world was young.

"So, you see," he said, a hint of the old humor returning to him, "I am no ordinary vampire. The sunlight does not harm me, nor does silver or blessed water. I am not bound by the rules that govern the younger of my kind."

I swallowed, the weight of his revelation pressing down on me. I had thought I was beginning to understand my situation, but now I realized that I was even more lost than before.

Ramses snorted, still looking over the scroll. "Yes, yes. Fae tales and all that."

Xaneth ignored him, and his focus was on me. "We are not demons, Lady. We are merely... different. Gifted, you might say."

I looked up at him, my heart pounding in my chest. "Gifted?" I echoed. "Is that what you call it?"

Xaneth's smile faded. "It's what we are. We are not human, Lady. We are more. More powerful, more enduring. And yes, more... dangerous."

Red eyes and long silver hair flashed in my mind.

"You had a companion with you...is he...?" I started to ask.

"Ronan. He is my progeny. I am rather proud of that one," Xaneth smiled. Even with his warm charm, his aura was cold, and I knew it was a mask. He was a predator, a hunter.

"Your... progeny?" I asked, the unfamiliar term echoing oddly in the room's silence. "Does that mean..."

"He is a vampire as well, yes," Xaneth completed my sentence with a note of pride. "I chose him. I... transformed him."

The image of Ronan flashed in my mind again—his silver hair, the strange, ethereal beauty about him. I thought of the mark on my neck and felt a cold shudder run down my spine.

"Did Ronan... did he...?" I couldn't finish the sentence, but Xaneth seemed to understand what I was asking.

"No, Ronan did not touch you. That was my doing and mine alone."

The relief I felt was overwhelming, but a new wave of fear quickly replaced it. If Xaneth had done this to me, what else was he capable of? What else had he done that I didn't remember?

"And what will happen to me now? Will I become... like you?" It didn't sound like a stupid question to me.

Both Ramses and he guffawed at that. Xaneth even slapped his knee in amusement. I felt my cheeks flush.

"I don't understand," I shook my head, my confusion growing with each passing second. "If you drank my blood, doesn't that mean..."

Xaneth shook his head, his laughter subsiding. "Drinking blood does not make you a vampire," he explained. "There is more to our kind than that. Much more. Imagine? Ha! There would be a swarm of them—like rats!"

I saw a shift in Ramses' demeanor, one that told me Xaneth had said something that irked him.

"His progeny is not like him. He couldn't join us this morning on account of the sun," Ramses pointed a clawed finger to the window. "You will have to forego the wine tonight, love."

My heart skipped a beat. He meant for me to be *aware*.

Xaneth flashed his teeth at me, the gold of his fang glinting in the light. "I will be gentle, dear."

"And what do you get out of this?" I asked the both of them.

Ramses raised a brow in warning.

"I get to taste the blood of the Furian Slayer. I get to know the woman who can crack the sky," Xaneth grinned at me. Xaneth leaned in, and I could feel the coldness of his breath. "You have a gift, one that you have not yet realized. I can sense it, like a storm on the horizon."

"Xaneth here... he has a penchant for collecting rarities," Ramses said.

"This is but a bonus," Xaneth said brusquely.

Ramses shifted uncomfortably, a frown creasing his brow.

"Tonight, then," I said, forcing a smile onto my face. "I look forward to it." I rose from the chair with a jolt and left.

●

The temple was a tempting escape, a place where Ramses and Xaneth couldn't reach me. But shaving my head and hiding among the priestesses wasn't a solution, not when it meant abandoning Vrys. And I had no desire to endure a "romp" with a Vampire Elder.

Instead, I found myself standing before the dragon's keep, a massive dome shrouded in mist and clouds. The framework glowed with ancient magic, each iron bar as thick as a tree trunk. From a distance, the dome seemed to swallow the sun and moon whole.

As I approached, the magical energy hummed through my veins, setting my skin tingling. The iron bars loomed over me, glowing runes etched into their surface. I reached out, hesitantly, and touched the cold metal. The magic flared in response, whispers of ancient spells echoing in my mind. Only such powerful magic could contain these creatures.

A dark thought clawed its way into my consciousness: I could release them. Unleash them upon Ember. A selfish, cruel part of me didn't care who would suffer.

A vision flashed before my eyes: fire raining down, innocent screams. I pushed the image away, forcing down that monstrous part of myself.

"Mother?" Vryseris called from behind me. I turned around, my hand still on the iron.

"Hello, Vrys."

"What are you doing here? Father doesn't want you around the dragons. They are dangerous," Vrys said. His comment carried a bit of worry and authority that I wasn't used to hearing.

"Just felt like a walk is all."

"Mother, you can't fool me," Vryseris said, crossing his arms over his chest. "You've never been drawn to the dragons. They *frighten* you."

And yet, I had been on their backs a handful of times.

The conversation with Corina about Aislinn's dragon echoed in my mind. I met Vryseris' gaze, seeing the shadow of Ramses' legacy in his eyes. Sorrow tugged at me – for the innocence he still possessed, despite everything.

I dropped my hand, the magic fading as I stepped back. "They are scary, true."

Vryseris stepped forward, his tall frame shadowing me. When had he grown so tall? "Or perhaps there's something else driving you here. Something or... someone?"

He had his father's keen intuition, or perhaps the foresight Ramses claimed he inherited from my father.

His grandfather.

"It's complicated, Vrys," I sighed, looking down at him. His features softened with understanding.

"The servants talk, you know. Say that father has you enjoying the company of other men," Vrys said, his tone clipped. He glanced at the scarf at my neck.

"I do not enjoy the company of other men," I snapped, avoiding his gaze.

"That isn't the only thing they say..."

"Gossip is just that." I turned my back to him, wondering how much longer he'd accept my lies.

Silence stretched out, his stare heavy on my back. "Mother, I'm not a child anymore. I can manage the truth."

I sighed, facing him. "Vrys, it's not about what you can handle. It's about what you need to know."

His teeth flashed defiantly. "I'm your son. If there's trouble, I have a right to know. I can protect you."

Shame washed over me. My child felt the need to defend me. I was supposed to be his protector.

I knew then that I couldn't avoid this confrontation. I'd hoped to shield Vryseris from the harsh realities of my world, but he was more aware than I'd thought.

"Yes, you're my son," I sighed. "But you're also the heir to your father's throne. And that means there are burdens you shouldn't carry."

Vryseris frowned. "So, there is trouble."

I nodded, struggling to compose myself. "Yes, there is. But I'm handling it, Vrys. Trust me."

He fell silent, his expression a mix of concern, doubt, and stubborn resolve. Finally, he nodded. "I trust you, Mother."

"Have you ridden on dragonback yet alone? Has your father given you permission to ride them?" A change of subject would be good.

Vrys smiled, gesturing for me to follow. "I've ridden Cirrok. He is smaller but fast!"

"Cirrok, the Swift Wind of the North," I said, smiling. I remembered the tales of the nimble dragon known for his speed and agility. "That must have been quite the experience."

He nodded enthusiastically. "It was incredible, Mother. The wind in my hair, the strength beneath me as Cirrok took flight... It was like nothing I've ever experienced."

Joy lit up his face. For a moment, I let myself bask in his happiness, forgetting the dire situation that had brought me to the dragon keep.

"He let me guide him too," Vryseris continued, filled with pride. "Father said it was a sign of trust. Cirrok wouldn't have allowed it if he didn't trust me."

"That's a significant achievement, Vrys," I said, placing a hand on his shoulder. "You should be proud. Not many can claim to have ridden a dragon, let alone guide one."

His chest puffed out at the praise, a grin spreading across his face. "Maybe one day, you could ride with me, Mother. I'm sure Cirrok wouldn't mind." Vryseris' sounded hopeful.

I never had the desire to ride a dragon alone, not that Ramses would ever let me anyway. He was particular about me not being alone with the dragons. Perhaps he was just worried about me flying off—or perhaps he was afraid I really would unleash them.

Not that I could anyway, with the entirety of the cage-like dome encased with magic. Vryseris led me to the gate, a lattice of iron guarded by Brotherhood soldiers. They bowed their heads as I passed, and I nodded in return. The gate was closed behind us, and we stepped out into the courtyard of the keep. We were greeted by the sight of a dozen or so of the Brotherhood soldiers, their hands on the hilts of their swords. One of the soldiers stepped forward, his voice echoing over the courtyard.

"Our lord and master, Prince Vryseris. Our Lady and Queen," he announced.

"The Furian Slayer," Vryseris added, a title that seemed to hold more weight than Queen. The soldiers saluted us, their fists over their hearts.

I walked beside him, feeling the Brotherhood watching me. I managed a small smile.

These people weren't my people. They were Ramses' people.

The courtyard was a riot of colors. Lush greenery covered the stone walls, and the sky overhead was a brilliant azure. Vryseris led me to the center, where a large fountain stood, gurgling softly. Encircling the fountain were stone benches, where a few soldiers sat, polishing their swords and sharing a quiet conversation.

Vryseris gestured for me to sit on a bench. "Wait here," he ordered, though his tone was gentle. He turned to the soldier who had announced us. "Captain, arrange for refreshments."

The captain nodded and dispatched a soldier, who disappeared into the keep. Meanwhile, Vryseris walked towards a group of soldiers engaged in a sparring match.

The soldier returned with a tray of goblets filled with wine. I accepted one gratefully. The wine was sweet and strong, a bit too strong for my taste.

Just then, a mighty roar echoed from the direction of the domed cage entrance. I jumped in my seat, nearly spilling my wine. The dragons were restless today.

Vryseris turned to look at me. "Don't worry, they are just eager for the flight exercise," he reassured me. "Every day at this time, they are let out into the dome, one by one, to spread their wings."

Despite his reassurances, I couldn't shake off the feeling of unease. The dragons were powerful, unpredictable creatures. And I was trapped with them, in this fortress, under the watch of the Brotherhood.

Vryseris waved his hand, and the spilled wine disappeared. I raised a brow. "When did you learn to do that?"

He beamed and said, "Recently. I am getting better at vanishing things. I let Commander Drian know we will be going into the dome."

"Oh-Vrys-we really don't have to."

"Don't you want to see me fly? I'll be going with Father beyond the wall again soon."

I swallowed at this, then sighed. "Fine. Okay."

The Brotherhood soldiers led us beyond the courtyard, down a winding staircase, and through a narrow corridor before coming to massive double doors. The doors swung open, and a gust of wind blasted through the hall. I was nearly knocked over by the force of it. Vrys laughed and pulled me along with him into the dome.

It opened up into a vast circular room. The domed ceiling was high and enchanted to look like an open sky. The floor of the room was a mosaic of colors, a patchwork of lush green grass and rocky terrains, mimicking a natural landscape. Scattered around were large boulders, presumably for the dragons to perch on. To one side, a large pool of water shimmered under the artificial light, casting dancing reflections on the surrounding walls. All along the walls, a series of hive-like giant holes, some larger and some smaller.

The dragons were nowhere in sight. The place felt eerily quiet, the silence only broken by the occasional gust of wind that echoed around the vast space.

He led me toward the center of the room, practically bouncing with excitement. "Wait till you see them in here," he whispered. "It's truly a sight to behold."

He held his hand up, his palm toward the floor. "Aegis."

A light shined from his palm and shimmered down to the floor, illuminating a mosaic of a glowing sigil.

As if on cue, a deafening roar reverberated through the dome, making the ground beneath our feet vibrate. A moment later, a dragon emerged from one of the hive-like holes, its scales glinting in the light. It was larger than any creature I had ever seen, its wings spread wide as it let out another roar, this time accompanied by a burst of flame that illuminated the dome. Its glowing red eyes fixated on Vryseris, who stood unfazed by the gigantic beast. It descended upon us, its wings beating the air and its tail lashing about. Sparks flew from my hands as I took a defensive stance and flung Vrys behind me.

"Mother—don't embarrass me," he hissed in a hushed tone, looking pointedly at the laughing soldiers.

The dragon drew nearer, its breath hot and acrid. Rows upon rows of spikes extended from its head, and its tail was tipped with a massive set of scythe-like blades. Silver scales ran down its neck and tail, giving it a metallic sheen.

Red eyes and silver.

Ronan. I shuddered.

"Steady, Aegis," Vryseris commanded. The dragon let out a puff of smoke from its nostrils before lowering its head in deference to the prince.

I watched in awe as Vryseris stroked the dragon's snout, whispering things I couldn't hear. Aegis could easily swallow us whole.

Its size was daunting, a reminder of the dangerous power these creatures held. Yet, there was a certain grace in its movements, a subtle gentleness in the way it lowered its head to Vryseris. He, for his part, seemed completely at ease, showing no fear or hesitation as he stood before the giant.

"Beautiful, isn't he?" Vryseris said, his hand still resting on Aegis' snout. I could only nod, unable to find a way to express my feelings.

"Would you like to touch him?" he offered, looking at me. I hesitated, my heart pounding in my chest. But something stirred in me, curiosity or perhaps a sense of adventure, and I found myself stepping forward.

With shaky hands, I reached out and touched the dragon. Its scales were smooth, cool to the touch, and surprisingly soft. Aegis turned his head slightly. There was intelligence in the way he looked at me, a depth of understanding that surprised me.

"He's... he's amazing," I managed to say. He smiled at me, his chest puffing with pride.

"Incredible creatures, aren't they?" he murmured. "And they are ours to protect and care for."

Aegis let out a low rumble, and I jumped back slightly. He watched me with a curious eye—red with splashes of green and blue.

"Aegis is gentle," Vrys said, grabbing roughly at Aegis' large fang tooth and pulling it playfully. Aegis opened his mouth, bared his sharp, serrated teeth, and sighed heavily.

"He seems annoyed," I said.

"Nonsense, he loves a good roughing up," Vryseris said with a laugh. Aegis let out another sigh and settled down on his haunches, lowering himself to the ground and turning his head to look at me. There were large spines on its neck and a row of spikes down its spine.

"How do you ride him?"

"Use the neck like a saddle. Better have strong legs," Vrys answered, pulling on leather gloves that had glowing symbols on the palms. "These keep your grip on the spines."

Things had changed since I had last been on dragonback.

The flight exercise began as Vryseris mounted Aegis, settling between a row of spines. The dragon spread its massive wings, creating a gust of wind that blew my hair back. With a powerful leap, they took to the air, soaring high above the domed enclosure.

I tried not to jump or shout for Vrys to get the hell off the dragon's back. Tried to remain calm and controlled.

Vrys and Aegis dove down straight to the ground, pulling up at the last second. They swooped past me, the wind from their passing whipping my hair around my face.

I settled down on the ground, where the sigil had appeared, watching them fly around the enclosure. There were hundreds of holes in the dome, each one housing a dragon. My fingers traced the sigil, and the symbols changed. As my fingers moved, the symbols transformed, morphing into legible names. The name 'Aegis' was the third on the list, illuminated with a light that made it stand out among the rest. I read the names slowly in my head, a strange mix of names, some familiar, like Balgeras and Rikandras, dragons used in the war before I was born.

Yet, among them, one name stood out. It was a name that had been brutally scratched out, overlaid with a harsh stroke to banish the name. The sight of it sent a chill racing through me, and yet, I found myself drawn to it, a moth to a flame. In a voice that sounded alien, even to me, I murmured the name out loud, the syllables echoing in the vast enclosure.

"Seraphix."

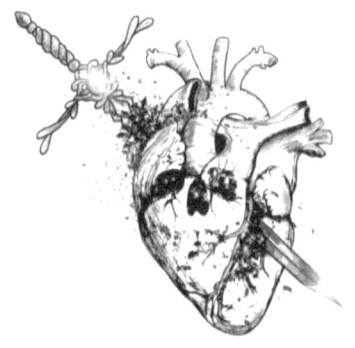

CHAPTER
TWENTY-EIGHT

T he name tore from my lips, and a crack echoed like thunder through the enclosure. The ground trembled beneath my feet as if in response to the shattered silence. A roar ripped through the air, making my heart stutter. It wasn't Aegis.

I spun around, my breath catching at the sight of another hive. This one pulsed with a malevolent red glow. The dragon that emerged was unlike anything I'd ever seen. Its scales were obsidian, sucking in the light. It was a terrifying beauty, a nightmare given form. Its eyes burned with the same red fire as the hive.

Vrys and Aegis circled back, caution replacing their usual grace. Aegis let out a low growl, but the black dragon just stretched its wings, unbothered.

"Seraphix," I whispered. The name felt wrong, like a secret that should have stayed buried. Ramses had never mentioned it, and I'd never heard the court whisper it. It was as if the dragon had been erased. But now, I'd summoned it. The black dragon's gaze locked onto mine, and I felt a jolt. It was like being pulled apart.

Was this Aislinn's dragon? Was this what Corina and I had been searching for? Vrys landed Aegis beside me, his grip on my arm tight.

"Mother, we need to go. Now." Aegis was tense, her tail thrumming. Even she was spooked. I hesitated, torn between the urge to run and the pull of the black dragon. Its eyes seemed to understand something. My hand reached out.

"Vrys, I—" The ground shook as the dragon's wings beat once. Dust swirled around us. I could hear the drums and horns from the palace. Soldiers on horseback poured through the gate. Everything seemed to slow down. The roar of Seraphix, the drums, the horns, it all blended into a deafening noise. Vrys was my only anchor.

"Mother, we're leaving!" he yelled. His grip tightened, and the world went black.

The sensation was disorienting. The sounds of the enclosure, the palace, everything faded. All I could feel was Vrys' hand and the rush of magic. One minute, the darkness was suffocating me; the next, I was gasping in the sudden silence of my castle room. Vrys' arms were still tight around me, his heart pounding against my back. We just held there for a second, our bodies humming with leftover adrenaline.

I didn't even have time to process what was happening. My door slammed open, the wood cracking against the stone wall. Ramses stormed in, his face twisted in a snarl. His aura blazed with this wild fury that made my stomach twist.

"Seraphix is loose!" he roared, barely cutting through the blaring alarms. I could hear the chaos from the dragon keep, even in here. My heart was racing again, my mind spinning.

Smoke billowed on the horizon, black clouds against the blue sky. The dragon keep was supposed to be this place of control, but now it was total pandemonium. Handlers and knights were running everywhere, trying to contain the disaster.

"Ramses," I began, ready to meet his wrath head-on. "We were there, Vrys and I. Seraphix—it's not like the others. There's something about it, something..." I trailed off, unsure how to explain the unsettling connection I'd felt.

"Something what?" Ramses snapped, his patience worn thin by the crisis at hand. "Do you realize what this means? If we cannot contain Seraphix, and he gets to the city, the destruction will be immeasurable!"

Before I could respond, a servant burst into the room, visibly distressed. "Your Majesties, the dragon is heading for the city! The handlers are trying to stop it, but it's too fast. We need to evacuate the citizens! Fourteen dragons have escaped!"

"Get Siorsen and Tiamut! Tell Servat to prepare the citadel!" Ramses shouted.

Vrys snarled, and my attention was drawn to him. His aura was....wrong. Tendrils of shadow flickered and writhed around him—then his irises blew wide. "Seraphix cannot be contained! He will destroy the kingdom! You have to let him go!" I realized that I had just witnessed him using his new magic.

Ramses gritted his teeth. "You couldn't see this coming before he escaped? How did you miss it?" "I can't just see things on a whim if I don't know what to look for! I felt something—a shift in the magic that binds the dragons to the keep. But it was unfamiliar. I've never felt anything like it before." Ramses rounded on me. "You had no business being in the keep in the first place!"

I felt a surge of power from him that sucked the air from the chamber, robbing me of breath. The walls shook, and the floor trembled. The room grew cold, and the flames in the hearth died out. "Ramses, please, you must understand—" I began, but he cut me off with a wave of his hand, his power crackling in the air like static.

Vrys stepped between us, his teeth bared. "It was me who brought her there, Father. If you must blame someone, blame me."

Ramses gritted his teeth. "Your newfound abilities do not give you the right to meddle with things beyond your understanding, Vrys." He studied Vrys for a long moment before turning to me. "Atreya, you should not have been there."

He raised his hand, palm up, and a swirl of energy formed between his fingers. "Servat, lower the wards. Let the beast out. It's better to have it out there in the wilds than here in Ember. Try to rally the other dragons, but don't fight." The light on his hands danced, then spiraled, shooting out and disappearing from the chamber.

My heart shattered. *So that dragon isn't the key to the wards. Servat is? Servat had the means to take us away this whole time?*

His title, The King's Shield, meant more than just being the General.

He was the actual shield.

•

I spent the next day avoiding the keep. My fingers fiddled with the crumpled drawing in my pocket, the edges digging into my thigh. I hadn't been back to Joslynn's room since finding it. Seraphix was long gone, and Ramses said he would deal with him later. Corina slipped into my chambers, her arms folded across her chest. A utility belt cinched at her waist held various pouches and sheaths, likely for weapons and other necessities a fighter might need at a moment's notice. She was paler than usual, with dark circles under her eyes.

"When I said we would find answers, I didn't mean for you to go and blow up the bloody keep." She glared at me.

"I didn't exactly plan on it," I muttered, avoiding her gaze. "Things just... got out of hand."

She scoffed, "Out of hand?"

"I didn't intend for any of that to happen," I snapped, finally meeting her eyes.

"I needed to let off some steam," Corina explained, noting my glance at her attire. "Sparring helps clear my mind. Maybe you should try it—might help with the tension you're carrying."

I couldn't help but smile. "Perhaps, but I doubt Ramses would approve. I haven't picked up a sword in years."

She sighed heavily. "You need to learn the art of suggestion. Make him think he thought of the idea. Men are simpletons that way. Even kings. How do you think I have gotten away with so much?"

I choked on a laugh.

"Ramses has been going on a tirade of trying to find this dragon. Seraphix. I don't suppose that was Aislinn Furian's dragon?"

I shrugged. "How was I supposed to know saying its name would release it? I could hazard a guess it is probably her dragon."

She rapped her fingers on her chest. "Have you tried the wards then?"

"No. I heard Ramses tell Servat to lower them. I think we were looking in the wrong place. It wasn't a dragon holding this place. It was Servat."

She frowned. "My cousin has such power and I know nothing about it?"

"Don't feel bad. I just learned my son has the gift of foresight and I wasn't told."

"But for Ramses to keep me out of the loop—failing to disclose the source of his wards to his advisor," she remarked with a bitter laugh. "Well, it would be rather simple. If that information were to get out, anyone could target Servat, leaving Ember without the wards."

I shook my head. It didn't make sense.

The wards had shown me a vision of the black dragon. It had spoken to me. Had that been Servat's doing all along? Was he warning me? Showing me something? I realized I was grasping at excuses to give him. There was no way to know. Not without asking him.

"I supposed that's a great reason why Ramses kept him alive and put him in such a high-ranking position. Servat isn't a legitimate heir to the throne, he's a bastard. Ramses found a use for him."

It wasn't fair. Another pawn on the chessboard.

"Even though he covets his brother's wife," Corina added with a sly grin.

"Shut up," I huffed.

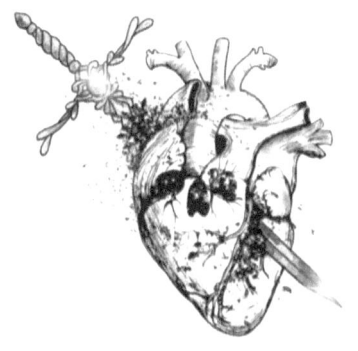

CHAPTER
TWENTY-NINE

That night, I returned to Joslynn's bedroom, the space echoing with memories. I ran my fingers over the intricate embroidery on her dresses, still hanging in the open wardrobe. My heart ached with a mix of longing and determination.

I fumbled through her desk drawer, a floating faelight illuminating the contents. My fingers traced the edges of the secret compartment, hesitating before pressing the hidden latch. The false bottom rose slightly, revealing the journal beneath.

Ramses claimed that both of my parents were dead. Joslynn knew something. She took a devastating secret to her grave, only depicting it in her drawings. It was evident that Ramses didn't want me to learn about them. Joslynn wouldn't have kept this from me. She knew how much I longed to know about them. So why didn't she?

Tears streamed down my face, the sound muffled by the thick walls that had once echoed with her laughter. She was gone, and everyone around me was harboring secrets and telling lies.

Memories flooded back as I sat with the journal open in my lap—memories of when I was whole before Ramses, when I was just a child in the gardens who didn't know better. In the wake of Joslynn's departure from this world, the vibrant light within me she had spoken of had begun to wane—and after the confrontation with Eldra, after being trapped in Ember's merciless grasp, that light had flickered out entirely.

With no way to get to Eldra, I lacked a purpose. A man like Ramses breaks a person down methodically, their tactics insidious and often invisible initially. He would say one thing and do something completely different. They feed on an individual's vulnerabilities, erode their self-esteem, and twist their perceptions until the victim doubts their reality. I often doubted mine.

It's a slow poison, a dance of manipulation and control in which he leads, and I follow, unaware that with each step, I am spiraling further into his web. He strips me of my identity and my purpose until I am nothing but an echo of his desires, a puppet whose strings are pulled with a master's touch. It wasn't like I was unaware of Ramses. But too often, I fell back into that web. I fell in love with honeyed promises and gentle touches. I fed from his hands the scraps of affection he would give to me like a starved animal.

I never had to beg Joslynn for love. She gave it freely. Joslynn loved me as if I were her own. Who fed me at her very breast. While her love was vast—Ramses' was a void. I became a hollow shell yearning for the love I once knew. And in that aching void, heartbreak was a silent scream. It was easier to tolerate him when she had been around.

I traced the lines of her drawings with my fingertips, feeling the spark of the old me in my chest. She would have told me the truth if she could. She did tell me. The only way she could.

"You could never speak of it." I whispered, realization dawning.

I scrambled to my knees, tearing the pages from the journal and arranging them around me. Joslynn had been telling a story—one that she could never speak of. Like the tongue-tie spell that had been used on the guards, they never spoke of what they saw, of what they heard. Servat took his pleasantries in making conversations obvious for that reason. Joslynn had been spelled from telling the truth about me. She wanted to get us out. She wanted to take me to Zay'Nath and had been trying to tell me the truth all along.

The reality of it hit me hard. Joslynn could have escaped at any point. She could have slipped away in the Hyperion Market at any time. She could have disappeared, and Ramses would have hunted her down—but she probably would have escaped. She never did. She always came back for me.

I raked through the pages once more, ingraining everything to memory. There was something odd in all of her drawings. At first glance, I didn't notice it. I thought the darkened smudge of a thumbprint on each page to be an accident. But as my gaze darted from one image to the next, the smudges seemed less like the incidental stains of a careless hand and more like deliberate markings placed with intention.

The smudges trailed over the drawings like breadcrumbs, leading me through a labyrinth of ink and parchment. I took out the drawing of my mother from my pocket and added it to the mess. I snatched a fresh paper from the journal and began replicating each thumbprint placement, marking them. Then, I moved onto the next page, moving the drawings together so the smudges made sense. And then the last thumbprint—at the center of the Solaris Sun Emblem.

I held my new page up, a series of dots and nothing more. I pinched the bridge of my nose and let out a laugh. I officially cracked. They were just smudges. Nothing else. No. No. Something is here. I am just missing it. I scanned all the drawings again, trying to piece together what I may have missed. There had to be something. Anything. I held each page up, examining them, faelight seeping through the semi-translucent parchment. I moved my glowing orb of light before me, lifting the pages up to it. Nothing. But then my eyes dropped down to Joslynn's crude rendition of Ferenz.

I brought the map closer to the orb, and this time, I overlaid my dot-covered paper on top of Joslynn's map, and the dots aligned perfectly with specific landmarks within the land of Ferenz. They weren't random at all. I wasn't crazy. I traced the path with my finger, starting from the center of the city of Ember, then down at the old abandoned watchtower just outside the city gates, then east, past what was once the Hyperion Market. The path snaked through the town of Vanhyn, cutting down to Calazar and through the Paladin Plains, then west to Ambrose Port. That last dot was floating in the sea: no land, no city, just a dot. The final smudge, the one at the center of the Solaris Sun Emblem, rested over that spot in the Sahari Sea.

My heart stuttered to a halt. Joslynn had drawn a map leading to New Solara. To Eldra. The realization was like a punch to the chest, knocking the wind out of me. My breath came in short, ragged gasps; my lungs had forgotten their purpose. My pulse quickened, a staccato rhythm pounding against my temples—too Loud. I couldn't breathe. I couldn't think. The walls closed around me, the shadows stretching across the room like phantoms. The pages fluttered like trapped birds, and the dots, the smudges, the secrets they held— A wave of dread crashed over me, and I was drowning in it. "You could never speak of it," I whispered to the empty room, to Joslynn's ghost.

"Were you on Eldra's side this whole time?" How many times had I ignored the signs, the silent screams for help?

The seizures. How she said that no healer could fix her sickness. Because it was never a sickness. The way she always spoke in cryptic messages—

"There is a beast within the walls."
Seraphix.

My hands shook as I clutched the map, the parchment crinkling under the pressure. The room spun, and I tried to steady the world that threatened to fall away from me.

Had she wanted me to go to Eldra? I couldn't ask her now, and she had gone to great lengths to ensure no one would find this. In my hands, I had the very thing that Ramses would kill me for. I swallowed thickly, breathing in slowly, talking myself through what I was about to do next. She was never afforded a proper burial. I took the drawings and placed them back into the journal. Then, I grabbed a cloth from the desk and carefully wrapped the journal—this would be her shroud. She will have the pieces of me with her. This secret was safe with me. Until I could use it to my advantage. I lit the hearth, and the flames flickered to life. I stared at the fire, my grasp on the journal loosening. Then, I tossed the journal into the fire and watched as they consumed the pages—my final farewell. I would never step into this room again.

●

I found myself in the courtyard closest to the city wall. White walls stretched out in front of me, broken up by a series of narrow archways. Hesitantly, I stuck my hand in the nearest archway. I was greeted by a blast of icy air and a wall of white. I sighed. I knew that would happen, but a part of me had hoped it wouldn't. That somehow, Ramses had been wrong, and that dragon controlled the wards. Some of me had even hoped I would see the vision of that dragon again.

Had it been Seraphix? Had he told me to wait because I was meant to release him?

"Don't suppose you're trying to climb over that wall?"

A man asked from the side of me, his silhouette illuminated by the dim moonlight as he leaned casually against a weathered stone pillar.

"Mind your business," I snapped, fixated on the daunting wall before me. "A soldier should know his place and speak when spoken to."

"I'm not a soldier. And I would think it is my business," he replied with amusement. "Anyone allowed to go over the wall would just walk through the grand iron gates. They would not need to climb it, especially not cloaked in the shadow of night."

"I am warning you!" I snapped, my patience dwindling.

"Warnings are not needed. Who am I to stop a queen from doing what she wants?"

That hauntingly familiar sound had been whispering inside my head for the last day. A light breeze rustled the nearby leaves, carrying the scent of blooming orchids. His scent.

"You-you! That night. You are Xaneth's slave," I stammered, recognizing him in the pale light.

At the mention of the word slave, his eye twitched as though struck by a sudden pain. "Yes. I do suppose I am," he admitted reluctantly. "I just didn't expect to see you here, in the dead of night, attempting to scale walls. What's your name?" he asked, pushing away from the stone pillar and moving closer.

"Does it matter?" I asked, crossing my arms over my chest defensively. "You should know it by now."

He chuckled lightly. "Perhaps not to you, but it matters to me. Yes. I know your name. But formal introductions are polite. I want to think myself a gentleman." He pointed a finger at his chest. "My name is Ronan."

I found myself staring at him. Ronan. "Atreya."

"Atreya," he repeated my name, rolling it on his tongue as though tasting a fine wine. The accent of his made my name sound prettier. "It suits you."

I didn't know how to respond to that. Was it a compliment? An insult?

"Why are you here, Ronan?" I finally asked. He looked at me for a long moment.

"I could ask you the same thing."

I sighed, feeling a strange sense of comfort in his presence. "I need answers," I admitted, drifting back to the imposing wall.

"Answers can be dangerous, Atreya."

"Not knowing is worse," I said. "Why are you and your master here? What information does he have that I am to be bargained with?"

Ronan's eye twitched again, his hands clenching into fists. "So it is true what they say about Blackwater women." He took a step towards me, his face inches from mine. "You think I'm important enough to know things? Are you not the king's wife? Shouldn't you know everything?"

I snarled at him, baring my teeth.

"Ah, the royal treatment," Ronan said sarcastically.

"You think this is a joke?"

"Far from it, Your Majesty," he replied, his lips twisting into a smirk. "I just find it fascinating that you, of all people, are asking me for help."

"I didn't ask for your help!" He raised an eyebrow, his smirk never leaving his face. "Oh? My mistake. I thought you were asking me about Xaneth's plans."

"I was asking why you are here!" My fists clenched at my sides. "Why are you and your master in my kingdom?"

Ronan shrugged, his hands tucked casually into his pockets. "Since you're so keen on knowing, we're here for the weather. Xaneth loves a good storm."

"That's not funny," I bit out, my frustration growing.

"Isn't it? I thought it was rather clever."

I shoved past him. "I have to get ready for your master's visit," I spat out. "I do hope he goes easier on you. Perhaps he will heal you after he feeds from you, this time," Ronan called out after me.

●

I was bathed until my skin was raw. The maids had taken their time with me, and the stinging of the water on my new neck holes was making me want to scream. I dressed and began wandering the halls, waiting to be summoned. The halls were deserted on the king's command. He didn't want anyone else to hear me.

The metal of my bracelet irritated my skin, the silk of my gown itched—I could feel my bones. Everything inside of me screamed. I could fight. Fight back. I could get myself killed. I could die. I could. Vrys. That single thought drove away the darker ones. Part of me recited what Joslynn had told me all those years ago.

That I was saved from poverty, that being a Queen came with its own set of duties. I could never imagine Vryseris putting his wife through what his father put me through. But I didn't know what Ramses was like as a boy. His mother died when he was young. Perhaps that was why he was so cruel.

No. I wouldn't humanize the man who put me in an arena to fight for my life. The man who beat me into a bloody mess. The man who gifted me to others to be used. I was a whore who wore a crown.

"Where has this ire come from?" I asked myself.

I never had such a temper. I traced my fingers along the cold stone wall as I pondered, the chill of it seeping into my skin. Maybe it wasn't anger, not really. Perhaps it was a realization, an awakening to the reality of my life, the life I had been forced into—the life I had accepted all too willingly in the name of survival.

A sharp laugh escaped my lips, echoing in the empty halls. How ironic it was, I thought, that I was surviving by slowly dying. Each day, a piece of me was being chipped away, leaving behind a hollow shell of the girl I once was. The girl Ramses had saved from poverty, only to be thrust into a life of wealth and misery.

My footsteps echoed as I walked, the sound of my heels against the stone floor the only indication of my existence. It was a deafening silence. It was as if the castle held its breath, waiting for something to shatter the calm. I wrapped my arms around myself, the silk of my gown providing little warmth against the biting cold. Ramses had never cared for my comfort or thought me worthy of even the slightest consideration. Unless it somehow benefited him or his image. I stopped before a tall mirror, my reflection staring back at me. I hardly recognized the woman who looked back: the hollow cheeks, the pale skin, the thin lips drawn into a harsh line.

"I am not a whore," I whispered to my reflection. "I am a queen."

I tried to keep from trembling. And as I spoke it, I felt something stir within me. Not anger, not resignation, but defiance. What I had been feeling all along. Why I continued to speak out of turn. Ramses wanted me to be complacent. To accept my lot in life and not fight back. My fingers found their way to my throat, feeling the healing scars there. My magic hadn't been able to heal them entirely.

Ramses wanted to take Vrys into a camp beyond the wall—to taint the innocence that still shrouded our son. In all my years with Ramses, he never allowed me beyond Ember's walls unless it suited him. He never shared his plans with me after that night with Eldra. He never discussed his ambitions with me outside of the usual rant. I had been relegated to the role of a trophy. A possession. A toy. Not even to dispatch rebels in the arena. But there was something out there, beyond the wall, that called to me.

Freedom.

Freedom...a word so foreign yet so compelling. It was a concept I had only ever dreamed—of a luxury I hadn't been allowed. But now, it was within my grasp, just beyond the imposing walls of Ember. And I knew where New Solara was. If Seraphix could get out, that meant I could. But Servat—he was just as responsible for keeping me here. All that talk of him wanting to get me out of here.

Why hadn't he? Why?

How could he say that if he could get me out of here, he would—only to be the very one responsible for keeping me here? I needed to convince him. I need to convince him that lowering the wards would be right for us.

The walls that had imprisoned me for so long suddenly seemed insignificant. They were but stones stacked high, a physical barrier that could be overcome. But the real chains, the ones that held me captive, were in my mind, and I had just shattered them. Ramses had kept me confined and had controlled every aspect of my life. He wanted to do the same with Vrys, to mold him into his image, to rob him of his innocence.

But I wouldn't let him. I wouldn't let Ramses destroy our son as he had destroyed me. I would take Vrys, and we would escape beyond the wall, beyond Ramses' reach. We would find freedom, a life where we could breathe without fear and live without shackles. Or I would die trying. The path to freedom didn't be easy, I knew. The world beyond the wall was unknown, possibly dangerous. But it was still a world of possibilities where we could be more than just Ramses' playthings. The pain, the humiliation, the control—I was leaving it all behind.

"I am a queen," I said to no one.

❋

I huddled in the center of my bed, arms wrapped around my knees, as I waited for Xaneth's arrival. My heart pounded in my chest. An Elder Vampire. I had no illusions about my chances against him. Survival was my only goal.

A soft knock at the door made me jump. I rose, my bed creaking in protest.

"Come in."

The door creaked open, and Xaneth loomed in the doorway. His towering figure blended with the shadows, making him all but invisible except for his piercing gaze. Finely tailored black velvet clung to his frame, matching the darkness outside. A shiver traced my spine, but it wasn't fear. Anticipation hummed through my veins.

"Good evening." His voice, smooth as silk, carried a chilling undercurrent. He stepped inside, his presence heavy in the suddenly cramped room. His movements lacked the grace I remembered, his step faltering on the threshold.

"I hope I didn't keep you waiting too long." A smirk played on his lips. Was his accent slurring his words, or was it something more?

I shook my head. "No, not at all."

He closed the distance between us. My heart stuttered, breath catching. This was it. The moment I'd prepared for. Yet, with it upon me, I hesitated.

Xaneth extended his hand. After a heartbeat's pause, I placed mine in his. His grip was a contrasting mix of firmness and gentleness. He pulled me close, his icy breath whispering against my neck, his beard prickling my skin.

Time to feed.

His fangs sank into my skin. I braced for pain, but instead, euphoria washed over me. A strange warmth spread from the wound, a life-for-death exchange.

He swayed, laughter rasping from his throat. I touched the punctures, and he collapsed to his hands and knees, still chuckling.

"Are you...are you okay?" I asked, confusion lacing my words.

"I may have overestimated Ember's nightlife," he gasped, wiping his mouth with a shaky sleeve. "Don't let it sour the mood. I can still perform."

My swallow was audible. This would be the last time I was vulnerable like this.

He gained unsteady feet, fingers fumbling at his belt. "The taste of your blood...so good. So fucking good."

His clothes hit the floor in a discarded trail. No shame burned in his gaze as it raked over me, only hunger – for more than just blood. He stalked toward the bed, primal intent in every step.

"I'm going to lick every inch of you." His voice was rough gravel.

I lifted my gown over my head, steeling myself. But before he could act, he stumbled, catching himself on the bed. Confusion replaced his smirk.

"What's wrong?" I asked, my heart racing.

Xaneth mumbled something to himself, attempting to right himself. But his legs gave out, and he crashed onto the bed, his weight pressing against my legs. I shook him. "Xaneth!" But his eyes fluttered closed, and he went limp.

I pushed and wriggled free, rolling him onto his back. His chest rose and fell with slow breaths, purple tinging his lips. Like Adderdale poison.

I stared at the discarded belt, then at the unconscious vampire. This wasn't how tonight was supposed to go.

With a sigh, I covered him with a blanket. I'd deal with this...this...thing in the morning. I slipped my nightdress back on, a strange mix of relief and concern churning in my stomach.

"Is he passed out already?" someone asked from the doorway.

My heart leapt. Ronan stood there, his long hair loose, framing his face. White scars marred his arms, a few trickling down his neck. Beautiful.

"What the hell are you doing here? How did you even get on this floor?" I demanded, trying to keep myself steady.

He shrugged. "I walked. Then I heard you calling out his name, but not in pleasure. You sounded...confused. Figured I would come in and give the man some pointers."

I raised an eyebrow. "You were going to give your master pointers?"

He shrugged again, a lazy grin spreading. "Well, someone has to. Clearly, he's not doing it right if he's passed out drunk on your bed. I have told him time and again to lay off the alcohol. Even vampires can be drunks."

"And you think you could do any better?" The question escaped before I could catch it.

Ronan winked. "Darling, I could do better in my sleep."

I pinched the bridge of my nose. "You're unbelievable."

"That's what they tell me." His grin never wavered. "Just trying to help."

I shook my head. "I think I've had enough help for one night."

"Fair enough," he said with a shrug. "Well, if you need anything else, and I mean anything, don't hesitate to call. Who knows, I might even show up sober with a salute."

"You could get him out of my room," I mumbled after a beat.

Ronan's grin widened. "Oh, so now you need my help?"

I wasn't used to this playful banter. Most avoided me. With Servat, it was always a careful dance. This...

"I didn't say that," I shot back, but he was already moving towards the bed.

With surprising strength, he hefted Xaneth over his shoulder. "You know, the first night, and he's already drunk. You sure know how to show a man a good time."

"Just get him out of here, Ronan," I snarled, my patience fraying.

He chuckled, heading towards the door. "As you wish."

I watched him disappear into the hallway, his laughter echoing back. The room felt suddenly empty, the silence deafening.

I collapsed onto the bed, relief washing over me.

But as I thought of facing Ramses in the morning, my relief turned cold.

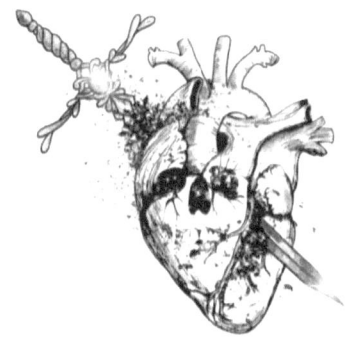

CHAPTER THIRTY

"**H**e says you didn't sleep with him," Ramses spat, his voice venomous from his throne. I'd endured a tirade from him already, and it wasn't even noon. "Did I not give you specific instructions to do so?"

I met his glare, relief etched on my face. "I tried. He was drunk and barely awake. I couldn't."

Ramses snarled, his tattoos seeming to writhe on his neck. "A street whore would have made it work!"

"I suppose you would know, wouldn't you?" The retort escaped before I could catch it.

Madness fueled my words. Ramses, with his wild red hair and disarmingly handsome face, inspired terror. I fought to keep that fear at bay, to cling to the resolve I'd found in the solitude of my room.

Everyone is braver when they can imagine victory.

Ramses' smile twisted, dangerous. "You sound... jealous?" He seemed pleased by my anger, misinterpreting it entirely.

"No, not jealous," I spat, fighting to keep myself steady. Fear was something Ramses fed on. "Just... disgusted."

His smile grew, showcasing sharp teeth. "Disgusted, hmm? And yet, here you are, arguing with me, defying me. Quite the compelling act, don't you think?"

"I'm not here for your entertainment, Ramses." I bit back a scoff. "I'm here because you ordered me to be, not because I enjoy your company."

Something flickered in his gaze – surprise, then amusement.

"Mother, look at Chansie's marvelous new knife!" Vryseris exclaimed, his voice cutting through the tension. I managed a neutral expression, grateful for the distraction.

Vryseris appeared before us, Chansie and Veren in tow. The twins offered me nervous smiles, Chansie proudly displaying a small obsidian knife. Veren shifted uneasily.

They're slightly shorter than Vrys, with a slight slouch to their posture. A splash of freckles littered their face.

"What a magnificent knife, Chansie," I murmured, forcing composure. "Where did you acquire such a treasure?" I already knew – Ramses always gave his bastards tokens.

Ramses' illegitimate children filled the palace, taking on meager roles. Sometimes, I wondered why he didn't make them my servants. I wouldn't have minded a few less of them.

I'm sure Vryseris knew, too. Maybe he found comfort in having so many siblings, even if he didn't acknowledge them as such.

"Stable Master Cornis praised me on my foaling efforts this year," Chansie said, beaming. "The King himself granted me a gift of my achievements and gifted me this glorious knife." Pride filled his face as he respectfully lowered his gaze. Veren shrank back.

Once, I'd been a jealous wife, wanting my husband to look at me with the same adoration he once had. Now, I sighed in relief when he didn't come to my chambers, when he occupied another. Now, I didn't grimace at the redheaded children or seethe at the obvious jokes about my inability to satisfy him. Joslynn said it was just their way—that even if Ramses weren't a king, he'd find his cock in someone else because men were fickle and bored quickly.

I suppose so.

"Indeed, it is a beautiful knife, Chansie," I forced a smile, glancing at Ramses. His focus was on his sons, his expression unreadable. Did he see himself in them, or only pawns?

Ramses finally spoke, his demeanor cold. "A knife is more than a gift, Chansie. It is a tool, a weapon, a friend. Make sure you treat it as such."

Chansie nodded, radiating awe and fear. "Yes, my king," he murmured, clutching the knife tighter. I saw the glow in him—excitement at being acknowledged. Veren held no such illusions—he cowered like a trapped animal.

Ramses turned to Vryseris. "And you, Vryseris," he began, tapping clawed fingers against his chin. "What have you got to show for your efforts?"

Vryseris straightened. "I have my knowledge, Father," he replied. "And the respect of my peers – and have broken in another dragon yearling."

Ramses scrutinized his son. "Knowledge and respect," he repeated, the words dripping with disdain. "Two things that can't be seen or touched. Interesting. As for the dragon," he paused, giving me a pointed look. "It does not make up for losing Seraphix. It's good you were there to save your poor mother; unfortunately, he escaped."

"Yes," I forced myself to say. "Vryseris' bravery is commendable."

Vryseris' jaw tightened. "It was my duty, father," he said. "As the future king, it is my responsibility to protect the people of Ember."

I hated the schoolboy tone. Ramses considered his son, then laughed—a hollow sound devoid of warmth. "Spoken like a true king," he said. "But remember, Vryseris, a king is nothing without his queen. And as of right now, you have none."

"He is but a boy. He doesn't need a queen now," I said, clicking my tongue.

"An arranged marriage would be beneficial," Ramses said.

I balked. "A-what? Arranged marriage? To whom?" I was on the verge of shrieking.

He ignored me. "Vryseris! Ready Aegis. You will be coming with me beyond the wall. Now."

My heart sank.

The implications were clear.

What would he have Vryseris do this time? Would he make him kill someone? Had he already found someone he wished to chain my son to?

Vryseris nodded, hiding his surprise well. "As you command, Father," he replied, his boyish features hardening.

I hated it. I hated how my son sounded like one of Ramses' yes-men. He turned to me, uncertainty flickering on his face before it was schooled. He placed his hand on Chansie's and Veren's shoulders and disappeared in a whirl of black.

Ramses turned to me, his teeth gleaming in the dim light. "It's time Vryseris learned what it means to be a king," he said.

He was cold, detached.

It was a threat. I knew it. I felt it deep in my bones.

Ramses may never touch me in front of Vrys – he may keep his transactions regarding me in hushed tones. But this.

This.

He would strip Vrys of his innocence to prove a point to me. That no matter what, he could hurt me, and it didn't have to be physical.

"And what does it mean to be a king, Ramses?" I scoffed, stomping toward him. "Does it mean ruling with cruelty? Or perhaps abandoning your flesh and blood and pretending they are not yours?" I gestured towards where Chansie had stood, now empty.

Ramses' gaze hardened. "Being a king means doing what is necessary for the kingdom's survival," he said flatly. "Even if it means making difficult decisions."

"Is that what you call it?" I half-laughed, unable to hide the bitterness. "Difficult decisions? Or is it simply your way of justifying your cruelty? The people outside these walls, in the land of Feranz, are still your people!"

He laughed, a harsh, cold sound that echoed around the room. "And you, my dear, are still as naive as the day I married you."

His hand struck me across the cheek. The sharp sting took me by surprise, and I stumbled back, my hand flying to my face. I pressed the cold metal of my gold bracelet against my cheek.

"I see you still have a knack for teaching lessons," I said hoarsely. I stood tall, refusing to let him see my pain. I licked the inside of my cheek, raking my tongue over my teeth to make sure they were all still there.

Ramses watched me, a cruel smile playing on his lips, eyeing the gold bracelet on my wrist – his wedding gift. "You always did have a sharp tongue, and it has become sharper as of late," he said. It seems I haven't been able to curb that."

"You can't curb a free spirit, Ramses," I hissed. "I may be caged here. You may strike me, but you will never break me."

His smile faltered, replaced by a look of annoyance. "Bold words for a woman in your position," he said with a low growl.

"And what position is that, Ramses?" I asked, "A queen? A wife? A mother? I am all these things and more. I am a woman who will not be cowed by a man who rules with fear. You cannot hurt me."

"Oh?" He struck me again. It was a blow that sent me stumbling back, my heels catching on my blue silk skirt and ripping. But I did not cry out. I panted, blinking rapidly. "I wonder which blow was your mother's last?" I mocked, standing straighter.

His mouth widened a fraction, his nostrils flaring.

The room went cold. My breath came out in clouds of vapor. Ice crystals formed along the stone and wood of the room, his throne – the twisted iron maiden, laden with frost.

"You cannot hurt me," I repeated, steady and cold as the ice that now frosted the walls.

I watched as he struggled to maintain his authority, his mask of control slipping. The air crackled with energy, and the walls of the room groaned under the pressure of his wrath.

As he lifted his hand again, the temperature plummeted further, and frost crawled along the surfaces, a creeping death threatening to encase everything in ice. His face twisted with rage and – grief.

"You know nothing of my mother's last moments," he hissed, the air around him shimmering.

I stared at his fist, ready to move. "I wonder how many men she had to endure before she was able to have you. Imagine. Growing in the womb of a woman who was filled to the brim with other men's seed...like a bowl of soup." I chuckled, the words flowing out of me easily and without fear. I was numb.

Ramses' face paled. For a moment, he was silent, his gaze locked onto me. Then he let out a low growl, "You're playing with fire," he warned. "Remember, you don't need your tongue."

His nostrils flared, a mixture of anger and surprise still etched across his face. He was not used to being challenged this way, especially not by me. There was a disagreement here and there, and he knew where I stood regarding his leadership.

But bringing up his mother.

Ha.

At that moment, time slowed as Ramses' fist hurtled towards me. I sidestepped smoothly, my body moving with a grace that belied the tension coiling within me. My muscle memory kicked in from all those years ago. Ramses' punch sailed through empty air, and his momentum carried him forward, off-balance.

Seizing the opportunity, I drove my knee upwards with precision, connecting between his legs. Ramses let out a pained gasp, his face contorting as he doubled over in agony.

Ramses' face was a mask of shock and humiliation, a rare sight from a man who wielded power like a second skin. It felt so good. I leaned close to his ear as he panted and said, "All men fall to their knees when kicked in the loins. Even kings."

I turned away, leaving him hunched in the grand chamber. I was surprised he just let me go.

I fully expected him to run his hand through me.

I was treading on thin ice, but at least I wasn't sinking. I had provoked him, perhaps more than was wise, but there was something liberating in making him angry.

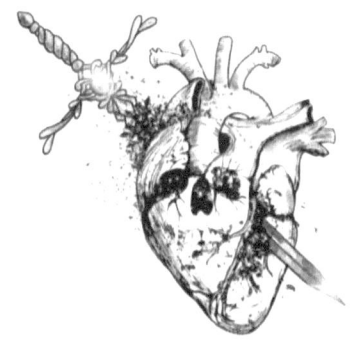

CHAPTER
THIRTY-ONE

Joslynn's map was ingrained in my head. I could see the path in my mind's eye. I just needed to break through the wall. Killing Eldra had been all I had ever wanted these last few years. If I handed over the information to Ramses, perhaps he would allow me back out into the world.

No. I would not. Joslynn had kept it hidden because she did not want Ramses to know. But how did Joslynn know of Eldra's whereabouts? Whatever answers Eldra had, I needed to carve them out of him.

Why had he sent his sentries of gold cloaks into the Hyperion Market to kill all those people—Joslynn being one of them? And yet, she had been protecting his secret.

"Nice bruise," someone commented nonchalantly.

I whirled around, my heart pounding in my chest, only to relax slightly when I realized it was just Xaneth's lackey, Ronan. "The hell are you doing out here?" I muttered, eyeing him suspiciously.

He was dressed in his usual black garbs, tightly fitted and blending into the shadows around him.

"I've licked a wound or two," he answered cryptically, his attention seemingly focused on picking at imaginary dirt beneath his clawed nails. His silver hair was braided neatly over one shoulder, adorned with odd gold trinkets that dangled and weaved through the strands. Some looked like arrowheads, while others resembled curved fangs. His red eyes were lined with black kohl, and I found myself once again drawn to him.

I absentmindedly touched my face, my mind racing with questions as to how he could have known I was ever wounded—the salves always leave me unmarked, and I had slathered on some before coming to the wall. "Go away," I snapped, turning back to the blank expanse of the wall before me. I reached out to touch it again and sparks flew up my arm. I gasped and retracted my hand, staring in disbelief at the score of tiny burns that now covered my skin.

"Enchanted still. Probably why everyone uses the gates," he snorted from behind with amusement.

"I don't need your help. You've caused more harm than good. A menace you are," I snapped, my anger flaring up once again.

"Oh, so you wanted to sleep with Xaneth? I've seen the man fuck. He can't. He also snorts like a pig when he climaxes," Ronan said, grimacing at the thought.

"I wouldn't have known any better. I would have just closed my eyes and it would have been over with," I replied. I would have just faded into the dark, safe spaces of my mind.

"I thought you were a queen?" he asked, his expression unreadable. I sighed heavily and turned to face him again.

"I am." This man was stupid—and annoyingly handsome.

"What you are describing is a whore," he deadpanned.

"I should cut your tongue for that!" I gasped, steeling myself against his jibe. He said aloud what I had only ever acknowledged in private. He shrugged his shoulders. I hated that he surmounted exactly how I felt.

"If you were so angry with my interference, you would rat me out," he said pointedly.

"Ah yes, putting me in an unfavorable light is such a pleasant touch," I hissed. "Thank you, oh so much for your help!"

"My apologies. I didn't realize you were so eager to sleep with Xaneth. Shall I lay you out a wet rag for when he's done making a mess on your belly? Or are you the type to let them finish off inside of you?" His eyes raked over my body in a way that made me feel dirty.

His words sparked a surge of anger within me, and I raised my hand, intent on slapping him for his insolence. But just as swiftly, he caught my wrist in his firm grip. His gaze was unyielding as he glared down at me, the moonlight casting an eerie glow over him. I could feel the dread seeping through my body like a shivering mouse cornered by a prowling cat.

"What do you think you're doing?" he growled menacingly, low and dangerous.

The darkness only seemed to amplify the sinister glow about him as he held me captive. His breath, warm and uneven, brushed against my face, sending chilling currents down my spine.

"Such a pretty thing," he whispered with sarcasm and venom that stung my pride. Ramses had spoken ill things to me that didn't incite such a reaction. "What a shame it would be if something were to happen to you."

And then suddenly, he let go. His grip on my wrist loosened, and he stepped away from me, leaving me trembling and bewildered. As I clutched my arm to my chest, nursing the tender skin where his fingers had dug into it, I couldn't tear my focus away from him—this puzzling enigma of a man.

"I could kill you," I hissed. He only smiled, his teeth a flash of white.

"Darling, I died a long time ago. You can do whatever you want with me." He laughed a short, mocking laugh and then turned his back to me.

I blushed at his implications, rage simmering in my chest. I raised my hand toward the sky and the crack of thunder broke the quiet expanse of night. My gold bracelet jingled against my wrist as I felt the cool drops of rainfall begin. Slowly, I pointed my hand toward him.

His composure didn't waver. He turned slightly to look at me and I felt my rage boil over. He looked bored.

This insolent man was bored.

Ronan's lips curled into a playful smile as he tilted his head toward me, giving a low, velvet whisper. "Tell me, dear Atreya," he purred with a subtle charm, "have you ever wondered what it would be like to dance under these starlit skies, free from the shackles of your husband?"

My heart ached as my name fell so casually from his lips. No one ever said my name like that. My hands clenched tightly, and a surge of lightning struck the earth just inches from his feet. The ground was seared and smoking. "How dare you utter such filth!" I tried to ignore that part of me that wanted to throw myself into temptation.

To have my name fall from his lips like that again.

He didn't even blink, merely fixing me with his sharp gaze. "Ah, my apologies. I failed to realize how near I was to breaching your fragile threshold of fury," he taunted with biting sarcasm. I readied myself to summon another bolt when he raised a hand in protest. "Do you truly wish to announce your presence to all of Ember?"

I demanded, "What do you want from me?" as my hand relaxed at my side.

A sinister smile danced on his lips as he leaned further into the shadowy pillar. "I wondered when you would ask. Naturally, I desire something in return."

My claws unsheathed as I charged toward him, baring my smaller fangs in rage. "You are in no position to bargain with me!" I snapped.

With the agility of a trained combatant, he sidestepped my swipe, and his laughter echoed through the desolate courtyard, sending shivers down my spine. "Let's not be overly theatrical, dear. However, you must first fulfill a request of mine. A bargain."

"You're a vampire. You can't make Fae bargains." I didn't know if that was entirely true or not.

Ronan chuckled. "I was once one of the Fae, bound by the same ancient rites and rituals that guide your kind. But let's not dwell on the technicalities of what I am or am not."

My claws were suddenly on his throat before I realized what I had done. I did not know this man aside from him being a vampire—and the full extent of a vampire's capabilities, I had no clue. His eyes widened a fraction of a second before a wide grin reappeared on his face. "Kinky," he purred, locking onto my mouth with an unsettling intensity.

"I'm not playing games, Ronan!" I hissed through gritted teeth, my claws pressing into his cold, almost lifeless skin. The moonlight reflected off his pallid complexion, making him look all the more ethereal.

"Neither am I, Atreya," he retorted. I detected a hint of amusement in his tone, but his face remained impassive.

"Speak now, or I swear I'll—" I began, my threat cut off short as he started laughing. It wasn't a cruel laugh but one filled with genuine enjoyment, as if my anger was the most entertaining thing he'd seen in centuries.

"You're adorable when you're angry," he said, his hand coming up to gently remove my claws from his throat. His touch was cold, sending shivers down my arm. "But let's not resort to violence, dear."

My heart pounded in my chest, my earlier bravado fading away. Truth be told, I had no idea what he was capable of. He was a vampire—an immortal being whose powers I could only guess at. But I couldn't let him know that I was second-guessing.

"I want to know what is going on beyond the wall. I want to go beyond the wall. I want to know why Ramses is so intent on more power. Why is Xaneth here?"

Ronan studied me for a moment, thoughtfully. "You're a mother," he said, not as a question, but as a statement. "I can see why you're so desperate."

"Desperate? I'm not desperate. I'm determined. There's a difference."

He laughed softly, the sound echoing in the night air. "I stand corrected," he said, raising his hands in surrender. "Determined, then."

I crossed my arms over my chest, my heart pounding. "So, can you help me or not?"

For a moment, he didn't say anything. Then, he sighed, running a hand through his silver hair. "Alright," he said with a sigh of resignation. "I'll help you. But you must understand, Atreya, what you're asking for... it's not going to be easy. Things are happening beyond the wall that you may not be prepared to face."

"I don't care," I replied with a shake of my head. "I need out. I need to know what Ramses is planning. I can handle whatever is out there."

I could get lucky and get to Eldra. Finish him once and for all.

He looked at me for a moment, a strange expression on his face. Then, he nodded. "Very well," he said, turning to face the wall. "But the journey will not be easy."

"I'm not afraid of a little hardship. Your request, what is it?"

He leaned in, his lips barely an inch away from my ear. "Promise me," he whispered, "that you won't run away from the truth."

His words gave me chills. I pulled back, analyzing him. "What truth?" I asked, my heart pounding. But all he did was smile, his crimson eyes twinkling in the moonlight.

"You'll find out soon enough, Atreya," he said, stepping away from me. "And when you do, remember your promise."

He disappeared into the darkness, leaving me alone in the courtyard.

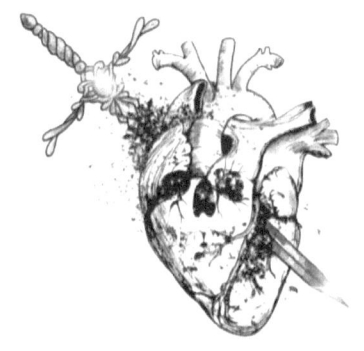

CHAPTER THIRTY-TWO

C orina was right. Men were simpletons, even kings. Ramses came to me the next day, straight-backed and proud with her in tow, telling me he thought of a great way to keep the people under control after Seraphix's escape.

He wanted to put me in the arena again. The Furian Slayer. No mention of me kneeing him in his balls. Instead, he gave me warmer smiles and gentler touches. More gifts were brought to my room. All things that would have broken me down before. But not ever again.

"It will remind them of the power we hold. Remind them of how you crushed the Rebel Queen," he said enthusiastically.

We. As if we were a team.

The idea of returning to the arena sent a shiver down my spine. The memories of the arena were still fresh, the weight of her dying gaze still haunting me. Those rebels that Ramses had chained by their necks—

Clang clang clang

But Ramses was relentless in his pursuit of control, and in his thought process, my victory was a symbol to be wielded—a reminder of the might of our kingdom and, more importantly, the might of his influence.

"Who am I to kill this time?" I asked him with a sigh.

"Just a show," Ramses said. "No bloodshed, not this time. You'll fight against a few of our best warriors in a mock battle. Make it spectacular, Atreya. Remind them why they should never rise against us."

Relief washed over me, though I knew this was only a reprieve from his more deadly impulses. Corina gave me an approving nod.

"And who would be my opponents in this... play of sorts?"

"Several volunteers," Ramses said quickly.

"Several volunteered to fight me? In the arena?"

They were stark raving mad.

"Servat is one of them," Corina interjected.

My mouth opened slightly. "You're joking."

"Servat was eager. It will take place tonight," Ramses added.

"Why tonight?" I suspected I knew the answer to that.

"We have to accommodate certain guests," he said pointedly. "So, put on a good show."

I wouldn't know how to put on a show. How does one fake fight?

"I'll get you fitted into some leathers and make sure you look the part. People are watching," Corina said. She whirled on her heels and was gone.

"This is just what we need to get the people talking. We need a distraction." Ramses smiled at me.

Fucking smiled.

That in itself unnerved me.

Corina returned promptly, her arms laden with the leathers and armors that would transform me. The dark material was supple yet sturdy, designed to allow for movement while giving the illusion of impenetrable armor. It had been a while since I had worn something like this.

I doubted that I could wear it as well as Corina did.

I dressed in silence, with Ramses leaving Corina fussing over how I should wear my hair.

"It is too long. You should roll it into a bun." She tapped her chin and flicked her wrist at my hair. The strands wove themselves tightly, and I felt a slight tugging on my scalp. "There," she said.

As I tightened the straps and adjusted the fit, Corina watched with a critical eye. "You look every bit the part," she said, nodding with satisfaction. "But looking the part is not enough, you must act it as well. The crowd expects a show, and you must give them one."

I met her gaze in the mirror, the reality of the situation settling over me like a heavy cloak. "And how do you propose I do that?" I asked, the idea of a staged fight still foreign to me.

"Simple," she replied with a sly grin. "You run around the arena, make it look like you're trying to evade them. They'll chase you, and you'll dodge. Make it dramatic. The people will love the dance of it, the suspense."

I snorted at the notion. "A dance? With Servat and the others chasing me down?"

"Yes," Corina insisted. "A dance with death, even if it is only an illusion this time. Draw it out, make them believe you could be caught, but always stay just out of reach. With the dragon having gone, the people are restless. There have been talks that Ramses is losing control. You can give them something else to focus on, even if only for a while."

"Why would I want them to focus on something else?" I smirked.

She sighed. "At least for now, cousin."

●

The dark corridor's wooden door remained closed, a barrier between me and the arena beyond. Muffled laughter and shouts penetrated the thick wood, a reminder of the crowd eagerly awaiting the spectacle to come. I leaned against the cool stone wall, my heart pounding in time with the distant drums.

Servat's boots echoed off the walls as he approached. His smile, a flash of white in the dim corridor, made my pulse stutter. "You look good, Furian Slayer," he said, low and smooth. His braided white hair gleamed in the faint torchlight, drawing my attention to my own tightly coiled bun. I suppressed a scowl.

"I don't need your flattery, Servat." I adjusted my leathers, the familiar weight of them a small comfort. "Let's just get this over with."

His smile grew. "Nervous, Atreya? Or perhaps you're not as confident in your...performance skills in the arena as you are in the palace?" His eyes glinted with amusement.

I shot him a glare. "What if I accidentally hurt you? Or the people?"

He chuckled. "Then it would be quite the show, wouldn't it? But we both know you have more control than that. Just remember, it's all a dance. Stay light on your feet, Furian Slayer."

I bristled at the title. "Stop calling me that."

"They are about to chant it out to you any minute," he said in a perfect mimicry of the crowd. "Fu-ri-an Slay-er."

My eye twitched. Before I could retort, a deep, resonant horn blared through the air, the signal to enter the arena.

"That would be our cue," Servat said, his expression turning serious. "Aim for two feet behind me while I am running. Always two feet behind. Not ahead."

"Why?"

"So that way, you are guaranteed to miss. I will do the same."

"What if we both miss, and I hit someone in the stalls?" I cringed at the thought.

He laughed. "After your destruction of the arena last time, they put in place a shield. Any attacks outside the designated area will be nullified."

If I had even thought to strike Ramses in the stalls, it would have done nothing.

"How will we decide who wins?"

Servat leaned in closer. "We won't. The 'fight' will end in a draw. It will appear as though we are evenly matched, and just when it seems one of us will claim victory, the master of ceremonies will call it to a halt, citing the kingdom's need for both of its champions."

I nodded, the plan making sense in the context of Ramses' desire for a show. It would keep the people entertained while ensuring no true victor emerged, thus preventing any shift in the balance of public favor.

"Remember, two feet," he reminded me, tapping a finger against the hilt of his mock weapon—a blunt-edged sword that gleamed dully in the dim light of the corridor.

"I don't have a sword," I said dumbly.

He raised a brow at that. "Do you need one?"

He knew as well as I did that I didn't need one.

"No, I don't need a sword."

His grin widened, approval shining in his eyes. "That's the spirit, Furian Slayer. Use your hands."

I could feel the warmth radiating from his body, the scent of his leather armor, and the faintest hint of his cologne mixing in the air.

"Though," Servat whispered in a low hum that vibrated through the quiet of the corridor, "I must admit, there's something else I've been wanting to use my hands for."

"Servat," I managed to say, steadying myself with great effort, "we can't. This isn't right."

Before I could process what was happening, he closed the gap, his hand cradling the back of my neck, and his lips found mine in a kiss that was soft yet full of intent. It was a fleeting touch, a whisper of what could be, and it left me breathless, my mind reeling from the suddenness of it.

We shouldn't be doing this, I thought. I shouldn't want this.

We promised.

As if hearing my thoughts, Servat pulled back just enough to look into my eyes, his own reflecting a tumult of emotions. "I know we shouldn't," he said roughly, "but sometimes what we should do and what we want to do are two very different things."

A memory hit me, and I felt my body shudder. I was back in my birthing room, drenched in sweat and wracked with pain.

The baby's wail was strong, but it was not his cry that captured our attention. Even the midwife gave pause. Joslynn's hand tightened over mine, her eyes darting from the baby to me, a silent communication passing between us as panic rose within me.

"Let me see him," Joslynn demanded. She stepped around, taking the baby into her arms.

Without a word, Joslynn handed the baby to me, still sticky with blood, then turned to the midwife. "You have served your queen well," she said calmly as she reached for a small blade on a tray of towels.

In one swift, brutal motion, Joslynn slit the midwife's throat, the woman's mouth wide with shock as she crumpled to the floor, clutching her open throat.

I held my baby to my breast, still too stunned to move.

Joslynn turned to me, wiping the blade with a cloth. "Of all da foolish tings," she started, "What is done is done." She pinched the bridge of her nose.

Joslynn's eyes met mine, and there was a steel in them that spoke of a resolve born from years of service and secrecy. The room, once filled with the cries of childbirth, was now heavy with the silence that follows violence. The midwife lay motionless on the floor, save for the occasional twitch, her lifeblood seeping into the stone.

"We never speak of dis day. Never. Do you understand me? We never speak of it." Her finger was in front of my face, pointing.

I nodded, pressing my nose to my new son and inhaling his scent. A crop of downy white hair crowned the top of his head.

"We will raise him to be strong, wise, and just," I whispered, kissing the top of my son's head, feeling the softness of his hair against my lips. "He will be a prince his people can be proud of."

"Pray for it," Joslynn said, "Pray for it with all your being." She held a hand over the baby, and a light began to glow from her palm around the baby's head.

It took me a moment to realize what she had been doing, and when she was done, I was grateful. of red, his hair was now black. Like mine.

I looked down at him, his small face a picture of innocence. "He will never know of this," I whispered, a promise to both my son and myself.

"You will promise me. Never to do dis again," Joslynn hissed. "It will be the death for da three of ya."

"We promised," I whispered against Servat's mouth, almost a whine. "Joslynn made us promise."

"Joslynn is dead and gone and I am tired of punishing myself for it. I'm tired of pretending that you do not have my heart. I am tired of watching you wither away into nothing because of my brother."

Servat's admission hung heavily between us, thick with the weight of unspoken truths and a past that clung to our skins like invisible shackles.

"We promised for Vryseris," I said, the name of my son wrapping around my heart like a vice. "For his protection."

Servat's expression hardened. "Vryseris is *my* son, and he is every bit the prince this kingdom needs, whether by blood or by name. He will not be destroyed. He is strong—our strength."

My heart leaped into my throat. "If the truth were to come out, it would bring a succession crisis the likes of which we've never seen. Your brother may be oblivious to many things, but even he cannot ignore the whispers of illegitimacy surrounding his throne. We will be found out."

Servat's jaw clenched, a muscle ticking in his cheek as he grappled with the reality. "Then we must ensure the whispers remain just that—whispers. I have played the part of the loyal brother and dutiful uncle for years, and I will continue to do so for as long as it takes—until Ramses is dead." He rested his forehead against mine.

"It's torture, seeing you every day, knowing what we once had—and what we must deny ourselves. I will get you out of here. I promise. No matter what it takes."

I thought of my bargain with Ronan. How I had planned to leave and find out for myself the truth of the outside.

Now those plans were changed. Because how could I leave Servat behind?

"Why didn't you tell me you were the shield on Ember? That it is your power that holds us here?"

The question lingered in the air, a testament to the secrets that had built walls between us. Servat's eyes held mine, the pain in them echoing the years of lies and silence.

"I couldn't," he said, barely above a whisper. "The shield was created to protect, to keep our enemies at bay, and to keep Vryseris safe. If anyone knew it was tied to me, it would put a target on my back—and by extension, on you and our son. But that has changed."

I let myself inhale him. I let myself run my fingers through his hair, my tongue across his skin.

"The King's Shield. Ramses has a way of making a mockery out of titles. Didn't you trust me?"

"I trust you with my life, Atreya," he answered. "I'll get you out of here."

In that moment, the world outside our whispered promises ceased to exist. The political machinations, the responsibility to the throne, the ever-present pressure of the court—all faded into nothingness as we clung to the last shred of our forbidden past, a memory that refused to be silenced.

Servat's breath was hot against my skin, his forehead pressed to mine, a barrier as thin as parchment between our thoughts. His words, a vow of liberation, sent a shiver down my spine. The intensity in his promise spoke of a future where we were untethered, free from the chains of duty that bound us to roles we never asked for.

And then, without another word, we surrendered to the longing that had tormented us for far too long. Our lips met in a kiss that was both a balm for our aching souls and a brand that seared us with its passion. It was a kiss of desperation, of yearning, of a love that had been denied the light but thrived in the shadows.

I lost myself in the sensation of Servat's hands in my hair, the taste of him on my tongue, the sound of our mingled breaths. For a fleeting heartbeat, we were not the queen and the king's brother; we were just two souls entwined by a love that defied the world.

But as the next horn sounded, a booming reminder of reality, we pulled apart, gasping for air. The horn's call pierced the air, a primal scream that shattered the fragile peace of the corridor. Our time was up; the masks of our roles awaited. The arena loomed before us, a monstrous stage upon which we would perform for the kingdom's ravenous gaze. Servat extended a hand, a gesture of false camaraderie. I took it, my palm slick with sweat, and allowed him to lead me into the blinding light.

The arena was an ancient beast, its stone walls bearing the scars of centuries. Banners of forgotten champions and fallen heroes draped the tiers, their faded colors whispering tales of glory and defeat. The air reeked of sandalwood and sweat, heavy with the weight of history. Lanterns and torches flared to life, casting a golden glow over the sunbaked sand.

A sea of faces stretched out before me, a mosaic of anticipation and bloodlust. In the royal box, Vrys sat rigid, Ramses and Corina flanking him. Xaneth looked bored, Ronan bemused. My heart stuttered. I hadn't set foot in this arena since that day, since I had refused to kill and sealed my fate.

As I stepped onto the sand, the crowd erupted. Cheers and jeers mingled into a deafening roar that shook the very foundations of the arena. I bit the inside of my cheek, fighting for calm. I was not a child, not prey. No one would die today.

The master of ceremonies bellowed our names, the sound like thunder. "The Furian Slayer! And the King's Shield, Servat!" The crowd responded with renewed frenzy, their cheering a tidal wave of sound.

The horn blared once more, its call echoing off the stone. From the gates opposite, a tide of fighters surged into the arena, their weapons glinting like deadly stars. The master of ceremonies didn't bother to introduce them; they were nameless, faceless. That was all they needed to be.

The first clash was a maelstrom of steel and screams, shattering the fragile calm. I wondered if these men knew this was a farce, a dance with blunt edges.

Servat engaged a hulking brute, his sword flashing like lightning as it parried a massive axe. Sparks flew, the impact ringing out like thunder. He danced back, fluid as a cat, and struck, his blade finding the gap in his opponent's armor and drawing first blood. The brute fell, clutching his side, and did not rise. At least he was not dead.

Servat gestured to me, his sword pointed like an accusation. It was my turn.

The sky above churned with grey clouds, heavy with the promise of a storm. I raised my hands, feeling the electric charge of the atmosphere coalesce around my fingers. It hummed through me, a raw and primal force that answered my call. It sent a thrill through my veins.

A pair of fighters charged. My hands crackled with sparks, and the crowd roared as lightning pierced the sky and sent the men flying. They were not dead, but they were no longer a threat.

The melee raged on, the number of combatants dwindling as the strong prevailed. The air was thick with the grunts of exertion, the cries of the injured, and the metallic tang of blood.

Clang clang clang

I blinked away the sweat that stung my eyes.

Two more men came at me. I unleashed the fury of the storm. Bolts of lightning arced from my outstretched hands, striking with the precision of a falcon's dive. I sent the bolts down, the sand exploding as they struck, leaving smoldering craters. The men were dragged away, not dead, but broken.

And then it was just Servat and I.

I aimed for two paces behind him, as he had instructed. My hands thrust forward, releasing the pent-up energy in a bolt of lightning that split the air with its fury. The electricity struck the ground with a deafening boom, hurling sand and debris into the air. Servat was already gone, anticipating the strike.

He swept around the arena, his sword at the ready, but never striking with intent to harm. It was all part of the act, the dance we had choreographed. The master of ceremonies watched, ready to signal the end of our farce.

Servat threw a knife at me, a blade of obsidian that whizzed past my ear. I whirled and ran, weaving in a zigzag pattern. Another knife sailed through the air, landing in the sand before me. I halted, my arm outstretched. Lightning barreled down, reverberating in the arena. With each pass, I aimed carefully, always two paces behind Servat.

Servat's throws were precise, each knife a dark streak against the leaden sky. He was an expert in misdirection, his movements a feint that kept the audience guessing. And as he threw, I responded, summoning bolts of lightning that answered the threat of his blades with a spectacle of raw power.

As he released another knife, I thrust my arms forward, calling down a bolt of lightning that was a crescendo of our performance. It struck the knife mid-flight, the enchanted metal and energy colliding in an explosion that sent a shockwave through the arena. The obsidian shattered, fragments catching the light as they fell to the sand, harmless as rain.

One more pass. I was panting, my brow laden with sweat. Servat was flushed, his breathing heavy. But he was still moving, so I had to keep up.

Another crack of lightning, two paces behind him.

But as the lightning descended, Servat's step faltered. His gaze met mine, and he smiled slightly, even as horror dawned on my face. He turned on his heel and strode straight for the bolt.

Time slowed as I watched, my heart plummeting into an abyss. Servat changed the routine, his body moving with a purpose I couldn't comprehend. The lightning, intended to strike two paces behind him, now found its mark on Servat himself.

The air was rent with the sound of the explosion, a blinding flash of light that seared my vision. When the brightness faded, Servat lay on the ground, his armor scorched and smoking, his body unnaturally still.

Panic gripped me like a vice. "Servat!" I screamed, shredding the stunned silence of the arena. I ran to him, dropping to the sand, my hands shaking as I reached out to touch him, afraid of what I might find. I placed my hand on his chest, searching for the rise and fall of breath, for any sign of life.

I heard Ramses' frantic call for the sentries.

Heard the startled cries of the audience as the shield around the arena fell.

Heard the screams of the people of Ember as the wards that safeguarded them fell like shimmering curtains of white.

And then I was encased in black, with Ronan's hands around my throat.

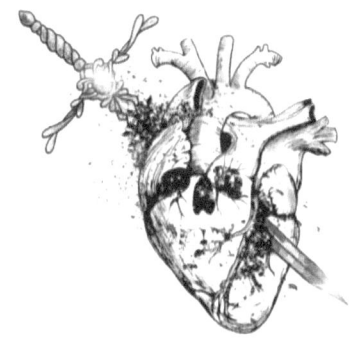

CHAPTER
THIRTY-THREE

ELDRA

"The wards have fallen. Now is the time for an attack!" Madsen yelled, pacing back and forth in the dimly lit underground chamber. Her boots echoed off the stone walls, each step a punctuation of her agitation.

"We aren't going to attack them, remember? We have a plan," I reminded her.

Madsen spun to face me, her eyes blazing with skepticism. "Are you certain we can trust this vampire, Eldra? Our entire plan hinges on the Furian Slayer's cooperation, and now we're to place our faith in a creature of the night?"

"I am aware of the risks," I said, meeting her gaze. My words were measured, chosen to soothe her fears without conceding the point. "But Ronan has his own reasons for wanting to bring the Furian Slayer to us. His motives align with our goals, for now."

Gaelin folded his arms, his brow furrowed in concern. "And what of those motives? We know little of this vampire save for the tales of his past deeds. How do we know he won't betray us the moment it serves his interests? He already betrays his master."

"I have something that he wants," I said, a shrug accompanying my words. "He has something that I want. If I do not get what I want, neither does he."

Madsen kicked at a small stone, sending it skittering across the floor. Her action was a testament to her frustration, her body language screaming of her disbelief. "And if the vampire's betrayal costs us everything?" She shook her head, her face a picture of incredulity. "Didn't she try to kill you? How the hell are we supposed to have her on our side?"

"Yes, she did try to kill me," I smirked, a wry twist of my lips.

Gaelin stared at me, his eyes narrowing. "You seem rather fucking happy about it. Tell me, Eldra, you wanna fuck this girl?"

Madsen's response was immediate, her pitch rising in outrage. "I'll tell Ameria on you, lad, and string your balls up myself!"

I pinched the bridge of my nose, my eyes closed in a bid for patience. "No. I do not desire her in that way. What matters is her potential to aid our cause and the common enemy we share in Ramses."

"You mean her husband," Gaelin said pointedly. "To whom she has a child with."

"You were there during the meeting in the forest with our mystery guest all those years ago," I reminded him, my words a gentle rebuke. "You were so certain that information was correct. You had even less of a reason to trust them than you do the Furian Slayer."

Gaelin grumbled at that, his body language a testament to his discomfort. "They have held up their end of the bargain, though."

"The stakes are high," I acknowledged, my gaze sweeping the room. "The entire revolution against Ramses hinges on the cooperation of the so-called Furian Slayer. Madsen's skepticism is not unfounded; vampires are notorious for their self-serving nature, and Ronan's history is stained with blood and betrayal."

"Ronan will bring her here," I continued. "She will turn on Ramses and work with us. And let's not forget the child. She will do what she must to protect her son, to secure a better future for him. That is something we can appeal to—our shared vision for a kingdom where the next generation doesn't have to live under the tyranny of a despot like Ramses."

"A child that is still within the walls of Ember," Madsen grunted, crossing her arms over her chest. Her body language was a wall, a physical manifestation of her resistance.

"And that child," I said resolutely, meeting her gaze, "is no longer bound by the wards that once held him to Ember. He will find his own way in time, and we must have faith in that. Our actions now will shape the world he inherits."

Madsen's reaction was immediate, her face purpling with rage. "What?" she squawked, slamming her fists onto the table. Her outburst shattered the fragile calm, sending shockwaves through the room. "What the fuck do you mean, inherit?"

My expression remained impassive, a mask of calm in the face of her fury. "I am not in the habit of dethroning children," I said flatly, my words a counterpoint to her outrage. "If it comes down to Ramses being killed, the boy would be the next king. It is the natural order of succession."

Madsen's face turned a shade redder, her aura blazing with indignation. "And what of you, Eldra? You lead us, you inspire us! You would make a far better king than some boy raised in Ramses' shadows!"

"This rebellion is not about placing a crown upon my head," I sighed, my words a gentle reminder of our purpose. "It's about freeing Ember from the grip of a tyrant. It's about creating a kingdom where power is not seized through bloodshed and fear but granted by the will of the people."

Madsen let out a frustrated huff, her body language a testament to her conflicted emotions. "But after everything Ramses has done, how can we trust the child won't follow in his footsteps? We tried this all before, Eldra, where the people chose. The people will always be divided. They will always choose the path that benefits them the most—even if it is the wrong choice."

"We cannot allow ourselves to be shackled by the fear that history will repeat itself," I said. "Instead, we must learn from it, and forge a new path."

"And what if the people choose Ramses? Again?" she pressed, "What if all of Ferenz sides with him?"

"He won't be a choice," I said, my words a promise, a vow that hung in the air between us.

Madsen's gaze narrowed, her eyes flashing with skepticism. "And what of the vampire, Ronan? A rot, that's what he is," she spat. "I've seen what the undead are capable of. Years ago, they swarmed a city, and the old kings had to sink the entire island just to stop them. I don't trust a vampire, Eldra, not one bit."

I flinched at her words, a flicker of pain crossing my face. One of those kings had been my father, a man whose legacy still haunted me.

"Our agreement is bound by more than mere words," I said, "It is sealed with magic that neither of us can afford to violate without dire consequences."

Madsen's brow furrowed, her gaze sharpening. "Magic?" she repeated, "He is not of fae, not truly. What kind of magic binds a vampire to his word?"

"A blood oath," I growled, the words torn from me. My gaze flicked to Gaelin, whose frown deepened in response.

Madsen's reaction was immediate, her face draining of color. "You did what...?" she hissed, a venomous whisper that hung in the air between us.

I rubbed my nose with my thumb and forefinger, fighting back a headache. "I am aware that it was not the most...optimal decision," I said, choosing my words with care. "But I had little choice. And it has bought us an ally, one who can aid us in our fight against Ramses."

Madsen's response was swift, a torrent of words that filled the room. She cursed at me in Arathi, a language she had learned from Emery. Her words were sharp, each one a dagger aimed at my heart. They carried a weight of emotion, of disbelief and betrayal, and they hung in the air between us like a challenge.

The room fell silent in the wake of her outburst, the only sound her ragged breathing. And then she was gone, stalking out of the room with a grace that belied the fury that still lingered in the air.

A long pause followed, the silence a heavy blanket that smothered the room. And then I turned to Gaelin, a wry smile twisting my lips. "That went better than I had expected," I sighed. "What do you suppose she said?"

Gaelin's response was immediate, his grin a flash of white in the dimly lit room. "Well, if I had to guess, I think she said, 'I am going to tell your wife.'"

I nodded, a single, decisive movement. And then I was bolting for the door, the sound of my boots echoing off the stone walls like a death knell.

Fuck.

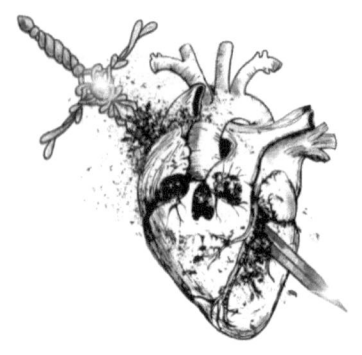

CHAPTER
THIRTY-FOUR

RONAN

I hum when I am nervous. I hum when I am bored. I sing quietly to myself when I am alone. The melody this time was a soft, disjointed tune, the notes rising and falling with the rise and fall of Atreya's chest as she lay unconscious beside me. I had whisked her away in shadow.

The wards were down.

I had taken her from the arena, from the horror of what had happened to Servat, from the screams and the panic and the enveloping darkness.

Eldra and his crew of rebels believed they had the upper hand with their plans and their blood oaths. Yet they knew nothing of the true game at play.

When I first met Eldra and his council, it had been quite against my will. The tavern near Tor was a place of damp wood and dim light, catering to the less savory characters of the night. In the midst of the foggy stupor brought on by the blood of a willing barmaid, I first laid eyes on Gaelinantis Otear—Gael, as he would later be known to me.

The taste of iron and life lingered on my tongue, the warm flow of the barmaid's essence a heady draught that dulled my senses to the outside world. I was not alone in my indulgence; Xaneth, ever the obnoxious one, reveled in the attention of our glamoured companions, their eyes glassy and vacant, yet bodies warm and yielding.

I was enjoying the haze of my blood-induced high, words slurred but ringing with the arrogance of our kind.

"The King of Ember has extended his hospitality to us," Xaneth boasted, his fangs glistening in the flickering candlelight. "We are honored guests within his realm, free to sate our thirsts as we see fit."

My master is stupid that way. Obnoxious and loud for no fucking reason.

The patrons were a mix of the enthralled and the too-drunk-to-care-about-what-the-fanged-man-said.

But Gael was not like that.

"Welcome, traveler," he called out in a smooth baritone. "What brings you to this corner of depravity? Besides the—well—depravity," he said with a chuckle.

Xaneth snarled, his fangs bared in warning. "Watch your tongue when you speak to us. We have been invited here by royal decree."

I rolled my eyes and languidly turned my head to look at him. A frock of blonde hair hung down around his shoulders, and his blue eyes glittered like mine when I found easy prey.

Gael's calm never wavered, even as the air around us seemed to crackle with the threat of violence. He was different, not cowed by our presence, which intrigued me.

"Peace, Xaneth. Let us not waste our time with pointless threats."

Gael's lips quirked into a half-smile, and he raised his glass in a mocking salute to me. "Wise words, my friend. Why not join us for a drink? After all, we're all here to indulge, right?"

There was something in his tone, a hidden challenge that made my blood sing with the promise of a game worth playing. I took a step closer, my eyes never leaving his.

"Very well," I replied, my smile mirroring his. "Let's see what this night has in store for us."

As I hummed that soft, disjointed tune beside Atreya's still form, I couldn't help but think back to that night. The game had only just begun, and I intended to play it to the very end.

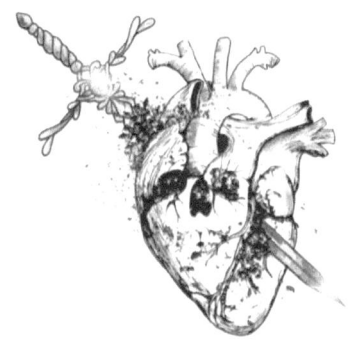

CHAPTER THIRTY-FIVE
FOLLOW THE AUTHOR

Stay up-to-date with the latest news, behind-the-scenes insights, and exclusive content by following Genesis Batista on social media:
Instagram: Gigixbites
Facebook: Genesis Xiomara
Twitter: Gigixbites
Tiktok: Gigixbytes
Scan QR Code to see updates on Goodreads, and leave a review!

www.ingramcontent.com/pod-product-compliance
Lightning Source LLC
Chambersburg PA
CBHW031428240626
47154CB00001B/252